CW01480933

# Ruth Wind

# JULIET'S LAW

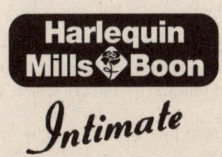

*Intimate*

First Published 2006
First Australian Paperback Edition 2006
ISBN 0 733 57304 5

Published by
Harlequin Mills & Boon
3 Gibbes Street
CHATSWOOD NSW 2067
AUSTRALIA

Printed and bound in Australia by
McPherson's Printing Group

**RUTH WIND**

is the award-winning author of both contemporary and historical romance novels. She lives in the mountains of the Southwest with her two growing sons and many animals in a hundred-year-old house the town blacksmith built. The only hobby she has had since she started writing is tending the ancient garden of irises, lilies and lavender beyond her office window, and she says she can think of no more satisfying way to spend a life than growing children, books and flowers. Ruth Wind also writes women's fiction under the name Barbara Samuel. You can visit her Web site at www.barbarasamuel.com.

For Madi Nance.
Remember, you are a princess,
and princesses can do anything they set their minds to.

# *Prologue*

"Juliet," said her sister Desdemona over the phone, "I'm in trouble. Real trouble."

Juliet, scrunched in a TV-watching coma on the couch, cleared her throat. "Yeah?" Desi's voice had been so bland Juliet didn't immediately see any reason to get excited. Or sit up for that matter. She chose an M&M out of the bowl in her lap. "What's wrong?"

"I have a shotgun in my lap," she said distinctly, "and I need you to tell me why I shouldn't shoot my lying pig of a husband when he comes through our front door."

Juliet sat up. M&M's scattered across the bare wooden floor, because until that minute, she'd been eating the candy and watching her new favorite soap opera. It was important, she had decided, to eat the candy in order of color: first brown, because they were so boring, then yellow, because that was close to brown, then green for grass, then red.

In order to keep herself from eating an entire king-sized bag in five minutes flat, she'd also made some rules about how to eat them, once they were sorted into colors. She could only put one in her mouth at a time, and she wasn't allowed to bite them—only suck the candy coating from the chocolate, then let the chocolate melt in her mouth. If she followed the rule, the bag would last through both *The Guiding Light* and *Days of Our Lives,* and then it was time for lunch.

Juliet liked structure. Since she'd been asked to take a leave of absence from her Los Angeles firm, there was no real structure to her life at the moment. She made do with what she could get—candy rituals, reliable television programs, meal times.

But this—! A crisis was even better than structure. In a crisis, there were steps to follow, a plan to make, a defined course of action. In this crisis, for example, she knew exactly what to do first. She put the bowl to one side and brushed blue M&M's off her lap.

"Desi?" she said gently. "You have a gun?"

"Of course I have a gun! I live in the wilds of the Colorado Rockies." She sniffed, the kind of thick-sounding snort that came after serious crying. "There are mountain lions up here."

"But you're holding it now? The gun?"

"Yes." Her sister now started to sob at the other end of the phone, that desperate, end-of-my-rope kind of crying Juliet had heard too often as a volunteer at a community center for immigrant women in L.A.

"Yes," Desi repeated. "He's out with his mistress and he knows I know it and I've told him to get out of my house and go get a divorce, but he won't do it, because he won't give up his half of the land, and I don't know what to do!"

"Desi," Juliet said, making her voice both smooth and authoritative, "take the bullets out of the shotgun and throw them out the window."

"He deserves to get shot," she insisted.

"No doubt," Juliet agreed, "but if you kill him, you'll go to jail. And that would be a very bad thing for you. Do you hear me?"

A sob came through the phone. "Who would convict me? A lying, cheating scumbag who will not move out of my house and instead is torturing me like this? This has been going on for three months! He deserves it!"

"Yes," Juliet said again. "Desi, please, sweetie, take the bullets out of the gun and go throw them out the window."

"They're not technically bullets."

"Whatever you call them, sis. Get rid of them."

There was a little rattle on the line, the sound of the receiver being put down. In the background, Juliet heard a clank, and Desi came back on. "Okay," she said in a raw voice. "I threw the shells out the window."

Juliet let go of her breath. "Good. Very good." She knew the very next thing to do, too. "I'll be there tomorrow, okay? Don't do *anything* until then. Promise me?"

Desi's voice was small. "Okay."

"Think of your wolves. Who will take care of them if you go to jail?"

A long quiet burned down the wire. "You're right," Desi said at last, and there was another kind of brokenness to it. "Please come, Juliet. I really need you."

"I'm on my way, sis."

# Chapter 1

The skies were heavy over the mountains of Mariposa when Josh Mad Calf fastened his daughter into her car seat in the half-back bench of his massive pickup truck. The four-year-old wore a blue knitted hat on her glossy dark head, and her eyes had the glazed blankness of mid-afternoon. "Sleepy, kiddo?"

"Don't call me that!" she said, glaring at him.

He chuckled and touched her nose. "Okay, rabbit."

"Not that, either!"

"Okay, wolf-girl."

"Dad-DEE!" she complained.

"Sorry," he said, grinning, and tucked a few bags of groceries around her feet—a handful of supplies for himself and his friend Desi, just in case the threatening snow turned into a blizzard. As he slammed the door firmly, he narrowed his eyes and looked up. Burly blue mountains surrounded the town, and clouds had moved halfway down their sides, hiding the entire line of ridges and most of the still-bare ski runs.

They wouldn't be bare long. A few cottony bits of snow were spitting out of the sky, but it would be a few hours until the heart of the storm moved in. By then he and Glory would be tucked into their snug house, a fire roaring in the potbellied stove, soup bubbling on the stove for their supper, a dog snoring on the hearth.

A good life. Good enough. In the old days, he'd imagined a woman for himself in that picture—a mother for Glory—but that had turned out badly. Very badly. As he headed away from town on narrow roads, he remembered to be grateful. Grateful for simple things like his daughter safe in his care, knowing she'd be fed well tonight and sleep in a clean, warm bed.

It hadn't always been that way. He looked in the rearview mirror and saw that she'd fallen asleep. Her cheeks were rosy, her dark eyelashes a half oval. He could never get over the fragility of her closed eyelids, the sweetness of her perfect skin, her tiny fingernails.

Several miles into the mountains, he turned off on an even narrower road, this one dirt, and bumpy. It looped around wooded landscapes alongside a stream, and opened finally into a pristine meadow, with spectacular views of the high, craggy peaks of the San Juan Mountains. Well, there was a view on clear days, anyway. This afternoon, only the blue lower skirts showed beneath blouses of thick clouds.

A collection of low outbuildings spread out to the east of the meadow. In the center was a small, neat house built of pine. Smoke came out of the chimney. Josh smiled to himself as he followed the driveway around to the front of the house. Desi would have the kettle on. Maybe he'd have a cup of coffee before heading home. She'd been going through a rough time.

As he rounded her house, his smile faded. A grim tableau was playing out in front of the little house. Desi, a tall sturdy woman with a glossy black braid, was standing on her back steps, a rifle in her hand. Her expression was grim.

The rifle was pointed at Claude Tsosie, Desi's soon-to-be-ex-husband, who also sported a long black braid. He wore a jean jacket and boots, and silver jewelry on his wrists. Josh shook his head. He'd never really liked Claude, an artist who lived too much on his talent and never spoke the truth if there was a way around it, but he didn't especially want to see him dead.

A third, unexpected player was a fragile-looking blond woman who stood by her car, frightened and obviously unsure of what to do. Her boots were the city sort—not high-heeled, especially, or pointed, but square and polished. Wouldn't be worth a damn in the snow that was coming. She looked over at Josh's truck, entreaty on her—he saw now—very pretty face.

From the glove box, Josh took his badge. He was a tribal policeman and technically had no jurisdiction off the reservation, but Claude wouldn't pay much attention.

He glanced over his shoulder to see that Glory was still sound asleep, and climbed quietly out of the truck.

* * *

Juliet stood frozen by her rental car, praying that Desi would not actually kill her husband. At the moment, the decision seemed to rest on Claude, who had by turns been cajoling Desi, then turning toward Juliet.

"Sister," he said in his reedy, sexy voice, his hands spread out in appeal, "can't you talk some sense into her? I just want to get a few of my things, and then I'm gone."

From the porch, Desi said, "Don't try to drag her into this. Get into your truck and drive out of here before I shoot you."

Juliet, once very good in a crisis, wrapped her arms around her ribs and tried desperately to remember how her old self would have handled this scene. She couldn't remember. Sometimes lately, it seemed there was a sinkhole in the center of her life, and all sorts of things were falling into it. Memories. Jobs. Maybe her fiancé.

How to handle a crisis.

So, when the big black truck pulled into the drive, Juliet was relieved. She wouldn't have to keep Desi from shooting Claude, or keep Claude from trying to take things that were not technically his. Juliet clasped her thin coat closer to herself—Southern California did not require the kind of coats you needed in Colorado—and gave the person in the truck an urgent expression: *help!*

In a moment, the door opened and a man climbed down and closed his door with odd gentleness.

Juliet blinked. He was obviously Native American, with hair the color of ink tumbling in a straight heavy gloss down his back. Tall, square-shouldered and lean, he wore a sheepskin jacket and jeans and had long, capable-looking hands.

But it was his face that captured her. Eyes as large and dark as a deer's, with a generous mouth to balance cheekbones as severe as a cliff. Not beautiful. Not even handsome, particularly.

Definitely compelling.

Especially now, as he advanced toward Desi and Claude. It was as if an aura came with him, a force field. Juliet wished—suddenly and fiercely—that she had learned that trick.

He moved without hurry across the yard. As he approached, he said, "Claude," and his voice rumbled out of his chest, as if a grizzly bear was doing the talking. The sound was low and full, an umbrella of protective sound. "You know you aren't supposed to be here."

"I just want to get my stuff," Claude responded.

"Get out of here," Desi said in a raw voice. Her face was blotchy with tears or anger or both. She raised the rifle to her shoulder. "Get. Out."

Claude raised his hands. "Take it easy."

From somewhere to the east came a howl, long and chilling, and then another and another—Desi's wolves, crying out from their sanctuary, as if they knew what was transpiring. The wolves were her special project, rescued from every imaginable situation, and the sound of their howls was chilling and primitive.

No one moved.

And then, as if the sky had been ripped open with a knife, it started to snow. Juliet looked up in amazement at gigantic flakes, as big and thick as slices of white bread, tumbling out of the sky. They stuck to the three dark heads to make lacy caps, and with that odd sense of disconnect that had plagued her so much lately, Juliet lost interest in her sister and the scene, and held out a hand to catch a snowflake. They touched her palm and melted white to silver. Pristine. Unspoiled.

The stranger's voice brought her attention back to the scene. "Desi, please put down the rifle. We all love you and need you and this is not the answer."

"Tell him to get off my land and I'll put down the rifle."

"It's not just your land!" Claude protested, taking a step forward.

Desi fired, striking the dirt by Claude's foot. He yelped and jumped backward, "All right. I'm leaving. Crazy—"

Desi calmly took another bullet out of her pocket and began to reload.

Claude climbed into his three-quarter-ton pickup truck, a vehicle even Juliet could recognize as fully loaded. The engine sounded like a semi as he fired it up and backed away. He rolled his window down. "Desi, babe," he said, one last attempt. "Can't we—"

"Don't *ever* talk to me again," Desi said.

The other man, the Indian, banged the flat of his hand on the truck, as if urging a dog or a horse to get along down the road. "Move on, Claude. It's done for today."

And, finally, Claude pulled away, his truck roaring down the dirt road. Not even gravel this far out, Juliet had discovered to her dismay. By midwinter, it would be practically impassable.

The stranger approached Desi, who stood on the porch with a blank expression on her face, and plucked the rifle out of her hand. With an expert gesture, he cracked open the barrel and emptied it. "I hate to leave you out here without protection, Desi," he said in that rumbling voice, "but I hate more to see you kill him, and end up in jail."

"You can't take my gun, Josh," Desi said. "I promise I won't kill him."

Josh kept on with his task.

At last Desi seemed to realize Juliet was there, and gave her sister a wan smile. "Hi, baby," she said.

The stillness broke around Juliet. She dashed across the yard and flung her arms around her big sister. "I'm here now," Juliet said. "We have each other."

And in a most un-big-sisterlike way, Desi broke down, tears streaming out of her eyes as she clung to Juliet. "Thank you. I'm sorry, I love you, I wish I could be stronger for you right now, but I'm just falling apart."

The man put his hand on Juliet's shoulder, and she startled violently, breaking away from her sister's hug, and backing away in a most inelegant way. Her left eye started that weird twitching thing it kept doing lately.

"Let's get her inside," the man said, appearing not to notice. "In case Claude gets mad and comes back."

Juliet nodded jerkily. She was oddly aware of the back of her neck, of the top of her head, parts of herself she never noticed. She looked at his shoes. They were sturdy, steel-toed boots. Serious and stable. He wore jeans that were just tight enough to show his lean, muscular thighs, and a sheepskin jacket that had been worn a few seasons. He smelled of leather and morning, an oddly compelling combination, and she wanted to lean closer, take that scent more deeply into her lungs. She swayed, dizzy from travel or danger or him.

He looked at her closely. "Are you okay?"

Fiancé, she told herself. Remember Scott. She nodded, a little too enthusiastically. "Fine."

"That was a tough scene to run into."

She nodded, lifted a shoulder. "I really am okay." Fear wasn't the problem these days, except the weird twitch and that exaggerated startle reflex. It was more this sense of not being able to really connect to anything that was driving her crazy.

The man said, "My daughter's asleep in the truck. Will you keep an eye on her until I take your sister inside?"

"Sure, of course." She pointed a thumb over her shoulder. "You want me to go stand there?"

But he'd already gone inside, nudging Desi along. Juliet stood on the porch and looked at the big truck, disappearing now under a thin covering of snow. It looked fake, as if someone sprinkled it out of some big box overhead, clumps falling out every so often to land with a puffy splash on the hood. She tugged her sleeves down over her hands and went to stand by the truck.

As if marauders might be coming to fling open the door and steal the little girl away.

Now that the drama had died down, the air was utterly, completely still. It almost held a sense of tension, as if the air were waiting for something. A gunshot? A cry?

No, none of those. Using a trick one of her therapists taught her, she pushed the dark thoughts away and willfully reached for good ones. The silence was waiting for what *good* thing? Laughter. Happiness. A bluebird.

She snorted to herself. Yeah, right. A little bluebird of happiness right here in the falling snow.

The man came out of the house, and she thought again what a sharp, strong face he had. A ripple of nervousness—or maybe attraction?—moved through her. His hair, straight and thick, was so black it sucked light into it. "Hello," he said, "I'm Josh Mad Calf."

"Metcalf?"

He grinned. His eyes crinkled gorgeously at the corners, sending a fan of sun lines into his dark cheeks. "Mad Calf," he repeated, enunciating carefully.

"Thanks for saving the day."

"All in a day's work, ma'am," he said, and winked. "I'm just going to get my daughter from the truck. Why don't you go in and keep your sister company?"

"Right. Yes. Good idea."

In the kitchen, Juliet put the kettle on the tiny, two-burner stove and turned on the fire beneath it, bemused by the bright blue flame that burst to life with a little pop. She had an electric stove at home. Gas seemed old-fashioned, though her friend the chef swore it was the only possible heating element for a serious cook.

Not that Desi—or Juliet for that matter—would ever qualify. Both had been too busy to learn to cook, really. And it wasn't as if their mother was the sort to have taught them. If Carol Rousseau had ever in her life cooked anything more complicated than a cup of tea, Juliet would be very surprised.

With the water on to boil, Juliet looked around to see what had changed since her last visit. The cabin was small, only two rooms; the kitchen/living area, and the sleeping area, with a bed and a futon and desk, plus the postage-stamp-sized bathroom. There was a very small generator for electricity, and the stove ran on propane. Two potbellied stoves, one in each room, provided heat.

Primitive, but not as primitive as it had been. At least there was a toilet and a tub now—things that had been missing the first couple of times Juliet had come to visit. Desi and Claude had built the cabin themselves, a little at a time, and the plan—at least until the marriage had started falling apart—had been to add a room every year.

Juliet found visiting fun for a week or two, but it got old to have to be so careful with everything she used so casually in the city, things a person took for granted. Water, electricity, heat. Desi didn't take long hot baths, as Juliet did in her old Hollywood condo, or leave the water running when she brushed her teeth, or play the television for company. Desi didn't actually own a television—she said they used too much power, and without a dish, there wasn't much reception anyway.

Despite the rustic aspect, the cabin was quite charming, with thick, western-themed blankets on the bed and futon, and a potbellied stove burning wood to warm the room. The windows framed views that were breathtaking on a clear day, and even now, the snow falling on long-needled ponderosa pines looked serene and inviting. As if to complete the picture, a huge dog with a thick, silvery coat wandered in through a dog door in the back, and came over to sniff Juliet's knee.

"Hey, Tecumseh," Juliet said, and bent down to rub his thick fur. "Long time no see."

He lifted his chin to let his chest be scrubbed, then wandered over to slump down by the fire. Desi was in the bathroom, and when she didn't come out fairly soon, Juliet went to the door and knocked gently. "Hey, sis, are you all right?"

"No," she said, the word muffled by tears or a towel or maybe both. "But I'll be out in a minute, okay?"

"I'm just going to go get my suitcase."

"Fine."

Juliet didn't move. She stood there, forehead against the door, and wondered what to do. Desi didn't make a habit of emotional scenes; in fact, of the three Rousseau sisters, Desi had always been the sensible, practical one. Juliet was the good girl. Miranda was the artist, the drama queen. Desi had always been the levelheaded person in any group, the scientist and practical one; picking up the pieces for other people, helping them put their problems into perspective. Desi got done what needed to be done.

One of the reasons, come to think of it, that it was a good thing someone had taken the gun away from her. If Desi was so despairing that she had loaded a shotgun and aimed it at her ex, if she was so overwhelmed that she was weeping in the bathroom, things were really dire.

Just this once, Juliet could be the rescuer in the family. "Josh will be back in a minute, too," she said through the door. "Wash your face and come out when you're ready."

Outside, Juliet was surprised by the density of snow. It already clustered on the steps like down feathers, so light the flakes scattered in front of her feet as she walked toward her car. Josh approached, carrying a car seat with a very, very conked-out little girl in it. Juliet smiled and went for her bag, and carried it back inside right behind him.

Just as Josh was settling the car seat down, the kettle started to whistle—loudly—and Juliet dashed into the kitchen area to pull it off the stove. She poured hot water into a fat yellow ceramic teapot she'd already primed. "Nothing like tea to cure what ails you," she said half to the man, half to herself.

"So my granny says," Josh said.

"Mine, too." She held out her hand. "I'm Juliet, by the way. Desi's younger sister."

Josh reached for her hand. His was a giant paw, the palm as big as her whole hand, and he raised his left, too, making a sandwich that covering hers completely. "Good to meet you."

"Not *that* much younger," Desi said, coming out of the bathroom. Her nose was red and her eyes were swollen, but she looked more like herself. "She's the middle child."

Josh looked over his shoulder, but didn't let go. As gingerly as possible, Juliet tugged her hand out of his grip.

He didn't seem to mind. "Sisters always fight about that," he said in a jovial tone. Juliet liked him for trying to create a sense of normality after the intense scene outside.

"Are you okay?" Juliet asked her sister.

Desi swiped hair off her face. "I'll live." She hugged Josh, and leaned into his chest. "Thank you."

He hugged her back, and in his bearish embrace, tall, square Desi looked tiny. Their mother had always called Desi an Amazon, and not in a nice way. It came out in sentences like, "You are such an Amazon you could never wear those shoes," or, "Will you try to stop clumping around like an Amazon, Desdemona?"

So mean, Juliet thought now, feeling a surge of fierce love for her sister. Their mother had been highly critical of all of them, but Juliet privately thought Desi had got the worst of it.

Lifting the lid on the teapot, she said, "I think it's ready now. Who wants tea?"

"Me, me, me." Desi sat down heavily at the round wooden table. "There are some oatmeal cookies in that jar over there, too, if you want to put a pile of them out for us."

Josh sat down next to her, rubbing his hands. "Oatmeal. All right!"

For all his size, Juliet thought he moved with a surprising grace, as light on his feet as a deer. She put the cookies down in front of him.

"Thanks," he said, and raised his eyes to look at her straight on. For a moment, Juliet didn't think to look away; and it was the *oddest* sensation: she felt as if she plunged into a vat of warm chocolate, seeing there in the long-lashed eyes a spirit of gentleness, beauty, something still and kind.

With a man like this at your back, nothing too

terrible could happen. She wondered where his wife was. There was no ring on his finger, but that didn't always mean anything.

Realizing that she stared, Juliet looked away, poured tea for Desi, and passed her a crystal bowl, stacked neatly with sugar cubes and a little pair of tongs. It had belonged to their grandmother, an east-coast blue blood; Daughters of the American Revolution, roots back to the Pilgrims. As she passed it, Juliet thought of long, quiet afternoons in the Maine "cottage," spent curled up in window seats, with the wind whipping the sea into a frenzy beyond, tea served late in the afternoon with tiny spoons and pots of cream and little cookies. It was a surprisingly rich memory. "So glad you have this bowl," Juliet said.

Desi nodded.

"Are you the artist sister or the lawyer?" Josh asked.

"Lawyer. Sort of." She flipped her shoulder against the thudding wound she sometimes felt over losing that, too, her job as a civil rights lawyer. Not fair. Not *fair!* "I'm taking some time off."

He picked up his tea. Blew on it. For one blistering moment, Juliet wondered if he knew her story, if Desi had told him. Her ears felt hot with embarrassment.

But of course Desi wouldn't tell Juliet's secrets.

Josh said, "It was nice of you to take time off to take care of your sister. She needs you."

"I do," Desi said, touching Juliet's hand.

"I'm glad to be here."

In the corner, the little girl in the car seat suddenly stirred. She kicked her feet, lifted her head, and peered at the adults in confusion. "Hi, Auntie Dez," she said. "Am I staying here?"

"Not this time, sweetheart. But I do have a cookie if you want to come get one."

"You got cookies?" The girl pushed out of her coat, discarded it in the middle of the floor. "What kind?"

"Glory," her father said, "What do we do with our coats?"

The child sighed, dropped her shoulders in exaggerated put-upon-ness, and clomped back to the coat. With rolling eyes, she picked it up and put it on the couch. She had a black braid that reached her hips, big dark eyes, and very rosy brown cheeks. She looked exactly like the kewpie Indian dolls they used to sell in tourist shops around here. Juliet wondered, suddenly, if such things were still sold.

Glory clomped back toward the table. Only when she rounded the corner of the counter did she catch sight of Juliet. The girl stopped dead, staring, her little mouth open in surprise.

"Hi," Juliet said.

The little girl still said nothing. She just gaped. After a few seconds, she frowned and her hand flew to her cheeks in what would be a mocking expression in an adult but was simply the most natural expression of surprise and shock a four-year-old could muster.

"Oh!" she said, as if she'd just figured it out. Her voice was breathy with awe. "You're the *princess,* aren't you?"

# *Chapter 2*

Juliet wasn't sure how to respond.

"The princess?" she echoed, trying to figure out what Glory meant. "Am I?" She glanced at Josh, raised her eyebrows in question.

He gave her a bewildered shrug. He didn't know, either.

Glory came forward, her eyes fixed on Juliet. She leaned on her father's knee, coquettishly flirting with both Juliet and her father. "Can I sit by her? The princess?"

"If she doesn't mind, that's fine."

"Of course I don't mind." Juliet moved over a little to make room, glancing up at her sister.

Despite her weariness, Desi gave a wan grin. "As a rule, she's not crazy about strangers."

"At all," Josh added.

Glory, oddly self-possessed, came around the table. With her hands folded in front of her, she said formally, with enunciation quite clear on each "t," "Is it all right if I sit here, Princess?"

"Yes," Juliet said, and patted the chair. "Please do."

The little girl sat down and spread a napkin over her lap. To the other adults, she announced, "The princess and I are having cookies."

"I see that." Desi blinked, and Juliet saw that she was very near tears again. Of all the things in the world she'd wanted a child most of all. She and Claude had been planning to adopt....

Juliet felt pierced, too, for reasons she couldn't pinpoint. There was something so innocent, almost magical, about the little girl's belief.

"They're very good cookies, aren't they?" Juliet said.

"My grandma makes better ones."

"This is your grandma's recipe, silly girl." Desi said, and gave her one. "I even put in the ginger."

"Listen," Josh said. "I don't want to interrupt, but we need to get some things ironed out here. Let me ask some questions of a purely practical nature."

Desi sipped her tea. Blinked hard. Nodded.

"Do you have a restraining order?"

"No. Not yet. I guess I was hoping I wouldn't have to do that. We've been together for fifteen years—I thought I knew him better than this."

"Princess," Glory said. "You aren't eating."

"You're right." Juliet picked up a cookie. It held absolutely no appeal, but she nibbled an edge anyway. She would have to get out her supply of M&M's. A girl had to eat, after all. Something about the small, bite-sized-ness of the candies appealed to her these days. M&M's, pistachio nuts in their shells, croutons, baby carrots—she lived on them. They also required no attention when one ate them while reading—a big plus. Food for the belly, food for the mind. Presto! Two jobs at once.

When in Rome, however, one did what the Romans did. She bit into the cookie and chewed as well as she could. "Desi, you need to get the paperwork done. You *have* filed for divorce, right?"

Desi examined her cookie, plucked out a raisin. "Not exactly. I guess I just kept thinking this was all going to be a bad dream."

"Time to wake up." Juliet had seen too many cases like this go awry, for all kinds of reasons. "I really don't want to see you lose the land."

"I know."

"I'll go with you," Juliet said. "I'll help you. We'll go to town tomorrow and take care of it, all right?"

Desi nodded. "Okay. Tomorrow."

"Princess," Glory said, touching her hand. "If you came to town, I could show you my shoes!"

"Shoes?" Juliet grinned. "Do you have a lot of shoes?"

"No," she said matter-of-factly. "But I have some red ones." She leaned in close and covered her mouth, whispering, "They have diamonds on them!"

"Wow. I can't wait." Caught in the moment, she bent and whispered, "I *love* red shoes."

"You do? Do you have some?"

"Not with me," Juliet said.

"Where are they?"

"I left them at home. At my home in California."

Glory's eyes widened. "Do you live by Disneyland? You can see Sleeping Beauty and Cinderella at Disneyland, you know."

As it happened—"I do live by Disneyland, actually. You will have to come see me and we'll go together."

"*That* would be good!" Glory looked at her father. "Daddy, do you think we could do that sometime, maybe?"

"We'll see, kiddo." Josh chuckled. To Juliet he said, "You've been anointed."

"Daddy," Glory said, "don't talk to her right now. She needs to eat." With great tenderness, she patted Juliet's hand. "Eat, Princess, I'll watch out for you."

The simple faith in the little girl's face was almost more than Juliet could bear. Sucking in a steadying breath, she bent down and patted the child's hand. "Thank you, sweetie."

Joshua Mad Calf was not a romantic kind of guy. He liked vigorous things, *manly* things like football and race cars and big trucks splashing through the mud. He tended toward the practical, and his job as a cop, as well as his history, had taught him that life was not sweet or nice or fair. In terms of women, he tended to go for a peasant type—strong and curvy, a woman who could work the land, take care of children, cook for twenty at the drop of a hat.

And yet, just like his daughter, he was enchanted by Juliet. He tried to avoid staring, but rarely had seen a woman so pretty. Not *beautiful,* which was too much, too intimidating, too much trouble. Not *attractive,* which was too sedate. Not even cute, which didn't bring enough weight to it.

Juliet was *pretty,* like a pink and white winter morning. Smooth, delicate skin, the softness of pale blond hair tumbling in waves over her slim shoulders, china-blue eyes. She looked exactly like the drawing of a princess in a storybook, right down to the red bow of mouth.

And like a princess under threat of a dragon, there was a vulnerable and fragile air about her. He hadn't missed the exchange of glances between the sisters, the unspoken communication that flowed between them. There was something going on here.

They were finishing their tea and Josh was thinking, reluctantly, that they'd have to take their leave when Glory said, "Auntie, can we feed the wolves?"

"They were already fed today, sweetheart, but we can go see them if your dad doesn't mind."

"Can we, Daddy?"

"You betcha."

It pierced him when Glory reached out and put her small brown hand over Juliet's pale white one, and lifted her guileless face. "Do you want to come, Princess?"

And what, he wondered, was that about, anyway? To say Glory didn't like strangers was like saying the *Titanic* was a big boat. It took months for her to thaw around a new adult, though she was fine with other children. What was it about Juliet that made Glory think she was a princess?

"Yes, very much." Her voice held much more weight

than you'd expect. It was strong and dulcet, well-modulated. He supposed that was at least partly from being in the courtroom, but it lent an oddly royal air.

*Get a grip,* he told himself. "C'mon, kiddo. Let's put your coat back on if we're going outside."

"I want Princess to do it," she said, throwing her arm around her body so he couldn't slip the coat on.

"If you're rude, we'll go home," he said. Quietly.

She flicked a glance toward him, perhaps gauging how serious he was. Something she saw convinced her he meant it. Lowering her arm, she said, "Princess, will you help me put on my coat? Please?"

Juliet looked up at him for permission. Something about the angle or the light made her pupils nearly disappear, which made her eyes look as if they were made of glass, like a doll.

Fragile, girlish. Not his type at all.

And yet, he kept noticing other things, too. There was nothing girlish about her breasts, full and bouncy beneath her sweater, or her mouth, which, despite the princess bow, was full and red, as sensual a mouth as he'd ever seen, or the roundness of her bottom in her jeans. The Rousseau sisters would never make the fashion runway, but he was glad there were still women in the world with some curves to them.

Down boy, he thought with some amusement, but still found himself taking one last look from the corner of his eye. Discreetly. Plump flesh beneath a thin purple sweater. Nice. Definitely nice.

Enough. Handing Glory's coat to her, he said, "Go ahead."

He turned away. There was no room in his life for a woman, and he had to be wary because of Glory, anyway. To make up for the nightmare eight months she'd spent with her mother, the little girl needed absolute stability, and no possibility of loss.

"Ready?" Desi said, tugging her long hair from beneath her coat. The dog got up and wagged his tail. She opened the door to let him go out.

They all traipsed outside in a line, Tecumseh the white wolf-Akita mix, then Desi leading with her strong walk, then Juliet and Glory, holding hands, and Josh in the rear. Snow still fell in heavy drifts, and he thought it was time they should get home.

First the wolves, then home for supper with his little girl.

Away from the sweet temptation of the princess.


Juliet had not been out to see her sister in nearly three years. They'd met several times in other settings. Once at their parents' house in Maine, once in New York City with their sister Miranda and once Desi had come to L.A. for a conference and stayed with Juliet.

Desi's beloved wolves, housed in the sanctuary that was the most important thing in the world to her, had been there the last time Juliet visited, as had the cabin. The path still wound through a thick forest of ponderosa pines and across a grassy meadow where once Juliet had seen seven elk grazing on a summer morning. A string of mineral springs tumbled down the hill, their clear green waters steaming in the cold day.

"Hey, Juliet, did you see?" Desi said, pointing. "We built a grotto, just for you."

"Oh!" Juliet halted in delight. In small clearing, surrounded by red-trunked pines that gave off the scents of butterscotch and vanilla, was a pool steaming boldly in the cold afternoon. Boulders clustered at one end, and Juliet could see the care they'd taken to make the rest of the rocks appear as if Mother Nature had tossed them there for the convenience of the bathers. There was even a small waterfall at one end. "It's amazing, Desi!"

"You'll love getting in it even more, I promise," Desi said. "Very healing. It'll be good for both of us."

Juliet ducked her head. She knew Desi meant well, but she didn't see how sitting in *any* kind of water could possibly heal a mental wound unless it could erase a memory.

"I can't wait."

"Put a little enthusiasm in you voice, there, sis," Desi drawled.

Wryly, Juliet smiled. "I'm sure it will be wonderful."

As if he scented the newcomers, a wolf suddenly howled, a mournful sound cutting through the snowy afternoon. Next to Juliet, Glory stopped and lifted her chin to the sky, letting go of an eerily beautiful howl finished with a series of little yips.

Juliet smiled. "What did you say to him?"

Glory dipped her head coyly, danced, holding on to Juliet's hand, and yipped some more. In the distance, the wolves answered.

Desi paused and turned around. "They're talking back to you, Glory. Do you hear them?"

"I know! That's why I said it!"

"Said what?" Josh asked.

The little girl looked upset and embarrassed and Juliet wanted to protect her from whatever was intruding on the pretty little story she was telling herself. "If it's a secret," Juliet said, "you certainly do not have to tell us."

"I was telling them," Glory said quietly, "that we were bringing the princess to see them!"

"Glory likes to be a wolf," Josh said, coming up beside them. "Sometimes she only speaks in wolf for a whole day."

Juliet chuckled. "I bet that's interesting for you."

"Oh, yeah." He glanced down at her, his dark eyes twinkling. "Since I don't speak wolf at all."

"And I would imagine that translators are somewhat hard to come by." She grinned, feeling her guard slip just a little as she met his gentle gaze. For a moment, she didn't look away, only allowed the slight, easy connection, liking the size of him, his broad shoulders, his legs like tree trunks, a surety of movement as he placed one foot squarely, solidly, then the other.

When the small group entered the clearing where wolves lived, the creatures set up a wild greeting, rushing to the front of their roomy, sturdy kennels, wolves and wolf-mixes bred with a dozen kinds of dogs.

"Wow!" Juliet paused, amazed at how much work Desi had done here, too. There were a lot more kennels— really wide-open, fenced spaces, and a lot more wolves, and Juliet could see that Desi had sunk some serious money into the center. Her love for the animals showed. It almost seemed to Juliet that the wolves got preferential treatment. There were sheds and shelters, trees and water troughs in each kennel—and most important, a lot of room to roam and run. Toward the north, on the flat side of the mountain, was a low, rambling adobe building. It, too, was new. The lights were on.

A youth of about nineteen, with a Prince Valiant haircut and the long limbs of a grasshopper, carried a bucket down the dirt alleyway between kennels. "Glad to see you, boss," he said as he approached. "The new bitch is not eating at all."

Desi nodded. "I'll go check her out in a minute. Alex, I'd like you to meet my sister Juliet. Alex is a wolf-charmer."

"Oh, no," the young man said, his cheekbones going red. "She keeps saying that."

"She doesn't give compliments lightly," Juliet said, extending her hand. "You must be very good."

"Desi's been dying for you to get here." He leaned over as he shook her hand, his knobby wrist sticking out of his coat. "Nice to meet you."

"Thanks."

"Hey, Uncle," Alex said to Josh, then to Glory, "And to you, too, little sister."

Glory danced, high on her toes, and held tight to Juliet's hand. She howled in greeting.

Alex howled back. "Do you want to help me with the water?"

"Can the princess come with me?"

Alex gave Glory a quizzical look. "The princess?"

"That would be Princess Juliet," Josh said, putting his hand on her shoulder. Heavy. Warm. Enormous.

"Ah. The *princess*. Sure, she can come. I bet you want to see the wolves anyway, don't you?"

"Absolutely."

He led them down the dirt alley between fences. Wolves ran over curiously, in groups of two or three, occasionally more. Juliet remembered that wolves, in general, liked to be in a family group. Some were fine with a pair bond; others liked a pack.

"This is Persephone," Alex said, pausing beside a kennel where a wolf with thick, black and white-speckled fur huddled to the back. She raised her head when she heard voices, the gold eyes showing hope. When she saw who it was—evidently not who she had been hoping for—she sighed and put her head back down on her paws, despondence dripping from every hair. "She's not doing well here. We're trying to encourage her to bond with some of the other wolves, but it's not working."

Juliet moved closer, drawn to the sorrow of the animal. "Where did she come from?"

"She was abandoned by her owner, and was killing rodents and other small animals down in Gunnison before animal control picked her up. The woman at the humane society there recognized that she was a wolf, not a dog, and gave us a call."

"Is she as depressed as she seems?" Juliet asked.

He nodded. "A wolf bonds for life, you know? And when humans abandon them, they can take it pretty hard. She's the worst we've had for awhile."

"Poor thing," Josh said. He stood right behind Juliet, and his voice resonated through his chest in a velvety roll she felt on her shoulder blades. "What do you do?"

"Sometimes, you can introduce a pup or another wolf and they get better. Sometimes, they transfer the bond to another human, though this one has shown no interest in anyone yet. Sometimes," he shrugged, "they just die."

Juliet snapped her head up. "They die of a broken heart?"

Alex nodded and looked back at Persephone.

"Wow." Josh moved, and Juliet found herself exchanging a look with him. Up close, she noticed that he smelled almost the same as the forest floor, of loamy ground and pine needles and that essential otherness of mountain earth. As if he were somehow shaped of the land.

*Quit it!* She shouldn't be thinking the things she was thinking about him. She had a fiancé! Feeling unsettled, she looked back to the wolf. "How did you know her name was Persephone?"

"We named her that," Alex said. "For the goddess who was taken under the earth by Hades before she was returned."

"Beautiful."

The wolf lifted her head for a moment, listening. It almost looked as if she'd weep. Juliet turned away, a thick sensation in her throat. "I think I'm going to head back. I'm pretty tired."

"Princess, will you come see me?" Glory asked.

"Yes," she said. "Soon."

# Chapter 3

$A$s the two sisters settled in over a supper of beef stew and crusty bread, Desi asked, "So, how're you doing, Juliet?"

"Fine." Juliet thought of the soap operas and M&M's and the routine of meals and forced a bright smile. "Good! Really."

"How much longer until you go back to work?"

Juliet chased a carrot coin with her spoon. "I'm not sure."

"Which means?"

"It was—um—a forced leave of absence, Desi. Until I can get myself together, I don't need to show up."

Desi put down her spoon, her dark eyes peering right by all of Juliet's defenses. "I see," she said. For a minute, it seemed she might say something else, but she only gave a small nod, picked up her bread and tore off a piece. "Well, then, I guess it's a good thing that you came out here to visit me."

"I'm so glad to be here, Desi." Juliet impulsively touched her sister's hand. Her nails were short and functional, the knuckles a little raw from scrubbing them so often. "You didn't have to wait until it was completely crazy to call me, you know. You don't always have to be the strong one."

Desi looked stricken. "I'm only getting divorced, Juliet!"

"Only? Desi, your whole life is turned upside down!"

"Oh, it's not that." She scowled at her bowl. A lock of wavy dark hair feel against a cheek that was too white. "I mean, it's rotten, the divorce. But it's not the same as being the victim of a violent crime."

"It's been a year. I'm doing okay. And it's not a contest, anyway. You've been with Claude for what, fifteen, sixteen years?"

"I was twenty-one when I joined the Peace Corps and we met the day I arrived in Africa, so—" she flipped her fingers, counting mentally "—fifteen years, I guess."

"That's a long time. And he's really been terrible."

Desi nodded.

Juliet picked up her spoon. "Tomorrow, we'll go to town and start the paperwork—first the restraining order, then we'll find a divorce lawyer in town to help you out."

"Thanks. That's a good idea." She buttered a corn

muffin and flashed a sideways grin, an expression that made an elusive dimple appear. "And you can stop in and see Glory's red shoes, Ms. Princess."

Juliet thought of the little girl's wide-eyed adoration with a sense of warmth. "She made my day, that kid."

"She really does *not* like strangers. It's weird how much she likes you."

"Gee, thanks!" Juliet said with a laugh.

"You know what I mean. She's afraid of strangers. Her mother kidnapped her and she was missing for nearly eight months. Josh only got her back a few months ago."

"That sounds grim."

"I haven't heard all the details, but I gather it wasn't great. No abuse, but a lot of neglect and a lot of people in and out." Desi shook her head. "I don't understand a mother who would put her child in danger that way."

"No, I don't, either," Juliet said. "So he's not married?"

"Nope. And says he never will be again. He and I have formed a Better Friends Than Lovers club." She raised an eyebrow. "One luscious creature, isn't he?"

"It's not that." Juliet felt the tips of her ears get hot. "Well, I guess he is, you know, but I do have a fiancé."

"Nothing wrong with admiring the scenery."

"True."

"How is Scott, anyway?"

Juliet pasted on her bright social smile. "Fine."

Desi blinked. "You are *so* lying."

Juliet ducked her head. "You're right. Things are just not good. I'm not sure why—if it's me or it's him, or both of us." She opened her hands, palms up, and stared at the pinkish flesh around the perimeter. "Or what."

"You have been to a counselor, haven't you?" She frowned. "Rape isn't something you just get over in a day."

"I know. And yes, I've seen a counselor. " Juliet shook her head. "I'm really okay, Desi. It's been a year. It's not like I walk around thinking about it all the time. I've got some issues, but I'll get through them."

"But Scott has issues, too."

Juliet nodded. "I guess it's not uncommon for men to feel unsettled by the rape of a wife or girlfriend."

"Is he pushing you away?"

"Not at all. He—" She paused. "Hovers. It drives me crazy."

"Have you ever told Mom?"

"No. And I won't." Pushing her plate away, Juliet sighed. "Can we not discuss this anymore? Honestly, my girlfriends tiptoe around me and everyone at the law firm acted like I was a very delicate egg they might break. I'm *fine*."

Desi looked at her for a long moment, the dark eyes probing and still. "Well, it's a good thing," she said at last, "because I am a wreck and I need you."

"So do your wolves. I'm so proud of you for that sanctuary."

"That sanctuary is why I'm fighting Claude so hard for the land."

"How does he have any right to this land at all?" Juliet asked in outrage. "You bought it, didn't you?"

Desi shrugged. "I put the original down payment on it, but Claude has done a lot of work to it—clearing and building. He does have some claim, but Juliet—you have to help me with this part. If he takes the land, he'll just sell it to developers."

"Usually, there's a split. Is there some sort of equitable split you can work out?"

"Not easily." Desi bowed her head. "Not and protect the wolves."

"Can you buy him out?"

A glitter danced in Desi's eyes. "Well, I'm sure that's what he wants." The dimple in her cheek appeared. "Real estate prices have skyrocketed the past five years, and there isn't much buildable land available. With the hot spring and the meadows, this really is extremely desirable, and there's a developer who has offered almost ten million for it."

Juliet's mouth fell open. "Ten million?"

"I can't believe it, either—that's about 60 times as much as we paid for it ten years ago."

"How vulgar," Juliet said with a grin, imitating what their mother would say whenever people spoke of money. Still, she whistled. "That's a lot of money."

"It is. But I'm not selling. If I did, I'd betray everything I've been working for my whole life. The land shouldn't belong only to the rich."

"You're right." Juliet frowned. The value of the land complicated the divorce in a very sticky way. "But if you think the pressure will ease, you're crazy."

"I know." She rubbed her face. "It's insane."

"What happened to kick the real estate value so high so fast?"

"Couple of things. One is just that Colorado is such a great ski center, and one by one, all the major recreational areas are exploding. This ski area has been here for about twenty years, but it's hard to get here and with so many other choices, there was no rush to get to Mariposa."

"Which is why you guys liked it, right? It was the mountains, there's a town, but it wasn't a big mass of tourists."

"Exactly." She stood up and carried the bowls to the counter and put a stopper in the drain. "That, and even for Colorado, it's amazingly beautiful." Taking a teakettle off the stove where it had been warming while they ate, she poured hot water into the sink. "It's a lot of things that made the land skyrocket, but the big one is that Johann Larsen—the skier—started training here about seven years ago, and then he won all those medals at the Olympics. Now it's becoming a center for training."

"Yeah, but that would account for the value tripling, or even quadrupling. Not sixty-times-ing."

Desi raised her eyebrows. "They built a casino on the reservation."

"Ah." That would do it, combined with everything else. Juliet pursed her lips in thought. "That complicates things a lot. But we'll figure something out."

"I'm tired tonight, though, and I'm sure you are, too. Let's make some hot chocolate and curl up with the dogs inside and tell ghost stories."

Juliet rubbed her foot on Crazy Horse, a black lab mix who had the sweetest eyes in the world. "Can Crazy Horse sleep with me?"

Desi grinned. "Absolutely."

"Let's get some rest then." Juliet had a feeling they were going to need it, to deal with all the layers of this sticky divorce.

It was only as she was drifting off to sleep that she realized she'd forgotten to call Scott. And the slight pinprick of guilt only lasted a second, while the recognition of Desi's situation sank in.

Ten million dollars.

Good grief.

Josh would never understand the vagaries of the human female, whether she was four years old or four hundred. The morning was cold and sharp as cactus needles, but what did Glory come out of the room wearing? A short skirt and sandals with flowers.

And a crown.

"Glory," he said, putting forks on the table, "it snowed last night. Snow is cold. Go back and find something warm to put on."

"Like what? Grandma says you should help me pick stuff out."

"Grandma is a troublemaker." His mother, Helene, wanted Glory to be spit-polished every morning, with matching ribbons and socks. Josh had neither the time nor the talent to make that happen. "Don't you tell her I said that, either." The water on the stove was boiling. He poured a cup of old-fashioned oats into the pan. Patiently, he said, "Every time I help you, you complain."

"I want help this morning."

"Okay, go get a pair of jeans and a—" he had to stop

and think. Did everything go with jeans? "A blue sweater."

"I want a yellow sweater."

"Yellow, then, I don't care."

Glory marched back to her bedroom, muttering to Pink and Ink, her imaginary friends. She didn't allow anyone else to talk to them, and she was disgusted if an adult pretended to see them. At the same time, they were quite real in Glory's universe. As far as Josh could figure, Pink was a fluffy girl being, and Ink was a boy, sleek as a seal. They were sister and brother.

"Spirit guides," his mother had pronounced in her I-am-the-Medicine-Woman voice.

"Named Pink and Ink?" Josh scoffed.

"Names don't matter."

He let it go. Helene was a sage and healer, in both "white" medicine and traditional native medicine. In the mainstream world, she was an emergency room nurse at the medical center, and on the reservation, she was a medicine woman, using a combination of spiritual and physical healing techniques like sweats and teas and spiritual journeys he no longer believed in.

But it worked for her. That was how he'd met Desi, actually, through his mother. They held women's sweats and drummings on Desi's land, in a sweat lodge by the hot springs. It was, evidently, sacred ground and Desi had been honored to help provide space.

"Hurry up, Glory!" Josh called. "Breakfast is almost ready."

Glory came out wearing a pink sweatshirt with a sequined butterfly over the front, and pale blue corduroy pants. Exasperated, he almost said something about the fact that she had not listened to his clothing advice, but let it go.

She handed him a brush. "Will you do my hair for me?"

"Definitely." He took the silver plastic-and-rhinestone tiara off her head and gave it to her to hold, then brushed out her long, thick hair. Sparks of static popped and flashed in the depths. When it was free, it fell past her hips in a perfectly straight waterfall of silk, but Glory liked it to be braided. He loved the cool weight of it weaving through his fingers. "You look very pretty," he said.

"I would like to get some curlers. Natasha has curls sometimes."

"Might have to take that up with Grandma. I'm not sure I know how to do curls."

She sighed, leaning against his knee as he braided her hair. "That's why a girl needs a mommy, too. Because dads don't know stuff."

She was only four. She didn't know it killed him to be so inept at the girly parts of parenthood. He did his best, but—again—he was a guy. He liked big messy things. Football games in muddy fields, big trucks with noisy engines, skinning fish. He didn't know much about making a living room look pretty or cooking anything beyond the basic meat and potatoes and oatmeal, though he was learning, painfully and slowly. He didn't know how to match clothes or do fancy braids.

He had, however, learned to paint her teeny-tiny fingernails. He'd even managed to get a miniscule star more or less centered on her thumbnail.

"Yeah, it's rough, kid," he said, fastening her braid. "You only have thirty-nine aunts and cousins and grandmas. One of them will know."

"The princess will know."

Josh felt a frisson of nervousness over his neck. Worry that Glory was flinging herself too much into this whole Juliet business, worry that someone else might let her down, worry that he couldn't protect her from everything no matter how much he might want to. "Well, if we see her, we'll ask her."

"We'll see her," Glory said. "She promised. Princesses keep their promises."

"I'm sure they do if they can, sweetie, but they have a lot of business to take care of, too."

Glory climbed up to the table. With a direct gaze that was much older than her years, she said, "We'll see her." She put the crown back in place on her head. "Stop worrying."

He chuckled and took the pot of oatmeal from the stove. "I'll do my best, kiddo. Do my best."

Juliet awakened to discover the warm breath of a dog on her neck. She didn't immediately realize it was a dog, only surfacing slowly to the warm weight of Tecumseh slumped against her body. She remembered his jumping up on the futon beside her during the night, and her welcoming his furry friendliness; she flung an arm around him and fell into the deepest sleep she'd known in months. No one could hurt you if they had to cross a seventy-five-pound wolf-mix to get to you.

But now that dog was panting against her neck. Politely at first, then with a cold nose against her ear, a quick nudge. When Juliet buried her head, Tecumseh put his paw on her shoulder.

"Okay, okay," Juliet said, and flung the covers back, wincing at the cold. The floor was freezing, the air as brisk as icicles. She spied Desi's down coat on a hook and put it on, and some boots that were resting by the stove, which had obviously either gone out or was very, very low. Juliet could see her breath. No wonder Desi had such long hair. She needed it for warmth!

Trying to move quietly, she shuffled toward the front door and let out the dog—well, dogs, now, since the other two were happy to have the chance to get outside, too. Desi locked the dog door at night. They moved gingerly, then one saw something in the trees and bolted. The other two followed in exuberant explosion, barking happily.

Juliet watched for a moment, then turned away to close the door and spied something out of the corner or her eye—a dark splash against the snow on the edge of the porch. She turned back frowning, and saw that it was a dead bird.

No, not just dead.

Murdered. Its throat had been cut.

Juliet yelped. Desi was at her side in two seconds flat, somehow alerted to danger by that small sound. She took one look at the dead bird and cursed. "Damn him!"

She stomped out on the porch, and picked the bird

up with a shovel. "I'm going to report this," she said, and settled the poor thing on top of the wood shed.

To Juliet's surprise, there was a tear in Desi's eye. "Are you okay?"

"No!" Desi said. "It's not okay to kill something to try to scare me, and I'm particularly fond of ravens, a fact that bastard knows, and used to hurt me."

Juliet hugged her. "Don't," she whispered. "Don't let him get inside of your head. He's being terrible, but one day this will all be over and your life will be good again."

Desi clutched her. "Promise?"

"I promise."

"Let's get ready to go to town." They dressed and did a few chores and piled into Desi's truck. "I'll treat you to breakfast before we get down to business," she promised. "Waffles and bacon?"

"Perfect."

Neither sister was particularly chipper first thing in the morning, and the dark spiritedness of the dead raven hung in the air. They rode in silence.

But after a few minutes, Juliet found herself admiring the scenery. It was so astonishingly beautiful it didn't seem real.

The storm had moved on, leaving behind enough snow to dust the trees and ground with a diamond sparkle. Sunshine beamed into the high mountain valley and the sharp, craggy peaks of the San Juans were newly touched with snow. "Do you ever get used to it?" she asked.

"The scenery? No way," Desi said. "How could you?"

"Good." She peered upward—up, up, up—to the

rugged red cliffs edged with stark white, and above them, the piercing blue of the sky. "I would hate to become immune. Every winter, I'd dream about being here. We never did come to ski, though, did we?"

"We begged enough, but I think our illustrious parents—" her voice was thick with irony "—thought it too plebian. If one were to ski in Colorado, it had to be Aspen, or at the very least, Vail."

"Is the camp still open?" All three sisters, Desi, Juliet and their youngest sister, Miranda, had come to camp in Mariposa every summer for years while their parents, afforded long vacations by their positions as college professors, stayed with friends in Crete, or hosted their set in Zurich, or ambled around whatever destination was approved for intellectuals that year.

"I think so. I see kids pouring into town on the bus every June."

"Poor things."

Desi laughed. "I loved coming to camp."

"I liked a lot of things about it, but I didn't like the bugs or the wild animals. I was scared all the time."

"You were?" Desi said in surprise. "I didn't know that. Why didn't you tell me?"

"Because you were always so brave about everything. Nothing scared you."

"I was always an outdoor kind of girl, though. You weren't."

"True." She admired the vividness of the sky. "What I really hated was being away from home all summer. It was really lonely."

"You poor baby!" Desi smiled. "You know me,

though—I loved getting away from…" She paused. "Oh, let's not be coy. I loved getting away from our parents. I couldn't wait. Camp seemed a thousand times more real and reliable than anything at home."

"I got used to it eventually." Juliet thought of those summers, her own wish to lean on reliable things, like the same room, the same stuff, the same friends, and Desi's adventurous heart, which had led to her travels abroad, and Claude. "What happened to Claude?" she mused aloud. "He always seemed like such a good guy."

Desi said carefully, "Do you think so?"

"Yeah. Don't you?"

"Yeah. I've just been wondering lately if I was blind or foolish or something." She gave Juliet a little shrug. "I'm glad you liked him, too."

Juliet reached over and touched Desi's shoulder. "You've always been wise and kind, Desi. Something changed Claude and his character didn't keep up."

"Thanks."

As they came down off the mountain and around a bend, they emerged suddenly from the trees and there was the narrow, long town of Mariposa. Five blocks wide, a mile and a half long. The sun had just climbed over the peaks to the east and now spilled into the valley, sparking on the snow-covered roofs. Juliet looked at her watch. Almost 8:30. "I bet it's dark on winter mornings."

"Very. The sun doesn't come up until nine." She swung onto the main street. Once it had been called simply Main Street, but it had been changed to Black Diamond Boulevard when the ski runs were built in the late seventies.

The tone of the town was half glitzy ski resort, half

mountain rustic. Stone bungalows built at the turn of the century populated the old part of town, along with buildings that dated back to gold rush days. At the ends of town, built to the very edge of the National Forest lands, were blocks of modern condos and faux Alpine shops housing restaurants and art galleries and shops selling sports gear and yoga clothing. Above it all rose the ski slopes.

"Uh-oh," Desi said. "There's Claude. Damn."

Juliet saw him ambling down the street in a black fleece vest and jeans and boots, his black braid shining. He held hands openly with a woman who wore what Juliet thought of as an adventure racer's uniform: tight stretchy pants with racing stripes down the side, a bright yellow thermal shirt, sunglasses on her tousled blond curls.

"Hey," Juliet said, recognition dawning, "isn't that Christie Lundgren? The skier?"

"Yep," Desi said, grimly. "Bastard! Now he has to make a fool of me in public?"

In alarm, Juliet looked up. "Just keep driving, Dez. You don't want any trouble."

But it was too late. Desi swung into a parking spot in front of the bank, and threw open the door before Juliet could so much as blink. Desi had something in her hands. Juliet couldn't make out what it was at first, but then she saw it was a phone. A camera phone. Desi dashed in front of the couple and snapped a picture, then another, before Claude managed to disentangle himself from his girlfriend.

Juliet got out of the truck, braced for anything.

But Desi grinned in triumph, waving the camera over her head. "Got you now, you sorry rat."

"What difference will a picture make?" Claude said.

"Date and time stamped? Plenty." She saluted the blond skier next to Claude. "Enjoy," she said, and headed back to the truck. Juliet, shivering in her thin coat, gladly headed back toward the truck. Out of the corner of her eye, she saw Claude make a sudden move. Juliet whirled.

Claude dived for Desi, who yelped, leaping a little to try to get away from him. He managed to grab the sleeve of her coat, and they slid around on the snow underfoot. Desi cried, "Juliet! Come get this!"

Juliet, shaken out of her surprise, dashed toward her sister. "Throw it!"

But Claude grabbed Desi close to him, and the two of them wrestled, slipping and sliding on the snow, and Desi couldn't get her arm free. "Let me go!" Desi cried.

"You owe me," Claude roared. "You're not going to cheat me out of that land. I bought it, too."

A crowd started to gather, across the street in front of the diner, and in the street. "I bought that land with my inheritance from my grandmother, and you know it." She yanked free suddenly, and started to bolt. "Juliet!" she cried, but Claude tackled her.

The two of them went down, slamming hard into the pavement. The girl with him yelped and plastered her back against the wall. Juliet saw blood spill brightly into the snow, but couldn't see who it belonged to. She rushed toward them. "Stop it, you two!" Juliet yelled. "Just stop it!"

Claude cried out and jumped up, the phone in his hand. Blood streamed out of cuts on his lip and cheekbone, and he wiped it away angrily. With a guttural cry of victory, he dropped the cell phone on the stone stoop and smashed it beneath the heel of his boot.

Desi, too, was bleeding from a cut in her scalp, and tears poured down her face. She struggled to her feet as Claude walked away. "I'm going to *kill* you, Claude Tsosie," she cried after him.

"You can try," he said, turning around to smirk at her.

Furiously, Desi bent down, picked up a rock, and threw it after him. It landed harmlessly a few feet behind him, but Desi slipped and landed on her bottom. Stunned, she didn't move, an expression of bewilderment and grief on her face.

Blood from the cut on her head stained the shoulder of her coat, and Juliet bent down with tenderness. "Come on, honey," she said gently, helping her sister to her feet. "Let's get you to the doctor."

A tall Ute woman with craggy dark features materialized on the street, a clean white towel in her hands. She pressed the cloth to the wound. "Desi, Desi," she said in a voice that sounded like the soft south wind, "you must let him go."

"I need to take care of the wolves," Desi said, wearily. "If he takes half the land, I can't."

"The law will be on your side," the woman said. She met Juliet's eyes. "Let's get her to the clinic. She's gonna need stitches."

Juliet nodded. "And then, we are going to file properly for divorce, and for a restraining order to keep you two apart until this is over, got it?"

Desi bowed her head. "Yes."

# Chapter 4

The scalp wound needed six stitches, but as it was Mariposa, a clinic that was supremely qualified to treat cracked heads, and it was the between season—between the high hiking and high skiing periods—it only took a half hour from start to finish. Then Desi, her friend Helene, the Ute woman, and Juliet were finally having breakfast at the Red Buffalo, a diner on Black Diamond Boulevard.

It was a busy morning. Several times, people stopped by the table to ask about Desi's bandaged head, and the trouble that had caused it. Others gave a quick nod and hurried by, and Juliet realized the town's people were taking sides. Some on Desi's side, some on Claude's.

Damn.

Desi noticed, too. "He's so damned charming and

good-looking," she said, matter-of-factly. "It's hard to get people to see beyond that."

"It's why some politicians can get so far," Juliet said.

"What's the feeling about Claude on the rez, Helene?" Desi asked. "They like him there?"

Helene lifted a shoulder. "Some do, the same ones who like him around town here. The ones who fall for charm and good looks fall for him, even in Indian Country." She stirred her coffee. Her wrist, flat and strong and brown, was ringed with three beaded bracelets in different colors. "There's some who like him 'cause he's been successful. Others don't because of the same thing."

"Why would they not like him because he's successful?" Juliet asked.

"Some people want everybody to suffer together."

Juliet frowned. "I'm still not quite getting why all this fuss about the two of you, anyway? Why does anyone care?"

"Because the land is so valuable," Helene said.

"But why would anyone on the reservation care about that?"

"In a town this small," Desi said, "everyone is intimately connected. Our fortunes are all mixed up together. The politicians will care what the Indian community wants because the casino is such a cash cow, and the Indian vote is huge."

"The lawyers will care because they want to be politicians," Helene said. "The townsfolk care because they need things to keep their tongues wagging, and everything financial ripples around the whole town."

Desi smoothed the empty spot on her left hand where her wedding ring had lived. "The businessmen will care because they court the Indian vote so the politicians will swing their way on land decisions."

"Are there businessmen trying to get the land right now?"

Desi snorted. "Oh, yeah. Developers of all kinds."

Juliet's head ached the slightest bit. "This is a lot more complicated than I expected." She rubbed the spot between her brows, thinking of what needed to be done.

First, she needed to do some research, both on local real estate law and practices, and on cases like this one in recent courts. "Have you talked to a lawyer at all, Desi?"

"Who can I trust around here, really? The lawyers all want to be politicians, the—"

"I get it."

A happy little cry cut through the gloom at their table. "Hi, Grandma!" said a girl who popped up at the edge of the booth.

"Glory, what are you doing here? Why aren't you at preschool?" Helene asked, clearly surprised to see her granddaughter. No more surprised than Juliet was to realize Helene was Glory's grandmother.

"My teacher had a toothache."

"Oh, that's too bad." Helene scooted over to let the little girl, with her long dark braid, into the booth beside her.

As Glory scrambled in, adjusting a tiara tucked with bobby pins into her hair, she happened to glance up and see Juliet. "Princess!" she screeched. "What are you doing here?" Before Juliet could answer, she whipped her head up to her grandmother. "How do *you* know the princess?"

"This is weird," Desi said.

Juliet liked it. She liked it even more when rumble-voiced Josh strolled up to the table and gave her a nod. "How are you, Princess?"

She smiled. His eyes were as warm and kindly as she remembered from yesterday. "Not bad. How are you?"

"Glad to see you. This little girl—" He took a breath. "*Believes,* you know?"

Juliet nodded. "It's okay."

He caught sight of Desi's bandaged head. "What happened to you?"

"Long story." Desi stood up, vacating the spot next to Juliet. "Sit down, Josh. I'm going to go wash my hands."

"I've got to get to the dojo in a few minutes—a home-school class is coming." But he sat down anyway, the long, solid weight of him warm against Juliet's side. His hands were as big as saucers, and he folded them together in front of him. He wore no jewelry on them. Juliet thought they were extraordinarily beautiful, the sinews and lines, the graceful length of his fingers, the oval nails.

In her fluting voice, Glory said, "Princess, do you want to come sit by me?"

Juliet looked away from Josh's hands. "Honey, we have to run some errands in a few minutes."

Her radiant face dimmed. "Oh."

Juliet leaned forward. "I'll be finished in an hour or two. I can come see you later, if you like. You can show me your red shoes."

"Hey! That's a good idea! Grandma, can you take me

to my house in a couple of hours so I can show the princess my shoes?"

Helene grinned, her eyes crinkling into angles. "I can do that."

"Okay."

"What happened to Desi's head?" Josh asked.

"She...uh...fell down."

He flipped a butter knife end to end on the table. "Claude somehow mixed up in it?"

"Yeah." Juliet glanced at Helene. "Your mom was there, too. You can hear more about it later."

"I'm not deaf, you know," Glory said. "I know about grown-up fights, too. My mommy had them all the time."

"Nobody is keeping secrets, Glory," Josh said. "But even if we were, you are a little girl, and little girls don't need to know everything. We like to keep things nice for you."

Glory sighed, long-suffering, and with a harrumph, leaned her cheek into her hand.

Juliet chuckled. "I like your tiara," she said. "And I can't wait to see your shoes later."

"Me, too." She suddenly perked up. "Hey! Princess, do you know how to curl hair?"

"Sure. You want your hair curled?"

"Yes," Glory said emphatically. "Natasha in my class always has her hair curled and my daddy doesn't know how."

Josh put one hand beneath the table and squeezed Juliet's hand lightly. "Thanks," he said very quietly.

"No problem." She pulled free delicately, and Desi came back to the table.

"Ready?" her sister asked, putting sunglasses on her head.

"I am."

A woman in a yellow jacket moved by the table and gave Desi a long, hard glare. Desi stared right back. When the woman continued toward the cash register, Desi and rolled her eyes at Juliet. "The dentist's wife," she said when the woman had gone outside. "She hates my guts."

"Because?"

"Because she's one of Claude's groupies, and in their eyes, I'm just a mean woman who doesn't understand him."

"Yeah," Josh said, behind them, "you old meanie, you."

Desi grinned, her eyes flashing in a way that made her sister wonder what had forged the bond between these two.

And was there something romantic brewing? "You better believe it, mister."

Did her sister have feelings for this man? He was sort of her type, after all, a rugged Native American, an outdoorsman. He had that adorable daughter who needed a mother.

Josh laughed softly, and Juliet felt the sound run down her neck like warm fingers. She resisted looking up at him, getting caught again in that dark, patient gaze. But even as she resisted, she felt the steady presence of him at her back, solid, steady, calm, and she couldn't help the wave of yearning it kindled in her. It had been a long time since Juliet had felt safe—if she ever had.

Scott was a good man—smart, supportive, ambitious—but she'd never felt sheltered by him. Josh, on the other hand—

With a popping little shock, she heard her thoughts. *Stop it!* She was engaged! It was one thing to admire the long, sturdy thighs of a man, or the grace of his hands. A woman had eyes, after all....

But it was something else again to be thinking of resting against that broad shoulder, to imagine taking a deep breath of relief as that deep laughter rang into the room.

Disloyal. In two directions if Desi was attracted to him, too.

Blindly, Juliet stood and walked towards the door, grabbing a green-and-brown-wrapped mint from a bowl on the counter. "I'll be right outside," she called back. Without waiting for a reply, she rushed out.

The door was in a little foyer with racks of newspapers and tourist brochures on one side. As Juliet rushed through, a man was coming in, and Juliet stepped aside, and—

Slammed squarely into her demons. She was never quite sure what happened, why she was flung back in time, but suddenly, she smelled a musky aftershave and margaritas, and there was a swooshing of all sound, as if her ears were covered. In real time, she ducked her head and managed to stumble around the man coming in the door, ignoring him when he said, "Miss, are you all right?" and got out to the sunshine in the street. Sweat poured down the back of her neck.

But even in the bright sunshine and open air, her throat felt constricted, and her breath came in ragged, tearing gasps. The worst was the sense of mindless panic urging her to *flee! flee! flee!* Her legs burned with the need, her lungs felt as if they would explode. With as much control as she could muster, she grabbed the stone corner of the building and leaned on it, trying not to fight the sensations nor give into them.

A heavy hand fell on her shoulder. "Hey, Juliet, are you—"

She screamed, slammed the hand away. Tried to back off, bumped into the wall.

Saw that it was Josh, and wanted to burst into tears.

He held his hands up, palm out to show he wouldn't hurt her. "Hey, hey, hey," he said. That rich gentle voice splashed into her panic, coating it like chocolate.

And just as suddenly as she'd been sucked into the flashback, she fell back out. With a soft noise, Juliet pitched forward, instinctively reaching for the sturdiness of his big, strong shoulders. Her head landed against his sternum, and she could smell the clean freshness of clothes hung out to dry on a line, and something deeper, his flesh. A gentle light hand smoothed her hair.

"You're okay," he said. "You're okay."

And it was true. After a moment, the dark memories retreated, and she could take a long, slow breath. Raise her head. Only then did she realize how close they were. Embarrassed, she tried to take a step back, and bumped into the wall at her back. "I'm sorry," she said, trying to duck to her left, afraid to look at him.

"Easy." He moved his big hand up and down her arm. "You don't have to go anywhere. Your sister will be here in a hot second."

"I'm—this is…oh, I'm embarrassed." She bent her head. "Thanks. I'm sorry."

"You don't have to apologize." His rumbling voice again rolled down her spine, easing the tension there, and his hands kept moving on her arms in a most soothing way. Steady. Gentle. "You don't have to say anything at all."

Juliet bent her head. He wore dark brown leather hiking boots, sturdy-looking with laces and hooks and eyes and a sole that looked as if it could withstand six inches of ice. Her feet in their thin California boots looked insubstantial, tiny even, and with a glimmer of pleasure, she thought one of the reasons to like a man so big was so that you could feel small next to him. And she was not normally a small woman.

She wanted to offer an explanation, to say something to excuse her weird behavior. The flashbacks were hateful, like a scar, and it made her feel overwhelmed to imagine telling him. Where to start? "Thanks," was all she said.

He released her and in the next instant, Desi came out, offering breath mints to everyone. Juliet moved away, vaguely aware of him watching her. "We'd better get to the courthouse," she said. "Get this taken care of."

"Yep. Let's do it. "

Juliet glanced up at Josh. "See you later."

His eyes were steady and sober and saw far more than she wished. "Right."

The homeschoolers left after their weekly practice, and Josh took advantage of the fact that he had a day off from his job as a tribal policeman on the reservation—they worked three on and two off—and the fact that his mother had Glory for the morning to do some cleaning at the dojo. He could have hired a service to do the work for him, but he found the rote actions of dusting, sweeping, mopping to be a healthy way to order his own mind.

He opened the doors and windows to the blaze of fresh mountain air, sweetened by the now-melting snow. In predictable autumn capriciousness, the sun was now warm enough to warrant the dread-locked boys taking off their shirts.

There were several layers of things on Josh's mind this afternoon. The first was Desi and Claude. It was a dangerous situation and getting more dangerous by the hour. Until now, Claude had kept his little assignations quiet, or at least somewhat under the table, and although some of the ex-mistresses were a little volatile, Claude had managed to keep them under control. The new one, Christie Lundgren, was a well-known professional skier, a woman much younger than Claude, and well known for her scathing and destructive temper. By all accounts, she was wildly smitten with her handsome, artistic, exotic lover.

Now Claude had gone public, humiliating Desi and, Josh was afraid, others. Claude's layers of women were like those Russian dolls, another and another and another. Someone had been cast aside for Lundgren.

On the plus side, Lundgren had plenty of money from endorsements, and Claude would no doubt want to keep her happy. Maybe he'd accept the restraining order with something resembling respect, at least until the divorce settlement could be hammered out.

Or not.

Trading a feather duster for a spray bottle filled with vinegar and water and a bag full of clean rags, Josh sprayed the first of the big windows in the room. It had once been a mother-in-law house behind a bungalow. Josh had knocked out most of the internal walls to open it up, and hung mirrors along the far wall. These old windows had ancient glass, with ripples and imperfections he genuinely loved, and he liked the action of making them shiny.

The next thing on his mind was his daughter's absolute refusal to speak of her time with her mother at all. Not with a counselor, not with her grandmother, not with him. But sometimes in nursery school, she drew chaotic pictures that frightened her teacher, and sometimes, she still awakened screaming.

It killed him. If it was not against his practice, he would hate his ex-wife. He didn't know, had no way to know, what had transpired in the long months Glory had been missing. She was found in Denver, finally, when the house they were living in caught fire, and they were transported, along with the other eight people living in the house, to the hospital. A nurse recognized Glory from a flyer in the newspaper, and called the police, who took the little girl into custody. Glory had been too thin, easily startled, but there had been no evidence of any sort of abuse. She'd been almost heart-breakingly happy to see her father and rarely spoke of her mother ever after.

Sunlight, captured by a bubble in the old glass, blazed in the window he washed. Josh rubbed a circle around it, thinking. The way Juliet looked after breakfast made him think of Glory's blankness when her mother was mentioned.

Which brought him to the last thing on his mental agenda—his discovery that Juliet was wounded. Obviously. Painfully.

Which, in a word, sucked. He'd done his time with broken birds. He drew them in flocks for reasons he could never quite figure out, and inevitably, he tried to mend their cracked wings and broken hearts. Inevitably, he failed, the most dramatically with his ex-wife.

These days, there was only room in his life for one wounded bird, and that was his own daughter.

The trouble was, Glory had made up her mind that Juliet was the finest thing to fall to earth in eons. Josh couldn't bear to deny her the pleasure of Juliet's company. Perhaps it would be a healing thing for both of them. Maybe the wounded birds would heal each other.

In the meantime, he'd just have to keep himself a bit aloof, apart. Much as he'd like to, he couldn't afford to explore the depths of the lovely Juliet.

# Chapter 5

Josh's resolve to stay aloof was immediately tested when Juliet showed up at the dojo an hour later. She'd obviously been shopping with Desi, because the pair of them came in wearing matching blouses, Desi in pink, Juliet in blue. He half grinned when they came in, laughing like girls. "Sorry, did we have a flashback to the hippie days?"

Desi laughed. Their blouses were airy Indian cotton embroidered with sequins and beads. "Everything in the stores is like this! It's like sixth grade all over again!" She spun around to model it, her long, long dark hair spilling down back, her curvy figure giving new meaning to the word *body*. "What do you think?"

"I think you ought to put on girl clothes more often."

He knew Desi rarely—if ever—indulged on clothes that could only be worn for fashion's sake, opting instead for more practical garb.

"That's what I told her," Juliet said.

Until she spoke, he'd managed to keep her blurred at the edges of his vision, a smear of blue and yellow in the corner of his eye. When she spoke, he had to look.

And then he couldn't look away. Everything about her looked floaty. Otherworldly, like a scarf that might blow away in a good wind. Her fine blond hair hung loose around her neck; the thin fabric of the blouse skimmed her slim shoulders and arms in a way that made him think of cobwebs.

She was…ethereal. Well, ethereal except the vivid turquoise of her eyes. And the lush, red bow of her mouth and the supple thrust of her breasts beneath the all-too-thin fabric. How could someone be so wispy and so lush at once?

"You look nice, too," he said. Did they notice the gruffness of his voice? He resisted clearing his throat. *Don't be an idiot, man. Ain't you ever seen a girl before?*

"Thanks." She held up the shopping bag she was carrying. "I hope you don't mind, but I brought Glory a present."

"You did?" He tried to hide his dismay, but evidently was not particularly successful. Juliet's cheeks turned red and Desi jumped in.

"It's my fault," she said. "We bought matching shirts for us, and for our sister in New York, and we decided to see if there was one in Glory's size."

"But it's okay, we can take it back, no problem," Juliet said. "It was presumptuous, I'm sorry."

"Naw, it's all right." He leaned on his broom, let a smile surface. "I'm just worried that she's gonna get her little heart broken, you know?"

Juliet put her hands to her chest. "Oh, I'd never break her heart! I promise."

She would never *mean to,* he could see that. He folded the rag in his hands, then refolded it, testing the sensation in his chest. Warning. But for was it for Glory, or for him? "She'll be tickled pink that you brought her a present, Princess."

"I've got to get some work done," Desi said, "check on a bull that was injured and touch bases with the clinic. You can stay here and visit with Glory, if you want. Give me a call on the cell—" She halted, frowned thunderously. "How am I going to function without a cell phone?"

Juliet raised her eyebrows.

"I'll have to go get a replacement." She growled. "That infuriates me!"

"Let it go," Juliet said.

Desi's hands flew in the air. "I know, I know." She pursed her lips. "Okay, when I get my new cell, I'll call you on yours, and then I can run by and pick you up later."

"Can I walk over to the clinic?" In addition to the wolf center, Desi had a traditional large animal practice in town. "I'd like to see it."

"Sure, it's at the east end of town, on the main road."

She gave walking directions. "Still, let me know you're coming, okay? So you're not stuck waiting for me forever and I don't even know. I'll finish up and then we'll head back to the house."

"Trust me," Josh said, "you want to call her."

"Okay. I've got the number programmed into my cell." Juliet pulled it out of her purse to show them. "You guys are acting like I'm twelve. I live in Hollywood, remember?"

Desi laughed, and Josh thought it was the easiest-sounding sound that had come from her in months. It was good for her to have Juliet around. "Did you get everything taken care of this morning?" he asked.

"Yes. Restraining order filed. Divorce papers picked up and will be filed by the end of the week, so we can get that rolling." She held up three fingers. "Scout's honor."

"Good work."

"Thanks." Desi put on her coat and headed for the door, rattling her keys as she waved. "See you kids later."

When she left, the bell over the door ringing faintly, Juliet looked at Josh and said, "I'm sorry about the little scene at the restaurant. That hasn't happened for awhile."

"You don't have to apologize," he said again. "It's okay."

She started to speak, then stopped, putting her hands in her back pockets. A pose that neatly illuminated the curve of her waist. For a long moment, she searched his face with narrowed eyes, and he had a chance to simply meet that blue gaze. He took in the tiny scar through her left eyebrow, and what looked like a chicken pox scar on her chin, barely visible and strangely appealing.

At last she nodded. "That's a relief. Thanks."

"No problem. Let's go find Glory, Princess Juliet."

Juliet stepped out into the day and blinked, wishing for her sunglasses. With one hand, she shielded her eyes and lifted her head to the brilliant blue sky. "Wow."

Josh raised his gaze, chuckled. "That about says it, all right."

Down the mountains spilled gleaming waterfalls of yellow aspens, vivid against the darker pines. It looked as if a pot of paint had tipped over. "I keep trying to name that color in my head—yellow doesn't really capture it, and lemon is too bright and it's not quite like butter."

"Marigold?"

"Closer," she agreed. "Saffron, maybe?"

"I'm not sure I know what saffron is."

"A spice. It's a little muddy, though. Marigold or sunflower are much closer." She dropped her hand, gave him a quick smile. "Sorry. I keep stopping to rhapsodize."

"Don't apologize. It's too easy to forget how amazing it is when you live here. We need the reminder to look around once in awhile." He gestured. "I never drive in town, so we'll just walk over to my mother's. It's not very far."

"I'm glad to walk. It's an amazing day." She felt buoyed, effervescent, and wasn't sure if it was the weather or the altitude or maybe the company of the very handsome man beside her. "The weather changed so fast!"

"And it'll change again this afternoon," he said,

pointing toward the south. "Those clouds might bring some more snow with them."

A pair of dogs, one black, one salt-and-pepper, loped by on some happy errand, bandanas tied around their throats. One stopped to bark at a third dog leaning his head out of the window of a pickup truck, a dog with an enormous head, who simply looked down at the Lab and yawned.

"I've never seen so many dogs in a town in my life," Juliet commented.

"They issue you one when you come to town."

Juliet laughed.

His eyes glittered. "Haven't you gotten yours yet?"

"Please, Desi has three *big* dogs. That's plenty."

"All right, we'll let you slide for a bit."

They walked in agreeable silence up a short hill. "So, what sort of martial arts do you teach?" she asked.

"Kung fu, mostly."

"I like the eastern arts," she said, and hoped it didn't sound too prim. "I studied yoga and tai chi for awhile."

"Yoga makes me feel impatient," he said, and gave her a rueful smile. "I think I need to move more than that."

They stopped at Black Diamond Boulevard and waited for the traffic to thin. "It's really busy for a small town," Juliet said.

"Wait until winter comes. You'll have to fight to cross this street, even with stop signs at every corner."

Juliet started to say, *I won't be staying that long,* but how did she know? She wouldn't leave Desi until everything was stable. "I'll keep that in mind."

The light changed and they crossed the street, and

into a small pocket of cottages and bungalows tucked between the main drag and the northern mountain. "Why aren't there ski slopes on both sides of the valley?" Juliet asked.

He flipped a thumb over his shoulder to the south. "That one faces north, so the snow gets deeper and stays longer and doesn't get as icy." He pointed to the one in front of them. "The sun melts the snowfall on this one much faster."

She grinned. "Cool. I love it when I learn something new like that."

"So, you got things taken care of this morning with Desi?"

"I think so. You're very worried about it, aren't you?"

He made a clicking sound with his tongue. "Well, I'll tell you. I've been a cop a long time, and that relationship has all the danger signs."

Juliet felt a prickling of dread, a sense of warning. "What do you mean?"

"They're very intense people, both of them. And at one time, I gather it was very passionate."

"Yeah, that's the weird part. I would have said they loved each other a lot."

"It struck me as something a little different." He turned his lips down in thought, and Juliet found herself admiring the angle of his cheekbone, the grace of his throat. She looked toward the cerulean sky instead.

"Possessive," he continued. "They *possessed* each other. Claude bagged an upper-class white woman with a social conscience, a pretty woman with a lot of heart who'd make him look good wherever he went."

"And Desi?"

He hesitated, then quirked an eyebrow. "She got herself somebody good-looking enough for her tastes, and exotic enough to give her cachet, and made sure he was an artist to piss off your parents."

Juliet laughed. "Very acute observation, Mr. Mad Calf."

"It's a kind of love, meeting needs like that. Relationships are complicated things."

"My parents taught us that very young."

"They sound like pretty complicated people."

"Mmm. Complicated is one word for it." She shook her head. "Or dysfunctional."

He looked down at her. "Why do you say that?"

"They're just…very intense. It's a very intense relationship. They fight and make up and swear the other one is killing them and then they go off on some big trip and they're crazy about each other again." She shook her head. "It would be exhausting to live like that."

"And it wouldn't leave a lot of energy for the children," he commented.

"Bingo."

"Still, love is a complicated thing, as you said. Why do we fall in love? It would be nice if it was always with someone who would be good for you, who'd take care of you, bring out the best, all that—but how often does it really happen?"

"Are you speaking from experience?"

His smile was wry. "Definitely."

She frowned, thinking of Scott. Whom she had not

been thinking of enough. Was that a relationship based on love or need?

Until recently, she'd believed she loved him, but maybe it *was* more been a matter of convenience and suitability. He was a lawyer, she was a lawyer. They both liked having someone to go out to dinner with and to accompany each to various business functions. They'd traveled to appealing spots together on vacation—the lesser known islands of Hawaii, the less-Americanized east coast of Mexico, Belize. They understood the demands of the work schedule of a busy professional and neither was particularly upset when the other had to work.

Tidy, convenient, pleasant.

Or was that fair? He'd stuck by her after the rape. But it was still just a very polite relationship in ways.

The very opposite of her parents' relationship. But was that what she really wanted? Maybe it was possible to have something somewhere in between.

A thick tension rose in her chest. She felt guilty, not loving him after all he'd done. She wished she knew why she *didn't*.

"Here we are," Josh said, gesturing toward a stone house nestled close to the mountain rising behind it. It was made of reddish stone, with a small turret on the ground floor and a small second story. A deep wooden porch was furnished with chairs and a table, and a pot of winter-brushed marigolds stood in the middle of the table. Homey. A dog barked from a front window, only visible in silhouette.

"I see you have your dog, too."

"Jack," he agreed. "Told you, it's regulations."

The door burst open and Glory rushed out, her long licorice hair scattering free over her arms and back. "Hi, Princess! Come in. We made tea, me and my grandma." She flipped her hair. "Hi, Daddy. You can have some, too. If you want."

"Gee, thanks."

The dog came leaping out, too, a mutt of indeterminate parentage with long red fur and a big black head, and a lolling, happy tongue. He nosed her hand and wiggled around in a circle around Josh. "This," Josh said, "is Jack."

"Too many J's," Juliet said.

He laughed.

Glory took Juliet's hand. "Come inside, Princess," she said, gazing upward with naked admiration, and brushed hair out of her face. The little girl's small fingers were cool and dry, but very sure. "Come sit down."

The house smelled of lemons and cinnamon, and beneath that, something Juliet couldn't quite name, a little sweet and exotic. They entered a large living room furnished simply with a slightly threadbare couch, two chairs and a giant ottoman, all gathered around a potbellied stove. A round table sat beneath a very old drop light made of frosted glass, and a large window topped with leaded glass looked down the street to a perfectly framed view of the town and a tumble of aspens above it.

She turned around. "Butterscotch," she said to Josh. He didn't understand immediately, then looked over her shoulder to the view of aspens, and grinned. "You're right."

The expression transformed his face. His eyes crinkled up at the corners and a fan of sun lines radiated outward into his high-planed cheeks. Big strong teeth showed in a wide smile. Juliet felt an electric little zing through her chest.

*Whoa. Careful there,* she thought. Flustered, she bent and petted the dog, who had followed them into the room. He lay down at her feet, sighing hard. Juliet chuckled when he covered one of her arches. "Silly thing."

"Hello again," Helene said. "You must be very special—nothing would do but the most special of our cookies." She gestured with amusement to the plate of sugar cookies dusted with cinnamon and slices of yellow cake. "I hope you're hungry."

"Definitely."

Josh put his hand on her shoulder. "I have a few errands to run, so I'll leave you to the care of the females in my world, if you don't mind."

"We'll be fine," Helene said. "Run along."

A wave of disappointment washed over Juliet, and she had to paste a smile on her face. "We'll be fine."

As she helped herself to the tea and cookies, she told herself it was better this way. The less she saw of him, the wiser it would be. Even if she didn't have a fiancé—which she did!—she had other issues. So did Josh.

To the little girl awaiting her opinion of the feast, she

said, "Glory, I have never tasted such a delicious cookie in my life."

Glory said in the way only a four-year-old could, "I know." She leaned her hand on her chin. "Will you marry my daddy, Princess? Then I could have a mommy who was a princess."

Helene said, "Glory, we don't ask such personal questions."

"It isn't personal."

Juliet said quickly, "Would you like to show me your red shoes before we forget?"

"Hey! That's a good idea!"

Over Glory's head, Helene mouthed, "Sorry!"

Juliet just shook her head and let a starstruck little girl lead her to the red shoes, feeling like a movie star or a...well, a princess.

After showing off her shoes and other treasures, including butterfly hair clips and a poster of Snow White, then having cookies and tea, Glory was glazed with overstimulation. Juliet tried to take her leave, thinking to make up an excuse so the poor thing could get a nap.

"Oh, don't go yet, Princess," Glory cried. "Auntie Desi's not here. How're you gonna get home?"

"What if you get me some books and we sit here and read?"

"Okay! Will you read to me? I have a whole book about princesses."

Helene chuckled.

"Of course," Juliet said.

Glory ran into the other room to find the book she

wanted, and Juliet helped Helene carry the dishes from the dining room into the kitchen. "She's a terrific little girl," Juliet said.

"Thanks. You must have experience with children. You're very good with her."

"I don't have any of my own, but I do some work at a center that offers services to displaced immigrant women. A lot of kids there."

Helene stacked plates into the dishwasher. "That sounds like interesting work. Do you like it?"

Scraping frosting and the shell of pistachio nuts into the trash, Juliet nodded. "Better than my actual job. That's a side job, pro bono work, but it feels like I'm really doing something when I'm there."

"Sometimes it happens that way—the side trip leads to the main road."

Startled, Juliet looked up. "I never thought of that."

Helene smiled and finished loading the dishwasher. She dried her hands on a cup towel. "Will you mind if I leave you with Glory now? Josh is supposed to be back within a half hour."

"That's fine."

Glory ran back into the kitchen, a picture book with a glossy cover under her arm. "I got my book."

"Okay, sweetie. Let's go read."

## Chapter 6

The room was warm, the fire crackling at her feet. Juliet grew sleepier and sleepier, and she could tell when Glory slumped against her in a heavy slumber. Juliet put the book aside. She thought about the slight shock she got from reading about princesses falling in love with a prince at first kiss, the whole myth and shocking suddenness of it. No wonder, she thought drowsily, there was so much discontent in the world of romance. They'd all been fed this nonsense of love at first sight for the whole of their youth.

*Cynic,* said a little voice in her head. But Juliet could find no words to protest. Glory's head nestled against her shoulder. The dog snored lightly. The chair was deep and soft, her feet cradled on an oversize ottoman.

When she startled awake some time later, she had no

idea how much time had passed, but it was the sudden cold spot where Glory's warm body had been that alerted her. She sat straight up, blinking, to see Josh carrying the very asleep weight of girl in his arms.

"Hey, sleeping beauty," he said, his voice very soft.

She waved vaguely, surprised at how deeply she'd fallen asleep.

"Be right back," he mouthed.

Juliet rubbed sensation back into her right arm, and yawned. She must have fallen *really* asleep. The room was gloomy with late afternoon, and the fire had gone very low. Desi would be worried about her!

Jumping up, she tried to remember where she'd put her purse, and finally found it by the table. She dug in the pocket where she kept her cell phone and pulled it out. It was off; with a stab of guilt she turned it back on. The screen told her there were five missed calls.

Five? Yikes! How had she missed five calls?

Then it came to her. She'd turned the phone off yesterday on the plane and never turned it back on. Guiltily, she pushed the button to review the numbers before she picked up voice mail. The first was Scott, yesterday at 4:00 p.m., about the time Desi had been pointing a rifle at Claude. The second was Scott, about 9:00 p.m. last night. The third, Scott, this morning. Desi, number four. Scott number five, just a few hours ago.

She was about to punch the number for voice mail when Josh came back into the room. "Don't bother. I saw Desi about ten minutes ago, and she said to tell you she left a message on the phone to tell you she's going to be awhile. A farmer with some sick pigs."

"Oh." She closed the phone, feeling suddenly the enclosed silence of the room, the pair of them essentially alone.

He seemed to notice it, too. "Where'd my mom get off to?"

"She had to meet someone. She said to tell you to call her later."

"All right."

Silence dropped between them. Juliet rubbed her hands together. "Um. I hate to be a pain, but I don't really have anywhere to go until Desi comes to get me."

"You don't have to go anywhere. We can just watch TV and read or something. Can I get you a beer?"

He was already headed for the kitchen. Idly, Juliet watched him go, and her eyes were on his long legs, and to her surprise, a very nice butt. Not just okay. Not just nice—spectacular. Which went along with everything else about him, really. She loved the glossy length of his hair, the darkness of his eyes, the—

She thought of all the phone messages from Scott and felt triply guilty. "I don't know if I should," she said in response to his offer of a beer.

Josh grinned at her over the door to the fridge. "It's not life or death, sweetheart. Just a beer."

"You're right. Sure. I'll have one."

"Excellent." He brought her a dark bottle. "Want a glass?"

"Are you having one?"

"Nope." He illustrated by taking a long swallow directly from the lip of the bottle. "Cheers."

"Cheers." Juliet raised hers and took a sip. "Hmm.

That tastes pretty great, actually." She sank down on the couch. "There's something about the mountains that makes everything taste twenty times better."

He settled in the chair and leaned forward, his hands loosely between his legs. A glitter lit his dark eyes. "Are you one of those people who feel better at high altitudes?"

"I feel better in mountains, absolutely, but doesn't everyone? The air is so fresh and clean. Makes me feel ten thousand times better. Clearheaded or something."

"Not everyone does feel better. A lot of people can't tolerate it at all—they get headaches and upset stomachs, can't sleep. But I had a friend once who wasn't much of a talker, and if you got him up in the mountains, he'd start chattering for all he was worth. It made him feel great."

"I guess I'm more in that category."

"Good." He smiled and lifted his beer again. His eyes were fixed on her face, and was it her imagination or was he looking at her mouth? He didn't look away, as was usual, just kept looking at her so directly.

Finally she said, "What? Do I have something on my face?"

"No." His expression grew more serious. "You just have a good face. I like looking at it."

Not "pretty," not "sexy." *A good face.* "I guess that's okay, then." In the warm lamplight, the hard bones and angles of his face were softened. Enormous dark eyes, that hawkish nose, full lips. "Yours is very strong."

He licked his bottom lip and to her amazement, Juliet felt a tiny shock of desire rush down her spine. It suddenly seemed there was dusky warmth in the room, something almost visible blooming right there in the air between them.

And she had no idea what to do with it, or even if she *wanted* to do something. Or not do something. One part of her brain was thinking, *oh, let's kiss him. Those lips are like cake!*

She could see, in the little way he rubbed his lip with the very tip of his tongue, that he thought of it, too. It wasn't as if he was doing it to cause a reaction, but more out of a meditative state, and that made it all the more alluring. He was so big and sexy and—

Her phone rang. "Sorry," she said. "I had this turned off for a whole day and I really should answer it."

"A whole day," he said with a slightly mocking lift of a brow. "Go for it. Do you want something to eat?" He stood up.

"Sure, anything." She flipped open the phone. "Hello?"

"It's about time," Scott said. "I was worried about you. Is everything okay?"

"The reception is patchy," she said, turning her engagement ring around and around in a circle, wondering what *else* she might end up lying to him about. "Sorry about that. I'm fine, but you may as well know I don't have reception at Desi's."

From the corner of her eye, she noticed Josh straightening in the kitchen, and against her will, she looked at him. His well-shaped legs. The long back clad in a heather-blue T-shirt, his amused, raised eyebrow.

The cell reception in Mariposa was spectacular. The well-to-do skiers who vacationed here insisted upon it.

She shrugged at him.

"I wish you'd check in regularly," Scott said. "You know you haven't been well."

A prickle of something moved over her neck. *You haven't been well.* As if she were a vaporous Victorian, prone to faints. "I'm fine, Scott. But I'll do my best to keep in touch. It's just not that easy." Lies, lies, lies. But she was tired of being fussed over and coddled and *watched.* "How is everything in your world?"

"It's good. As a matter of fact, I have to go to dinner with a client, but I thought I'd try you before I left."

"Okay, thanks. I should go, too. I'm at the house of a friend of my sister's."

"Call me soon, then."

"I will. Take care."

He clicked off, and Juliet looked down at the phone, thinking. When had they stopped saying *I love you?* When had they ever had any passion?

"That's not the happiest expression," Josh said, coming back into the room. "Boyfriend troubles?"

She waved the ring. "Fiancé."

Instead of sitting on the chair, he carried a tray of Vienna sausages, string cheese, crackers and grapes to the coffee table and sat down beside her. He smelled of pine and sunshine. "Not the most elegant stuff around, but you know, I've got to feed a four-year-old."

"I didn't know they still made Vienna sausages."

"I eat Spam, too."

She looked a him. "Really."

"I'm a guy," he said, popping a squishy little sausage into his mouth. "We don't have to eat right."

Juliet found a chuckle rolling up from her chest. "Ah. I'll have to remember that."

He gestured toward the phone. "Now, you were saying…fiancé troubles?"

"I don't know." She sighed. "I'm not sure it's working out, but I don't really know why."

"Sometimes, things aren't right, that's all."

"Right." The crackers were grainy, the cheese in neat, white slices. Her stomach growled. "I don't know how I could be hungry. I ate pancakes for breakfast, all that cake and cookies for lunch with your mom and Glory and now this."

"That's not that much food." He made a masterpiece of layering a two-inch sandwich of crackers and cheese and sausages. "But then you're one of those California girls, aren't you? A spinach leaf for lunch, a grain of brown rice for dinner and all the chardonnay you can drink?"

She dropped her jaw in exaggerated shock. "Ow!" Raising a quick eyebrow, she said, "You must know some of my girlfriends."

"They all come here to ski."

"Of course." His knee was only a few inches from her own, and she poked it with one finger. "But not all of us are Hercules, you know, able to down 12,000 calories a day."

"True." He rubbed his broad chest happily. "It's good to be a guy."

She found her gaze on that big hand, the chest beneath it. His fingernails were clean, flat ovals. At the opening of his Henley, the skin was the brown of good wheat bread, very smooth. Absurdly, richly, she imagined her mouth on that sleek triangle of skin.

Lost in a spell of newborn desire, she raised her eyes and found him looking back at her.

In that second, the thickness bloomed around them again. An atmosphere as humid as a cloud, fragrant with possibility. The only thing in the world for a moment was Josh. The lavishly fringed eyes, his quirky mouth, those giant hands that she'd seen could be so gentle.

He leaned forward and put the crackers down, and carefully brushed his fingers clean. Lacing his hands together, he leaned on his knees, putting his face much closer to hers. "Is it my imagination," he said, "or is there something clicking here between us?"

"Clicking is not the right word," Juliet said quietly. Blooming, maybe. She looked at his mouth, and could not even remember when she had so longed for a kiss. His mouth entirely filled her vision—full lower lip, sharply cut upper. Black whiskers, a few millimeters long, grew around his mouth in a sparse goatee shape, and it occurred to her that he probably didn't grow much beard.

"It isn't your imagination," she said, and swallowed.

"That's what I thought," he said, the voice rumbling out of that deep chest with the depth of a drum. His nostrils flared as he looked at her mouth, at her breasts, which pearled embarrassingly, back to her face, all without touching her. "Probably shouldn't do anything about it, though."

"I'm engaged," she offered.

"So you said." He moved one hand and touched her

diamond, just the ring, then the knuckle right above it. "There's more though. You have something in your past."

Juliet swallowed. "Yes."

"And so do I."

"Oh." She looked at him. "What do you have?" Then she waved a hand. "Never mind. You've given me privacy. I'll give you yours."

"It's all right—mine is pretty common. An ex-wife who is unstable and dramatic and kidnapped my daughter."

"I'm so sorry. That's why you're worried about Glory."

"That's right."

She loved the simple straightforwardness of him, the way he met her eyes, the directness of his speech. He was real in a way she hadn't encountered in a long time. In L.A., everybody seemed to feel a need to play to the audience. Not this one.

Honestly, what was this? This narcotic spell he cast? Would he kiss her? Would she let him?

"I can be strong, Princess," he said, "but not if you keep looking at me like that."

"Sorry." With effort, she stood up and walked away. Shaking her head, she turned, donning her lawyer self. "Let's just not do that. Too much going on."

"Agreed. Come eat your crackers and cheese."

She sat back down. "Is it all right if I ask what happened to your ex?"

"It's fine. Nobody knows where she is." He cleared his throat. "Unfortunately, she's an alcoholic and doesn't seem to want to get help, so she's just out there."

"I'm sorry. That's hard."

"It is. And it's especially hard for Glory, who loves her."

Juliet settled a slice of cheese precisely on a single grainy cracker, and balanced it in her fingers. "I assume she was not an alcoholic when you met her."

"Right."

"So, what did the two of you give each other?" She got ready to bite the cracker. "Was it love or need or— what? Why did you fall in love?"

"Hmm." He gave her a look. "Right for the heart of things, huh?"

She shrugged. "You don't have to answer. I'm just thinking about these things."

"What things?"

"Love things." She took a bite of her sandwich.

"Love things," he repeated, and took a breath, looking into the middle distance. "Andy—my ex—is very beautiful. I was just getting out of the army in Colorado Springs and I met her at a nightclub. She was the most beautiful woman I'd ever seen. Glory looks just like her."

Juliet was surprised to note a ripple of jealousy, which she hoped she was hiding.

Josh went on. "She was Indian—Sioux and Cherokee—and proud of it. She was—" he frowned "—somebody I could bring home to my mom, you know? An Indian woman who wouldn't mind the rez. She was a shawl dancer, and had beaded her own moccasins and—" He rubbed his face. "It seems kind of shallow now, but I thought that's what I *should* want."

She wondered what he wanted when he wasn't following shoulds, but she said only, "Ah. And what did she get from you?"

"I don't really know."

Juliet had a lot of experience with people who didn't particularly know the truth, those who were hiding it, and those who had hidden it from themselves. She smiled gently. "Yes, you do."

For a moment he looked at her. "Yeah, I guess I do. I offered stability. She'd spent her childhood moving around. She liked the fact that I already had a job lined up here as a tribal cop, that we'd have a whole community she could just plug into."

"So what happened?"

"It bored her to tears." He grinned. "This a very slow, quiet place in a lot of ways. She'd spent her whole life in cities, and didn't know how much she'd hate the way everyone knows your business, all that stuff."

"I get it." It was a common enough story. She took a sip of beer, dared herself to ask the other question. "So what do you like about women that you don't feel you should?"

"Blondes," he said distinctly. "And lots of cleavage."

Juliet laughed. "Very original."

"Not at all." Rakishly, he raised his beer to her. "To you, Princess."

Heat ran across her cheekbones and the bridge of her nose. "Thanks."

"What about you," he asked. "What do you like that you shouldn't?"

"Other than being wildly attracted to a man who is not my fiancé, you mean?"

"Wildly, huh?"

A knock came at the door, and Juliet frowned, worried it would awaken Glory from her nap. Josh jumped up and hurried to open it.

Desi stood there, fuming. "You know what he did now?" she said, coming into the room.

Juliet put a finger to her lips. "Glory is asleep, sis."

"Sorry." She made a low growling noise, put her face in her hands. "He's just making me so crazy I can't stand it."

Josh rubbed her shoulder. "What happened, Desi?"

"He agreed to sell the land to a developer. His *half!* What the heck does that mean, his half? He also is threatening to get an injunction to keep me from operating the wolf shelter until the land dispute is settled."

"Did you see him?"

She slumped in the chair, stared at the crackers. "No, he called me. He said it looks bad for his business to have a restraining order, and if I wanted to get nasty, that's what he'd have to do."

"So he hasn't actually done anything about it yet," Juliet said.

"I don't know what he's done." She picked up a piece of cheese, examining it as if she'd found it in the Dumpster instead of on a tray in her best friend's living room. Her face brightened. "But I also heard that there are some other people who aren't too happy with old Claude."

"Gossip," Juliet said. "Always good. Who is it?"

"Kay Turner, the dentist's wife—you saw her this morning—is widely known to have a crush on him.

And she's very put out that he's dating Miss Ski Queen of the World."

"But she's married!"

Desi waggled her eyebrows. "I gather her husband's none too happy with any of it, but what can he do?"

Josh scowled. "This is a mess. I want you to just go home tonight and forget about all of it, okay?"

Looking deflated, Desi nodded. "I will."

"Promise?"

"That's what I'm here for," Juliet said. "To make sure she doesn't do anything rash."

"Good," he said. But he didn't look particularly comforted.

As they were getting ready to leave, he touched her shoulder lightly. "I'll be thinking about what you said."

She met his eyes, conscious of Desi's close interest. "Me, too," she said.

"You guys stay out of town for a day or two, huh?"

Juliet nodded. "Will do."

"I'll be by tomorrow to check on her."

There was nothing else to do. Juliet followed her sister down the sidewalk to the truck, feeling his gaze touching her back, her hair, her neck. When she climbed in the front seat and closed the door, she looked back and saw him still watching, his face sober.

She raised a hand and resolutely turned her face away.

## Chapter 7

When they got to the cabin, Desi said, "Let's get some wine and go up to the hot springs. That'll burn off some stress."

"It's getting dark, though."

Desi gave her a half smile. "It's not very far, Juliet. There's a trail the entire way. We have flashlights."

"But what about…animals? Like bears and cougars?"

"We'll bring the dogs. Trust me, this is a wonderful thing, these hot springs at night."

"Okay."

Dusk was closing in as they hiked up the hill, carrying thick towels and flashlights and cans of natural soda Desi fished out of the cupboard. At the clearing where the pool bubbled up, Desi dropped her things and stripped off her shirt, then her jeans, folding them neatly and putting them on a rock nearby.

Juliet had done this before, soaked naked in the hot springs with her sister, but it suddenly seemed unwise. Foolish, even. She stood there, hands at her sides, unable to move. Her eye twitched, once. Twice. The smell of earth and minerals rose up from the water, and in the growing dusk, she could see steam rising from the surface.

"C'mon, silly," Desi said, reaching for the straps on her bra.

"I don't think I can this time," Juliet said. "I feel weird about being naked outside."

Desi didn't say anything for a minute, but Juliet felt her measuring eyes. "It won't hurt anything to leave on our bras and panties if that's easier for you."

"I should have brought a bathing suit," Juliet said. "But Colorado, winter, just didn't think I'd need one."

"No big deal. I'm cold, though, so I'm getting in." She stepped into the pool, then submerged and gave a groan. "Oh that's good. C'mon, girl. Climb in."

Juliet shucked her coat and blouse and jeans, hungry for the feel of the water. For a minute, she wished she could be naked, but she decided to not beat herself up about it just this minute, and climbed in. As the hot, scented water enveloped her limbs, she groaned. "This is fantastic!"

There were ledges at various levels, formed cleverly with flat rocks when they built the pool, and Juliet chose one and leaned back, closing her eyes. "It's like having your own spa," Juliet said.

"It is my own private spa," Desi said. "The good mud pools are by the wolf kennels, but I'll show you those, too."

"I know women who would pay a lot of money for this."

"Oh, trust me, one of the developers who wants the land is a guy who wants to do just that. Put in a spa."

"It would make a fortune, Desi."

"That's not what I'm about."

"Well, of course not, but there's nothing wrong with money, is there?"

"No. I just don't think that every square inch of the earth needs to be developed. It's important to keep some of it wild."

"You're right," Juliet said. "Pass me a soda, will you?"

"Absolutely." Desi snapped it open and handed it across the water.

Juliet took a long, cooling swallow, then settled the can on the edge of the pool and let herself slide down further into the water, tipping her head back to rest it against a grassy pillow so she could gaze up at the sky. It had gone velvety with black night, and the darkness glittered with a million zillion stars. The sight made all of her issues and problems seem very, very small.

Desi asked gently, "What happened to you outside the restaurant this morning, honey?"

Because of the big sky and the uncountable stars, Juliet could answer without too much pain in her chest, "Flashback. They keep happening, and I never quite know what will trigger them."

Desi splashed, sitting up. "Why didn't you tell me?"

"There's nothing to tell, really." Juliet let her arms and hands float in the water, free and loose, as if they were not attached to her at all. "They just kind of show up now and then."

"That must be hell. And what an awful sister I am to need you to take care of me when I should be taking care of you."

Juliet, soft boiled and relaxed, shook her head dreamily. "No, don't worry. My counselor said they'll go away eventually."

"What triggered it today?"

"Maybe the doorway. Or maybe the smell of margaritas. I don't know. It's hard, because then I'm not me, standing there, I'm the me I was that night when I got raped."

"I hate him," Desi said fervently. "I'd like to kill that guy."

"Desi!" Juliet sat up. "That's not who you are."

"Oh, yes it is," she said. "Hurt one of mine, and you are dead." She peered through the dark at her sister. "You don't want to hurt him in revenge?"

"I don't even feel that much for him. I just don't care." It was as if there was a wall around the whole miserable incident. "It's like it happened to somebody on television or something, and I can replay it with the sound turned down, but why would I?"

"You know, it doesn't seem to me that you've ever gotten angry over all of this. If I were you, I'd be furious."

"I'm not."

But as if her body and her mind were expressing different things, Juliet felt her throat close, as if there was a scream lodged inside it and she couldn't seem to get it out. Taking a sip of her mandarin lime soda, she said, "I just wish they would have caught him. I hate it that he got away with it."

"Yeah. And he's probably doing it again."

The idea made Juliet feel sick to her stomach. "Don't even say that."

"Sorry." Desi leaned back and tipped her head toward the sky. "Look at those stars, will you?"

Juliet tipped backward, again, too. Between the shadow arrows of pines, she admired a night sky wholly unlike the one she knew at home. This one was deepest black, with no gray or pink on the horizon, and across it were thousands and thousands of twinkling points of light, tiny pinpricks to glowing planets, close and far. At home she could only see a few.

It made space seem incomprehensibly vast, and by comparison, her own problems seemed very small. "I'm so glad to be here, Des," she commented, and rolled the cool can over her forehead.

"I'm glad, too," Desi said. "I was losing it."

In the soft dark, Juliet asked, "Desi, what happened with you two? You used to be so in love."

Desi sighed. "It was never what you thought it was, Juliet." Her voice sounded unbearably weary. "We just got locked into some dance and we couldn't stop."

"Like Mother and Daddy."

"Yes." She took a sip of her own soda. "It doesn't thrill me to say that, I can tell you, but I pretty much reproduced their relationship to a T. The brainy female scientist and the dashing upstart artist."

"Good grief. I never saw that before."

"You're kidding. I saw it years ago, but as I said, we were locked in this dance, and it was very difficult to get out of it once we started."

Juliet thought of the women she worked with, the sorrow in their haggard faces as they spoke of husbands, boyfriends, brothers. "At least you're done now. Or will be soon."

"I know." She was silent for a long time. "I feel like a fool, Juliet. I really do. I'm smart and well-educated and our parents showed us how destructive this kind of union can be, and yet—I did it anyway. I fell for the myth."

"What myth?"

"Oh, I don't know. The fairy tale, I guess. I'm just so angry with him right now!"

"He's behaving badly, sis. You have a right to be angry."

Desi sat up suddenly. "You know, we should get a car from a junkyard and beat the hell out of it with sledgehammers."

Juliet laughed, envisioning the pair of them in old jeans and tattered flannel shirts swinging sledgehammers to the sound of some twangy music. "Or we could try out for roller derby."

"I'm serious. It would be a lot healthier than pretending you're not absolutely furious."

Juliet said, "I'll think about it."

But she didn't see how swinging a hammer at an inanimate object would help, either. It wouldn't give her back her innocence. Anger wouldn't give her back a sense of courage.

* * *

They got back to the cabin around eight, and not long afterward, Desi got a phone call. The way she started barking questions about blood flow and gashes, it sounded like she was dealing with a wounded animal. As she talked, she was taking out warm clothes—jeans, thick socks, sturdy boots.

Juliet busied herself stoking the fire. There was an art to building a good fire—something Claude had taught her back in the old days when he had been a nice person. This one still had embers, so Juliet layered in some medium-sized sticks and thinner kindling and waited for them to catch before she carefully added two logs about the width of her thigh.

Behind her, Desi barked out, "How long ago?" and then, "Where did you see him?"

Desi had a bellows she'd found at an antique fair once, and Juliet used them to fan the flames, watching as they turned bright yellow and started to crackle.

Desi hung up by snapping her cell phone in half. "I'm going to have to take off for a little while, sis. Emergency."

Juliet rocked back on her heels and rested her hands on her thighs. A slight sense of dis-ease rippled down her spine, but she said, "Okay."

"Are you going to be all right?"

"Desi, I'm thirty-two years old. I think I can handle a few hours by myself."

The elder sister smiled ruefully. "Sorry. Maybe I'm projecting. I'm worried about my own ability to cope. You're doing fine." She dressed in the layers of warm clothes, and put on some boots. She attached her replacement cell phone to a clip on her belt. "If you need me, feel nervous, even just want a little reassurance, don't hesitate to call, all right?"

"I'll be fine, I swear."

"You'll have the dogs here. They're great protectors, but don't get nervous if they bark at something. Every so often, they pick up the wolves howling and go nuts."

Juliet put a hand on Sitting Bull's hindquarters and dug her hands into his long thick fur. He groaned and licked her wrist, then fell back to the floor.

Desi opened a long closet and took out a rifle and a box of what Juliet assumed were shells or bullets or whatever. She frowned. "I thought Josh took the gun away from you."

"Please." The word was droll. "He needed to feel better because he's a cop, but there's no way I'd be out in the woods without a rifle."

"What do you need it for?"

"The emergency is a cougar that's been stalking goats. He got one tonight, and injured two more. The rancher shot it, but it took off and now he's worried. If I'm out there looking at bloody goats, I want to be sure I'm not that cat's next meal."

"Desi! That sounds dangerous."

"I'll be all right." Desi put on her heavy coat and tugged her braid out, flinging it over her shoulder like a rope. Juliet liked the sturdy, capable aura that surrounded her sister, and she wondered how it would feel to know how to stitch up an injured goat or do surgery on a wolf or deliver a colt. "I doubt I'll even see the cat, but if he's injured badly, he might be very dangerous."

"Be careful."

"Always."

After Desi left, Juliet dragged the futon mattress to an open spot in front of the fire, bringing dogs and a book with her. There were things Juliet did not love about her sister's cottage. Taking fast, somewhat chilly baths got on her nerves pretty quickly. She sometimes felt anxious about not using too much power or water and knew Desi eyed her excesses—or at least she felt eyed—with disapproval.

But she *loved* the woodstove. The smell of it, that wispy, smoky, woodsy scent; the flickery warmth of it, the sound of it crackling, popping. Desi kept piles of pillows and blankets around and it was easy to pile them up into drifts, then camp down with a book and a cup of hot chocolate and a good novel and read and read and read.

With the dogs. Which was the other thing she loved about the fire and pillows and reading experience— puddles of dogs surrounding her like a moat. All of them were wolf mixes, of course, dogs Desi had adopted over the years, but they were very different animals nonetheless.

Tecumseh had the best fur, thick and fluffy and white, and he liked to speak in little groans and mutterings that Desi told her were indications of the husky portion of his parentage. He loved cuddling, too, which is why she liked him being on the bed with her. She hugged him like a stuffed animal.

Crazy Horse was a fluffy, nervous mutt with big paws and silky black fur and a head that seemed too big for his body. He startled easily and liked to bark, but charmed Juliet by putting his head down and huddling close to her body for attention.

The beauty of the three was an aloof gray-and-black dog named Sitting Bull. He had burly shoulders and a thick tail, and ears that stood alertly on his elegant wolf's head. He didn't speak much, but he was devoted to Desi and brought her tidbits to share now and again, various massacred small animals. He was clearly the alpha. The other dogs deferred to him. He usually slept a bit to the outside of the pack.

Alone in the cabin, with the fire and the dogs for company, Juliet gazed toward sky visible through the window and at the stars twinkling so far away, and the day leaked back into her mind for review.

The day—Claude and his girlfriend, the confrontation on the street. Helene and Glory. Joshua Mad Calf. She smiled. Speaking of alpha wolves!

The flashback, which had been so violent and intense—maybe one of the worst she'd had so far— replayed, too. She pressed cold fingertips to her twitching left eyelid and tried to think about it calmly. It was just a memory replay, nothing to worry about. Time healed wounds like this, and hers would be healed, too.

But the truth was, the flashbacks seemed to be getting worse, and she wasn't sure quite why. The rape, as these things went, had not been particularly terrible—Juliet had been horrified by some of the stories a few women had told in the group therapy sessions she'd attended. Terrible rapes, involving torture or violence or scarring. By comparison, Juliet's had been a very ordinary rape.

She'd been on a business trip in late winter. That was part of the irony, of course. For months, she'd been going to a grim neighborhood in Long Beach to work for the immigrant center, and had never even been frightened.

The business trip was to Albuquerque for a deposition on a civil rights case involving illegal immigrants and their employers. The day had been a long one, and Juliet had a slight headache by the time she got back to her hotel. As always, she was staying in an upscale hotel, with above-average security measures, and as always, she paid attention to her surroundings.

But it was such an ordinary night. An ordinary business hotel. An ordinary hotel restaurant and an ordinary sandwich she ate while she read the newspaper and nursed a single glass of red wine. There were quite a lot of family groups in the restaurant itself and she sat at the bar to give them room. A crime drama played on the television in the corner, and there were a handful of other business travelers in the lounge area watching it.

A businessman at the bar, well-dressed with gray at his temples, asked if she minded if he smoked. She apologized but admitted that she did mind. He politely stepped outside. When he came back in, Juliet was devouring a French Dip and he gave her a smile. "It's a gorgeous night out there," he said. "The patio is enclosed, you know, so it's safe."

"Thanks."

She finished her meal and paid for it, and headed for her room. The door to the patio area stood open, and she thought, *what the heck*. She still had a headache. Maybe she needed a little fresh air.

It was dark, but there were lights around the pool, and a couple sat at one end of the area, so she felt safe enough. She'd just walk once around the pool, then go back upstairs and take a hot bath.

She was nearly back at the starting point when someone grabbed her from behind, one hand slapping around her mouth and the other around her waist. She had time to make a soft ulping sound before her attacker dragged her backward into a dark copse of trees. A branch scraped across her arm painfully, and his hand was cutting hard into her mouth and she couldn't quite figure out what was going on.

At first, she thought, "this is probably not as bad as I think."

He was not a big man, but he was strong. "Don't say a word and it will go smooth and easy. If you make a single sound, I'll hurt you."

Terror bloomed in her chest, spread through her limbs, making her feel weak.

She could only whimper softly. He maneuvered her to the ground, shoved a handkerchief into her mouth, and unzipped her dress. She froze.

It was going to happen. He was going to *rape* her.

She began to shiver violently, uncontrollably, and he shook her, once. "Stop that! I won't hurt you if you just cooperate."

Her dress fell down her arms, and he did something—she later found out he cut it—so her bra fell off.
The night air struck her exposed skin, his hands
clutched her breasts, and she nearly gagged, feeling
physically sick at the invasive touch of this stranger.

Tears dripped down her face. Shame. She squeezed
her eyes tight against it.

"Stop crying," he growled, and jerked her into place.
"I hate that."

But however much he hated it, she couldn't stop, not
the crying or the shivering. She shivered as he ripped
off her panties and shoved himself into her. It hurt. It
took forever and it made him mad. He shoved her this
way and that, hands grabbing, groping, twisting.

Bizarrely, she heard the sound of diners just a
stone's throw away, the clatter of silver against plates.
The smell of margaritas and cigarettes filled her
nostrils. He finally finished, and she wept harder in
relief and in more fear—would he do it again? Would
he kill her?

He pushed her down to the ground facefirst and
picked up her clothes. He hit her once, very hard, and
she didn't move for a minute, terrified he would do it
again. His footsteps disappeared almost eerily fast.

She lay there, stunned, for an indeterminate amount
of time, then slowly she moved one arm. It functioned
normally and she spread it out, looking for something
to cover her nakedness. She found her dress, but everything else was gone, including her shoes.

There was no help for it. She shook out the dress,
tugged it over her head then stood there a moment,

trying to get her bearings. She felt light-headed and strange, as if she'd run too long on the treadmill or something, but some still-coherent lawyer part of her brain insisted she look around for anything that might be a clue. She tried to figure out how to mark this exact spot, and finally broke a branch and stuck it in the ground where the grass was already springing back around the imprint of her body.

That done, she made her way out of the trees and looked for the couple that had been sitting at the end of the swimming pool. They were gone. In dismay, she had to go back into the doorway she'd come out of, and go back into the restaurant.

The bartender took one look at her, and picked up the phone. "Get the police here," he barked, then slammed the phone down, came around the bar, and managed to snag Juliet and lead her to a chair before she fell down.

"Breathe, honey," he said. "You're all right now."

She bent over and put her head to her knees. Then it came to her that she must look frightening, her hair mussed and shoes off, and she didn't want the children in the restaurant to be frightened. "Maybe," she said, straightening slightly, "I should just go in the other room, out of sight?"

"I can take you to the office," he said. "Lean on me."

So they went to the restaurant office and someone brought her a drink of water.

By the book, she thought now, running her fingers through Tecumseh's thick fur. She'd done absolutely everything by the book. The police came and took her to the hospital to be examined, evidence collected. As these things went, she had escaped without much damage. Some bruising. A black eye and a split lip, and scrapes down the front of her body. The nurse tended her gently, directed her to a rape counselor.

Juliet had attended the counseling sessions, including the group sessions her therapist recommended. She talked it out with people she trusted, cried and got it out like that. She even escaped the looming specter of HIV and STDs and could finally move on with her life.

Or so she thought.

It was little things that went wrong. She couldn't remember things very well, like where she parked her car or what time an important meeting was. She dropped the ball in court one day when a man reminded her of the businessman in the restaurant that night.

She couldn't sleep at night and couldn't stay awake in the daytime. She didn't want to have sex, and at first, Scott was patient, but he understandably grew frustrated as time went by. In sympathy, she finally gave in. It wasn't traumatic, she didn't *mind* it, particularly, but she didn't feel anything, either.

Maybe she never would. Sometimes it felt like something was broken inside of her when she was raped. Some unnamable part, an invisible spiritual limb that now lay in shards, jamming up the emotional works.

As if he sensed her distress, Crazy Horse sighed and snuggled closer. Juliet clasped his furry warmth and buried her face in his warm fur and wondered what it would be like to be a wolf in a pack.

Safe, she thought. Safe and warm.

# *Chapter 8*

At 4:21 a.m., Josh's cell phone rang. "Joshua Mad Calf," he said gruffly.

"Josh, we found a body." It was his boss, Dave Jiramillo, on the reservation. "You need to get down here."

"Body?" Josh croaked. "What body? Dead of what?"

"Not sure yet. There's some mauling, but we're not sure if it's the cause of death. Looks like he's been shot."

"What?" Josh swore. "Murdered, you mean?"

"Looks like it."

Before he could help himself, Josh swore again. He put his head down into the pillows, listening to directions to the location, his heart thudding heavily in his chest. Unease. Warning. This was not going to be good, he could feel it.

"An animal's been at him," Dave said, "so it's not a particularly pretty crime scene."

"I'll be there as soon as I can."

He dressed, called his mother to let her know he'd be bringing Glory over, then wrapped up his sleepy-headed child into a thick blanket and carried her two blocks. The moon was high over the Mariposa ridge, spilling cold light down the grassy slopes, illuminating the ghostly quiet of the middle of the night. No one was about but a pair of dogs ambling down the empty streets. In the distance, an owl hooted.

Appropriate.

His mother was waiting, bundled in her robe. She pushed the screen door open and Josh carried Glory into the room she used there, made sure she was settled, and went back to the main room. "I don't have time to talk," he said in a quiet voice, kissing her forehead, "but they found a body up on the reservation, and I've gotta go check it out."

Helene took a breath and crossed herself, half-Catholic after all these years. "Go," she said.

With dread, he pulled his hat close down on his head and headed out, a bad feeling sitting hard in his gut. The reservation started at the edge of Mariposa, forming the western border of the town and stretching for 1900 square miles into the San Juan mountains, inhospitable and difficult country that was too steep for farming or most ranching. There were no passes through the mountains, not even many jeep tracks. Until a few years ago, the people had been distributed in seven very poor villages that based their livelihood in sheep farming, wool, and loaning out bodies to the hotel and ski industries during the winter months. For most of the twentieth century, it had been one of the poorest reservations within U.S. borders.

Then gambling swept through the Indian nations, one after the other, and the Mariposa Utes had finally approved the measure. They raised capital through elections and by leasing several hundred acres of prime land to developers, and built the casino. It had been wildly successful. The nation was no longer poor.

Crime had increased, but not dramatically, and certain crimes—namely Indian on Indian—had even decreased.

Murder on the rez, and even in Mariposa, was not unheard of, but it was rare. A few years ago, there had been a dramatic family crime—two teens killing their parents and two friends—and there were the usual spousal murders. Josh couldn't think of a time he'd ever been called to an outdoor crime scene with a murdered body.

This one was not far into the rez, only a couple of miles from town, a field bordered by public forest and open grazing. When Josh arrived, the area had been secured with yellow police tape, and a police cruiser from Mariposa had come in with floodlights to illuminate it enough for an investigation, but even given the drama, there were not many people there—a few deputies, the coroner, the Mariposa county hard crimes detective, and two tribal officers. They were all waiting, respectfully, for Josh to arrive. He settled his hat and stepped out, slamming the door smartly.

He didn't like dead bodies much. He'd done his time

as an MP in the first Gulf War and had witnessed enough violent death there to see him through to the end of his own days. It was the biggest reason he'd chosen to come back home to the reservation rather than take a job in the cities.

But even out here, there was sometimes something ugly. This scene, for instance. Stark white light blistered the body into sharp black and white lines. It sprawled facedown in a sloppy patch of mud, the clothes shredded along the upper back and around the shoulders. Josh could see a long braid, but out here, that could be male or female, though this body looked male.

"Do we have an ID?" Josh asked.

"'Fraid so," the deputy said, a stout young woman with high red cheekbones. "Claude Tsosie, a Navajo enrolled on the tribal rolls at Tuba City. He's been shot, in the chest."

Claude.

Josh shook his head, the sense of dread doubling, tripling. "Estimated time of death?"

"Coroner thinks maybe about 10:00 p.m."

"And who found the body?"

"Paul Martinez, over there. He was walking home from his girlfriend's house and saw the white of the shirt."

Josh nodded. "Who have we talked to?"

"Nobody yet."

"All right." Josh stepped in to take a better look. His training, cold and analytical, kicked in as he took notes and barked out orders and collected evidence, but a little voice in his head prayed silently: *please let Desi have a good alibi.*

\* \* \*

Juliet awakened to the sound of her cell phone ringing Alicia Keys' song about "a real man," her signal that it was Scott calling in. Jolted guiltily out of sleep, she pushed the dog off of her and scrambled in her socks to the counter, where her purse sat, and managed to snare the phone before it stopped ringing.

"Hello?" she said breathlessly.

"Hi, Juliet," Scott said. "Did I wake you?"

It was freezing in the cabin and Juliet scurried back to her piles of pillows and blankets and dogs. "I guess you did. What time is it?"

"Eight here, so nine there."

"Wow." She looked over her shoulder—Desi was already gone. "My sister must have just let me sleep."

"So, you're at the cabin? I thought you didn't have reception there?"

Wincing at how very quickly her lie had come back to haunt her, Juliet said, "You know how it is with cell phone reception. Sometimes it's great, sometimes horrible. Maybe it's a very clear day."

"Well, at any rate," he said, "I'm glad to finally be able to talk to you. I miss you."

Juliet plucked at the yarn used to quilt the enormous blanket over her legs, emptiness crashing through her. "Me, too."

"You must be getting some excellent rest."

"I really am. Desi and I got a lot done yesterday, too—restraining order and some legal paperwork filed."

"Good. I know you've been worried about her."

"How are things with you? Tell me about the Whiting case."

She made small talk with him, pretending it all mattered somehow. Once it had. She tried hard to call up his face, his eyes, his hands. Nothing seemed real. He seemed like a character in a book she'd read a long time ago, thin and vague.

As he talked, she could feel how hard he was working to keep her attention, and a clear, sudden recognition settled on her: it was not fair to keep this up, this masquerade of the Juliet Who Felt Something. Breaking up hurt, but not as much as lies.

But how to begin?

When a slight lull fell between them, she said quietly, "You know, Scott, I've been thinking I might not be coming back there." The words ran like electric shocks down her nerves, rippling down her spine and arms— surprise. "To Los Angeles."

It stunned them both. A long silence, filled with the implications of what she'd just said, fell.

"You're going to live in Mariposa?" he asked finally, his voice thin. "Why would you do that?"

"I just don't think I want to live in L.A. anymore. I don't want that job or that life or—anything."

"Or me?" his voice sounded hollow, like an empty restaurant.

"It's not you, Scott," she said, knowing it was a cliché even though she meant it. In the middle of her chest was a dull burn, a recognition of the pain she was causing him, but even as she rubbed the heat of it, her shoulders suddenly didn't feel as hunched. "I just don't know what I feel anymore and it's not fair to you to keep you hanging on this way."

"But we're engaged!"

"I know." She rolled her shoulders. "I think it's time that we are not." She paused. "Engaged. Anymore."

"This seems rash," he said.

"It's not rash, and you know it if you're honest with yourself."

"Juliet, it's been a little weird the past few months or so, but you've had a hard time, and you probably shouldn't make any big decisions."

"Scott, I want you to be free to date other people. I have no idea when I'm going to get my head together."

"I don't want anyone else."

Juliet took a breath. "Scott, I'm so sorry, but I can't see you anymore."

"Don't do this," he said, blustering. "You can't do this to me!"

"*To* you? I'm doing it *for* you!"

"I've been here for you. I've been really patient."

"You have."

At the other end of the line, he sighed. "You're really doing it aren't you?"

"I really am. I'm sorry."

"Stop saying that, like I'm some pity case or something. You're the one who needs pity, not me!"

He hung up on her.

Juliet fell backward. "That went well," she said to Tecumseh, scratching his head. "Maybe we need to get some coffee."

The phone rang in her hand. Scott's number came up

on the screen and she hesitated. Maybe she should just be done with it. And yet, what if the situation was reversed—wouldn't she want to have her say? She flipped the phone open. "Hi, Scott."

"I'm sorry. I lost my temper."

"It's okay. But let's not do this, okay, the back and forthing. I'm really breaking up with you and there isn't anything you can say to change my mind." She almost added, *I'm sorry,* but remembered in time that it had upset him.

"Just let me ask this one thing," Scott said. "Have you met somebody?"

Unbidden came Josh's face, the harsh slash of cheekbone and jaw, the licorice black of his hair. Guilt, the color of bile, burst through her. "No," she said.

"Will you do me one favor then?"

"If I can."

"Give it a little time. Don't give up on all of this until you've had time to heal."

Juliet bowed her head. "I can't do that favor, Scott. This is final." She breathed the phrase anyway. "I'm sorry," she said, and hung up.

Coffee. Definitely coffee was in order. She slid into a pair of jeans and tugged wool socks over her toes, let the dogs out, and padded into the kitchen. There was no automatic coffeemaker, of course, only an aluminum percolator you put on the stove and boiled the old-fashioned way. Juliet liked it quite a bit, loved the crystal percolator button on top, and the sound of it bubbling up, like an old television commercial, and the smell filling the kitchen like some heady cologne.

Sunlight streamed in through the window by the sink, and the bars of yellow light falling over the polished pine framing gave the moment a depth of serenity Juliet found surprising. She crossed her arms, leaned a hip against the counter, and wondered what it was that made it seem so lovely. Through the window, she could see pines and blue sky and the jagged line of mountain rising high.

She felt lighter than she had in months. How could she have not realized how much she wanted to break up with Scott, all this time? What else was in her life that she wanted to let go?

She called up her life, and really, there wasn't much to it, was there? Scott, her condo, her job. Essentially, the job was gone, and she'd known it the minute she'd lost what should have been an easy win. The lives at stake were too important to risk on a sloppy lawyer, which was what she'd become over the past year, sadly enough.

In time, she'd be ready to go back to work. When she had her head together. When she could think about a courtroom without thinking of her rapist being on trial.

She liked working for the people, trying to even things out between the little guy and government or business, but a person could do that in many different ways.

She might miss her friends, but this wasn't her first big move. *If* it ended up being a move. Which left the condo in old Hollywood, her pride and joy, with all its Art Deco touches and glowing woods. It was a beauty, with a fireplace, within walking distance of shopping and restaurants and the bus line. She'd paid a pretty penny for it, but the value had nearly doubled since

then. If she sold it, could she buy something in
Mariposa?

Would she even want to?

Maybe it was better to just stick with the condo for
awhile. Not too many changes at once.

Humming under her breath, she poured coffee and
thought about how to spend this beautiful day.

Josh drove to Desi's ranch with a heaviness in his
gut. Of course it could only be he who delivered the
news, and he didn't expect Desi to take it particularly
well.

It seemed incongruous to be bringing such bad news
on such a great day. Melting snow dripped from the
trees, pattering and dazzling on such a bright day. Most
of the snow was gone, but he knew there was meant to
be more tomorrow afternoon. He made a note to be
sure they had plenty of supplies in case of a blizzard.

He parked under his favorite tree and got out. Desi's
truck was not in its usual place. He'd hate to have to go
find her at work to deliver this news, and had tried to
get here a little sooner, for precisely this reason. Reluctantly, he crossed the gravel, steering clear of a puddle.
Three dogs came running through the trees, barking
first in warning, then in welcome when they saw who it
was.

He knocked on the door. In seconds, Juliet swung it
open, and Josh was awash, once again, with the
luscious, somehow innocent sensuality of her. Her pale
hair was slightly mussed, as if it had not yet been
brushed, and her face was absolutely bare of makeup,

showing pale smooth skin only lightly freckled across the nose. She wore a flowered Henley with three buttons and long sleeves and no bra, which he tried mightily not to notice, but there was such a delicious loose sway of breasts beneath thin cotton that he couldn't help it. Her feet were bare.

"Hi, Josh."

"Hi," he said, and cleared his throat. "Is Desi here?"

"I think she went to work already. Do you want to come in?"

"Um." He tried to think. The smell of coffee blasted out of the kitchen, thick as a giant arm snaring him around the neck. "God, that smells good. Yeah, I'd love some of that coffee."

She moved away from the door, leaving it open for him to come in.

As he entered, he saw the pile of covers and pillows before the fire, still rumpled from her sleep, and damned if he didn't feel a little heat in his sex, a wash of awareness over his lower belly, a wish to have her back in those mussed covers, naked, with him on top of her. Kissing. Bare-chested, bare-hipped, legs tangling—

"Cream and sugar?" Juliet asked.

"What?" He blinked, aware of a graininess behind his eyes, in his throat. It had been a long night. "Yes, please."

"You don't look very well, Josh," she said. "Come sit down. Is there something wrong?"

He settled on a bar stool. "Long night," he said, reluctant to go into it just yet.

"This will help." She came around the counter and

put the cup down beside him, then rested her hand on his shoulder. "Can I get you something to eat? There are eggs, some bread."

Up close, he smelled her skin, something vaguely meadowlike, the slightest bit spicy, like crushed grasses. He found himself noticing the hollow of her throat, the rise of collarbones on either side, her breasts, with raised nipples burning through the cloth. He felt dizzy with the desire to touch her, weigh her breasts in his palms, taste her mouth, feel her body close to his own.

With a sense of near-despair, he wanted more than anything to just be held, and it shamed him.

"It must have been terrible," she said. Her voice was smooth and deep, like a hot spring pool, and her hand moved on his hair, as if she petted a dog.

He bent his head, trying to maintain a sense of propriety. Her hand moved on his neck, smoothing the skin over the tense muscles there, and he felt the touch through his whole body.

Josh lifted his head, and Juliet swayed forward and pressed a kiss to his brow, put her hands on his face. "What can I do?" she asked, and there was her pricelessly pretty face, so scrubbed and lovely, and he put his hand up around her neck and pulled her closer, between his knees. Her breasts touched his upper chest, surprisingly full and soft, and their eyes locked for a long, long second, hers smoky and sure and vibrantly blue. Her fingers were cool, almost cold. He put his hands on the small of her back, nudged her closer, and lifted his face to receive the kiss she bent down to offer.

It was one of those moments that would not come

again, and Josh tried to gather as many details as he could. The sway of her back beneath his palms, the smell of her skin, the cold tips of her fingers against his cheekbones.

The very good taste of her mouth. A good mouth. Plump lips, breath that tasted of sugar, a sweetness he expected and a heat he hadn't. He let her lead, let her just do whatever it was she was doing here. One moist kiss, two. His chest ached and he wanted to pull her more closely against him, but something told him not to.

But it was funny how it seemed there was light flowing between them. Not just nerves and excitement and arousal, but actual light, as if her lips flipped on some switch inside of him.

She raised her head. Her thumbs moved on his jaw, sweeping lightly against the bone. "Did that help any?"

"What about your fiancé?"

She pulled a hand from his face and showed him the bare space on her left hand. "We broke up. This morning."

"I'm glad," he said, and meant it.

"Me, too." She stepped away. "Let me get you some coffee and eggs."

"I need to—uh, tell you something, Juliet. This morning—" His voice, always gravelly, gave out on him. He cleared his throat. "I have something else to talk about. The reason I came here."

"Okay." Trouble came over her eyes, clouding the vivid blue. She stepped out of his embrace. "What is it?"

"First, do you know where Desi is?"

"She must have gotten up early. I haven't been up

that long, really." She glanced over her shoulder at the bed. "Why?" she said suddenly in alarm. "Is she hurt or is there an accident or—"

"No, she's not hurt. When was the last time you saw her?"

"Last night. She was called out to an animal emergency and I went to bed."

Josh's belly dropped. "What time was that, do you remember?"

A quick shrug. "I don't know. About nine, maybe?"

Mentally, he swore. This would not look good for her at all. It might not *be* good. He had to remember to think like a cop, not like Desi's buddy. What if she had killed him? "And you haven't seen her since?"

"*No.* I already said that. You're scaring me, Josh. What happened?"

He squared his shoulders. "Claude is dead, Juliet. We found his body out on the rez last night."

Her hand flew to her mouth. "Dead? How? Like murdered? Or in a car accident or something?"

"We're waiting for the autopsy, but it's pretty clear he was shot to death."

Juliet went so white he was afraid she'd faint. Carefully, she sank down to a stool, and let go of a breath. "Do you have ideas who did it?"

"Not yet."

She raised her eyes. "It's not Desi, you know. She might seem as if she'd like to kill him, but I know she wouldn't really do it."

"I know that, too," he said, and realized it was true. He could see her shooting Claude during a confrontation, but not stalking him to shoot him dead, or luring him out to some deserted place. "But it's not going to look good for her, not after that run-in yesterday in front of half the town."

Juliet pressed her lips together. "Damn."

"And the trouble is, she has the most motive. Who would blame her for killing him?"

"Right," Juliet said grimly, and looked at him hard. "I hear what you're saying, but there's no way she did it." She rubbed her palms on her jeans. "Do you know the land is worth ten million dollars?"

He whistled. "There's motive."

"Talk that one up," she said, and he suddenly realized he wasn't dealing with soft Juliet, but a tough lawyer who probably did very well in court, thank you very much. "Let me find my cell and I'll try to call her."

"I already tried," he said. A headache throbbed at the back of his skull, low, right over his neck. "No answer."

"We need to find her."

Josh nodded and then asked the question he had to ask. "Are you sure she even came home last night?"

# *Chapter 9*

Juliet darted a glance at the bed. What she had not noticed upon awakening was the yellow sweater, inside out and sleeves akimbo, that Desi had flung there last night. Juliet remembered her tugging it off over her head, her hair coming loose in a heavy tumble.

"Maybe she wasn't here last night," Juliet admitted.

"Did she tell you anything about the call?"

"Yes." Juliet frowned. "Goats. Some goats were attacked by a mountain lion. She had to take—" Another wave of guilt swamped her and she halted, the salty taste in her mouth.

"Had to take what?"

"Her rifle. For protection."

Josh pursed his lips. "It's not surprising, considering." He dropped his head in his hands. So weary.

Juliet didn't know if she should comfort him or protest or weep. She crossed her arms over her chest and waited.

He raised his head. "What do you remember about the call? Do you think it was really an animal call?"

She thought back. "We'd just gotten out of the hot springs, you know. I was tired and not paying much attention." She narrowed her eyes, trying to recreate the moment in her mind from the things she could remember. The yellow sweater. The fire in the grate. The sound of Desi's voice, murmuring, pausing.

*Where did you see him?*

In a split second, Juliet chose her sister over any other thing, even the truth. "I'm absolutely sure," she said.

"All right." He pulled his cell phone off his belt and punched in a number. "Let's find out who keeps goats."

The only possibilities, according to the main vet office, were Alvin Taylor, Pauline Two Tree and John Crum. The first was a wealthy rancher, sitting on about fifty million dollars in land in a flat strip between the two mountain ranges. He turned out to be on an extended vacation and his ranch manager didn't have a record of anything happening to goats the night before. They had, however, seen the mountain lion several times in the past few weeks.

Two Tree lived on the edge of the reservation. Her goats, used for their hair in her weaving, were fine, as carefully tended as small children.

Which left Crum, an ex-hippie turned farmer on the outskirts of town. Josh turned in to his drive and a dozen creatures skittered out to see who had arrived—dogs, goats, a couple of sheep. Chickens squawked and chuttered from their coop, protected from prey behind two layers of fencing.

"A mountain lion would have a good time here, all right," Josh said.

"Poor things."

He gave a little shrug. "It's just nature."

A man with a beard combed neatly to his waist came out of the house carrying a rifle. He wore jeans and a cowboy hat and heavy work boots. Juliet wanted to laugh—he looked like a cartoon version of a mountain man. "I didn't think people like him still existed," she said quietly before they got out.

"Don't you dare make me laugh," Josh said with a glance.

"I'll do my best."

They got out of the truck and Juliet held out her hand for a big shaggy dog to sniff. The man stood there suspiciously. "Can I help you folks with something?"

"We're looking for Dr. Rousseau, the vet? Her office thought she might have come here last night," Josh said.

"Yeah, she was here, but I ain't seen her since she stitched up the goats."

"Do you remember what time that was, sir?"

"Must been ten, ten-thirty, I guess. I just missed the news."

Juliet felt a sense of mingled dread and relief. Relief that Desi actually had been called out to tend some wounded animals, dread that she had been out all night. "Did she say anything about what she was planning to do when she left here?"

"Yup." He lifted his hat, pulled it down tighter over

his ears. "She was gonna go track that blasted cougar while the tracks were fresh."

"Damn," Josh muttered under his breath. Then, more loudly, "Where?"

"She headed out to the reservation. Said she thought she might know where it had its den."

"By the reservation," Josh repeated dully.

The man hawked and spit. "Wasn't that she wanted to kill it, you know. I shot it. She was afraid it might be dangerous."

"All right." Josh held out his hand. "Thank you."

For a moment, the man just stood there, then abruptly stuck out his hand and stiffly shook Josh's. "I gotta protect my critters."

"I understand, sir. A rogue cat can take down a lot of livestock." He tipped his hat. "Take care now."

Back in the truck, Juliet put her hands in her lap, clasped tightly together, and started straight ahead.

"I'm scared," she said, and looked at Josh. "Where is she?"

His mouth could never look tight, but there was grimness to it. He shook his head slowly. "We found the body out there. It was mauled by a big animal. Could have been a cat."

"Maybe somebody shot him accidentally, aiming for the cat?"

"Sure, I mean, it's possible." He seemed to notice her fear and reached across the seat to take her hand. "We'll find her. There's a perfectly reasonable explanation she's missing. Keep the faith."

She nodded.

"Try her cell phone again."

"Good idea." Juliet pulled the phone out of her pocket, jabbed the speed dial. It rang once, then again. Again. Again. The answering machine picked up, and Juliet left a message. "I'm getting seriously worried, Desi. Call me." She hung up and looked at Josh. "Now what?"

"I'll take you home."

The phone rang shrilly and Juliet answered urgently. "Hello?"

"Juliet," Desi cried, "Where are you? It freaked me out to get home and find you gone."

"Where am *I?* Where are *you?* I've been worried to death about you."

"I'm fine. Are you in town? Where did you go?"

It suddenly occurred to Juliet that her sister did not yet know the news, of course, that she was still living in a world where Claude Tsosie was a pain in the neck, but still alive. "I'm with Josh," she said. "We're on our way back there. Don't go anywhere, okay?"

"No way. I chased that lion halfway around the world last night."

"Did you get him?"

"No." She sighed, and Juliet could imagine her rubbing her hand across the back of her neck, a gesture she'd repeated at moments of exhaustion since childhood. "He's wounded, and likely very dangerous, and I'm really worried that he could be a problem. I want to get some wildlife officials out there to sedate him and bring him down so we can fix him up."

"Will they do that?"

"I don't know. We'll see."

"I'll be there soon, sis."

Josh held out his hand for the phone. Juliet handed it to him, and he spoke to Desi. "I'm beat, Desi. Make some coffee, will you?"

Juliet couldn't hear her sister's reply, but Josh clipped the phone closed and handed it back to her.

"Listen," Josh said, "I know this is kind of weird, that life is all in a tangle, but before we go in there and face the way your sister is going to feel about her ex getting murdered, I'd like to know if that kiss this morning means maybe we can figure out a way to see each other. Sometime. Soon."

"It is kind of weird," she said. "But, yeah, I'd like that, too."

He smiled. "Have I told you I have a weakness for blondes?"

"That's because we are princesses," she said, and promptly felt guilty. But there was something about him that made her want to just stop struggling, stop building up defenses, and just rest with him. "I mean, of course there are brunette princesses as well—"

He laughed, the sound as rich as coffee, as chocolate, all things dark and tasty. "Now you know what kind of trouble I get into liking blondes. It's *so* politically incorrect."

Juliet laughed softly and as it rolled out of her chest, she realized it had been a long time since she'd heard it, her own laughter. How odd that it should arrive now, when there had been a murder, when she was dreading the look on her sister's face when she heard her ex was dead.

And yet, why not? Something about this gentle giant

eased her, and she'd been tense so long she was starved for that simple pleasure.

"I won't be able to leave Desi today," she said. "Let's play it all by ear."

"Maybe Glory and I can make supper for you one night. How about that?"

"I'd like that." Juliet smiled. "Glory. What a kid. How did she get that name?"

His nose wiggled in amusement. "My ex liked the song, 'Angels We Have Heard On High.'"

She laughed.

"She was a little strange," Josh acknowledged, "even before she started drinking."

"Glory is a pretty name, and it suits her. She's such a glorious little girl."

"She is."

They stopped at a traffic light. "Her kidnapping...that had to be pretty hard for you."

He touched his nose with the pad of his thumb. "It was brutal. Every single minute." He shook his head. "Who knows what it was like for her?"

"She seems all right, though."

"So far so good. She's with me now, and that's the important thing."

A vision of Desi's face crossed Juliet's imagination, and she pressed a palm to her belly. "I'm so worried about how Desi will take this news. She really did love him, at least she did at one time. I think it's going to break her heart."

"I'm a lot more worried that she might be arrested for it."

"Arrested!"

"Yeah. She has no alibi, and there really aren't many leads at the moment."

Feeling airless, Juliet pressed harder against her stomach. "That would be *so* bad."

"I agree." He cleared his throat. "Let's not cross that bridge just yet. One thing at a time."

"All right." Fingering her phone, Juliet said, "I guess I'm going to have to call my other sister, let her know what's going on. She gets very upset if she gets left out of the loop."

"The artist sister, right?"

"Yes, Miranda. She lives in New York."

He turned on the road toward the cabin. "Shakespeare, huh? Miranda, Juliet and—what's Desi short for?"

"Desdemona."

"Ah." As if he sensed her nervousness, he said, "Is Miranda older, younger?"

"Youngest. The redhead. There's a blonde, a brunette and a redhead. She's the fiery one. More the child of our parents than we are, really." The truck rocked over a deep rut, and Juliet grabbed the door. "Not that she ever sees them. I get the impression that she does everything she can to distance herself from them."

"It's not like you and Desi are living in the old family home, producing grandchildren."

"That's true." Juliet thought of her mother, Carol, her long dark hair and piercing eyes, and felt a pang. "They weren't the best parents. And probably Miranda got the worst of it. They went through some drama when she was in high school. I've never really heard the whole story, but it wasn't pretty for her." She glanced at him. "Sorry, I'm babbling."

"It's interesting. Desi doesn't talk about your family, except you."

"We were pretty close as kids. She was the brave one and I was the coward."

He grinned. "I don't believe that."

"Trust me, it was true. I was afraid of everything— snakes, spiders, all the outside stuff. Desi never was." The cabin came into view. "Oh, dear. Here we go."

They pulled into the circular drive and Juliet couldn't help but think about the first day she'd come here, when Claude had been trying to coax Desi into seeing things his way, and she'd been promising to kill him if he took another step.

What if Desi really had done it? Killed Claude?

No. Juliet set her jaw and got out of the truck. No, she wouldn't allow that possibility. As they came in, she called out, "Hello! Anybody here?"

Desi sat by the potbellied stove, drying her hair. "Just us elves."

Juliet paused, letting one more placid moment pass in Desi's world before they shattered it. Desi sat on the floor, on a pink and paisley cushion. Sitting Bull, glum as ever, sat beside her. Desi's hair, her glory, fell in splendid lushness over her shoulders and down her back. Juliet forgot, because Desi kept it braided, how beautiful her sister's hair was. Yards of it, deep brown like earth or bark, shot through with gold and threads of copper. It flowed down her back like the hair of some medieval queen.

"Desi," Juliet said. "I have some bad news."

Something in Juliet's voice must have conveyed the depth of the bad news, because Desi put down the brush and looked up. There was a scratch on her cheek and marks on her forearms. Pale blue bruises ringed her eyes.

"Well, don't just stand there," she snapped. "*Tell* me!"

Behind Juliet, Josh tensed, as if waiting, and the lawyer in Juliet knew he was probably going into cop mode. What would Desi do? How would she react?

Juliet sank down on her knees. "Claude is dead."

"What?" Desi sounded irritated, impatient.

"Claude is dead," Juliet repeated. "I'm sorry."

For a long moment, Desi waited, as if for the punch line, some other words to change the reality of what Juliet said. Her brown eyes, luminous as the moon, searched her sister's face. "He's dead?"

"Yes." Juliet felt relief rippling through her at Desi's bewilderment.

"Which means what, exactly? Does that pseudo-sale go through and I lose half the land?"

"I don't know. Desi, what does that matter right now? He's dead."

"I heard you." Suddenly, she crumbled forward. "How? Car accident?"

"Murdered," Josh said, that grizzly bear voice making the word even more harrowing.

Desi's head jerked up. "*Murdered?* That's impossible. Who would kill him? I mean, aside from me, of course."

"Don't even joke about it," Juliet cried.

"I wouldn't really kill him. You know that." Desi jumped up. "What happened?"

"He was shot," Josh said. "Last night some time. Found his body on the reservation."

Desi's jaw went hard as she looked at her friend. "Last night," she repeated. "How did he die?"

"Shot," Josh repeated patiently, understanding Desi's shocked and disconnected reaction.

"Damn," Desi whispered. "This is not good for our team at all, is it?"

Grimly, he shook his head. "Half the town heard you tell him you'd kill him."

She took a breath. "Well, then you'd better get out there and find out who really did it. I'll be damned if he ruins my life, that bastard." She shook her head. "What a lousy day." She bent her head and started to cry. "That poor cat is still out there in agony and I'm worried sick that he's going to hurt someone."

Juliet sank down beside her sister, putting her arms around her and whispering, "Shh. It's okay. You'll be all right."

"Find out who killed him, Josh," Desi said.

"I will," Josh said. "I promise."

The skies were getting heavy by midafternoon, when Desi came in from tending her wolves. "I think it's going to snow for real tonight," she said, shedding her down coat and hanging it on a hook. "We have plenty of food, but do you have enough reading material?"

Juliet looked up from the paperback she was reading, curled up in a nook by the windows, Crazy Horse the dog beneath her knees, like a furry pillow. She scratched his forehead idly as she read, nibbling little foods like pistachio nuts and small candies, as she had all her life. Reading and nibbling were always her favorite things. As a child, she'd sometimes read a book a day, happily inert in some corner. In those days, it had usually been a cat who curled up with her.

"Very funny," Juliet said, because they'd bought a paper bag full of novels at a used bookstore the day before. "I think I'll live."

Desi smiled, and it lightened the dark circles beneath her eyes, though there was only so much to be done. "Let's make some cookies, shall we?"

"Definitely an excellent idea." Juliet yawned and put her book down. Crazy Horse groaned and fell to one side. "Did you call Miranda? Let her know what happened?"

"Yes. And Mother and Dad. They're in Greece and send their love." With an exaggerated smooching sound, she kissed the air, then rolled her eyes. "I told them not to interrupt their trip for this. We were divorcing anyway."

Not, Juliet thought cynically, that they would have anyway. They'd never been fond of Claude, which had probably been at least part of his appeal. Desi had never been able to resist needling her mother at every possible chance, a repayment for the endless, endless prodding and poking the eldest daughter had endured from their elegant, blue-blooded mother. She plopped down on the bar stool by the counter and plucked a chocolate chip out of the bag Desi had opened. "What did Miranda have to say? How is she?"

"Fine. I told her you were here and she sent her love." Desi settled a bowl on the counter. "Does she know about the rape? I wasn't sure."

Juliet shook her head. "Can that just be our secret? I hate how people look at me after they find out."

"She's your sister. She won't look at you that way."

"Why burden her with it? There's no point, and it will just upset her."

Desi lifted a shoulder. "What if she'd been raped? Would you want her to tell you?"

With excruciating care, Juliet lined three chocolate chips up into a triangle. "Yes," she had to admit. "I'd feel left out if she didn't tell me."

Desi nodded. "Exactly."

"I'll think about it," Juliet promised.

"Before we start the cookies," Desi said, wiping her hands, "I worried about this all night last night—come here and let me show you how to operate a pistol. You probably will never need to know, but there are some times you might need to have a gun, and I'd feel better knowing that I'd showed you."

"I don't want to shoot a gun, Desi!"

Desi rolled her eyes. "Don't be a baby. Just let me show you." She opened the gun cabinet and went through the steps of loading and firing both the rifle and the handgun. Juliet went along with it, but she couldn't imagine ever really using either one of them.

"Guns kind of give me the creeps," Juliet said.

"That's because you're in the city and people use them to kill other people. In the mountains, they make up for not having large, savage teeth and long claws."

Even Juliet had to chuckle at that. "I'll just hope I never have to use them then."

"I'm sure you never will." She went back to the

kitchen and popped a handful of chocolate chips in her mouth. "I'm so tired I could sleep for a year!"

The dogs exploded into a frenzy of barking, all of them racing to the front window that looked out toward the driveway. "Who's that, I wonder?" Desi said, wiping her hands on her apron.

Juliet was the first to see the flashing red lights. "Uh-oh."

She rose and went to the window, where she saw two vehicles with official Mariposa county shields on the sides. Lights on. "This looks official," she said, and turned around, lifting a hand, palm out, to caution Desi. "Don't say a single word, Desdemona, do you understand me? Not a word."

"You don't think they're arresting me, do you?" She widened her eyes. "I'm a vet! A *doctor.* We don't kill things, we save them. They can't really think I'd kill him?"

Juliet opened the door to the sheriff and two deputies, each dressed in green and khaki uniforms. "We're here for Desdemona Rousseau," one of the officers said.

# Chapter 10

"She's here. You know her, right there."

"Desdemona Rousseau," the sheriff said, "You're under arrest for the murder of Claude Tsosie."

Looking stunned and shaky, Desi said, "I can't leave my sister. She doesn't know how to live up here in the mountains. By herself."

"Then she'd better get to town."

"Somebody has to look out for the property," Desi said. "The wolves—"

Juliet raised her palm. "Stop talking, Desi. I'll call Josh. You just go with them, we'll get you out in no time."

The sheriff snorted unpleasantly. "Not this time. Not in this town."

With hands that trembled visibly, Desi untied her

apron and came around the counter. She reached for her coat, hanging by the door. The sheriff pulled out a pair of handcuffs. Her face was the color of the flour on the counter.

Juliet protested. "Are handcuffs really necessary? She's obviously cooperating."

"Regulation," he said, but Juliet doubted it. He just wanted, for whatever reason, to make this more humiliating for her sister.

Once she had her coat on, Desi held out her wrists. The sheriff gruffly ordered her, "Turn around."

Desi's nostrils flared, a sign when they were children that you should clear the area. She turned around woodenly, and met Juliet's eyes as the handcuffs were fastened. "Don't stay alone," Desi said. "Call Josh, right now."

"I will," Juliet said. "Don't *worry.*"

Handcuffed, head down, Desi was led to the SUV. Over her shoulder she said, "*Now,* Juliet."

But Juliet waited until the SUVs had gone down the road into the pinkening dusk, her heart pounding so hard it felt her ribs would break. The case was circumstantial, it was true, but it was a very good circumstantial case. If they didn't find out who had really killed Claude, there was a very good chance Desi would at least go to trial. In a town so severely divided, that seemed like a very bad idea.

Whistling for the dogs, she headed back inside with the pack. She wondered if she ought to just go ahead and drive into town and find Josh rather than call him. But then she'd have to drive back up the narrow, twisting road in the dark. And, judging by the sky, the snow.

Josh's cell phone number was on the list taped to the wall and she dialed it with purposeful stabs. There was no answer until a voice mail message said, "This is Joshua Mad Calf. Leave a message."

Odd that he didn't answer the cell, especially as a cop. She frowned and said quickly, "Josh, this is Juliet Rousseau, and they just arrested my sister. I need your help."

She hung up and held the phone in her hand for a long moment, trying to decide what the best course of action would be. They'd have to set bail fairly quickly, but maybe not until Monday morning, which would mean Desi would molder in jail all weekend.

Beyond the uncurtained window, snow suddenly started to float down.

Great. Just great. She'd never learned to drive in the snow. And she *would* have just broken up with her boyfriend, who knew all sorts of things about criminal law that were unknown to her. She made a face. Who else could she call? Most of her friends were in entertainment or civil law.

No blinking neon sign came on in her imagination. No dancing choir came kicking through the room with placards around their necks. Outside, it was quickly getting dark, and the snow would begin to pile up, and her sister was going to jail for a crime she didn't commit.

Juliet hoped she hadn't committed, anyway. She was 99.9% sure, but her study of the law had shown her people did some pretty crazy things sometimes. Even people devoted to healing. Scorned lovers, in particular.

Her stomach plummeted. If she, Desi's sister, could think such things about a woman she'd known and loved all of her life, what would a jury think?

The phone in her hand rang suddenly and Juliet answered it breathlessly. "Hello?"

"Looks like your sister is finally going to get what she deserved," said a woman's voice.

For a moment, Juliet was stunned into silence. The line held a faint buzz, eerie and somehow menacing. "Who is this?"

But of course the threatening party didn't answer. Just hung up. Juliet pressed *69 to see if she could get a number, but the robotic voice simply said, "That number is unavailable."

Outside, the gloaming edged the peaks and the tops of the trees with an opal stain. Juliet wished she could enjoy it, but she walked over to a lamp and turned it on, her throat getting tighter and tighter. The idea of driving into town, without any clue of who she would seek out or what she'd do when she got there, seemed intimidating. Even worse was the idea of driving back here after she'd done whatever she'd done in town. Driving through the snow. On dark mountain roads in a little rental car not particularly designed for the task? No, thanks.

But even worse than that was the idea of staying here in the cabin alone. The uncurtained windows showing the whole world she was here by herself. The distance to town if anyone or anything—

What? She said to herself. Attacked? This wasn't a horror movie, with a deranged serial killer lurching through the high mountain forests of the San Juan range, or a rabid bear so hungry for blood he'd smash through windows and back doors.

And even in the event of murderers or wild animals, there were three dogs, wolf mixes that were enormously loyal to protect her. Three *big* dogs.

Still, she stood with the phone in her hand, her throat so tight she could barely breath, her heart pounding wildly. Tears stung the backs of her eyes and furiously, she blinked against them.

She was so tired of being afraid! Tired of being frozen. Tired of giving her whole life up to the possibility that something bad would happen again. Inside her head was a voice screaming: *just do something!*

And yet her body could not break free of its prison.

As Josh drove back to town from a call to a domestic dispute in the wilds beyond Mariposa Falls, he listened to Bonnie Raitt. He loved her better than any singer alive, loved her smoky voice and the richness of her sorrow. In her expressions of lusty love, lost and found, he connected with the sense of the mystical, as deep as any worship service. It was a passion he'd shared with Claude, actually. They'd spent many an enjoyable hour drinking ginger ale and listening to Bonnie. It was hard not to like Claude when he'd turned on the charm, and Josh, though he held himself aloof, had wanted to like the man.

What an absolute waste of a human being, he thought now. Claude had been born with talent, intelligence, charm and a very pretty face. He could have done anything, gone anywhere, and he'd actually started out on that path—earning a scholarship to college, working his way through, going into the Peace Corps after graduation. All the right things.

And yet, somewhere, he'd let himself get twisted into a parody, a Coyote thinking he knew more than he did.

Now he was dead.

Josh had taken himself off the case. He was too close to Desi, and the signs were pointing too hard toward her. He'd never be able to be objective about the evidence if it ended up pointing to her. Worse, he was afraid he'd ignore things he ought to notice.

Sometimes it wasn't possible to be both a good cop and a good friend. Josh had chosen friendship.

As the truck descended through an aspen grove in full blaze, the phone on his hip suddenly trilled with the message signal. A phone call had come in while he'd been out of range.

He punched the button to reach voice mail and held the phone to his ear. There were six new messages. *Six?* Good God.

The first two were from his mother, who told him that Glory had chipped a front tooth and had a dentist appointment on Monday morning—did he want Helene to take her? The second one was that Glory had asked permission to spend the night with one of her nursery school playmates and Helene was pretty sure Josh wouldn't want her to, but she'd promised Glory she would ask.

The third was a hang-up. The fourth was his boss with a very gruff order to call him immediately. There had been some news on the Tsosie case. The fifth was his boss again, repeating the message.

The sixth was Juliet, her voice wobbly as she reported the news that Desi had been arrested. He swore and pulled over to make phone calls properly.

Damn! He'd only been in the mountains for an hour and a half. How could so much have happened in such a short time? This morning, the skier Claude had been involved with had come in to make a report, and Josh had been concerned about her swollen eyes and shaky hands. She was pretty young, and it had to be traumatic to have a boyfriend murdered. Her alibi was airtight— she'd been drinking at The Black Crown with a group of Germans who were hiking the Mariposa trail. By the number of witnesses that had come forward, half the town must have been in the pub that night.

First, despite the urgency of everything else, he called his mother. "Is Glory all right? How did she chip her tooth?"

"She went down the slide facefirst before anyone could stop her." There was a mix of exasperation and pride and weariness in Helene's voice. "She has a mind of her own, that girl. It's not bad," she added, "and it's a tooth that'll come out in a year or two."

"Okay." Josh took a breath. "Mom, they arrested Desi a little while ago."

"Oh, no!"

"I'm going to the jail and see what I can find out, then go up and see her sister, and I'll be back after that."

"Why don't you just let Glory sleep here again? You go and get some real sleep. You sound beat."

He nodded. "All right. I'll let you know if I hear anything more."

"If you talk to Desi, give her my love."

"Will do."

When he hung up, he called Desi's home phone, and Juliet answered wearily. "I just got your message," he said. "Are you okay?"

"*I'm* fine. I'm worried about Desi, though. When will they have her arraignment? When can we get her out of there?"

"I'm going to town right now to see what I can find out." Snowflakes were floating out of the sky, sticking to his windshield and he frowned. "I want you to look around the cabin to make sure you have everything you'll need for three or four days, too. It could snow a lot with an Albuquerque low like this."

"You mean I could be stuck for three days up here by myself?"

"Easy." He turned the heater knob to defrost to melt the snow collected in little tufts over the windshield. "Look around and see what you might be missing. Water, food, firewood. We'll make sure you're prepared."

"You mean Desi might not get out of jail for *days?*"

He hesitated. The truth was, he doubted she'd be able to make bail at all if this shook out the way he thought it was going to. "Maybe, maybe not. Don't get all worked up about it just yet, though. Let me do some talking and see what I can find out."

He heard her take a breath and consciously release it. "Okay. Thanks."

"I'll be there in a little while."

He put the phone away and drove into town, worried on some low level at the way Juliet sounded. Not exactly frightened. Not panicky, which he could actually understand, given that she was a city girl and the mountains could be intimidating.

Something else. Hushed. As if a hand were pressing down on her. With a scowl, he resolved to get this taken care of as fast as possible, and then get up there and check on her.

And, he thought, maybe he should gently try to discover her story, whatever had traumatized her. It was obviously not resolved.

Juliet tried to pretend it was a normal night. She put some music on her MP3 player and stuck an earphone in her ear, determinedly singing along with the Black Eyed Peas and Dido as she creamed sugar and butter for the cookies Desi had started before she was arrested. The supplies were fine—she could survive for weeks on the food in the cupboards.

Outside, snow started to fall in a sturdy, determined way that seemed very different from the dinner-plate-sized flakes that had fallen her first night here. Once she'd read that the aboriginal peoples of Alaska had many names for snow, and this seemed a place where you'd want different names for it, too: Plate snow. Flurries. Blizzard snow. She stirred chocolate chips into the mix and stared out the window. This would be rain snow. Small flakes that were heavy enough to make a little bit of noise when they were falling steadily, as they were now. It was collecting more slowly than the other snow had, but with greater determination.

What if she was stuck here for three days, all alone?

*Don't think about it.*

Dropping spoonfuls of dough onto the cookie sheet, she tried to remember what it had been like to be brave, long ago. What had made her brave? She'd gone to college far away from her family, lived alone in an apartment in Berkley when she'd gone to law school, found her condo in Hollywood and lived there alone, in a neighborhood that was both good and bad, for several years. She'd traveled all over the U.S. by herself, stayed in hotels, navigated strange cities without much distress.

How had she done it?

The sound of a truck engine came to her as she took the last batch of cookies out of the oven. Juliet saw Josh, snow catching in his long glossy hair, headed across the yard.

He looked grim. Furious.

Beautiful.

His beauty struck her across the solar plexus, blazed into her throat. Against the snowy forest, with the very last of the daylight hanging in the clouds, he looked like an enchanted and ancient being emerging from the trees to visit the mortal realm for a moment. She wanted to put her hands in his hair, touch his cheekbones, kiss his throat, breathe in the enchantment.

She pressed her hand to the hollow of her throat, tried to brush the startling recognition off her face with her palm, and opened the door. "Did you see my sister?"

He shook his head, his mouth tight. "They wouldn't let me."

Gesturing him inside, she asked, "What did you find out? When will they set bail?"

"Very earliest is Wednesday. The judge is out of town until then."

Juliet narrowed her eyes. "Was that deliberate? The deputy who arrested her seemed to want it to be a very humiliating experience."

"Probably." He met her eyes. "It's a closed community in some ways. Desi has been accepted more than some because she is a great vet, but Claude made some enemies." He sounded calm, but his anger made his back too straight, his face stiff.

She offered a plate of cookies and Josh helped himself to a handful. "Wednesday! I hate thinking of her in there for so long."

"Me, too." He took a bite, then said, "I don't think you should stay here. It's pretty isolated and you're not used to it."

Relief moved through her like a wave of wind, cooling her fear. "I don't want to. But where will I go? I have to take care of the dogs, of the property, of—"

"You can come to my house. I have a big couch."

A ripple moved on her skin. She thought of kissing him earlier, thought of the flare that had burst over her nerves at the taste of his lips, the thrust of his tongue. To her embarrassment, her nipples pearled and she crossed her arms, hoping he hadn't noticed. She hesitated, picking up a cookie, then putting it down.

"I'm not expecting you to sleep with me," he said. "It's not like that."

Juliet blushed. "I didn't think you were."

"I just don't think you need to be up here by yourself."

"What about the dogs?"

"We'll bring them with us. Alex, the kid Desi loves so much, will take care of the wolf sanctuary. He's very capable."

Juliet really didn't have to weigh it out. Stay up here, terrified, or go to town with Josh? "I'll be right back," she said, going to pack a bag.

## Chapter 11

Snow was really beginning to fall by the time they got to town. Juliet stood outside in it for a moment, the dogs leaping and dancing all around her as they heard Josh's dog, Jack, howling inside. In spite of everything, Juliet could not resist the delight of turning in a circle, looking around and up at the sky. It was enchantingly beautiful. "Snow is so magical," she said.

He chuckled. "See if you feel the same way in April."

There it was again, the assumption that she'd be hanging around. "I'm sure it loses some of its appeal."

"Let's get inside. I'll make us some supper. Unless you already ate?"

"I'm pretty sure fourteen chocolate chip cookies don't count for dinner."

The dogs tore inside and greeted Jack, and then Josh put them out in the backyard, which was fenced, to let them burn off some energy. "We'll have to take them out for a walk in the morning. Walk over and pick up Glory from my mom's house."

"Walk?"

He grinned, shrugged a little as he pushed his sleeves up on dark, smooth forearms. "Snowshoe, maybe. Have you ever tried it?"

"Nope."

"I need to give my mom a quick call," he said. "Go on into the kitchen if you want."

She followed him into the kitchen, a small room dominated by glass-fronted cabinets and a butcher block island in the center. Stools sat on one side, and the stove was in the middle of the island. The colors, peach and magenta and white, were a little weird, but in general, she liked it. In the hallway, Josh talked to his mother, explaining what had happened to Desi. He asked if Glory was still awake.

Then, "What?" he said. "I can't believe you let her go, Mom. That wasn't your decision to make."

Silence, the faint sound of a voice on the other end. "All right. I guess you're right." He paused. "Thanks, Ma. I don't know what I'd do without you."

Juliet pulled the sleeves of her sweater down over her hands, an old habit from childhood, and wondered with a pang what it would be like to have the kind of relationship with her mother that Josh obviously had with his. Her mouth curled at the corners in a bitter smile. Carol, the brilliant physicist with her tweeds, and blue blood, and trim waist, had better things to do than roll around in the emotional quagmire of children's needs.

Josh came into the kitchen. Juliet turned. "Everything okay?"

"I was hoping to go get Glory and bring her home before the snow, but my mom let her spend the night with a friend on the rez."

"And that's a problem?"

He lifted one shoulder, quickly, as if he knew his feelings were unreasonable. "I don't like her to be with anyone else but me or my mom. I only started letting Desi keep her a little while ago."

"Because of everything that happened with her mom?"

A terse nod. "It's all right. My mom has a point, too, that Glory needs to get to normal life. Part of that is spending the night with friends. My mom knows the family and trusts them." He blew out a breath. "It's hard for me to trust anybody these days."

"Yeah." Juliet found her mouth twisting again. "Yeah. I know what you mean."

"I noticed that." He reached for a pan on the stove. "Can you talk about it?"

"Not right this minute, if you don't mind." Like a curious dog, she rounded the perimeter of the kitchen, worrying her sleeves. "Is the color scheme your doing?"

"Hardly." He snorted. "Real estate is stupidly expensive around here, but there are some rentals set aside for the workforce. Most of them are down the valley quite a ways, but this whole section of blocks is rentals owned by the town. We have a place on the rez, of course, but it's a long way out, pretty isolated, and I need to be in town for Glory's sake." He pointed with a knife he'd taken out of the drawer. "My mom lives a couple of blocks over. She's the librarian."

"That's very convenient."

"No kidding. We worked at it." He sliced ham from a butt he'd taken out of the fridge, and dropped chunks of butter into a heavy cast-iron skillet. When the butter started to foam, he dropped the ham into it and sprinkled it lightly with brown sugar.

"That looks great," Juliet commented. "Can I do anything?"

"There's some canned pineapple in that cupboard to the left of the sink, if you want to get it out and open it. Can opener in the drawer below it. No, one more over."

He turned the heat down and let the butter and sugar caramelize with the ham. When Juliet opened the pineapple, he forked rings out and laid them on top of the ham slices, sprinkled them with a little more brown sugar and dots of butter, then turned the heat very low. "I'll let it just get good and hot. Do you like corn? Carrots?"

"Both." She leaned on her elbow. "I have to admit I was expecting something like a sandwich or something, not this actual supper."

He grinned. "Once upon a time, that's what it would have been. I had to learn to cook easy, healthy things so I could feed Glory."

"Lucky for me." She watched as he took frozen corn from the freezer and poured some into a bowl he put in the microwave, then filled a plump white teakettle with water and set it on another burner.

"Tea or milk or hot chocolate to drink?" he asked,

and opened a cupboard to reveal neat colorful boxes of tea in stacks.

"Oh, tea, definitely," she said, and chose a spice blend.

When they were settled over the very satisfying meal, Juliet said, "So, what will we do about Desi? Who else could have killed Claude?"

"Let's start with the people we know didn't do it," he said, buttering a chunk of hearty dark bread. "It wasn't Christie Lundgren, the girlfriend. She's got a rock-solid alibi. It wasn't you. It wasn't me."

Juliet raised her eyebrows. "That leaves a few possibilities."

"Right. I've done some poking around, and the trouble is—" He paused.

"The trouble is?"

"Claude made a lot of enemies the past couple of years." One thick brow cocked. "Mostly women and a few disgruntled boyfriends."

"I see." Juliet cut a triangle of ham, carefully layered a triangle of pineapple on top of it. "Criminal law isn't my specialty, but usually a crime of passion kind of murder seems to happen in the heat of the moment, or at least in the heat of the affair."

"That's true."

She ate the bite of ham, perfectly balanced salt and sweet, caramelized sugar, rich butter, crisp pineapple. "This," she said with deep appreciation, "is very good, Josh."

"Like it, little girl?" He winked. "I have many special dishes up my sleeve."

"Really." The word was droll. "As exciting as the

Vienna sausages and saltine crackers we had the other night?"

He laughed. "Point taken."

"So, anyway," she continued. "Who are the most recent scorned lovers?"

"That will take some digging, but it seems to be the dentist's wife. Who, in my opinion, would have been more likely to shoot Christie."

A little pause fell. "What about the developers who want the land? What if they've gone out of their way to frame Desi or something?"

Josh nodded, considering. "It's possible. There's a lot of money at stake, but we'll have to look into that some more. Might not be a bad idea to amble over to the Black Crown and see what the gossip around town has been."

"Is it open tonight?"

He raised his head. "Sure. You want to go?"

"What else is there to do, really?"

The corner of his mouth lifted, very, very slightly. "Nothing at all."

The Black Crown occupied a pub that had been serving libations to Mariposans as far back as the gold rush, though it had been called Molly's Tavern for most of that time. An ex-pro rugby player from New Zealand had purchased it two years ago and renovated it into a classic British-style pub that specialized in beers from around the world and old-fashioned pub food like hamburgers and shepherd's pie and even a ploughman's platter with cheeses and pickles that Glory loved.

Josh wasn't much of a drinker, but he liked Tamati Neville and his pub. Rugby jerseys lined the walls, and the jukebox had a great selection, and Tam kept order with a jovial smile backed up by muscle when necessary.

It was fairly busy tonight, especially for a night in the between times—between the summer tourists and hikers, before the winter ski crowds—and Josh glanced around, wondering why. A big group of skinny, tough runner types lounged in one corner, empty plates scattered on the table before them. One had an orange-and-white flag on his T-shirt: orienteering. Another group, mostly women, were dressed in athletic clothes, their leathery skin, sturdy thighs, and no-bullshit air giving away their adventure racer status.

Tam was behind the bar as always, a tall, athletic man with thick curly hair and bright, wolflike green eyes. "Hello, my friend Joshua," he said in his clipped Kiwi accent. "What can I get for you two?"

"Gossip is what I'm here for," Josh said, "but I'll have a bottle of whatever is on special tonight."

"And you, miss?" Tam asked. "We have beer from everywhere, but other things, too. What would you like?"

"What do you like best?"

"Well, I must admit to a soft spot for my native Tui."

"Okay. I'll have that." Juliet settled on the bar stool and glanced up at Josh, at which point he realized he'd been staring at her. The low light of the pub washed her blond hair with shimmery gloss, and he wanted to stroke the length of it, bury his hands in the softness. "What?" she asked.

He shook his head slowly, and lifted one hand to her hair, touching it very lightly with his palm. "Your hair is beautiful."

A flicker moved on her face. "Thanks."

Tam came back with their beers, and Josh raised his to toast Juliet. "Cheers," he said. She tapped his bottle with her own and they both drank.

"This is Juliet Rousseau," Josh said. "Her sister is the vet in town, and she runs the wolf center."

Tam said, "The one who was arrested today."

"Yep."

"I am sorry," Tam said, his accent slightly formal. "How can I help?"

"Claude drank in here, didn't he?"

Tam rolled his eyes. "Yeah. There was a bloody bastard, if there ever was one." He glanced at Juliet. "Sorry."

She smiled. "No problem. I agree with you."

Josh felt a sudden wish to puff out his chest and strut, or fling his arm out and claim her. Irritated with himself, he said, "So, did he bring his women in here?"

"Sure. Different bird every week."

"Anyone recently?"

"The skier. Before that, nobody in particular. All summer, he was feeding on the hikers with the tours."

Josh nodded. A local tour group brought hikers from all over the world to walk the Mariposa Falls Trail, part of a 238-mile loop that wandered through the Sangre de Cristos and the San Juan mountains. "Have you heard anything else?"

Tam leaned on the bar and his arms rippled. "I'll

keep my ears to the ground, mate, but not at the moment."

"Right. Thanks."

"Tam!" a tall, lovely blond woman cried from the other end of the bar. "A refill, love."

The big man grinned. "Duty calls." He started to head down the bar, then turned around. In a low voice, he said, "There was a woman with him a bit, off and on all summer. I dunno who she was, but she had money."

Josh took a notebook from his pocket. "Description?"

"Dark hair, green eyes. An accent from Europe. Maybe Germany or Poland or one of those, you know. That kind of accent."

"All right." Josh scribbled notes. "Age?"

He lifted a shoulder. "Maybe early thirties." With a swipe at the bar, he leaned in toward Juliet. "Ye ain't with this guy, are you?"

"Hey, man," Josh began.

But Juliet grinned. "Well, he's not as gorgeous as you are, but he's got great eyes."

"I reckon." He spotted the bar. "Come back under better circumstances."

Juliet shot a look up toward Josh, her eyes as blue as turquoises. A fine glitter danced there, a tease and a challenge. He let his gaze drop to her mouth and thought again of her kissing him, of the cool feel of her fingertips against his cheek, the plushness of her breasts against his chest.

"You're gonna have to quit looking at me like that," Josh said, and even he could hear the rumbling sound of his voice.

"Will I?" she asked, and put her small hand over the back of his big one. Beneath the bar, their thighs bumped. "Why?"

In other circumstances, he would have leaned over and accepted the invitation of that mouth. He would have thrust his tongue between her lips and laced his tongue with hers and inquired, in the most physical way possible, if she wanted to invite him in elsewhere. He was aching to touch her, undress her and look at her breasts and taste her pearling nipples. She had beautiful hair and beautiful eyes and a luscious mouth, and he wanted with a burning sort of energy, to explore her skin, see if it was as smooth as it looked. He loved blond hair. He loved pretty lips. He loved natural breasts, the squishy feel of them, the juicy jiggle. He imagined her nipples would be as pink as her tongue. Or perhaps dark and—

"You're looking at my breasts," Juliet said. "In American culture, that's considered rude."

"It's not rude in other cultures?"

She shook her head. "Not at all."

"Can we pretend we're in those other places?" He grinned. "I like looking at your breasts."

Juliet shifted, leaning back a little. "Better?"

He inhaled slowly, trying to calm his arousal. Leaning forward, he put his lips close to her ear and said quietly, "I could spend a whole evening on just your breasts."

"Could you?" she said, just as quietly. "Doing what?"

He raised his head and looked her in the eye. "It would be a lot more fun to just show you."

Juliet stood. "Okay."

Josh threw a ten-dollar bill on the bar and raised a hand at Tam. "Let's go."

She laughed softly and put her jacket on, tossing the long locks out of her collar and down her back, and headed for the door.

He knew the exact instant her flashback seized her. Her shoulders went rigid and she had a faint vacantness to her face. With an unnerving speed, she bolted through the door.

Damn. Josh bolted after her, catching up just as she skidded in the snow outside and fell flat on her belly, hitting hard enough he heard bones jar.

"Juliet!" He knelt at her side, tried to help her up.

But she fought him, her arms flailing, a dark noise coming from her throat. She gasped for breath, and he realized the wind had been knocked out of her. He blew in her face, as he did when Glory was a baby and cried so hard she lost her breath.

It didn't help immediately, and it was hard to hold on to her. The sidewalk was slippery with the slowly piling snow, and he skidded twice, feeling as if he was holding on to a fish that didn't want to be caught, or a wild horse. She bucked and flipped and twisted, fighting as if for her life. Blood came from her nose, and her hands were skinned raw, and she didn't seem to even notice.

Finally he grabbed a handful of snow and aimed for her face. She dodged and the bulk of it landed against her neck and chest, and for whatever reason, it did the trick. With a gasp, she caught her breath and her eyes focused on the moment. This moment.

"Hey," he said, sinking down against the wall. The street was deserted, the air filled with tiny steady pellets of snow. She was draped across his lap, blinking.

"Hey," she said, and swallowed. The tension in her body eased. "Sorry. I did it again."

"Can you walk?"

"Yeah. It's all mental, not physical." She stood up, brushed herself off, felt the blood on her face and looked at her glove. "Is it bad?"

Blood smeared from her nose and a cut above her eyebrow. He took snow from the window ledge and offered it to her. "We're only a few blocks away. Let's go get you cleaned up."

"Okay," she said. It seemed impossible it was the same word she'd uttered in such a saucy tone a few minutes before.

With as much gentleness as he could offer, Josh reached out and took her hand. She didn't pull away.

Juliet felt the stinging in her hands more acutely than anything. The palms were skinned raw, in a way she hadn't done since she was a child and had fallen on roller skates.

Depression crept in as they walked back, a sense of things going wrong, to never be put right again. Her sister rotting in jail, her own mind claimed by some wretched moment in the past. She felt doomed and defeated.

When they got to the house, the dogs rushed forward, sniffing her hands curiously. Josh's dog licked the stinging palms helpfully, and when the other dogs slumped by the fire, Jack padded behind the humans when they went to the bathroom.

It was a wonderfully old-fashioned room, with glass brick and tiny, art-deco era tiles on the walls. Jack trailed in after them, sniffed a corner, then the edge of her shoe, and settled in the hallway just outside the door as if keeping watch.

Juliet avoided looking at herself in the mirror, and turned on the water in the sink. "I can do it," she said.

"I know you *can*," Josh replied. "Why don't you let me help you? I'd really like to."

Embarrassed, she lowered her eyes and plopped down on the toilet. "Okay."

A smile edged his voice. "You say okay a lot." He dipped a wash cloth in warm water. "Lift your chin."

She did, but still managed not to look at his face, instead focusing on the buttons traveling up his shirt. Off-white buttons in a green corduroy shirt. "So is the pub guy a friend of yours?"

"Acquaintance, I'd say. He was with a crew of smoke jumpers who were fighting the Hayman fire a few years back. You remember the Hayman fire?"

"No."

"It was a bad forest fire, the worst we've had in Colorado in decades. They were fighting it for weeks, and it took a lot of manpower." Gently, he wiped blood from her face. "Tam and another guy had a bad landing—he broke his leg and his friend died. Don't move."

He ran cold water over the cloth and pressed it to her eyebrow. "This one is bleeding pretty good. You might need a stitch."

She didn't say anything, remembering another night,

another time her face was gently wiped clean of blood. Her throat felt tight.

"It might be a good idea to talk about this," Josh said. "Maybe tell me what happened?"

A half hour ago, she'd been thinking only about how it would feel to have Josh's arms around her, taste his mouth, feel his hands. She'd been thinking about what his body would look like without clothes and how it might feel to have the attention he promised—*an evening on your breasts*—and then, some wretched something had yanked her back in time again, and it had been bad, this time, a sense of panic so acute and over-whelming that she'd barely been able to breathe.

"I feel so cheated," she said dully.

He sank down on the bathtub, putting their faces on the same level, and brushed hair away from her forehead. "Cheated how?"

His eyes were that soft deer-brown, the lashes so very long and childlike, softening the hard lines of cheekbone and jaw. His hands, brushing that hair away, were gentle as feathers. "I haven't been able to feel much of anything for a long time, and there I was, wanting you in a real way, wanting to kiss you and—" She lifted a shoulder. "And then something in my brain or memory kicks in and it's like I've made no progress at all."

"Were you raped?"

She bowed her head, ashamed. It was so humiliating, every time, to have to admit it. "A little more than a year ago." With exasperation, she said, "I don't know why I can't seem to get over it, process it, be done with it. I mean, he barely even hurt me. As these things go, it wasn't that bad."

"Oh, Juliet," he said, taking her hand and carrying her knuckles to his lips. "That's like saying you were only murdered with a single gunshot instead of knifed. It's horrible."

She shrugged. "Maybe."

He pressed the cloth to her eyebrow again. "Have you had any counseling for PTSD? They have some better techniques these days."

"I've had counseling. I really think I'm doing okay. It's just that a couple of times lately, I've had some bad moments."

"Right. I can see that you're pretty functional. Smart. All that stuff." He smiled. "But you're also having some pretty serious flashbacks and that's going to make life tough to manage."

"Have you had some training in PTSD or something?"

He raised his eyebrows. "I studied it on my own. In case Glory had symptoms, I'd know what to do."

"I see."

"Tell you what," he said. "Let's go make some hot chocolate and look through the video collection and see what looks good. What do you say?"

"I'm not an invalid," Juliet said with some irritation. "I don't need special treatment."

"Okay, Hop-A-Long."

She scowled at him. "What does that mean?"

He stood and held out a hand. "Come on. Let's go make something good and watch television and let the rest of the world go by for a couple of hours. How does that sound?"

For a moment, she hesitated, then put her hand in his and let herself be hauled to her feet. "Pretty damned good."

The dogs, excited, ran for the back door, looking over their backs to make sure the humans were getting the message. Juliet let herself laugh, let the day shake free from her shoulders. "Think they might want to get out?"

They all traipsed down the hall, into the kitchen, and Josh opened the back door. He whistled. "Well, it's coming down now. Look at that."

She peeked out over his shoulder. "Dinner plate snow!" she cried. "It's so pretty."

"It is. Now don't you think hot chocolate seems like the right idea?"

"Yeah," she said. "It does."

As she stood there, she thought of her sister, out in the darkness last night. "I am so worried about Desi," she said quietly.

"So am I," he said.

"We have to find out who did this," Juliet said. "I keep worrying that it looks bad for her. That if *I* can think the worst—"

"The worst?"

Juliet raised her eyes. "That she killed him." There, she'd said it.

He took a breath. "We have to find out the truth."

"Are you afraid of what you might find?"

"Maybe a little," he said, and brushed a lock of hair off her cheek, tucked it behind her ear. "But it's always better to know the real truth of a thing."

"Is it?" she asked. A fierceness rose in her. "I'd lie to protect her, Josh."

His smile quirked sideways. "So would I. So would my mother and her cronies. So would a lot of people. Let's cross that bridge when we come to it, huh?" He took her hand. "Come on, let's get some refreshments."

# *Chapter 12*

Josh built a fire and made a tray with cookies, cups, a fat pot for the hot chocolate, even some marshmallows. While he was getting it ready, Juliet dutifully flipped through his extensive DVD collection. It contained a fair number of race-car and football movies, along with what appeared to be every James Bond ever made, and all the original *Mission: Impossible* television series. There were Disney cartoons she assumed belonged to Glory.

But Juliet was also delighted to discover her favorite kind of movie: big dramas, not the usual black-and-white comedies so many people seemed to collect these days, but war movies and tragedies. She saw *The English Patient* and *Dangerous Liaisons* and— "*Dr. Zhivago!* You have actually seen this movie?"

"Oh, yeah. My mother loves it. I've watched it with her a million times." Kneeling by the fire, Josh grinned over his shoulder. "Julie Christie is hot."

Juliet grinned. "She's blond, right?"

The lights flickered suddenly. Went out. "Uh-oh," Josh said. "I forgot to mention the power is a little wonky during heavy snows. The lines are still all overhead in this part of town."

Juliet leaned back on her heels. As always, the quiet left behind by a power outage always amazed her. The hush filled the rooms, and then the lights blinked back on. They wavered, then held.

"I'm going to get some candles," Josh said. "Go ahead and put the movie in if you want."

"Really? You'll watch *Dr. Zhivago?*"

"Sure, why not? We might lose power, but we might not."

"That's not what I meant." Juliet handed him the case. "I am *so* not going to argue with you. Pop that baby in before you change your mind."

He chuckled. "I won't change my mind." He headed into the kitchen, and came back with three fat candles on saucers.

Settling on the couch in her socks, Juliet plucked a marshmallow off the tray. "If I ever told my friends that a guy watched *Dr. Zhivago* with me there would be a line of women from your door around the block."

"Yeah?" He put the DVD in and came around the coffee table to sit next to her. "All this time, that was all I had to do? Tell women I loved sappy old movies?"

Juliet thought about it. "Yes. Pretty much."

"Damn. Somebody should have told me." He held the remote control in his hand, put his other hand on her leg. "Are you okay now?"

"Yes. Play the movie."

He did.

She knew it was just a distraction, a way to keep her mind off Desi, but Juliet loved *Dr. Zhivago*. Loved everything about it—the music, the costumes, the handsome, tortured face of Omar Sharif, the beautiful landscapes, the sad, sad story.

It was delicious to be curled up on the couch in front of a fire, watching it with Josh, too. They nibbled cookies and popcorn, drank hot chocolate. At one point, he put his arm around her, and Juliet did not object. She snuggled into his broad side and let the smell of him fill her, enjoyed the pleasure of his body next to her own, so warm and real. It was both comfortable and arousing to be so close.

It felt wonderful, and she tried to remember a time she simply watched a movie on video with a guy.

When the movie ended, so tragically and so poignantly, Juliet was wiping tears away surreptitiously when Josh handed her a tissue and stood up. "I'll be back with your pillows. Do you want anything to drink?"

Disappointed that he was headed off to bed so abruptly, Juliet shook her head. The lights flickered, and she suddenly wanted them to go out, for the room to be plunged into blackness only lit with the embers of the fire and candles. She wanted to kiss him, to explore his mouth and those broad shoulders and—

Well, whatever else.

And really, what was stopping her from taking the initiative?

Did she dare? She did. Standing up, she turned off the lamp, then lit the candles on the coffee table. The fire had gone low, and she padded over to it in her stocking feet to see if she could figure out how to feed some more wood to the flames.

"This is nice," Josh said, coming back into the room with pillows and blankets. He had to step around and over dogs, who groaned in pleased ways when he nudged them, and dumped the linens on a chair. "Does this mean you might not be ready to go right to sleep?"

Juliet smiled over her shoulder. "Maybe. I just kept wishing for the lights to go out and I decided maybe it would be okay if I just turned them off." She held a smallish log in her hands. "Is this the right size to feed it right now?"

"Perfect." He came around the coffee table and knelt next to her, picked up the poker and sent sparks sailing up the chimney. "Put another one on, too, in case we do lose power."

Juliet felt a low singing pleasure rising through her veins as she put the log on the fire. Flames began to lick the new wood and heated her skin on the front of her body, and she leaned back on her heels, putting her hands on her thighs. "Beautiful, isn't it?" Juliet said.

Kneeling next to her, Josh brushed hair away from her face. "Yes," he said, and leaned down to kiss her.

Juliet met his lips eagerly, and they kissed for a long time, just that. Lips weaving together, sliding, sipping.

Tongues dashing out, dipping in, lacing together. Just lips, his and hers, and the languorous rise of sap in her blood, delicious and almost forgotten. The rush of sensation over her spine, the softening of her thighs, the catch in her breath as she imagined his hands on her. She shifted, raising a hand to his jaw and he made a low, pleased noise, and tumbled her sideways to the floor. They laughed a little as they landed.

"If we're going to make out in front of the fire, maybe we ought to get a blanket," Juliet said, amazed at the throatiness of her tone.

"I just happen to have one right over here," he said, and leapt up, grabbing the thick down comforter from the chair and spreading it in front of the fire, then kneeling down and pulling Juliet onto it with him. He tossed a pillow down and Juliet nabbed it, smiling up at him.

For one minute, he looked demolished and overwhelmed. "Juliet, you are so beautiful."

"Am I?"

"Oh, yeah." He kissed her lips, lightly, and her chin. "Can I ask a question?"

"Sure."

"Do you have any issues with sex? I mean, not that we have to do anything but lie here and kiss, but if there are things I should know, maybe you should tell me?"

Juliet gazed up at him. "I don't have any that I know of. All I know is that I feel something when you touch me, and that's new."

His eyelids grew sleepy. "Yeah? What do you feel?"

"Kiss me again and let me see if I can tell you."

He made a soft noise and covered her mouth with his own, a hot tongue and hot lips lighting tiny explosions of peppermint fire over her brow, and a smoky surprise at the base of her throat, and an electric zing down her spine. "Oh," she whispered, "I feel like kissing you for about a hundred years."

"We can do that," Josh said, and kissed her again. "And if I kiss you here?" he said, pressing his lips to her throat. "How is that?"

"Oh, I don't know," she said, her breath coming a little higher in her throat. "You might have to do it again."

"I can do that," he said, and opened his mouth and dragged his tongue down the column of her throat, lingering in a circle over the hollow between her collarbones. Slowly, slowly, he made his way back up, his tongue making lazy circles on her flesh, his mouth pausing to take little sharp sucks. Juliet closed her eyes and luxuriated in the pleasure he gave, letting her hands move on his broad shoulders. The fire warmed her feet and lent a quiet counterpoint to the sound of their breath and the little exclamations of surprise and discovery.

He worked his way back to her mouth and plunged this time with barely concealed passion, his tongue thrusting, his body hard against hers, his hands on her shoulders.

Juliet ached to feel his chest, taste his skin, and she pushed away enough to put her hands on his shirt. "I need this off," she said. "I want to see."

He rose on his knees and stripped the shirt off, his eyes fixed on her face. Pale orange firelight spilled over his naked torso, illuminating his broad shoulders, his lean waist. She lifted a hand and traced the round of his navel, and the silky hair against her finger sent a shock wave through her body, straight between her legs. With a boldness that was unlike her, she sat up and kissed his belly there.

"Now you," he said.

Juliet knelt, too, and started to unbutton her blouse. "Let me do it," he said, and she dropped her hands. He reached up to unfasten the first buttons, then the next, the next, and spread the cloth open to show her belly, her bra. He did not move fast, seeming to relish every moment of revelation, and Juliet felt a wild wave of desire washing over her, wave after wave making her dizzy and hungry. "Touch me," she whispered.

His smile was very small. "All in good time." His hand glided beneath the fabric of her blouse, across her shoulders, then down her sides, skimming the shirt off of her. The bra was a back closure, and he reached around and undid that, too. Juliet arched her back and held her arms down so he could take it off, feeling her breasts spill into freedom, into firelight.

He tossed the scrap of fabric aside and put his hands on his thighs, simply looking at her toplessness, at her eyes, then her shoulders and neck, then her breasts. She gazed back at him, at the black crown of his head, the beauty of his well-formed shoulders, the sleek nakedness of skin just inches away, and thought she would faint dead away of desire. It buzzed through her mind, through her forehead, her groin, pearled in perfect, beaming lights at the tips of her breasts which wanted—

He bent and opened his mouth around her right

nipple and suckled lightly. Juliet cried out softly. He raised his head. "Is that okay?"

"Yes." The word was a breathy whisper.

He bent and did it again, opened his hot, wet mouth and settled it with no hurry and great skill on her nipple. He sucked lightly, and wound his tongue around it, and let go, and started again on the other side. At just the moment she felt she would fly away if he didn't somehow ground her, capture her, he raised his hands and cupped her flesh in his big palms and kissed them all over.

"Your breasts are beautiful, too," he said with a raw sound, "as beautiful as your hair and your eyes and your mouth." He gathered her up into his lap and kissed her lips, and Juliet cried out at the explosion of feelings that brought, flinging her arms around his shoulders, pressing them close together. He pulled her hips down and into his aroused member, thrusting slightly upward. His hands skimmed up and down her back, buried themselves in her hair, and Juliet felt as if she was a being of pure light, radiating heat and desire and relief.

His hair. Heavy and cool, like the skirt of a bridesmaid's dress she'd worn once. Juliet lifted her arms so she could feel it on her skin and kissed him, over and over.

A huge noise slammed into the placid moment, and both of them grabbed on to the other, looking to see what happened. The lights did go off.

"What was that?" Juliet cried.

Josh grabbed the quilt and tugged it around her shoulders, wrapping them up closely. "I don't know." He was still, listening, and Juliet listened, too, hearing only the fire and the wind outside. "I should go look around," he said.

She nodded, climbing reluctantly off his lap. He kissed her head and moved away in his bare feet. Juliet watched him go round the house, beautiful and strong and gigantic, a man she could fall in love with.

But with a rush of disorientation, she thought, *how did I get here?* With a man she hadn't even known existed a few weeks ago, taking off her clothes with him, getting ready to—as they used to say to each other—go all the way?

One of the dogs got up, Jack, and wandered over to sit with her, falling down beside her with a great, wuffling sigh. Juliet put a hand in his fur and stared at the leaping, crackling flames, feeling suddenly dizzy. She'd broken up with her fiancé. Her sister had been arrested. Claude, who had been her brother-in-law for more than ten years, was murdered.

"A tree fell over in the street," Josh said, coming back into the room.

Juliet looked up at him. Nodded.

He sat down beside her. "You okay?" He put a hand on her back, just one flat hand.

It was enough. As if someone flipped a switch, Juliet felt the panic rise up in her, the unreasoning need to flee, and she gripped the dog's fur more tightly than she intended. He yelped and gave her a wounded look, and Juliet, horrified, let go. Blindly, she reached for Josh. "Help!" she whispered.

He grabbed her hand and held on tightly. "It's all right, Juliet. I'm here. I'm right here."

And this time, it faded fast. She took a breath. "You must really think I'm wacko."

He put his arms around her, the blanket between them. "No. I wish I knew how to help."

Juliet didn't speak for a moment, letting herself rest against his broad chest, feeling the solid strength of his arms around her. She raised her arms and put her hands on his wrists, and they stared into the orange-and-yellow fire. "I feel safe with you," she said finally, and pressed her lips to his wrists. "But in general, I'm *so* afraid, all the time, and I'm so tired of it. It's exhausting."

"I know." He nestled his head close to hers, kissed her shoulder. "Do you want to tell me about what happened?"

Juliet paused. "People don't really want to hear about it, Josh. You think you do, but then the reality is boring and ugly and it changes the way you look at me."

"That might be true of some people," he said, "but I'm a cop, remember? It won't shock me and it won't make me think differently about you." He made his legs into a diamond that fit around her knees, so she was entirely protected with his body. "All that said, if you don't like or don't want to talk, it's okay. It just kinda seems like maybe you've got a boil that needs lancing."

"Maybe so," Juliet said. She took a breath and said, "I was on a business trip for my firm. I'd just had dinner at the hotel restaurant and I went outside."

In a steady, plain voice, she told him the story, factually and without elaboration or hysterics. As she got to the end, when she was finally home, two days later, and could not go to sleep in her own bed, she realized tears were streaming down her cheeks, and Josh was ever-so-gently rocking her, side to side.

She was half-naked beneath the blanket. Her sister was in jail. Claude was dead and she'd broken up with Scott, and nothing seemed the way it should…except Josh. There was something so unbelievably, perfectly right about his arms around her, his gentle rocking, the feeling of his nose in her hair as she wept. Wept and wept and wept, for all the darkness in the world and all the women who had ever been raped and her sister who had a broken heart and Claude, who was dead.

And all through it, Josh held her. A blessing.

When Juliet was finally spent, her tears leaking out of her in a long, slow stream, never noisy, never hysterical, but steady and seemingly endless, he helped her into a T-shirt from his closet and put her to bed in his own bed.

Exhausted, she said, "Thank you," and fell asleep so hard he thought she'd probably be there a long, long while.

He, too, was exhausted, and slipped between the covers next to her, cradling her curvy self into his belly. She shuddered in post-weeping release, and allowed herself to be cuddled, lifting his hand to her mouth before falling back over the cliff to her rest.

And then, he too, was asleep, carried away into a restless world of vivid, violent dreams where a cat was tearing apart a rapist, where Desi was sitting in a jail cell crying out his name, where the silence seemed vast and endless and terrifying. Over and over, he surfaced the slightest bit to discover the Juliet part of the dreams was real, that she was still in his bed, still sleeping soundly, protected and safe in his arms.

When he started awake suddenly to find that circle empty, it was light outside, and he heard Juliet in the bathroom, running water. She came back out, and when she found him awake and looking at her, she paused.

"You look so beautiful," he said, and it was true. Her hair, the shimmery color of the lemon crayon in Glory's box, was mussed and tumbling over her slim shoulders in the plain white T-shirt and a pair of underwear.

"Do I?" she said with a laugh and looked down. "I was coming back, if that's okay. I didn't mean to wake you."

Wordlessly, he flipped the covers back and made a place for her. As she crossed the room, her breasts, bare beneath the T-shirt, swayed and bobbled, a sight that made him instantly, furiously hard.

At the edge of the bed, she showed him a small foil packet. "I hope you don't mind," she said, "but I found this in the bathroom cabinet."

"I don't mind," he said. If there was any more blood in his organ, it would explode, but more surged in when she reached down, grabbed the bottom of her T-shirt and pulled it off over her head.

For one moment, she stood there, pink and white and blond, her skin smooth and pale, her tummy slightly rounded, her shoulders delicate like butterfly wings, and her breasts, white and round and full, tipped with pearly pink nipples.

He pulled the covers further back, showing his bare upper body and the raging hard-on in his briefs. Lightly he touched himself and said, "See what you're doing to me?"

One impish eyebrow lifted. "Very nice."

Josh said, "Come here."

She did, flowing forward to put her body against his, naked chest to naked chest, legs tangling, mouths open to absorb, inhale, meld. Hands tangled in hair, his and hers, hers and his. He tasted her lips, her chin, her neck. She straddled his erection and he groaned at the heat and pleasure of her rubbing against him. He held her hips and rose up, bending her slightly backward in his lap so he could take a nipple into his mouth and play with it, teasing with his tongue, sucking and letting go, using his fingers on her other one, until she was whimpering softly in longing, her hips moving restlessly against him, hot and damp and ready.

But not as ready as she would be. He slid his fingers between them, beneath her panties and into the layers of folds beneath, all trembling and shivery. His organ throbbed in furious desire as he rubbed her, slowly, deeply, bringing out a rhythm of cries, a bucking hunger. When he knew she was very, very close, he stopped.

Her blue eyes flew open. "Josh," she panted. "I've never…this is—"

He kissed her, thrusting his tongue deep into her mouth, and rolled them over until he was on top, it took a moment of fumbling to get rid of the fabric between them and another moment to sheath himself properly, but Juliet was like cake falling to pieces beneath him, and when he nudged her legs apart, reached down to ease himself into her, she cried out in guttural pleasure, that rich, panting sound of mindless, pure, physical enjoyment. His own flanks quivered at the pleasure of her around him, the beauty of that tousled hair on his pillow, her pink and white breasts straining upward for his mouth, her legs wrapping around him and pulling him home with surprising strength. She pulled him in with strong arms.

They kissed, and it was a rocket of sensation, touch, sound, movement, a pleasure so profound and rich and earthy Josh wanted to stay right there, an orgasm building in his loins by degrees. Go go go go, nerves, lips, legs, hands, tongues. Her hair tangling in his fingers. Her breasts, her belly, her sex pulsing like a squeezing fist around him as she came, crying out with a high, blistered keening. He tumbled right after her.

And then it was the next best thing, the first moments afterward. He kissed her and kissed her, her breasts all sweaty against his chest, their breath still coming fast, his organ doing that last little throb, uh uh uh, and she was pulsing around him now and then, the little aftershocks.

"Wow," Juliet said, blinking up at him.

He grinned down at her. "Have a pretty good time, did you?"

"Uh, yeah." She raised a hand and brushed hair over his shoulder. "You're amazing."

"It's you. Or us." He realized how heavy he must be and made a move to slide sideways. "Or something."

She sighed as he left her, making a sound of soft regret. "Come on back now, anytime," she said, and laughed, putting her head against his arm. It was a giggle, a sound of pure, unfettered pleasure.

"You sound pretty happy."

"Wonder why?" She put her finger on her cheek, looking exaggeratedly vacuous. "I've only just had great sex with the sexiest guy I've run into in years—"

"Only years? Is there someone better than me out there?"

"Okay, ever. And I slept like a baby, and it snowed a lot less than I thought it was going to."

"Really?" He flipped the covers off his body and jumped up to peek outside. The snow was spitting a little, but he could tell from long experience that it wouldn't be long until the sun burst through the clouds. Snow had definitely piled up in corners, but it was more the sort of accumulation that came of wind. "It should be gone by suppertime, I'm guessing. Maybe sooner."

She'd propped herself up on the pillow and inclined her head, frankly admiring him. "You, Mr. Mad Calf, have very, very nice legs."

He grinned, and turned around. "Yeah? Anything else you like?"

Her eyes looked suddenly smoky, and there was the faintest betraying flare of her nostrils. "Everything," she said distinctly.

It was cold. He dived back into the bed. And they did it all again.

After a long, luxurious, *hot* shower, Juliet found Josh in the kitchen, watching the news on a tiny white television set. The scent of bacon frying and coffee brewing perfumed the air, and there were agreeable piles of food lined up on the counter—eggs, cheese, apples.

But for a moment, Juliet was seized with a sense of

surprise, looking at Josh himself. At his long, powerful legs, his graceful hands, the thick black fall of his hair.

She'd taken a new lover! How amazing!

And what a lover—every cell in her body felt properly tended for the first time in a very long time, as if every inch of her had been taken out, washed, dried, brushed, and put back into place.

Her mind, her heart, all those places that ordinarily sent out objections and got so noisily involved in these things, were strangely silent. "What's your pleasure, my lady?" Josh asked, gesturing toward the supplies on the counter. "Omelets with cheese, bacon on the side?"

She grinned. "A girl could get used to this."

He wiggled his dark brows. "Promises, promises."

"What are you having?"

"Omelets, bacon on the side, coffee."

"I'll have that, too. Do you want some help?"

He gave her an ironic grin. "You just sit there and look purty, little lady." From the cupboard, he took a cup and poured coffee into it. "Milk's right there."

On the television, a newscaster showed the ski slopes in Aspen, and a shot of a beautiful blond woman. "Josh, look! It's Christie Lundgren. On the news. Turn it up!"

The newscaster said, "—Lundgren was said to be in a heated relationship with the artist who was murdered two days ago in the glitzy ski resort town of Mariposa."

Josh pointed to a banner below the picture. "It's an old picture of Christie," he said. The banner read photo January 2004.

"Prominent Aspen art dealer Renate Franz has issued a statement that her collection of Tsosie art will be on display through the end of the month, when she will hold an auction."

A photo of an elegant, tiny woman with a wealth of dark hair stepped in front of the camera, visibly upset. "We're all grieving," she said. "The world has lost a major talent and a man we will mourn for years to come."

Josh said, "German accent, you think? How old do you think she is?"

"Thirties?" At first, Juliet didn't make the connection. Then she turned back to the screen. "Ah! Do you think she might be the one Claude was with last summer? An art dealer?"

Josh frowned. "I think she had more than art on her mind."

On the television, the newscaster wrapped it up. "Investigations are continuing, but Tsosie's wife, Desdemona Rousseau, has been arrested."

Juliet's stomach flipped. She wondered if her sister Miranda had seen this story. "I've gotta call my other sister after breakfast."

"We need to go talk to Desi, too, make sure she's all right."

Spiraling tension rose through Juliet's chest, tightening and compressing her lungs. *Breathe,* she told herself. They would get to the bottom of this. She stood up, shaking off the anxiety, and peered out the window. There were still heavy clouds overhead, but the snow had stopped falling. The tiny pellets, the rain-snow, had not particularly piled up, though the wind had blown it into drifts here and there.

It was plenty for the dogs, however. They pranced

around in it happily, dancing, dodging, almost laughing aloud. "The dogs look very happy," she commented and watched them as they played with each other, bowing down, throwing up tufts of snow, getting covered with it. "I was never much of a dog person before Desi got so wrapped up with the wolves, but there's really nothing like them."

At the stove, Josh turned slightly to indicate he was listening. "What do you mean?"

She lifted a shoulder. "They're so…fluffy and happy and devoted." Faithful, she wanted to add, but didn't, afraid it would be too leading. In the yard Crazy Horse dashed away from a charge by Tecumseh and she could almost hear him laughing. "They make me feel protective and protected."

"I love dogs. When I was in the army, it was impossible to keep them and it was terrible. I missed having a dog every single day." He smiled. "I love it that I can leave for five minutes, come back, and there's Jack, at the door, dancing around like I've been gone for three days."

"I'll have to get a dog when I go back to Hollywood."

His head jerked up. "Are you going back?"

"I have a life there." Used to have a job. "A condo."

"Right. I get it."

Juliet looked at him. "You sound angry." She had considered not going back, but what did his reaction mean? Did she want to get so involved?

"Sorry." He focused on the eggs, very gently flipping them over their filling. "I'm not. I just have to remember not to let Glory get too attached."

Juliet crossed her arms and sat down. "Maybe you

should drive me back up the mountain before she comes home."

He brought the pan over to the island and slid the omelet out on to the plate. "Do you have any idea how much snow is up there right now? We'll go get her this afternoon, but you're not going up that mountain for at least a day."

Juliet looked at the steaming eggs and her stomach growled. He passed her a plate of bacon. "So what do you want to do?"

"Just don't give her any false promises," Josh said. "That's all."

The back of his neck looked stiff and she wondered if she'd been rash to sleep with him. "I didn't mean to lead you on, Josh. I thought we were grown-ups here.... I..." She looked at him, feeling both rejected and pleased at his jealousy and pierced at the possibility that—what? He wanted her here? "I'm sorry."

With a thud, he put the pan down and came around the island. With a sexy, vulnerable forcefulness, he took her face in his hands and kissed her. "No, I'm sorry," he said. "I'm being an ass. It's not your fault that Glory thinks you're a princess. It's not your fault her mother let her down. It's not your fault that I wish you lived here instead of in California."

She put her hands on his, holding him there, aware of a thudding something in her chest—some strong, unacknowledged emotion. "Josh, I'm pretty much a mess right now. I lost my job. I haven't been able to do anything much for a year. I don't know that I'm ever going to be any better, okay?" A wave of that volatility she'd felt last night struck the back of her eyes and she blinked hard. "Please don't make me cry again."

He kissed her. First her mouth, then her eyelids, one at a time. He raised his head and looked at her. "Can I tell you, Juliet, that you really are getting under my skin? I'm not used to it."

"Me, either."

"You are one of the prettiest women I've ever met."

She smiled. "You can tell me that anytime."

"And I love your mouth. And your breasts. And your eyes."

"All those things."

His dark eyes looked serious. "You also have a lot of heart. Like a lion." He touched her nose lightly. "And I've been known to be just a little bit…intense."

She captured his wrists before he could pull away. "You have given me more peace in twenty-four hours than I've had in many, many months, Josh. I just don't know myself well enough to know what any of it means today. Is that okay?"

"It's fine." He let her go and went back to his side of the island. "Let's eat, then I'll find out where Glory is and maybe we can go snowshoeing or for a walk, depending on how the paths look. What do you think?"

"Excellent," she said, and cut a generous piece of omelet. "Not, however, as perfect as this."

"Don't suppose you brought any hiking boots down with you."

Juliet tossed her hair over her shoulder. "No. But I have a credit card. I bet there are hiking boots for sale somewhere in this town."

"You'll pay with blisters if you do that."

She shrugged. "We don't have to hike to Timbuktu, do we? I mean, I like hiking, but it's been awhile, and maybe just a *little* hike would be fun."

He grinned. "That's a possibility." He, too, busied himself with the food. "I'm starving."

Juliet laughed, and the sound was as much like a giggle as she ever gave. "We did have quite a workout."

His eyes crinkled up. "So we did." He took a big gulp of milk. "Do you think you could curl her hair?"

"Glory's?" Juliet asked. "I don't know. What do you have around here?"

"Nothing I know of."

"We can always use rags. I know how to do rag curls. Or we can buy curlers in town."

He nodded. "The other thing we need to talk about is what to do about Desi's bail."

"Setting it? Or getting her out?"

"Paying it once it's set."

"The land is worth a fortune," Juliet said. "But I think she'll protest using it as a guarantee for bail."

"Might not have any choice."

Juliet thought about it for a few minutes. Thought of everything Desi had gone through to secure that land, hold on to it—and not for herself, but for her wolves. "No," she said. "If we have to, I'll use my condo. It's worth plenty."

Josh put his knife and fork neatly over his plate, tines down. "What about your parents? Sounds like they have a few resources."

"They do, but they don't particularly like to dip into

them. They'd be horrified over the scandal attached to this."

"Who are these people?" Josh asked in an irritable tone. "You and Desi both make them sound like monsters, but they raised both of you. You're not monsters, either one of you."

Juliet nodded. "I know. There's the paradox. I can't explain it, either." She touched her napkin to her lips. "My mother is an old-fashioned WASP, a blue blood back to who knows when. Trouble is, she had this amazing brain for physics and she thought she should pursue it, and instead of marrying some Massachusetts-blooded stallion, she met my father, a poet, who swept her off her feet."

"That's romantic."

Juliet shrugged. "I guess. They think it is." He looked so bewildered she shook her head. "They're great at being scientist and poet and grand lovers to each other. They were just rotten at being parents."

Josh crossed his arms, his beautiful mouth taut with skepticism. "Rotten how? Did you have to spend too much time with the nanny or something?"

"Are you being a snob, Mr. Mad Calf? If you have your physical needs covered, everything's all right? Is that it?"

"I made you mad, I'm sorry." He took a breath. "But to be honest, it is kind of a stretch to believe that you suffered much."

"Honestly, I didn't suffer as much as the other two. Not sure why. I was always such an innocent, you know, that maybe some of it just didn't get through." She met his eyes. "But for example, my mother does not know

I was raped, and she won't. She'd hate to know about it, and it would end up being my fault somehow, and I'm just not going to go through all that."

"You can borrow my mom if you want."

"I just might." With a sigh, she said, "If you ever meet them, you'll see what I mean."

"I believe you."

"No, you don't," she said. "But that's okay."

## Chapter 13

The morning was pristine, and once they moved out of Josh's pocket neighborhood, there wasn't as much snow as it had first appeared. In town, business seemed a little slower than normal, but the ReNew café and the pancake house were open for business, shoveling snow off the sidewalk into the street, where a fast-moving stream of melting snow ran down the gutter.

"It's weird how fast the weather changes around here," Juliet said. "Blizzard to sunshine in five seconds flat." She kicked the slush on the sidewalk. "How long will it take to melt?"

"A day at these temperatures," he said. "But it won't be long until there's snow everywhere, all winter." He gestured to an outdoor wear store. "Let's get you some boots, huh? We'll hike up to the shrine. It should be fairly accessible."

"The shrine?"

"Our Lady of the Butterflies. She's famous. You don't know about her?"

Juliet nodded. "I know. We used to come to church camp here." That was something Juliet's father had won, after all. "Despite my mother's wish to turn us all into good little Presbyterians, my father was a French Catholic, and he insisted that his daughters would all be raised in the church."

"Have you ever been up there?"

"No." Warily she shook her head. "But there's so much to do. How do we get money for bail? What about—"

"Shh." Josh smiled, very slowly. "It's a perfect hike. We'll take an offering for Desi." He moved closer and took her hand. "For you, too, if you want."

Juliet looked up at him, at the breadth of his shoulders, the kindness of his deer eyes, and felt a squeezing in her heart that was both wonder and fear, hope and despair. "We'll see," she said. And although she wanted, in some ways, to leave her hand cradled in his, something bigger made her pull away. "Let's get my shoes. You can help me pick out good socks."

"All right."

She saw that she'd wounded him a little, but better a little wound now than a bigger one later. Despite her pleasure in his company, and her very real passion for him, there wasn't anything really alive inside of her to share, and he was right: he had a little girl to think about.

\* \* \*

Juliet chose a pair of sturdy, lace-up boots that felt both warm and comfortable, along with thick woolen socks and something Josh called gaiters, a sort of thick nylon sock to tie over her jeans as they walked, to keep the snow out. Since she was there anyway, she also bought a good coat, much warmer than the one she'd brought from California. Who knew coats came with so many features? she thought happily, snuggling into it. Josh asked the girl in the shop if they could leave the old things there and pick them up on the way back, and she tucked them beneath the counter.

The jail was only a few blocks away, and they walked there after the trip to the store. The sergeant in control was pretty lax and let Desi come out to the table without handcuffs. Juliet gave her a paper cup of coffee she'd brought from the local coffee shop, flavored with vanilla and raw sugar, just the way Desi liked it.

Desi was not particularly open to being cheered up, however. She looked dull and distant, her face swollen as if she'd slept hard after crying hard. Her hair was in a braid, slightly mussed at the top. "You have to get me out of here," she said, and it seemed her voice came from somewhere deep in her chest. "I get panicky in that cell."

"There's no arraignment until Wednesday," Juliet said.

Desi narrowed her eyes. "That's not soon enough. You need to go see Judge Behrens, out on the County Line road and tell him what's going on. He'll get me out faster than that."

"Okay. We'll call him right away." Juliet touched her sister's hand. "Don't panic, honey. Just let it go. Everything is going to be okay."

"Is it?" Desi asked in a dull tone. She raised her eyes. "I didn't kill him, Juliet. I might have wanted to bash his head in. I might have been angry with him. But I wouldn't have shot him."

Juliet felt the beat of her hesitation went one half second too long. "I know," she said.

Desi raised her head and looked at her. She didn't say anything, just looked.

"I'm sorry," Juliet said. "I'm just worried about you."

Josh put his big hand on Desi's shoulder. "We'll get you out of here, babe."

She put her hand on top of his, looking worn and weary. "I know."

From outside came the sound of chanting. All three looked up and then the sergeant was in the room. "Sorry, you're gonna have to go back to your cell now."

"What's going on?" Desi lifted her chin. "Juliet, look and see."

But Josh was already across the room. "Protest," he said, "but I can't tell who or what. I think it has to do with you."

The sergeant nudged Desi along. "Come on," he said. "You need to get back in your cell before I get my ass in a sling."

"Yessir." She looked over her shoulder at Josh and Juliet. "Judge Behrens," she said. "Remember."

"We're on it," Josh said. "Don't worry."

Outside, it was plain that the anti-Desi contingent had organized the rally. A small knot of mostly women, led by a tall brunette in a yellow jacket, stood by the jail steps. Remember Claude Tsosie, a placard read. It showed a picture of Claude when he was a bit younger, and a reproduction of one of his paintings.

"What, he's a *political* cause now?" Juliet hissed to Josh as they came down the steps. She slowed, feeling an argument on her lips, but Josh took her arm.

He said gruffly, "Keep moving. The last thing we want is more attention brought to this whole thing."

Juliet glared at the brunette as they walked by, and the woman glared back, but they left it at that. "Let's make the phone call," Josh said, and stopped at a pay phone with a phone book on a metal cable. A tiny phone book, Juliet noticed. It was about the size of her address book back home.

Josh found the name and dialed it on his cell phone, and outlined the situation to the person on the other end. The judge obviously asked for clarification several times, and Josh offered facts. There was a short period of "yes," and "no" and "not that I know of."

Finally he said, "Thank you, Your Honor. Right. I'll call you later."

He hung up. "He's going to do what he can, he said. He thinks he can get her out on Monday, anyway."

"Good." Only two nights more. It was misery, Juliet knew, but it was better than a week or two or ten.

"Still want to hike?" Josh asked.

"Yes."

"Let's go." He'd brought a small day pack with him, and they headed straight west, to the box-end of the box canyon. Snow melted with dizzying speed, making pattering noises as it melted off the trees and ran into the creek. They crossed it on a little wooden bridge. When they got to the middle, Juliet had to stop to admire it for a moment—the blue-white snow piled up in the shadows, the rushing stream in its rocky bed, aspen coins gleaming through wherever the snow had melted. The air smelled of earth and pine and something elusive, that note that always said, simply, *mountains* to Juliet.

As she stood there, sunlight spilling over her head from that brilliant sky, something in her eased. "When we came here to camp, I loved that smell. I loved coming to camp," she said to Josh, breathing in the scent of the water. "Well, maybe not at first, because I was afraid, but I got to the point where I loved it. All three of us did. We always said we were going to grow up and come live here."

Josh said, "And Desi did it." He gestured up the sunny side of the canyon. "That way."

"And this is her home. I hate it that this has happened to her. She was so happy to be here."

"We're going to make this work. I promise."

They climbed on a gravel path, not terribly muddy, thanks to the gravel, but it was slippery enough Juliet was glad to have the hiking boots with their good tread. A signpost made of wood read simply, Shrine, 1.4 miles, and pointed the way.

"Do you think she killed Claude?" Josh asked.

Juliet jerked her gaze up to his face. "Do you?"

He pursed his lips. "Honestly, I don't know."

"Me, either," Juliet admitted. "The case against her is circumstantial, but it's a pretty strong circumstantial case."

"I do know that she will die if she goes to jail."

"I know. We have to get her out." Their feet crunched on the snow. "My gut says she didn't do it. That she might be really mad and she might have shot him if he'd tried to take something from the ranch, but I don't think she would ever kill anyone."

Josh took her hand. "We'll find the right guy."

She squeezed his hand. Let go. "Thank you."

"So, what did you like about camp, back in the day?"

"Everything." Juliet grinned. "Well, no, that's a lie. I loved a lot of things, but not all of it. There were a lot of bugs. I was afraid of the spiders in the cabins and the possibility of rattlesnakes and afraid of lightning and afraid of drowning in the lake." She gave him a rueful look. "Scaredy-Julie, that was me. Still is, I guess."

"You're not a scaredy-cat. You're brave. Very fierce, fighting for your sister."

"Really?" She looked at him.

He half chuckled. "You sound so surprised."

"We were supposed to find totem animals at camp. There was this whole process we went through, making a medicine bag, listening to the stories of the elders, writing down our dreams. There were even elders who came in from the Mariposa Utes, now that I think about it."

He nodded. "There's an education and outreach arm of the government. I'm sure that's who it was."

"Probably." Juliet flung her hair back from her face. "Well, we were all supposed to be open to animals who came to us, and I was so worried it was going to be something stupid for me, you know? Like a rabbit or something, all timid and shy."

"All animals have their places," he said.

"Yeah, but I'd had enough of being a rabbit. And there were my sisters—Desi was a wolf, surprise, surprise, and Miranda was a dragonfly, which is at least beautiful. But nothing came to me. I didn't have any dreams, didn't find feathers. I was a total failure at the whole vision quest thing."

He laughed.

"So, just before the end of the season, I was out in the woods and I found this skull and a claw. I was so excited and ran it back to camp to show my counselor who didn't really believe I'd found it, that somehow I'd planted it, because it was—ta da—a mountain lion."

"No kidding!"

Juliet shook her head. "No. Everybody was jealous and it seemed like a big joke because I really was so afraid of everything that a rabbit would have been a lot more accurate."

"But the mountain lion chose you."

"That's what the elder said. That your totem finds you."

"I see that lion medicine in you, Juliet."

"Thank you."

"Now you should be brave enough to let life in."

She paused. "I'd like to try."

"That's all a man can ask."

They walked along in the warming day, and Juliet noticed the most curious sense of well-being spreading through her. It had to do with the sunlight and the woods, the quiet and the birdcalls, the scent of pine trees and the scent of Josh. All of it. She liked it that they could walk together in silence, without having to fill it up with chatter. She liked the feeling of safety she had in his company, and the way he'd felt around her last night.

Sneaking a glance at his profile, she let that memory come rushing back through her, along her skin and the nape of her neck and the backs of her knees—he'd held her close all through the night. As if she were precious. As if she were beloved.

She'd never had that feeling before. It scared her.

And yet, she wasn't alone in risking things, was she. Tentatively, she reached out and slipped her hand into his. When he looked down, she gave him a little smile. His lips quirked slightly.

He didn't let go. They walked up and up, around a switchback and another, beneath aspens with fluttering leaf-coins spinning around over their heads, beneath pine groves, along open spaces where the snow from the night before had melted.

"What do you know about the shrine?" Josh asked.

"Not a lot, really. I know a lot of people come to see it, that there was some sort of miracle attached to it. Aren't there hiking tours that bring people to it in the summertime?"

"Yep. One path, actually, goes right over the corner of Desi's land."

"And what's the miracle?"

"There was a young girl—"

"Is there always?"

He grinned and related the story of a young girl who'd been born with club feet who promised the saint that she would walk to the falls if her feet could be transformed. It had taken her three days to make the trek, but she'd done it, and when she got there, ten thousand butterflies had swirled up out of their sleep and touched her all over. The girl was healed.

"And now," he continued, "every year, people make pilgrimages here, usually at a point of transition in their lives."

"That's beautiful."

He paused, catching his breath. "And now, we're here."

"Where?"

With a secret little smile, Josh led a few more steps and turned the corner, and the path dead-ended in a small, open meadow surrounded by trees.

"Oh, my!" Juliet sighed.

The shrine sat at the foot of a waterfall, which splashed into a hot springs that send up a steamy spray. A mist covered the ground in a thin layer. Stationed above the hot spring was the shrine, a large, old statue of the Virgin Mary, but not like any Juliet had ever seen. This one had the sweet, somehow robust face of a Guadalupe, with the lush, curvy body of a siren. Her arms were spread wide, and a faint smile curled up her lips. Flowers, real and artificial, were scattered at her feet, and a plethora of candles and candleholders stood in a sheltered little glass building, like a small greenhouse.

But most breathtaking were the butterflies. Thousands of them, attached to the trees and rocks in a thousand different ways; butterflies made of cloth and embroidered with beads and braided out of ribbons; painted and carved and fashioned from rocks; tiny and large. Expressions of gratitude and petitions for intercession. For a moment, stunned into silence, Juliet thought she could hear whispers, of praises, prayer, petition, thanksgiving.

"It's so beautiful!" she cried.

"In the summertime, there are thousands of mourning cloak butterflies," he said. "It's unbelievable."

"What do they look like?"

"They're black, with a little ribbon of yellow around the edges of their wings, and a blue spot on each wing."

Just then, as if called by his description, a butterfly looped upward on a warm draft from the hot springs, its wings shimmery and beautiful.

"How is that *possible?*" Julie cried.

"They can last over the winter," Josh said. "Hold out your hand."

"I'm afraid! It'll feel weird!"

"It's half asleep. They have to warm up their wings before they can fly."

"No, no. You do it."

He chuckled and extended his hand. The butterfly lazily circled and landed on his finger, wings working. "Now you," he said. "Hold out your hand."

Juliet obeyed. The creature swooped and landed, as if a benevolent spirit were visiting, and to her surprise, she felt some intense, unnamed emotion rise in her throat. "It's beautiful!" she whispered, afraid to so much as breathe for fear it would fly away again. So close, she could see butterfly eyes and the pattern of scales on his wings and the long feelers.

Amazing.

In a moment, it lifted off and swirled lazily upward, as if carrying prayers toward heaven. Juliet swallowed. She didn't meet Josh's eye as she moved forward, and took a candle from the box by the little housing. Josh stepped away and Juliet was grateful for the privacy as she lit the candle and put it inside the safe house. Looking up at the sweet face of the saint, she whispered an urgent prayer. "Let her get through this safely. Please."

After a moment, Josh came forward. "My turn," he said, and Juliet gave him the same privacy. As she stood beneath the trees, waiting, she couldn't help but sneak a small glance backward at him, at his tall, sturdy frame, his walnut-colored skin, his beautiful cheekbones. An arrow went through her chest—*I'm falling in love with him!*—and then she turned away.

He came up behind her. "Are you ready to go back to town? I'm going to have to get Glory home pretty soon."

"Sure." She looked at the heavily dripping snow. "I wonder if I should go up to the cabin tonight. It looks like it will be fine up there, doesn't it?"

He met her eyes. "I can take you if you like, but the cabin is above 9000 feet. There will be a lot more snow up there than there is down here."

"You're the expert." She cleared her throat. "I was thinking, in part, of Glory. Like giving her the wrong idea."

"It'll be all right." He raised his chin, scanned the horizon. "It's not like we're all over each other or anything."

Again she had the sense that his feelings were

wounded. There was a faint stiffness around his jaw and mouth. "Josh, I'm not sure what—"

"Don't worry about it, all right?"

Stung, she said, "Fine."

Josh was aware of a knot in his chest the size of Montana as they went through the rest of their errands. They stopped in the drugstore so that Juliet could get some hair rollers, then by the store where they'd stashed their things from earlier. Only then did they walk to Helene's house to pick up Glory.

His mother had obviously been cooking, and the house smelled of her trademark corn fritters and potato soup. She came out, wiping her hands on a cup towel, rangy and lean, and not at all a grandmotherly-looking sort. "Hello, Juliet!" she cried. "What a nice surprise."

Josh bent down and kissed his mother's cheek, handed her a bag of supplies, and called out, "Glory, I'm here!"

"I'm looking at a book right now!" she yelled from the kitchen.

Helene lifted an eyebrow. "She might not have had as much sleep as usual, spending the night with her friend."

"We're gonna have a talk about that," Josh said gruffly.

"No, we are not," his mother replied serenely. "You're too protective. Time to lighten up."

"Glory!" Josh yelled. "I brought somebody who knows how to curl hair."

"She wants her hair curled?" Helene asked. "Why didn't she ask me?"

"Because you have *short* hair, Grandma!" Glory

said, coming out of the kitchen. She carried a book, with her fingers stuck between two pages. She would be five in six weeks, and he was pretty sure she had taught herself to read quite some time ago, but she pretended she didn't know how if anyone asked. She always said was just looking at the pictures with Pink and Ink.

"Silly me," Helene said, plucking at her thick, cropped hair. "I still know how to curl hair."

"I've never seen you with a curl."

"True." Helene waved a hand good-naturedly.

Glory had not caught sight of Juliet yet. Juliet waited by the door, looking oddly nervous, her mittened hands smushed together. As Josh looked at her, his senses were slammed again, a winding depth of memory, yearning, desire, braided together. Her lips were a little swollen from their kissing last night, and he only had to look at her to remember the way she tasted, when they'd—

"Princess!" Glory squealed. "Hi!"

"Hey, sweetheart." Her low, well-modulated voice poured like butter into the room. "I'm so happy to see you."

"You haven't been to my grandma's house before! Are *you* going to curl my hair?"

Juliet smiled and held up a plastic bag from the grocery store. "I've got the rollers right here."

"Can we do it right now?"

"Wait until you wash your hair, kiddo," Josh said. "After supper. Juliet is going to stay with us until tomorrow because she's not used to being all alone in the mountains, and Desi is—" He scowled "—away for the weekend."

"You're going to stay in *my house?*" Glory said.

"Just for tonight, if that's okay?"

"Yes! We can read stories, maybe. Or if you want, we could watch *Snow White* or *Cinderella* or—" she leaned on Josh's leg "—what other ones do I have?"

Her face was awash with light and excitement. Josh put his hand on her silky head. "We have a lot of DVDs," he said. "I'm sure we can find one to watch together."

Juliet looked up, and he saw for the first time the slight bruising beneath her eyes, the weariness and strain of the past few days starting to show. "I'm really looking forward to it."

"First, we're going to eat some of the best corn fritters you've ever tasted," Josh said, and picked his daughter up. "Who makes the best?"

Glory raised her hands above her head, a cheerleader move. "Grandma!"

"It's not ready for a little while," Helene said. "Maybe another twenty minutes on the soup."

"No problem." Josh wiggled Glory in his arms. "Whatcha want to do?"

"Wash my hair."

"Then we'd have to go home with it wet. Not a good idea." He shook his head sadly. "Your hair would turn into icicles and fall on the ground and break into pieces. Not great."

"Na-uh!" She narrowed her eyes suspiciously. "That sounds like a story."

"Let's go read the book, kiddo."

"Okay. You want to read with us, Princess?"

Josh spoke up before Juliet had a chance. "The princess is going to hang out with Grandma."

"I am?"

He nodded firmly. When she just stood there, awkwardly holding the bag of drugstore hair rollers and barrettes and such things, he took it from her, nudged her shoulder. "Go on in there and sit at the table, Princess. I'm going to let you borrow my mom for a little while."

As Juliet stripped off her coat and sat down at the big wooden table in Helene's roomy kitchen, she suddenly felt exhausted. Not just a little bit tired, or stressed, but absolutely, bone-deep demolished. Everything seemed to catch up with her at once—Desi's arrest, the emotional storm from last night, the sudden and surprising connection to Josh and all that stirred up. Not to mention all the purely physical things they'd been doing—hiking, making love, walking all over town.

"You look all done in, honey," Helene said, touching her hair. "Can I get you a cup of tea?"

"That would be wonderful."

From the doorway, Josh said, "Ma, remember my friend Agatha, from the Ute School?"

"Sure."

Josh looked at Juliet, significantly. Nodded.

Juliet scowled. "Don't make secret gestures around me," she said irritably.

He half grinned. "The princess needs a nap."

Helene shooed him out of the kitchen. "He's my one and only," she confessed as she poured water into a red enameled teakettle. "I might have spoiled him a little. He thinks he knows what's best for everybody all the time."

Juliet couldn't even muster up much of a smile. She nodded, was caught by a massive yawn, and covered her mouth. "Sorry! We hiked up to the shrine so I could light a candle for Desi. I think I'm pretty tired."

"Have you seen your sister this morning?"

"Yeah. She's not doing well."

Helene said, "She's a wolf—jail will kill her. We have to make sure she gets out. We're going to drum for her tonight, her sisters and I."

"Sisters?"

"Spiritual sisters, I guess you'd call it. We sweat together. To heal ourselves, each other, the earth."

Juliet could think of nothing to say to that. "I see."

"Maybe you'd like to come sometime."

"Maybe." She wasn't sure what it entailed and it seemed a little bit intimidating.

"You can think about it." Helene sat at the table, her kind, strong face as calm as a mountain morning. Her hands, long-fingered and graceful, were very much like her son's, and she folded them in front of her the same way. "I am a healer, Juliet. May I take your hands?"

"Um. Okay." Juliet put her hands on the table, and Helene enfolded them in her own. Her fingertips were cool at first, but as she held Juliet's hands in her own, Helene's hands warmed up, getting hotter and hotter with every passing second. When it seemed it would be uncomfortable and Juliet would have to pull away, the heat suddenly stabilized and Juliet let go of a breath.

"You're worn out," Helene said.

Juliet nodded. She had a sudden vision of herself crawling into a cave and curling up by a fire to sleep and sleep and sleep. Hibernating.

"Winter," Helene said, her voice sounding more lyrical somehow, "is the time we can rest. Sleep more, eat more. Like the earth, we're being more quiet. You can use this winter to let all those wounds heal, and by spring, you'll feel much better."

Juliet thought about saying, "I'm not wounded," but it would have been such a blatant lie that she would shame herself uttering it aloud. Instead she heard herself say, "I lost my job a month ago. I worked so hard to get it, and then—"

"Then?"

She dropped her gaze. It wasn't that she didn't want to say anything more; it was that she couldn't seem to focus on just one thing to pull out and offer as an explanation. *I was raped* seemed as valid as *I am not sure that was ever what I wanted. I think my mother wanted it for me.*

Finally she said, "I don't know. I don't seem to want to do anything to get it back. It doesn't matter. Or—it matters, but it's not *my* job." Which sounded stupid, so she added, "Or something like that." Frowning, she said, "That doesn't make any sense."

"It makes a lot of sense. Maybe there's something else you need to do now."

Juliet thought of the mothers she'd met at the immigrant center, both earnest and weary, with their children clinging to their legs. How satisfying it had been to help them find work, housing, food for another day or two! "The law doesn't move very fast," she said. "I was growing more and more frustrated with the way that worked in people's lives."

Helene nodded. Patiently, she kept her hands around Juliet's, her eyes steady and calm, her face smooth. "What brought it to a head?"

"I was raped," Juliet said simply. "A year ago."

No ripple of judgment or shock or slightly prurient interest. Helene simply nodded. A quiet radiance came from her, and it felt like it was spreading to Juliet, a silvery energy that radiated upward from her hands, through her arms, into her tight, weary shoulders.

She would have said she didn't believe in hands-on healing, but it was impossible to deny there was something going on with Helene's hands. It was pleasant enough she didn't feel the need to do anything about it. For long moments, they simply sat at the table, her small hands enfolded in Helene's larger, rangier ones.

The kettle began to whistle. Gently, Helene pressed Juliet's hands together. "Let me get the tea."

As she poured water into the kettle, Juliet asked, "What happened to Josh's friend at the Ute School?"

"She was abandoned by her mother."

"Oh." Juliet felt a ripple pulse through her, a sense of having been recognized, seen. Josh hadn't focused on the rape at all, but on her feelings of not being able to reach her mother. It took her breath for a moment.

Why did people fall in love? Was that what was happening here? And if it was, why was Juliet so skittish?

Somewhere in the house, a phone rang. "Uh-oh," Helene said. That's Josh's phone. Usually means trouble."

Josh looked grim when he came into the kitchen a few

minutes later. "That was my friend on the sheriff's department, who called earlier to let me know they got a search warrant to go through the cabin for possible evidence."

"They can get a search warrant but they can't get a bail hearing?" Juliet asked with annoyance. "What *is* that?"

"They took her rifle and some clothes, maybe some other things." He touched his nose with his thumb again, that thinking gesture. "The ballistics test was inconclusive."

"That's good, right?"

"It doesn't clear her," Josh said gravely. "The bad news is, they found Claude's blood on some of her clothes."

## Chapter 14

For one long second, Juliet couldn't breathe as the reality of Josh's words sank in. *They found Claude's blood on some of Desi's clothes.*

It made her dizzy. A thousand scenarios played out in the space of moments—Desi in prison, ankles chained, eyes hollow with despair, the wolves euthanized one by one, the land turning into a retreat for the very, very rich. She made a noise of protest and covered her eyes. "Dang it."

"If you have any high-powered criminal lawyer contacts," Josh said, "This would be a good time to call them."

With an ironic twist of her lips, she said, "My old boyfriend. Who probably isn't talking to me."

"Call him," Josh said.

Juliet glared at him. "You have a bad habit of ordering people around, you know that? I'm not a child and I'm not one of your minions on the police force, and if you want something from me, you need to ask politely."

Helene grinned.

Josh took a breath. His eyes glittered suddenly as he gazed down at her, and his tongue laced out and touched his lower lip. To her amazement, the sight of that healthy pink tongue, the tip that had given so much pleasure, the plumpness of lower lip, gave her a jolt of yearning.

He took a step closer. "Yes, ma'am," he drawled, a country boy without guile. "Your sister needs a lawyer. A very good lawyer. Do you have any contacts you can lean on?"

"Better." She raised her chin. "I just might." Taking her phone out of her bag, she flipped it open and punched in a number. "Alicia," she said to the voice mail of her friend, "this is Juliet Rousseau. My sister is in criminal trouble in Colorado and we might need the names of some good lawyers here. Give me a call when you can, on my cell phone."

"Good work," Josh said as she hung up.

She found herself preening just the tiniest bit. "Thanks."

After feasting on soup and fritters, Josh, Juliet and Glory walked through the gilded late afternoon to Josh's house. The dogs had been romping the fenced backyard all day and were very happy to see the humans arrive. They set up howls of greeting as they stepped onto the porch.

Nothing would do but Glory had to have her hair washed and set right now, and Josh excused himself to make phone calls, promising to see what he could find out, how much information he could gather from various sources.

Meanwhile, Juliet let the very female pleasure of giving Glory a bath and washing her hair take away the sting and worry of the day. Dozens of toys were collected in a laundry basket by the big bathtub, and Glory picked out a few to toss in the tub as Juliet started the water and adjusted it. "Do you want bubbles?"

"No, then I can't see my toys."

Juliet chuckled. "Ah." She started humming under her breath, stirring the water around to make sure it was the right temperature, and she unlaced Glory's braid. Her hair was thick and cool and elegant, and Juliet luxuriated in the feeling of it, spilling over her hands. "You have very, very pretty hair," she said.

"I got it from my daddy." Glory stripped out of her clothes and gingerly stepped into the tub. "My mommy has really yellow hair."

"She does?"

"It was really supposed to be black, but she didn't like being Indian."

"Oh, I'm sure she did," Juliet said.

"No. She told me she didn't." Matter-of-factly, Glory filled a cup with water from the running tap and poured it into a bowl. "I like being Indian."

"I'm glad."

"My Daddy says I look like Pocahontas. Do you think I do?"

"Absolutely. Do you have that movie on DVD?"

"Yeah! You want to watch that one with me tonight?"

"Sure."

The smell of the soap and the shampoo, the easy pleasure of sitting on the closed lid of the toilet, making small talk with a little girl, made Juliet feel peaceful. She washed Glory's back, then her hair, and rinsed it with detangler, and helped her out into a big, fluffy turquoise towel. When Glory was dressed in her footed pajamas—pink, of course, with little kittens all over them—Juliet led her into the living room to sit by the fire, where she brushed Glory's hair to get it mostly dry before she put it on the rollers. Josh's voice came from the kitchen in low tones, only the odd word coming through here and there.

"My sister has very long pretty hair," Juliet said. "We use to brush each other's hair all the time."

"So does Pink," Glory said. "But hers is red."

"Who is Pink?"

"She's my friend. Not like Natasha at school. Pink and Ink are in my room. Or if I want, they'll come along in my pocket."

"I see. Like imaginary friends?"

"Sometimes, grown-ups pretend they can see them, but I know they can't." Glory held very still as Juliet rolled the first section of hair into a curler. "Grown-ups can't see angels anymore, can they?"

"I guess not." Juliet secured the roller, and picked up another section. In front of them, the fire crackled and snapped. Two dogs—Crazy Horse and Tecumseh, snored nearby, tuckered out by their long day playing outside. "Pink and Ink are angels?"

"Yeah. Pink is a girl and Ink is a boy. They were brother and sister before they died and went to heaven. They came to take care of me when my mommy stole me." Glory gave Juliet a long-suffering look that was well beyond her years. "My mommy wasn't very good at taking care of me."

Juliet had a sense, suddenly, that Josh was listening. "So, how did Pink and Ink help you?"

"A lot of ways! They showed me how to get on the counter so I could get some cheese and bread. They showed me how to lock the door when I was all by myself."

"Really! All that. Very good angels."

"Yeah," she said with a shrug. "They are. I mostly liked it when I was scared and they came and slept with me. Grandma says they're my spirit guides and when I get older, they'll be the ones to help me find out what I'm gonna do when I get big."

Josh ambled into the room, deceptively casual, and sat on the couch. "I never knew that, about Pink and Ink," he said. "They took care of you?"

"They always take care of me, Daddy. You know that."

"I do?"

"Yeah. You said your prayers, so God sent angels to watch over me."

Over Glory's head, Juliet met Josh's eyes. If only, she thought, it was that simple. And yet, hadn't she gone this morning to light candles for Desi?

Josh looked stricken. "So I did, honey. So I did."

"Can we watch *Pocahontas?*" she asked.

"I'd love to." He looked at Juliet. "Suit you, too?"

She nodded. When all the rollers were in place, Juliet dried the curls with a blow dryer, then let them out and curls fell in beautiful ringlets over Glory's shoulders.

Juliet couldn't help but grin. Glory looked like a vision of an angel, or a Victorian drawing.

"Wow, kiddo," Josh said. "You sure do have a lot of hair."

Glory stood for a long time in front of the bedroom mirror, the only one she could see into without help or standing on something. She flipped her hair over her shoulder, smoothed her hands over it, walked very close to the mirror and nodded. "I look pretty," she said.

"You definitely do," Juliet agreed, and wondered when girls lost the ability to do that—announce she looked good without hemming and hawing about it.

They all piled together on the couch, Glory sandwiched between the two adults. Tecumseh came and pushed himself beneath Juliet's feet, slumping happily asleep with her feet on his side. Jack, Josh's dog, whined until Josh let him up on the couch. Crazy Horse, not to be left out, curled up close by.

It was slightly overwhelming, Juliet thought. It was warm. It made her feel loved and protected.

And the way Glory held her hand, and kept looking up at her as if to be sure she was really there, made her realize she had to be very, very careful with this little girl's heart.

After Glory was settled in bed, her new curls protected with a scarf, Juliet took her phone out of her purse and held it for a long minute before she flipped it open and dialed Scott's number. It rang in her ear, then his voice mail picked up. "It's Juliet. My sister is in trouble and I could use some advice if you are not too annoyed with me."

She hung up and looked at Josh, sitting in his chair, whittling with an expression of deep concentration. "That's that, I guess."

He nodded. All evening he'd been very cool and distant, and Juliet had put it down to keeping things cool in front of Glory. But there was no Glory around now, and he was still locked tight inside his own little world.

"What do we do now?" Juliet asked. Nudging him.

"Wait. Watch television. Read a book. Knit."

"Oh, sure. I have my knitting right here."

He shrugged. "I'm thinking about what Glory said about Pink and Ink, protecting her. That was pretty wild, wasn't it?"

"What a survivor she is, your daughter!"

"What do you mean?"

"She found a way at—what, four?—to get her needs met. She created a world where she had help when she needed it."

"I didn't think of it like that."

"I don't think you have to worry about her, Josh. I think she's fine."

"Really?"

"Really." She touched his hand. "She's a great kid."

He leaned back on the couch. "She is that. I'm worried that she worships you."

"Me, too. She asked me to marry you the first day."

He grinned, showing those big white teeth. "You didn't tell me that."

"Pretty funny."

"It is." Josh took her hand, worried her fingers. "The other thing on my mind tonight is the blood on Desi's clothes." He shook his head. "It's a nightmare. If they can put her at the scene—and even if they can't, it's well known she was chasing the mountain lion that mauled him—then there's not a damned thing we can do about it."

"I have to keep believing it's going to work out," Juliet said. "Don't you dare give up yet."

"I'm not giving up. I'm talking to you as a cop. This is bad."

The doorbell rang and Josh scowled, then put down the wooden block and stood up to answer it. Juliet heard voices, then Josh returned with another man behind him—the bartender from the Black Crown, the pub they'd visited last night.

Something about him was jovial and upbeat, even under such gruesome circumstances. "Hello" he said, "you're Juliet, isn't that right?" His accent was the slightly drawling New Zealand British.

"Yep." She stood. "Was it Tam? How are you?"

"I heard some gossip I thought might help you."

Josh gestured toward the couch. "Have a seat. Want a beer or something?"

"No, thank you." He settled on the couch, laced his fingers together. "I've been seeing a woman who—" he tsked, inclined his head "—might be a bit of a gold digger. Not looking at me, 'course, though I've got the pub, it's not on the order of the payoff she's lookin' to find, you understand."

"Not uncommon around here."

Juliet widened her eyes. "Really?"

"Just wait, sweetheart, for the ski season to get going." His sentences ended on questions. "You'll see what we mean."

"So, the one you've been seeing?" Josh prompted.

"Right. Elsa." He looked at his palms. "She's Norwegian, a beauty and after a rich man. There's a developer in the pub who's promising her the moon and more, and he was talking this afternoon about how the land with the wolves will be so much better spent as a spa."

"Not sure what that proves."

"Nothing, mate. But it's gossip. Could help."

Josh nodded, his mouth grim. "Have you heard other developers speculating about the land?"

He lifted a finger. "I have, and it's better." His pale green eyes had a directness Juliet found appealing. "There's some talk of an enclosed aquifer, a hot spring, beneath the wolf center."

Josh straightened. He let go of a long, low whistle.

"Just rumor," Tam said. "But worth mentioning."

"I don't understand why that would be a big deal," Juliet said.

"It could be tapped for energy," Josh said. "Steam heat that can be recycled back into the earth. Theoretically, it's an eternal energy source."

"Worth billions, likely," Tam added.

"Wow."

Josh nodded. "She made the deal of the century with that land, I'm telling you."

"She really did." Juliet pressed a hand to her diaphragm. "It scares me."

"The good news is," Josh said, "it's a lot of motive for murder, and to frame Desi. That's what we need right now."

"Yes," she said. "Thanks, Tam."

He winked. "No problem."

Tam left and for the second time in two nights, Josh brought the quilts and pillows out to the couch. Last night, when he had returned with the pillows, Juliet had lit candles and built up the fire, an invitation in her eyes. Tonight, when he returned, she'd tumbled sideways, clutching a pillow, and stared at the fire with a melancholy expression.

"You look like you've lost your best friend," he said, settling beside her. With an easy gesture, he rubbed her arm.

"Long day." She looked at him. "Thanks for all your help."

"You're welcome."

They sat there. The fire crackled. Her cheek, curved and white, invited his fingers, and Josh resisted. Her throat, long and smooth, invited his lips, and he resisted. "I guess this is…uh…good night."

"Okay." She shifted to look at him. "It's awkward, Josh, but this is probably the right decision for now. With Glory and all the stuff with Desi and—"

He kissed her, cutting her off. He didn't even know

he was going to do it until he was bending over her, claiming that lush and seductive mouth.

And if she had resisted, if she had protested or pulled away, he would have respected that and taken himself off to bed.

But she didn't. With a little cry, she met his kiss and flung her arms around his neck, pulling him close to her. They had been slow in previous times and easy with each other. Josh had been mindful of her wariness, and she'd had a fragile way about her that was tentative and quiet.

Not now. It was as if their kiss let free the tigers of hunger and yearning and need that had been circling all day. Her mouth opened wide, inviting the hard, fierce thrust of his tongue; her hands laced into his hair tightly and pulled him close.

"Not here," Josh murmured, and picked her up and carried her, easily, into his bedroom, where they shed their clothes in a tangle and a tumble, tossing them wherever they landed until both were naked, and shivering and Josh drove himself home between her thighs, into slick heat and quivering warmth and the surprising strength of her grip.

And when they were spent, they were both so worn from the long day that they simply curled together.

"We can't keep doing this," Juliet said thickly, her head nestled against his chest.

"I know." He pressed a kiss to her hair.

But they would. He'd finally understood a simple truth about Juliet Rousseau. It wasn't only her feelings about the rape that were buried, it was her feelings about everything. He held her, quietly, and thought about the things she'd said about her mother. "I think you need to tell your mother what happened to you, Juliet."

"Why?"

"Because I think you need to confess it to her."

"Confess? Like a sin?"

"No," he said quietly, brushing hair from her forehead. "Like a sorrow."

"She won't understand."

"It doesn't matter. It's not for her. It's for you."

Her hand moved on his chest, slow and easy, as if she was drawing comfort from the feeling of his skin. "I'll think about it."

"Will you also consider a support group?"

She was very quiet for a long stretch. "I don't know. We'll see."

They fell asleep, naked and exhausted, in each other's arms.

After breakfast, Juliet went to see Desi at the jail. If possible, Desi looked even worse, her skin the color of gruel, her hair unbrushed. Juliet hugged her, tightly. "Don't give up on me, Desi. Josh talked to the judge yesterday and he thinks you can be out tomorrow morning."

Desi nodded dully. "I had so many dreams last night. That mountain lion is haunting me. I swear I heard him last night."

"Do you want me to call somebody?"

She shook her head. "No, there's nothing they can

do until he shows up somewhere. I just hate that he's in pain for so long. There was a lot of blood out at the ranch."

"Is there anything you want? Anything I can do?"

Desi roused herself to give Juliet a wan smile. "Just watch out for my dogs."

"That I can do." She paused. "Desi, can I talk about something kind of frivolous?"

"Please," she said, sipping the latte Juliet had brought to her.

"I broke up with Scott."

"You did? When?"

"Right after I met Josh." She bit her lip. "The thing is, I just can't seem to get to my feelings. Not any of them. I mean, I think I was very attracted to Josh and that's what made me realize that Scott and I were just drifting. But then Josh kisses me and I can feel things while his hands are on me, but the minute I move away, it's like a wall snaps into place."

"I'm glad you broke up with Scott, first of all. I never liked him. He was too uptight."

Juliet smiled. "I know."

"And Josh—well, if I were to pick any man in the world for you, I couldn't do better than him. But you're going to have to do your healing work or nothing is ever going to be okay again."

Juliet took a breath and confessed her secret. "I don't know how."

"Just be with it," Desi said. A little color came back into her cheeks as she counseled her sister. "When you're afraid, just be afraid. When you're mad, be mad. You don't always have to be the good girl."

The advice held a stinging rightness. Juliet nodded. "I'll try."

"That's all anyone can do."

# *Chapter 15*

Josh drove her home in the late afternoon, at Juliet's request. After her conversation with Desi, Juliet knew that her instinct to stay alone and face her mostly insubstantial fears was a good one. If all went well, Desi would get out of jail tomorrow morning—this would be a chance for Juliet to spend one night alone in the mountains.

It worried her a little that there was more snow in the forecast, but there were plenty of supplies, and she wouldn't even technically be alone, after all; the dogs would be with her. Josh went through the cabin with her, made sure she understood how the various things worked, and he carried in several armloads of firewood for her, not listening when she protested that she knew how to do it. "I know you do. It doesn't hurt to take some help, either."

At last, he paused at the front door. "You don't have to do this," he said. "There's nothing to prove."

Juliet nodded. "Yes, there is. I need to prove to myself that I'm not going to be afraid forever."

He seemed as if he would say something else, then just shrugged. "Okay. Call me if you need me."

As the mountain darkness enveloped the cabin, Juliet determined to keep herself busy. She boiled pasta and grated cheddar for macaroni and cheese while she listened to Celtic tunes on her MP3 player. While the macaroni and cheese baked, she tidied up the cabin, which took all of six minutes, since they had not been there the past couple of days. The fire was going nicely in the potbellied stove, and she had already piled up her nest of pillows and quilts so she could read after dinner.

One of the dogs went outside, then another, then the last one, but Juliet didn't fret. The blackness of the un-curtained windows was bothersome, as always, and Juliet wondered with some annoyance why Desi had never made any curtains.

Well, aside from the fact that you didn't technically need them since there were no neighbors, save for the odd bear.

And the views were spectacular.

Still, at night, it was creepy to know anyone else could see inside and she couldn't see out.

*Anyone else being who, exactly?* a voice in her mind asked. The odd werewolf, the rapist who had followed her from California to here to rape her again in the high mountains in an isolated cabin that no one knew existed?

Something like that. Vampires, rapists, crazed serial killers.

She rolled her eyes at the absurdity of her thoughts and wished she could turn on the television for company. That was how she got through the loneliness and fear back home—she turned on the television and let the chatter and advertisements and constant, on-demand companionship blunt the terror she felt, the sense of her own isolation, even in the midst of a big city. She had done it as a child, too, taken refuge in the world of game shows, soap operas, movie of the week. Her mother had disapproved, but it kept Juliet out of her hair, so she looked the other way.

The bell on the stove dinged and Juliet took out a small, beautiful casserole, the top lightly browned. As if she called them, the dogs all reappeared, sitting politely along an imaginary line Desi had drawn for them as if to say, "Are we not the best dogs you've ever seen?"

Juliet chuckled. "You are great dogs and I will have some treats for you in a little while."

She set the table and ate supper, reading the novel she'd started before Desi's arrest. It was enjoyable enough. The wind started to blow outside, and a little while after that, it started to snow lightly. The silence was vast, apart from the wind that blasted against the window panes every so often. When she'd finished her macaroni and cheese, she gave the waiting dogs the leftovers and they took them politely, delicately, as Desi had taught them.

Desi. Juliet carried the dishes to the sink and thought about her sister. And the one thing Juliet was most afraid of was that Desi really had killed Claude. Her blood on his clothes. The inconclusive ballistics report, the fury Desi had been feeling.

*Be with whatever you're feeling.*

Juliet's eye twitched as she thought of other things: Desi's desire to kill Juliet's rapist, the fact that Desi could not account for her whereabouts that night.

A night Juliet had spent alone, now that she thought about it. The difference had been that she hadn't realized she was alone. She thought she'd only be by herself for a few hours, and she had dogs to protect herself.

She and the dogs padded over to the stove and settled into the nest. Juliet pulled the quilts around herself, propped up against the wall with pillows, and stared into the fire, dancing yellow and orange against the gloom.

Desi had always been unlike other women. She was stronger, tougher, smarter. She strode through the world like some ancient goddess, the hunter Diana with her dogs. She'd been bolder, fiercer than her sisters, traveling boldly, learning things like how to hunt and fire a rifle. She'd gone to the Peace Corps, moved to the mountains, started a sanctuary for wolves.

Unlike anyone else.

Juliet's throat felt tight as she imagined the disaster awaiting Desi if it turned out she really had killed a worthless scumbag of a man, a charmer and a user who'd taken advantage of entirely too many women over the years.

No.

She didn't, in her heart, believe Desi had done it. Which meant someone else had. Which meant Juliet just had to find out who. In the morning, she would go talk to the girlfriend, and see about any other girlfriends who might have something to share. The one thing Juliet was good at was talking to women, even hostile women. Why hadn't she thought of this before?

Because she'd been too busy being afraid, focusing on fear and all the terrible things that could happen instead of all the good. She thought of Glory's faith, the angels who had protected her through a dark time, the angels that had brought her home safely to her father.

Where had her own faith gone? Juliet wondered now. Had it been so fragile it could be demolished by a single person with an evil agenda?

Her cell phone rang, and startled one of the dogs, who barked wildly for a minute. Juliet laughed and rubbed his head. "It's okay, silly. It's just a phone." She flipped it open and said, "Hello?"

"Hi, Juliet." It was Josh, his voice like dark toffee.

She let the sound of her smile enter her voice. "Hey, Josh. What's up?"

"I was just thinking about you and thought I'd give you a call."

"Yeah? Were you worrying?"

"No."

"Good." She twisted a piece of hair around her index finger, leaning back more comfortably on the pillows. "Because you really don't need to. I'm having some pretty deep thoughts up here."

"Am I interrupting?"

"No, actually," she said in a more serious tone. "You're part of what I'm thinking about."

"You're thinking about my parts?"

Juliet laughed. "I am. Big, juicy parts."

"Me, too."

A softness of silence fell between them. The fire crackled and the wind blew and the dogs snored. In her mind was his angled face, his thick dark hair. "I was thinking, honestly, about how safe I feel around you. I don't know that I've ever had that feeling before, with anyone, and it's kind of weird."

"Is it bad to feel safe?"

"No. I'm just not used to it."

"Well, you make me feel the opposite of safe, Juliet. I've been pretty well protected, and you slammed right by my walls. Like they weren't even there. I'm worried about that."

"Worried why?"

"Because you have a whole life in L.A., not here. Because you're a city girl and that's who screwed up my life last time. Because my daughter thinks you hung the moon and she doesn't need to get hurt again and I don't know how to protect her from it."

"The truth is, Josh, you can't." Juliet rubbed her foot along the back of a dog. "The world isn't safe. Not for any of us."

"I know. But you can cut the risks."

"Maybe." Juliet paused. "I am a girly girl, by the way, not a city girl. There's a difference."

He chuckled, the sound low and warm. "I stand corrected." He fell silent again, and Juliet was surprised by how much she liked knowing he was there, just on the other end of the phone. "It's not all that easy for me to talk about feelings, Juliet, but you're not like anyone I've ever met. It's like you smell right or something."

"I know what you mean," she said, and realized that she'd been breaking up with Scott in her mind within minutes of meeting Josh. The look of him, the sound of him—even, yes, the smell of him. But it was something deeper than physical, something unnamable, a recognition. "I felt like—" She realized she'd been about to say something really stupid and halted. "Never mind."

"Come on, be dopey with me, huh? If the girl doesn't start, the guy can never go there."

"Okay. I felt like I'd known you before," she said.

"Good," Josh said. "Me, too."

In the distance, a wolf howled, and then another. The dogs, apparently comatose up to that moment, sat up, ears pricked to alertness. Another round of howling went up, a series of yips and yowls that made the hair on Juliet's neck rise.

"Hold on," she said, and put the phone down to her chest, dancing over to the window to see if there was an animal in view.

"Sorry," she said, coming back on. "The wolves are going nuts up there."

"Might be an animal," Josh said.

"What kind of an animal?"

"I don't know. A bear. A deer. A mountain lion. It is the mountains, you know."

"A bear? Yikes."

"If it worries you, give Alex a call, see if he's seen anything."

"Good idea, thank you." She paused. "I guess I'll talk to you tomorrow, then, all right?"

Tecumseh jumped up and padded over to the window, where he went absolutely still, then growled at something he saw.

"Uh-oh."

Tecumseh bolted for the dog door in the back of the kitchen. Juliet didn't hesitate—she dropped the phone and ran for the door, trying to get there before Tecumseh bolted through. "Damn it!"

Desi would never forgive her if something happened to these dogs. She was seconds too late—jamming her index finger in the process, eating dog fur as she slammed into the door. "Damn!" she cried.

The other two dogs, alerted, leapt to their feet, nails skittering on the floor as they, too, bolted for the dog door to see what the commotion was all about. Tecumseh followed on Sitting Bull's heels before she could stop him. She managed to tackle Crazy Horse before he got out, yelling "no!" as authoritatively as she could manage. Before he got out, she flipped the lock— then felt immediately guilty. What if they needed to retreat by coming back inside?

But while the other two were easily wolves when it came to the hunt, Crazy Horse was more of a dog, and she didn't want him hurt.

In the distance, the wolves howled and cried in an eerie cacophony of sound. Closer in, she didn't hear the other dogs, but Crazy Horse dashed for the window and whined, a low, eerie sound that made the hair on her neck stand up. "Come on, baby," she said, taking him by the collar and leading him into the bathroom. He wasn't happy about it when she closed the door, barking in protest, but she needed to think about what to do.

Back in the living room, she turned off the lights and peered out the window. The dogs were nowhere in view. The night was cloudy, and very dark—impossible to see anything.

Something yipped, a sound like an animal in pain. One of the dogs. Damn! Juliet instinctively ran for the cabinet where Desi kept the guns. The only thing left was a handgun, but there was a box of bullets right beside it, and when she looked at it, it looked like it had bullets in it.

From her cell phone on the floor came a tinny voice. "Juliet! What's going on?"

She dove for the phone, picked it up. "Josh, it's okay. There's an animal out there, the dogs are freaking out. How do I shoot a gun if I need to?"

"Holy Mother of God," he breathed. "What kind of gun?"

"Handgun, pistol. I don't know. It's heavy. It has bullets in it."

Another pained animal sound, and Juliet whirled around, wishing she had x-ray vision to see what was out there. A bear? A coyote?

"I'm here. I've gotta do something." Without waiting for an answer, she dashed for the dog door and flung the lock open, whistling for Sitting Bull and Tecumseh. Sitting Bull bolted through, and Juliet saw immediately that he had blood on his face. He howled, and in answer, Crazy Horse cried out in the bathroom.

"Oh, baby," she sobbed, reaching for the big dog. He whined, and came over to her, and she could see he'd been cut, and blood was soaking into the fur above his eye, but the actual cut didn't seem dire.

"Come on. You, too." She opened the door to the bathroom, and Crazy Horse bolted out, running past her with a frantic, fierce bark, a charge she would never have expected from him, and he was out the dog door in three seconds.

"No!" she cried. "No! Crazy Horse! Wait!"

But he was gone, and the house was suddenly silent. She swallowed and stood still, peering into the yard. A break in the clouds allowed the faintest of moonlight to spill through, illuminating the shape of the dogs, and— maybe a coyote?

The animal cried out, the unmistakable, ragged, pained cry of a mountain lion. It gave a warning cry, low and long, and Juliet felt tears spring to her eyes, tears of fear, of empathy, of horror and a weird, sharp relief of understanding.

The dogs and the lion were intimately connected to her sister. Juliet desperately needed to do the right thing. What would Desi do right now?

The lion was desperately injured and in pain. It had been carrying a bullet around for days, and had to be half mad with pain by now. The dogs were only protecting their pack, the house, Juliet. They had to be her first priority—she couldn't let anything happen to them. Desi had lost enough.

She looked at the gun, remembering her sister's instructions about the safety, and she saw that it was on. She switched it off. Held the cold, heavy weight of it in her right hand. Her heart was pounding as she went to the door of the cabin and pulled it open the slightest bit.

The mountain lion bawled out a miserable cry, and she wished, desperately for another answer. "I don't want him to die," she said. "I hate this." Tears filled her eyes, her throat, her heart.

Juliet thought of her sister, tracking the poor beast all night long, tirelessly, all through the dark, snowy forest, cold, hungry, smarting, putting herself in danger to either save or put the animal out of pain. She pulled the door open and stepped on to the porch. The lion made a loud, agonizing sound, and she saw him on the ground, unmoving, as if he were dying.

The dogs howled, as if warning her or sending out a call to the other wolves, to the pack that no doubt paced restlessly in the runs at the sanctuary. They were so close to the dying mountain lion that she couldn't take a chance on firing from this distance.

It was dark. Her heart filled her throat, and tears ran down her face, making it hard to see well. She halted and steadied herself. It was important to forget herself and her fears right now, to act as Desi would act, to be selfless for the sake of the animals.

For *this* animal, who had no one else but her right now.

This wild, beautiful creature, stained and dirty with its travails the past few days lay on the ground, unable to move, and looked up at her. Its yellow eyes were full of misery, and Juliet almost felt as if the creature asked for release. She held up the gun, steadied her hand, and fired.

It lay still. Sitting Bull sat back on his haunches and lifted his nose to the sky, letting go of a long, singing howl. In the distance, the other wolves answered. Their cries rolled into the still night, as if to accompany the spirit of the mountain lion home, and Juliet, overcome, sank down beside the beautiful creature and wept.

And she would never tell a soul, but she swore she felt the animal's spirit move through her, in her chest and through her belly, velvety fur and fierce paws permeating her very cells, becoming one with her.

"Thank you," she breathed.

Sitting Bull and Crazy Horse, sensing her sorrow, came over and lapped her face. She stood up. "Come on, guys, let's go inside."

Josh drove up to the land an hour later, to see the lights were on inside, though he could see no sign of humans or dogs. It was the low, flickering light of a fire, and when he went inside, he found Juliet and the dogs lumped in a pile around the fire, all fast asleep.

He would have come sooner, frantic as he'd been with the sounds he'd heard over the phone, but it had taken some time to get hold of his mother, and he couldn't risk dragging Glory to a scene of mayhem.

But there was no mayhem. Relief, deep and wild, bolted through him, making his legs weak, and he sank onto a chair. One of the dogs had some blood on his face, and he could smell the lingering scent of overwrought wolf in the rooms, but for the rest, the scene was peaceful. Maybe he should go and let her sleep in peace.

Except—

She lay there so sweetly asleep in her nest of dogs and blankets, looking like the only thing he'd ever want again all his life. The soft tumble of her hair, shining in the reddish light, the curve of her shoulder, her pretty mouth. Voluptuous and wounded and strong and somehow innocent in spite of everything.

He fed the fire and took off his boots, then crept close and touched her arm. "Hey," he said quietly.

She opened her eyes. "Hi!" She blinked sleepily, peered at him with some confusion. "I told you everything was okay. You didn't have to come all the way up here."

"I know. I needed to make sure."

She blinked sleepily. "It was the lion," she said, drifting away.

"A lion?" He pictured the king of the beasts, roaring on the African veldt.

"Yes. I'll tell you about it in the morning." She shifted, pushing Tecumseh to one side. "Do you want to go to sleep with me?"

"Yes," Josh said, and took off his shoes and climbed in beside her. It was sudden and surprising and there were a thousand reasons not to fall in love, but it didn't appear he had a choice. He never wanted to sleep in a bed without her in it ever again.

When he settled beside her, she eased across the slight space between them and tucked her head into his shoulder. "Just right," she said. "Just right."

# Chapter 16

In the morning, Juliet took Josh outside the back door to see the mountain lion. He squeezed her hand. "My mother is going to have some things to say about this."

"Did I do something wrong, do you think?"

"No way." He shook his head. "Let my mother talk to you. She's the medicine woman."

Juliet felt a sense of peace, looking that still body. In memory, she could hear the agonized cry, the wish for an end to pain. "Not sure what a person is supposed to do with such a thing." She looked up at him. "But it doesn't feel like an accident."

He made no comment, letting her find her own way through her thoughts.

"It was such a profound experience, and I'm not

sure what it all means yet, but I did figure out a lot last night, Josh."

"Like what?"

"I've been paralyzed by fear the past year, and I'm tired of it."

"It's normal, Juliet. People—"

She held up a hand. "Wait. I know it's normal to take some time to recover from a trauma. What's been hard for me was not the trauma itself, but the fact that I'm a good girl. I follow the rules. I did everything right and something terrible happened to me."

He nodded, listening. "Right."

"And now something terrible has happened to Desi, who doesn't deserve it, and—" She took a breath. "I just want to help her. Help other women like her, but I don't want to do it in a big, lonely city anymore. I'll find a way to serve women and the law here." She bit her lip. "I hope that's okay with you."

"It's very okay with me."

"I know it's soon, Josh, but I've fallen in love with you." She faced him, put his hand to her face. "It feels like I knew you before, that I've just been waiting for you."

He bent and hugged her, sighing. "Me, too," he said, and Juliet felt his voice through his chest, in her ear.

Juliet felt the losses and tensions and terrors of the past year suddenly flow out of her. Josh was home. "I love you," she said.

"I love you, too."

"How are we going to handle Glory?"

He chuckled. "I suspect she'll just handle us."

Juliet laughed. "I suspect you're right."

"Come on, let's get to town and report this, and go see Desi so she doesn't get too depressed."

Juliet nodded. She whistled for the dogs, and turned to find them sniffing something on the front step, a black shape. Tecumseh picked it up politely and carried it over to Juliet, depositing it at her feet with a happy grin. "Good dog," she said, automatically.

When she saw what it was, a blast of insight burned through the cobwebs in her brain. "Desi didn't kill Claude," she said. "The blood came from the altercation they had the other morning, remember?"

"Of course!"

She pointed to the dead raven at her feet. "And this is the third or fourth raven Desi has had on her porch. She thought it was Claude. Obviously it wasn't."

"We have to find out who it is."

Juliet nodded. "Yeah. We do."

# Chapter 17

On Monday morning, Juliet drove her rental car down the muddy road to town to pick up her sister at the jail. The judge had set a $10,000 bond, secured by the land, and had apologized that he couldn't make it lower, but there was pressure on him from other sources, too. He also dismissed a request for an injunction by the now-deceased Claude Tsosie to force Desi to sell half the ranch.

Desi looked tired and pale when she emerged, but she came right to Juliet and hugged her hard. "I'm so proud of you!"

"For what?"

Desi laughed. "For the mountain lion. You did the right thing."

"Did I? I was so scared, Desi, but I was trying to think what you would do."

"Josh took the lion's body to Helene, and she's going to help you make a medicine bag if you like."

"A medicine bag?"

"She'll use some of the fur and the teeth and claws. The lion came to you, and you took care of her, and you have earned the right to call her your totem."

"My totem?" Juliet said in a whisper.

"Lion medicine," Desi said, brushing back her sister's hair. "You look like a lion, you know. You always have."

Juliet felt a press of emotions in her throat. She thought of the feeling of the lion moving through her, the breath of the creature in her lungs, and she promised herself she'd never speak of it. But it appeared she did not have to. "Thanks."

Desi punched her. "Pretty powerful totem, kiddo. I'm impressed."

"I didn't do anything, Desi. I tried to think what you would do."

"You were very brave, Juliet. You faced a situation that was way out of your league and handled it very well, with great compassion and empathy. The cat chose you. Don't dismiss it."

"No," she said, and it seemed she could feel the lion's heart within her. "No, I won't."

They walked into the bright day and Desi stopped on the sidewalk, and tipped her face up. "I wanted to die in there," she said quietly. "I can't go back. I *can't*."

"I know." She took her hand. "We will not let it

happen. I promise." She smiled with her secret. "Come on, let's take a little walk up to Josh's house. Glory wants to tell you something."

"What?"

"You'll see."

The day was clear and busy, the sky arching like a turquoise balloon over the little town. As they passed the path that led to the shrine, a black-winged butterfly floated dizzily through the air. "Amazing how they live through the winter," Juliet said.

"The natural world is a great thing."

In quiet they walked up the street and down to Josh's house, where Glory waited on the porch in a fuzzy red coat, wearing a crown. "Desi!" she cried and flew off the porch into Desi's waiting arms. "I'm so happy you're out of jail!"

"Me, too, kiddo!" Desi kissed the little girl's cheek. "I hear you have something to tell me."

"I do! Where's my daddy?" Glory wiggled and Desi put her down.

Josh came out on the porch, and Juliet met his eyes, feeling as if the sun expanded to twelve times its size. He took his daughter's hand.

"Guess what?" Glory said.

"What?" Desi asked.

"My daddy is going to marry the princess!"

Desi shrieked. Literally, happily shrieked, then covered her mouth, and hugged Juliet so hard she thought her ribs would break. "Finally," she said, "a plan that worked out!"

"What plan?"

Desi laughed. "Never mind." She held out an arm to Josh and Glory. "Come on, let's have our first family hug!"

They embraced, Glory in the middle, Josh and Juliet side by side, Desi and Juliet hugging. Jack barked happily from the porch, then dived down the steps and slammed into Juliet's legs.

Juliet could not remember being happier and thought it was impossible to feel more until Josh leaned over and whispered in her ear, "I love you," and gently, sweetly, kissed her ear.

She raised her eyes. "Me, too."

\* \* \* \* \*

Special thanks and acknowledgment are given to
Kathleen Creighton for her contribution to the
CAPTURING THE CROWN miniseries.

The Kingdom of
*Silvershire*

River Dane

Dunford

Leonia

Perth Castle

Port of Perth

Weston Manor

Silverton Kairn River

Barton

Lake Lodan

42 km. (25 mi)

# Kathleen Creighton

## THE REBEL KING

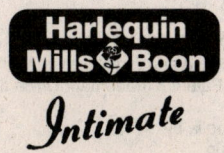

**Harlequin**
**Mills & Boon**

*Intimate*

First Published 2006
First Australian Paperback Edition 2006
ISBN 0 733 57304 5

Published by
Harlequin Mills & Boon
3 Gibbes Street
CHATSWOOD NSW 2067
AUSTRALIA

Printed and bound in Australia by
McPherson's Printing Group

## KATHLEEN CREIGHTON

has roots deep in the California soil but has relocated to South Carolina. As a child, she enjoyed listening to old-timers' tales, and her fascination with the past only deepened as she grew older. Today she says she is interested in everything—art, music, gardening, zoology, anthropology and history, but people are at the top of her list. She also has a lifelong passion for writing, and now combines her two loves in romance novels.

This book is dedicated to the victims and heroes
of Hurricane Katrina, to those who lost so much,
and to those who've given so much in an ongoing
effort to bring aid, comfort and hope to the devastated.
I am in awe of you all.

# Chapter 1

He'd always been a little in love with Paris. She was the village eccentric, that mysterious lady reputed to possess a past both lurid and glorious. True, she was a bit blowsy now, not terribly clean and beginning to show her age, but beautiful still. And while she may have been mistrusted and reviled—and secretly envied—by her more conventional neighbors, one knew she was always ready to welcome a lad in need of refuge with open arms.

And there had never been a lad more in need of a refuge than Nikolas Donovan. His life had recently gone careening out of control with the dizzying speed of a sports car traveling down a steep and winding mountain road without brakes. It seemed to him a ride that could end only one way: with a calamitous plunge off a cliff.

Though at the moment, he had to admit, all the turmoil of the past several months seemed far away. It was an early September evening in Paris. Rain was expected later, but now the air was warm and soft with humidity. The trees were still green, with only a few leaves, harbingers of the autumn avalanche to come, tumbling and skittering like playful kittens under the flying feet of the children playing soccer among the chestnut trees in the Tuillerie Gardens. He felt pangs of envy as he watched them and listened to their grunts and scufflings of effort. He envied them this time, this age when a boy's only concern was whether he could kick the football between the makeshift goalposts before darkness and his mother's voice calling him to supper put an end to the game.

As he turned reluctantly back toward the flat he'd been calling home for the past few days, he was conscious of a certain irony in the fact that innocent children's games should be played in this spot where so much blood had been shed during France's chaotic march through history. It occurred to him that maybe there was a parallel, too, between those bumps and unexpected turns that were a natural part of growing children into adulthood, and the war, violence and turmoil countries seemed destined to endure on the way to becoming peaceful, democratic nations.

Certainly, in the past several months, Silvershire, the island country of his birth and of his heart, had experienced more than its share of that violence—murder, blackmail, attempted murder, conspiracy, terrorist bombings and assassination plots against the ruling family. Acts of violence in which he, Nikolas Donovan, had been suspected, if not openly accused, of complicity. Now the country seemed poised on the brink of outright rebellion—a rebellion Nikolas was assuredly guilty, at least in part, of fomenting.

He hadn't wanted rebellion.

Change, yes. He'd worked all his life for change. But not by violence. Never by violence.

But now change had come, and with a vengeance. Catastrophic change. Just not quite the way he'd expected.

The temporary lightness of heart he'd enjoyed while

watching the soccer game sifted away, and he felt it again—the cringing coldness in his chest, the hollow tapping of a pulse deep in his belly—the symptoms that came to him now whenever he remembered his life had been turned upside down.

Dusk had fallen. Lights were winking on in the trees and bridges and on the tour boats cruising up and down the river, and lovers were strolling the pathways along the riverbank hand in hand, taking advantage of the lovely late-summer evening. Paris would always be a city for lovers. Feeling more alienated and alone than ever, Nikolas quickened his steps toward home.

On a quiet tree-lined street not far from the Eiffel Tower he paused to look up at the third-floor windows of the borrowed flat that was his temporary refuge now. He wasn't sure what made him do that—perhaps a habit of caution learned from his life as a rebel with a cause, accustomed to watching his own back. Or maybe simply stealing a moment to appreciate the charm of the grand old buildings with their balconies and tall mullioned windows framed by creeping vines. Whatever the reason for that quick, casual glance, the move that followed it was launched by pure instinct, and it was not in the least casual. He slipped into the shadows between trees and parked cars and became utterly and completely still while he studied the window of his supposedly empty apartment where, a moment before, he was absolutely certain he'd seen something move.

The movement didn't come again, but never for a moment did he believe it had been a trick of the eye. Unlikely as it seemed, someone or something had just entered his flat through the balcony window.

All his senses were on full alert as he quickly crossed the street and let himself into the building. Inside he paused again to listen, but it was quiet as a mausoleum; most Parisians would still be out and about this early on such an evening, at least until the forecast rain arrived.

The quaint old staircase with its ornate wrought-iron balusters and railings that spiraled up through the center of the building seemed to hang unsupported above him in the shadows as he curled his fingers into a fist around the keys and began to climb. His heart was pounding, sweat trickling coldly down his back, and not from the exertion of the climb. Nikolas made a point of keeping himself in shape. He was no adrenaline junky, but with everything that had been happening in Silvershire lately, a certain amount of paranoia seemed not only healthy, but prudent—perhaps even vital.

He mounted the last flight of stairs on tiptoe and moved soundlessly down the hallway, footsteps swallowed by the carpet runner. At the door to his flat he paused one last time to consider the situation, which was, the way he saw it, as follows: Someone had entered the flat through the balcony window. That someone either was or was not still in the flat. If not, he'd have a little mystery to solve at his leisure. On the other hand, if someone *was* in the flat, odds seemed against whoever it was being there for friendly purposes.

It had been a good eight years since his military service and commando training, but he was gratified to feel his mind and body shifting gears, settling into that particular state of quiet readiness he thought he'd forgotten. He could almost hear the hum of his heightened senses as he took hold of the doorknob and silently turned it.

The flat was in shadows, the darkness not yet complete. He'd left no light burning, but everything seemed as he'd left it. Aware that the slightly brighter backdrop of the hallway must cast him in silhouette, he stepped quickly into the room and closed the door behind him, checking as he did so for a body that may have been flattened against the wall behind it. Then he paused again, the old-fashioned metal key gripped in his hand like a weapon, and sniffed the air.

The room was empty now, he could feel it. But moments ago *someone* had been here, someone who had left traces, a faint aura…a scent too delicate and ephemeral to be aftershave or perfume.

Something about that scent jolted him with an untimely sense of déjà vu. But before the feeling could coalesce into thought, he received a different kind of jolt entirely—a shock-wave of pure adrenaline.

*There—a movement.* Swift and furtive, just on the edges of his field of vision. The window curtain, stirring where no breezes blew.

Nikolas was naturally athletic and very quick for a big man. Moving swiftly and soundlessly, like a creature of the night himself, he crossed the room and slipped through the open casement window onto the balcony. In the fast-fading twilight he could see a figure dressed in black standing frozen beside the balcony railing. He heard a sound…saw a hand come up and extend toward him…and before the sound could become speech or the hand activate whatever death-dealing object it may have been holding, he launched himself toward the intruder, going in low, aiming for the knees.

He was a little surprised at how easy it was. There was no resistance at all, in fact, just a soft gasp when he drove his shoulder into a surprisingly slim midsection, then a somewhat louder *"Oof!"* as his momentum carried both him and the intruder to the balcony's plaster floor. With that slender body pinned half under him, Nikolas caught both wrists and jerked them roughly to the small of the intruder's back.

It was over just that quickly—so quickly, in fact, that it took another second or two for Nikolas's senses to catch up with his reactions, and for him to realize that, A. his would-be assailant carried no weapon, and B. wasn't a "he" at all. Wrists that slender, a bottom so nicely rounded and fitting so sweetly against his belly, that elusive scent…those could only belong to a woman.

The revelation didn't induce him to relax his vigilance or ease his grip, however. If there was anything he'd learned from the recent events in his homeland, it was that assassins came in all sizes and both genders. And that no one—*no one*—could be trusted.

"I expected someone with a bit more in the way of fighting skills," he said through gritted teeth, his face half-buried in the woman's warm, humid nape. The smell of her hair made his head swim.

*That scent…I know it…from somewhere.*

"I have skills…you can't even imagine," his prisoner replied in a breathless, constricted voice. "Just didn't think… it'd be smart…to kick a future king…where it'd hurt the most. Not exactly…a brilliant career move, you know? Plus… there's that little matter…of you being required to produce an heir…"

That remark, as well as the fact that the woman's accent was distinctly of the American South, barely registered. "Who are you? Who sent you? Was it Weston? Carrington? *Who,* damn you?"

"Neither. Well…sort of— Look, if you'll get off me and let me up so I can get to my ID…"

"Not a chance." An ingrained habit of courtesy under similar physical circumstances did induce him to take some of his weight off the woman—a concession he made sure to compensate for by tightening his grip on her wrists. She wasn't showing much inclination to resist, but he wasn't ready to take anything for granted. "I'll get it. Where is it?"

She gave an irritable-sounding snort. "Oh for God's sake. It's in my jacket—inside pocket. Left side. Just don't—"

He was already in the process of shifting both himself and his prisoner onto their sides so he could slip his hand inside her jacket, which was leather and as far as he could tell, fitted her like her own skin. It closed with a zipper which was pulled all the way up, almost to her chin. "Don't…what?" He found the tab and jerked it down, impatient with it and with his own senses for noticing and passing on to him at such an inopportune moment how supple and buttery soft the leather was, almost indistinguishable from her skin, in fact…and how warm and fragrant her hair…*and what was that damn scent, anyway?*

He thrust his hand inside the jacket opening…and froze.

"Never mind." A rich chuckle—hers—seemed to ripple down the length of his body as his hand closed—entirely of its own volition, he'd swear—over a breast of unanticipated voluptuousness. Furthermore, the only barrier between his hand and that seductive bounty was something silky, lacy and, he felt certain, incredibly thin. A chemise? It seemed to him an unlikely choice of attire for an assassin.

And the nipple nested in his palm was already hardening, nudging the nerve-rich hollow of his hand with each of her quickened breaths in a way that seemed almost playful. As if, he thought, she were deliberately taunting him. Testing his self-control.

A growl of desperation and fury vibrated deep in his throat. He tried again to shift his weight to give his hand more room to maneuver inside the jacket and only succeeded in bringing her bottom into even closer contact with the part of his own anatomy least subject to his will.

"You're not going to have much luck finding it where you're looking," she remarked, her voice bumpy with what he was sure must be suppressed laughter.

"I'm so glad you're finding this entertaining," he said in his stuffiest, British old-school tone, feeling more sweaty and flustered than he had since his own schoolboy years in that country. "Forgive me if I don't share your amusement… These days I don't consider— *Ah!*" With a sense of profound relief, he withdrew his hand from its enticing prison, a thin leather folder captured triumphantly between two fingers. "Yes—*here* we are."

"How are you going to look at it? It's dark out here." The woman pinned beneath him now seemed as overheated and winded as he, and her body heat was merging with his in steamy intimacy that should have been unwelcome between two strangers—or, he thought, at the very least, unsettling. Exotic. Instead there was that odd familiarity, as if he'd been in this exact same place, with this same woman, before.

The situation was becoming intolerable. Nikolas levered himself to his feet, hauling his unwelcome visitor with him. "Come on—inside. Now." His natural bent toward gallantry deserted him as he hauled her none too gently through the casement window.

"This really isn't necessary," she panted, and he was grimly pleased to note there was no laughter, suppressed or otherwise, in her voice now. "If I'd wanted to leave we wouldn't be having this conversation."

"Yes, and then the question becomes, why are you here at all, doesn't it?" He quick-marched her across the shadowy room to the light switch beside the front door, and flipped it on, filling the room with the soft light from an art deco chandelier. "Now then, let's see who… Ah—the Lazlo Group. I say—I'm impressed. And you are—" And he halted, the ID in his hand forgotten…or irrelevant.

*That face.*

The face he'd half convinced himself must be a fantasy.

She was the fantasy every heterosexual male past the age of awareness must have entertained at least once. The impossibly beautiful woman who came from out of nowhere to land—almost literally—in his lap, proceeded to make passionate love to him and then…vanished without a trace.

*The summer between his second and third years at Oxford… Nikolas was interning with Silvershire's diplomatic mission to Paris. He'd been to a reception at the embassy in honor of the newly appointed ambassador from Spain, where the wine had flowed rather freely. He returned to his hotel in a not entirely unpleasant state of fuzzy-headedness. The weather had turned hot and muggy, and that combined with his mild intoxication had made him too warm to sleep, so, in the hope of clearing his head and cooling his body, he'd stepped out onto the balcony.*

He was leaning on the railing, enjoying a breathtaking nighttime view of the Eiffel Tower and contemplating the possible sobering effects of a cold shower when it happened. Someone—a body—a woman's body—clad all in black and lithe and supple as a cat's, seemed to fall right out of the night sky. Fell on top of him and knocked him flat.

Perhaps it was the wine he'd drunk, but he didn't feel terribly alarmed by this odd occurrence. Merely—understandably—a bit surprised. As he lay on his back gazing up into what he was certain was the most beautiful face he'd ever seen in his life—rather feline, like the rest of her, he decided, with wide cheekbones and pointed chin, and exotically tilted eyes— the woman placed her finger against his lips and whispered, "Shhh…" Then she lowered her head and kissed him.

Not a casual brushing of the lips, meant to be an expression of thanks for breaking her fall, perhaps, or even a droll bit of teasing. No—this was the kiss of fantasy; deep and warm and lush, it seemed to vault right over all those bothersome—to a young lad's way of thinking—preliminary stages of intimacy, and plunge straight to the heart and soul of the matter: Sex! And the lithe and supple body squirming into even more intimate alignment with his seemed to second that idea most heartily.

Nikolas's state of shock-induced paralysis didn't last long; his was not a passive nature. But as his body was flaring to life like a gas burner under a lighted match, he heard a preemptory masculine voice somewhere above his head say loudly, "Excuse me, you didn't happen to see— Oh, I say!"

Opening his eyes and aiming them—as much as was possible under the circumstances—in the direction of the voice, Nikolas saw a man's head hovering atop the half wall that separated his balcony from the one next to it.

"Terribly sorry—excuse the intrusion—Pardon, Monsieur…" The head disappeared, and the string of apologies died to an annoyed but unintelligible mutter on the other side of the wall.

*It was several more enjoyable—and volatile—seconds
before the woman detached her mouth from his, and even that
process she managed to turn into a sensual adventure. With
her lips separated from his only by their warm mingled breath,
she murmured a pleased and rather surprised, "Hmm..."
And then she lowered her mouth again.*

*He suspected she meant it to be a briefer kiss this time, a
sweet, perhaps regretful, farewell peck. But Nikolas had had
enough of games, at least the way this one was being played—
according to her rules. Before she knew what he was about, he
tightened his arms around her and rolled her under him, and
knew a fierce, hot shaft of pleasure at her gasp of surprise.*

*"Who are you? What the hell is this?" he asked in a rasp-
ing whisper. He could feel her heart beating a wild tattoo
against his chest.*

*And her catlike eyes narrowed and tilted with her smile as
she whispered back, "Serendipity."*

"Rhia de Hayes," Rhia said, eyeing her assignment as she
might a tiger who'd stopped suddenly in midspring and begun
instead to purr and rub his head against her legs. The smile that
had flared so unexpectedly in his fierce gray eyes to spread like
sunlight over his rather austere features was intriguing, for
sure, and she had to admit she liked it a lot better than the frown.
But she didn't trust it for a moment. What it reminded her of
was a limerick she'd heard somewhere, about a young lady
who'd smiled as she went for a ride on a tiger. As Rhia recalled
the limerick, when they'd returned from that ride the lady was
inside, and the smile was on the face of the tiger.

*What is he smiling about? As if he knows something...as
if he knows me. But we've never met before. Have we?*

Uncertainty wasn't a condition Rhia suffered often, or
well. But so far this whole assignment hadn't gone as expected, and that had her feeling off balance. She liked losing
control of situations even less than she liked being unsure of

herself, and she meant to remedy that state of affairs as quickly as possible. Rhia de Hayes had never failed to complete an assignment successfully, and she wasn't about to sully that record now.

Of course, none of her previous assignments had been quite like this one. Her specialty within the Lazlo Group was retrieving lost children of the rich, royal or famous, and while it was true that this was undoubtedly the offspring of a man who could claim to be all three of those things, there was nothing even remotely childlike about Nikolas Donovan.

*Except for that damn smile. There's mischief in that smile. Reminds me of a kid hiding a big ol' bullfrog behind his back.*

"So, Rhia de Hayes…they've sent you to 'bring me in,' I expect," he said as he handed back her ID. His eyes were veiled now, and his voice was that languid upper-class vaguely British drawl she'd always found so annoying. "What were you planning to do, conk me on the head, heave me over your shoulder and haul me back to Silvershire?"

"I was *plannin'* on checkin' the place while you were gone," Rhia said, leaning heavily on the nasal Cajun twang of her childhood; she could out-drawl just about anybody on the planet, if that was the way he was going to be. She glared at him as she tucked the ID back in her inside jacket pocket, inadvertently allowing him another glimpse of the silk chemise that had apparently so unnerved him before. And she reveled in the spark of response that flared in his cool gray eyes. Veiling the triumph in hers, she said accusingly, "You came back early. I figured you'd be havin' supper out."

"It was going to rain," Nikolas said with a dismissive shrug, "and I didn't have an umbrella. So, what was it you hoped to find hidden away amongst my socks and tightie whities? Guns, knives, explosives? Leaflets inciting the violent overthrow of the monarchy? Evidence of what a dangerous fellow I am?"

"Oh, I think I know what a dangerous fellow you are," Rhia said, and instantly wanted to bite off her tongue. Not only was it an inappropriate comment to make to a royal heir, but the voice that uttered it had turned low and husky, become almost a growl. It wasn't as though she'd never heard such a sound coming from her own throat before—on…certain occasions, yes, but never under these circumstances. Not while on a job, put it that way.

She wasn't sure which surprised her most, that or the small vibration that had begun to hum somewhere deep inside her chest.

Half angry with herself, she tore away the clip that had held her hair clubbed tightly to the back of her head and shook the thick dark waves down to her shoulders.

"You could easily have beat a hasty retreat when you heard me at the door," Nikolas remarked in a relaxed, conversational tone. "I assume you had an escape route planned. Why didn't you use it?" As he spoke, his gaze followed the motions of her hand and hair, his gray eyes heavy-lidded and amused, as if he knew exactly the effect he was having on her.

*Of course he knows, dummy.* Rhia repressed a shiver as she became intensely conscious of the cool silk of her chemise licking across her hardened nipples. How could he not know, when the evidence was right here in front of his face?

But to zip up her jacket now would be an admission of awareness she wasn't willing to make, and besides, she'd never been shy about her body. If it was going to go shivery and shameless over Nik Donovan, well…so be it. It wouldn't affect her ability to do the job she'd come to do.

And, if it came to that, she was also well aware of the effect her body had on members of the opposite sex, and she wasn't above using it to distract an opponent, if the occasion demanded.

*When did the assignment become my opponent?*

She faced this one unflinchingly and inhaled deeply, and smiled at the slight but unmistakable hitch she detected in his breathing. "I'd planned on coming back and knocking on your door. Talking to you—you know, like a civilized human being, one to another? Figured since I was already here I might as well save some time, see if I could persuade you to do the right thing and come back with me voluntarily."

Nikolas folded his arms on his chest. He was smiling too, now, a lazy, arrogant smile that caused an immediate and automatic elevation of her hackles. "And if that didn't work?"

She gave her head an airy toss and broadened her smile to a 'gator grin. "I planned to conk you on the head, throw you over my shoulder and haul you back to Silvershire."

He laughed, briefly but out loud, something she suspected he didn't do often. He made no comment, though, as the promised rain chose that moment to announce its arrival with a rush of cool wind that set the curtains to dancing and carried a mist of droplets into the room. Nikolas straightened and strode quickly to the balcony doors. He closed and latched them and twitched the curtains across the black rain-spangled glass, then turned to give her a leisurely up-and-down appraisal.

"It would appear you also are without an umbrella," he said mildly, lifting one eyebrow—an ability she lacked, and coveted. "I seriously doubt you'll find a taxi just now. Since I suppose this means you'll be staying for dinner, may I offer you a glass of wine?"

She shook her head, both in bemusement and in refusal of the offer of wine—she had no intention of letting anything slow her reflexes or cloud her judgment, not with this man. And although he seemed completely at ease, now, and was being effortlessly charming, she thought again of the smiling tiger.

She decided it wouldn't be necessary to tell him she had no intention of calling a taxi, or, in fact, of leaving him at all. Fact was, she wasn't about to let Nikolas Donovan out of her sight until she had delivered him safely into the arms of his father, the king of Silvershire.

## Chapter 2

Rhia stood in the entrance to the apartment's tiny kitchen and watched the recently discovered "lost" heir to the throne of Silvershire take a stoppered bottle of wine out of the tiny refrigerator.

He turned to make an offering gesture toward her with the bottle. "Are you quite certain you won't join me? It's rather nice for a rosé, actually. Fellow who lent me this flat comes from a wine-making family down in Provence—he's left an apparently bottomless supply."

She shook her head, and he responded with a shrug that seemed to her more French than British. It was what came of growing up in an island kingdom located halfway between those two countries, she thought, as she watched him pour himself a half glassful and lift it to his lips. She couldn't imagine why observing that mundane activity should make her mouth water; she wasn't terribly fond of wine. She seldom drank at all, but when she did, she preferred bourbon whiskey. Straight.

His eyes, meeting hers above the rim of his glass, crinkled suddenly. He lowered the glass. "Oh, hell—of course, you're on the job, aren't you? Do forgive me. Perhaps a glass of water? Cup of tea?"

"I'm from South Louisiana," Rhia said drily. "We Cajuns aren't all that much for tea." Well, hell, if he was going to play the British fop again—badly overplaying it, in her opinion, and she didn't know what his game was or whether to be amused by it or annoyed—she figured her trailer-park Cajun could trump his Oxford Brit any day of the week.

"Ah, yes—coffee would be your drink of choice, I imagine. Made with—what's that other…" He snapped his fingers impatiently.

"Chicory," she grudgingly supplied, then tilted her head. "How'd you come to know a thing like that?"

His chuckle was dry, his smile sardonic. "I know a little about a great many things, my dear." He waved the wineglass in a sweeping gesture. "My education has been…shall we say, eclectic? Wide-ranging?"

"An education fit for a man who would be king," Rhia said softly.

He snorted—a most unprincely sound. "An education attained courtesy of some very good scholarships and a lot of hellish hard work, which I doubt could be said of most royals." He paused, and his lips curled with disdain he made no effort to hide. "Not the one I knew personally, at any rate."

"Reginald, you mean. Yes, you two were at Eton together, weren't you?"

"And Oxford." Nikolas gazed at his wine as if it had gone sour. "Look, I am sorry he's dead—God knows I wouldn't wish for anyone to be murdered that way—poisoned, I mean—but the man was an arrogant, insufferable prick, if you want to know. And not fit to govern a frat house, much less a country."

"Ah," said Rhia, smiling slightly, "but he never got the

chance, did he? And, as it turns out, he wasn't even the prince after all."

Instead of answering, he took a quick gulp of wine and set his glass down with a careless clank. Turning abruptly, he opened a cupboard door and took out an espresso maker which he placed on the countertop, plugged into a wall outlet and set about filling with an ease and efficiency that spoke of some degree of familiarity with the process.

Watching the movements of his hands, Rhia felt again that odd little quiver beneath her breastbone. His glossy dark hair might be in need of a trim, and a day's growth of beard might be shadowing his jaw, but there was no denying the grace in the lines of his body, the power in the breadth of his shoulders, the authority in the set of his chin, the intelligence in those intense gray eyes. And all of it, she thought, completely natural to him.

*It must be in his genes. Even here, in this little bitty kitchen, making coffee for uninvited company, he looks like he was born to be a king.*

"You can come in and sit down—I promise not to bite you." He threw the brittle invitation over his shoulder as he worked, and Rhia gave a guilty start, as if his long list of royal attributes might include the ability to read minds.

She shook her head and smiled, but stayed where she was. Prince or not, the kitchen was too small a space to hold two people who weren't already on intimate terms.

*Intimate.* The word sprang into her head from out of nowhere and sat pulsing in her brain like the neon lights on a Mississippi River casino boat.

"Tell me something." He gave her another look, this one as sharp and keen as any scrutiny she'd ever received from Walker Shaw, the shrink who'd done her psych evaluation when she joined the Lazlo Group. "How does a nice American girl from Louisiana come to be working for Corbett Lazlo?"

She gave him back a smile she knew would dazzle but tell him nothing. "Ah, that's a long story."

Still his gaze lingered, intent enough to kick-start that hum in her chest again, and, as they often did when she felt ill at ease, her fingers went of their own volition to the small silver charm that hung from a narrow chain around her neck, nestled in the hollow at the base of her throat. She rubbed it idly as she watched Nikolas shrug and go back to measuring dark roasted coffee beans into the grinder.

He switched it on, and for the next few seconds the racket made conversation impossible. The grinding completed, Nikolas poured water into the espresso machine, closed and secured the lid and punched a button. He turned back to her, then, and picked up his glass of wine and the thread of conversation he'd temporarily put aside.

"Might I ask what your specialty is with the Lazlo Group? You do seem an unlikely choice of field agent to send after a notorious suspected terrorist." This time a smile crinkled the corners of the eyes studying her across the rim of the wineglass, though it didn't diminish their intensity one bit.

"My specialty?" Her smile was small and wicked. "I locate and retrieve lost children."

Caught in mid swallow, Nikolas gave a sputter of laughter and quickly lowered his glass. He touched the back of his hand to his mouth and managed to say in a choked voice, "A lot of call for that, is there?"

"Unfortunately, yes." She wasn't smiling now.

"I'm well aware of the sad state of the world," Nikolas said, matching the new seriousness of her tone as he stared at the contents of his glass. He'd been enjoying himself entirely too much, he realized, given the fact that it was this woman's intention to fetch him back to Silvershire whether he wanted to go or not. That he could enjoy himself at all, under any circumstances, was surprising in itself. It had been rather a long time since he'd found anything in his life amusing. "I meant in the context of the Lazlo Group, of course. Isn't their clientele pretty much limited to the rich, royal or famous?"

"Theirs is," she replied shortly. "Mine isn't."

"Meaning?"

"Meaning, the ability to take cases pro bono when it suits me is one of the conditions of my...shall we say, employment agreement."

"I'm impressed." He was, too. He hadn't thought there was anybody on the planet who could dictate terms to Corbett Lazlo, and that included royalty. He sipped wine while he studied the woman lounging with easy grace in his kitchen doorway. Tall and lithe, but curvy as well—truly an amazing body, as he had ample reason to know, and he really did need to discipline his mind past those recent memories of her. Under the circumstances, they were proving entirely too distracting. He couldn't afford to be distracted with this one; he had a feeling if she'd intended to take him by force he'd already be hog-tied and on a plane bound for Silvershire, so it was a safe bet she must have something else up her sleeve. "I gather, then, that you're quite good at what you do. Might I ask how you go about it—this business of finding lost children?"

She smiled, the enigmatic little Mona Lisa smile he'd seen before. "Oh, the Lazlo Group has resources you can't even imagine." The smile vanished again—fascinating, the way it came and went, like the sun playing hide-and-seek with clouds. Something he couldn't identify flickered in her eyes, and her hand went again to whatever it was she wore on that silver chain around her neck. He couldn't quite make out what it was—something oddly shaped but familiar as well—and it was beginning to intrigue him.

"And then," she went on in an entirely different kind of voice, "I suppose I probably just have the knack."

"The knack?"

She shifted, as if the door frame against her back had grown uncomfortable. "Instinct. You know—a sixth sense. I just always have been good at finding people. Particularly kids."

"Ah. You mean, like second sight?"

She gave him a brief, hard look. Suspected him of mocking her, he imagined. Which he wasn't; he'd seen too much of the world and of things in it that defied logical explanation to scoff at the unknown and unproven. When it came to the mysteries of the human mind, he preferred to keep his open.

The espresso machine chose that moment to erupt with a gurgling, hissing cloud of fragrant steam, and the last thing he saw before he turned to attend to it was Rhia's lush pink lips tightening and her long slender throat rippling as she bit back and swallowed whatever it was she'd been about to say.

*Second sight? Yeah, that was what Mama called it. Her gift to me. Now it's the only thing I have of her, except my music and my memories. And this necklace.*

Rhia fingered it briefly as she watched her assignment—and host—pour steaming black liquid into a tiny cup and place it on the table along with a spoon and a bowl filled with sugar cubes, and was thankful for the lifelong habit of self-control that made her keep those thoughts inside.

"I don't suppose you'd have any hot milk?" She kept her voice as bland as the request.

He lifted that damned eyebrow. "Milk? Sorry."

"That's okay, I'm adaptable." She pushed away from the door frame. It was only two short steps to the kitchen table, but her pulse quickened as if it was a tiger's den she'd entered.

She sat in the nearest of the two chairs and shifted it so the small arched window and its rain-blurred view of the Paris lights was at her back. She stirred a sinful amount of sugar into the espresso—she hated cubed sugar because it always seemed as though someone might be keeping count. *How many, dear, one lump, or two? Yeah, right. How about...ten?* Then she settled back with one elbow propped on the tabletop to watch the future king of Silvershire take eggs and a variety of other things out of the fridge and scatter them across the sink and countertop with the reckless abandon of a gourmet chef.

*The future king…* How remote and unreal that seemed to her now, with her pulse tap-tapping away and that strange little vibration humming somewhere deep inside her chest and an intense awareness of silk slithering over her naked skin—because what, after all, could be more of a turn-on to a woman than watching a smolderingly handsome and mysterious man cook dinner for her?

She took a cautious sip of the potent coffee—though Lord knew she didn't need any more stimulation—and tried to coax her mind into placing the man presently whacking merrily away at a pile of mushrooms into his proper setting, one that included his royal peers—the Grimaldis of Monaco…the DuPonts of Gastonia…the Dutch and the British royals. But her rebellious mind kept returning, like a drunk to his bottle, to the memory of what his body had felt like, out there on the balcony, lying full-length on top of hers.

And why did that memory kindle another, one that flared bright for frustratingly brief moments, then before she could grasp it, vanished into the darkness of her mind like a lightning bug in a bayou summer night?

"I'd give a lot more than a penny to know what you're thinking right now."

Rhia blinked the heir to Silvershire's crown into focus and found him studying her with—naturally—one eyebrow a notch higher than the other, and a similar tilt to his smile.

"It would take more than you've got to find out," she retorted, and gave up, for the moment, trying to think of him as royalty. After all, she reminded herself, at the moment he was merely Nikolas Donovan, college professor, rabble-rouser, rebel and fugitive, and she was the special agent hired to bring him in. "But," she added after a moment, "since

you're cooking me dinner, I guess I can give you one for free."
She paused. "You have to know I feel a little odd about that—
you fixing me dinner. Considering you're the future—"

"Look," he interrupted, before she could say the K-word
again, "You're here, it's time to eat—what did you expect me
to do?" A smile slashed crookedly across his austere features
again. "Ask *you* to do the cooking?"

"I've known men who would," Rhia said drily.

"Ah. Well." He watched his hands maneuver the knife
across the chopping board. "Since I grew up without benefit
of a mum, I suppose I never acquired the prevailing attitude
that a woman's primary purpose is to serve a man."

"Oh, wow," she said in an awed tone. "You really are a rev-
olutionary, aren't you? My mama would have loved you."

He glanced at her, his eyes unexpectedly gentle. "*Would*
have. She's gone, then, your mum?"

She nodded, and found to her surprise and dismay that it
was the only answer she was capable of giving him just then.
Where had it come from, she wondered, this bright shaft of
pain and loss, like a lightning strike out of a clear blue sky?

Nikolas watched her struggle with it, soft mouth and
pointed chin gone vulnerable as a child's, those exotic golden
eyes fierce as a tiger's, and her fingers once again fondling
the tiny silver charm at her throat. Something shivered through
him, a new awareness, a magnetic tugging he was pretty sure
had nothing to do with sex.

"Sorry to hear that," he said, careful not to let too much
softness into his voice, suspecting it wouldn't take much in
the way of sympathy to send her scurrying for cover. "When
did she die?"

"When I was eighteen."

"Ah—well—" he broke an egg and plopped it into a bowl
"— at least you had a chance to know her."

He heard her take a breath, sharp and deep. He knew she
had herself in hand again when she said with a soft, breathy

chuckle, "What I remember most about my mama is her laugh, you know? She had this great big laugh, and when she laughed, her eyes sparkled. She laughed a lot, too. My mama did know how to have a good time."

He broke a few more eggs into the bowl. "You had a happy childhood, then." He glanced up when she gave a bitter-sounding snort.

"Yeah, I did. Until my father came and took me away from it."

Before Nikolas could reply, she rose abruptly, frowning. If she had been a cat, he thought, her tail would surely have been twitching.

"Mind if I use your…what do you Silvershirers call it? The loo?"

"Do you mean the bathroom?" He said it with the deadpan courtesy of a butler he'd once known and gestured with the whisk in his hand. "It's that way—next to the bedroom."

She slipped from the room like a cat through fog, and left him with a bowlful of eggs on which to beat off his bemusement and frustration.


"You're a pretty good cook, Donovan, even if you don't have any Tabasco," Rhia remarked, studying the last bite of her omelette before popping it into her mouth. As she chewed, her expression grew thoughtful. "Not that that surprises me— you cooking, I mean, not the Tabasco. I imagine you're good at whatever you take a mind to do."

"Thank you," Nikolas said, with only a hint of a smile. He was glad to see she'd recovered her aplomb, since he'd found she was a much nicer person when she felt she had the upper hand.

"Tell you what does surprise me, though," she went on as if he hadn't spoken. "I never would've taken you for a coward."

It took some doing, but he kept his expression bland. "A coward, you say. Really."

To his further bemusement, she wiggled in her chair and said in a testy tone, "Oh, stop it. I hate it when you do that."

"Do what?" The woman did have a way of keeping him hopping off balance. He didn't know whether he found it amusing or demoralizing.

She waved her finger in a circling motion. "That...that *thing* with your eyebrow."

"My *eyebrow?*"

"Yes. It goes up. Just one. The other doesn't. It's damned annoying, if you want to know."

"Really." He leaned back in his chair and gazed at her, trying his best not to elevate any of his facial features. "I had no idea. Well, I shall endeavor to keep my various body parts under better control, if it offends you. Now, what was it you were saying about me being a coward?"

She returned his gaze with a narrow stare of her own, as if she suspected him again of mocking her. Then she gave a shrug and pushed back her plate. "Well, you did run away."

"Ah. Yes. There is that." He scrubbed a hand over his face, as if doing so could rub away the tiredness and confusion that were like a veil of cobwebs over his brain at times. Then he tried a sardonic smile. "I prefer to think of it as a strategic retreat."

"Look—Nikolas—"

He held up a hand to stop her there. "Miss de Hayes—Rhia. Try and put yourself in my shoes. Six months ago the heir to the throne of Silvershire is found dead in his mountain retreat—murdered. So who do you suppose shot directly to the top of the list of probable suspects? Right you are—an organization bent on doing away with that very same monarchy, an organization known as the Union for Democracy, of which I happen to be founder and de facto head."

"Yes," Rhia said, frowning, "but your group was considered an unlikely candidate for Reginald's murder, since it's well-known you've never advocated the use of violence."

"Ah, but that didn't stop the rumors, did it? Especially

after the king's collapse due to the grief and strain of his son's death. There were rumors Reginald was being blackmailed, rumors of terrorism, of hostile invasion or violent revolution. Rumors of a split in the UFD, with a violent faction taking over control. Even after I met with Russell—Lord Carrington—to reassure him—"

"Just because they're called rumors doesn't mean they can't be true," Rhia said quietly.

Nikolas looked at her for a moment in silence. Then he pushed his plate aside and leaned back in his chair with a careless wave of his hand. "It's true there've been some... things going on in the UFD I'm not happy about. There've always been members of the group who are somewhat...shall we say, less than patient with the slow-grinding wheels of change, which is what we've advocated up to now. That faction seems to be growing of late. But I see that as a *result* of the unrest surrounding the monarchy, rather than the *cause* of it."

"Sort of a We-should-strike-while-the-iron's-hot attitude?"

His smile was brief and wry. "Something like that."

"How did you get involved with the organization?" She asked this in a conversational way, leaning forward with an expression of great interest, though Nikolas was fairly certain whatever dossier the Lazlo Group had on him would have included that bit of information.

Still, she was a treat to look at and fun to spar with, and he didn't mind playing along once again. So he settled back, outwardly relaxed but inwardly alert, and replied, "When I was in college, actually. That's when we got organized. Before that, my uncle Silas—the man who raised me—had already gotten me interested in the idea of bringing about an end to monarchy in Silvershire."

"You say...your uncle. That would be..."

"My father's brother."

"Ah," she said, those feline eyes of hers intent again, "but now we know he couldn't have been your father's brother, could he?"

An expected surge of anger hardened his voice. "So *you* say. So *they* say. If you ask me, it's all ridiculous nonsense." *Please, God, let it be so.*

*This is hard for him,* she thought. *His whole life, who he is, his perspective—everything has changed.*

She knew how that felt. She'd had only a few short years to be Rhia de Hayes in a Louisiana trailer park with her mama and her big laugh and sparkling eyes, where there was always music and dancing and good things to eat and she could run barefoot all summer long. Then one day everything had changed, her world and everything in it—her home, her school, her friends, her clothes, even her name had changed. As everything would change for this man.

She wondered if he was thinking now, Who the hell is Nikolas Donovan? Who am I?

She said gently, "I'm afraid it's not nonsense. You are the biological offspring of King Henry Weston and his late wife, Queen Alexis. DNA proves that, and DNA doesn't lie, Nikolas."

He said nothing, only burned her with his smoldering eyes.

"I'm curious, though. What did your—uh, Silas Donovan—tell you about your parents? That they were dead, I assume, but what was supposed to have happened to them?"

His mouth hardened. "My parents were patriots—some would say traitors, I suppose. Insurgents—anti-royal activists—call them what you will, it was Weston's people that had them killed. It was supposed to have been a road accident. Their car was forced off the road—went over the cliffs near Leonia into the sea. Their bodies were never found."

"Oh, ouch." Rhia winced. "So you were pretty much programmed to hate King Weston from birth, weren't you?"

"I don't hate the man." He rose abruptly, swept up her plate along with his and carried them the two short steps to the sink.

*No...I don't think you have it in you to hate.* Rhia studied him thoughtfully, quivering inside again with that strange sense of recognition. *But where do I know you from, Donovan? I know we've met before. I know it.*

"I don't even think he's that bad a king," he said with his back to her, and she could see the tension in his neck and shoulders, hear it in his voice. "I just don't think something as important as running a country should be determined by an accident of birth. Can you imagine Silvershire in the hands of that spoiled, selfish twit, *Reginald?*"

"Well, it didn't happen, did it?" said Rhia. "Someone made sure of that. What do you think of the current regent, Lord Russell Carrington, by the way? I know you've met with him. He seems to be doing a decent job filling in for the king while he's been out of commission."

"Carrington's a decent man. Probably make a decent head of state as well." He jerked around, eyes gone dark and fierce, and she was aware once again of how small the kitchen was, and how big Nikolas Donovan seemed standing in it. "Look— that's not the point. No man should have the right to rule without the consent of the people he's ruling. This is the twenty-first century. The people—"

Rhia held up both hands in mock surrender. "Hey, you don't have to explain democracy to me—I'm an American, remember? Anyway, back to the issue at hand. You're going to have to face this sooner or later, Nikolas. You do know that, don't you?"

"Of course, I do." He was silent again, staring past her at the rain-splashed window glass. She waited, and after a moment he drew a breath and shook his head. "It came at me too damn fast. I needed to think a bit." Another pause, and then he drilled her with his intent gray eyes. "I went to ask Silas, you know. It was the first thing I did when I heard the...rumors. I suppose I wanted him to explain, or some such thing." His eyes went bleak.

"And?"

He shrugged, and his mouth twisted and settled into

hard, angry lines. "Couldn't find him. Wasn't at his apartment in Dunford, hadn't been to his job at the college in days. Don't know where he's got to. I know I want to hear it from him, and until I do, as far as I'm concerned it's just that—rumors."

It was Rhia's turn to be silent and thoughtful as she watched Silvershire's reluctant prince run hot water and scrub egg off frying pan and dinner plates. She was remembering the rich, velvety voice on the phone that was her only contact with her boss, the founder and head of the Lazlo Group.

*Nikolas Donovan can be a hard man. Never forget that. He's also intelligent, resourceful, charming and suave.*

*I've heard he's something of a fanatic,* Rhia had said.

*Not a fanatic,* Corbett Lazlo had responded after a brief pause. *He's too intelligent for that kind of insanity. Donovan's a reasonable man. Focused, yes. Passionate...but capable of iron self-control. It would be a grave mistake to underestimate him.*

*Wonderful,* Rhia had thought then. *Just what I need—another powerful, bullheaded man determined to have his way.*

A small shiver passed through her body now, as she gazed at the broad and powerful shoulders, the rich sable hair curling slightly on the back of a smooth sun-bronzed neck. So far she'd seen the suave sophisticate, the smiling charmer, the intelligent man, the hard man. She wondered what the passionate man would be like...and what it would take to test his iron will.

"Lord Carrington was ready to arrest you," she remarked. "I assume you knew that when you ran. Were you aware that Danielle Cavanaugh—the assassin known as the Sparrow—named *you,* before she died, as the man who hired her to kill Reginald?"

His laugh was brief and harsh. "Nothing much surprises me these days, you know." He turned, drying his hands on a dishtowel. "Considering what's happened in Silvershire over the past few months." He held up a clenched fist, one finger extended, a sardonic smile curving his lips. "One—the crown prince gets murdered practically on the eve of his marriage to the princess of Gastonia and his ascent to the throne, thus saving Silvershire—*and* the princess—from unimaginable disaster." Up went another finger, along with the errant eyebrow. "Two—the reigning king collapses from shock and grief, and Lord Russell Carrington, off in Gastonia to escort the bride-to-be to her nuptials, rushes home to assume the king's duties—but not before falling in love with and ultimately marrying Reginald's erstwhile intended, the lovely Princess Amelia."

His smile was all teeth. "How'm I doing so far?"

"You must read the *Quiz,*" Rhia murmured. "You're certainly up on all the royal gossip."

"Hmm, yes, well, I do try to keep informed. Particularly when my name is being bandied about as the most likely candidate for royal murderer."

"You haven't mentioned the part where it's discovered during the royal autopsy—through routine blood typing, I assume—that Reginald could not possibly have been the biological child of either King Henry or Queen Alexis."

He gave her a quelling look. "Hush. I was coming to that."

He held up a third finger. "The plot thickens. Scandal follows mystery, follows intrigue. We learn Reginald has an illegitimate child by the illegitimate daughter of the prince of Naessa—ah, those randy royals!" The fourth finger shot up. "Next, we have a bloody great explosion right next to where the king is lying in a coma. He's not injured, thank God, but I understand the same can't be said for his personal physician. I'm told the lady—Dr. Smith, is it? Something exotic—Zara, I believe—was rather badly injured."

Rhia nodded. "She was. A head injury. She had amnesia for a while. Fully recovered, now, though, and marrying the psychologist for the Lazlo Group who helped bring her back. Walker Shaw—I know him personally. He's a good man." She paused. "She's the one who discovered the vault, you know."

Nikolas gave her a sidelong look, narrowed and wary. "Vault?"

"Oh, mah goodness," Rhia said in her sweetest Southern, "I thought for sure you'd know 'bout that. That's where the DNA evidence came from that proves—"

Nikolas's teeth snapped shut. He closed his fist and punched the air with it as his voice raised to override hers. "Yes, and then we have *the Sparrow*. An assassin by trade. This woman makes a deathbed confession *you* say, in which she names me—"

*"Donovan."* Her voice was quiet, now, but firm. "She said she was hired by someone named Donovan." She paused while he stared at her, hot-eyed. "There's more than one Donovan in this story, Nikolas."

"Silas…" It hissed from him on an exhaled breath as he leaned back again against the counter. He shook his head. "Yes, and what could he possibly have to do with any of this?" He pressed the heels of his hands hard against his eyes as if they burned even him, but when he looked at her again his eyes were cold. And hard. "They'd have arrested me anyway, wouldn't they." It wasn't a question. "And they sent you to find me."

"Well, my Lord, what did you expect? Look, there are questions that need answering. And naturally the king wants to meet you—since you appear to be his long-lost son and all. Carrington has questions…doubts…suspicions, maybe, but you've met him, talked with him, you know he's a fair man. If you're innocent—"

"Carrington *is* a good man—and I *am* innocent."

"Then why," Rhia said on a gust of exasperation, "won't you come back with me and prove it?"

He passed a big, strong-boned hand over his eyes again, and this time when they emerged from cover they were no longer hard. They looked tired, she thought. Wounded. Still, when he spoke his voice held the ring of cold steel.

"I have questions of my own that need answers. When I have them, I'll go back. Not until then."

"Well, then," Rhia said briskly, getting to her feet, "I hope you have a comfortable couch and a spare bath towel or two, because my orders are not to come back without you. And since I'm not about to let you out of my sight now that I've found you, I'm afraid I'm going to be staying right here until you're ready to go home."

# Chapter 3

"What happened to throwing me over your shoulder and hauling me off to see the king?"

Instead of being annoyed by her announcement, Nikolas's voice and smile betrayed amusement, and even his eyes had lost their steely glitter. Rhia wondered if that was simply more evidence of his legendary self-control. For all she knew—could only hope—the man was seething inside.

"Sorry to disappoint you," she said tartly, annoyed herself at the hum that had come again from nowhere to warm her chest and quicken her pulse.

"You have, actually," he said in a faintly surprised tone. "I was rather looking forward to the experience."

"Oh, don't worry, it may still come to that. For right now…" She shrugged and turned away to hide the heat she could feel rising to her throat…her face. *His* face was entirely too attractive when he smiled at her with that rakish charm, his eyes heavy-lidded and gone unexpectedly soft… "The fact is, I have a little leeway—not much, but a little. You say you need some time, I'm willing to give it to you—to a point." Faking a huge yawn, she paused in the kitchen doorway to lift her arms over her head in a sinuous catlike stretch, knowing that motion would lift her jacket as well, and reveal a good bit of silky chemise and the skin on the small of her back, and hint…just hint…at everything below that.

Two could play the subtle tease, she thought.

"Hmm—pardon me. It's been rather a long day for me," she murmured huskily. "If you don't mind, I think I'd like to take that couch, now. If you'll just throw me a blanket and maybe a pillow…"

"Nonsense," Nikolas said grandly, "what kind of host would I be? You shall have the bed, of course. I'll take the sofa." He slipped past her with the quickness that seemed so unexpected in a big man, touching—apparently casually—her waist as he did so. The sensation of his warm hand on her bare skin sent an entirely involuntary shudder of pleasure coursing through her. "After all—" for a moment his eyes, bright with laughter, stared straight into hers, and for that moment her brain seemed to cease all function "—I do have a certain reputation to maintain…as a gentleman, that is."

My God, she thought, what's the matter with me? I was warned about this man!

"Hold it." Recovering quickly, she caught up with him as he crossed the living room with his long-legged athlete's stride and tapped him on the shoulder. "Not so fast, Your Highness. Don't think for one minute you're going to stick me off in a bedroom behind a closed door and leave you free to slip out and away the second I nod off. This couch right here will do me fine, thank you very much."

Nikolas tilted his head and gazed thoughtfully past her. "Slip out…and away…do you know, it's a pity the idea hadn't occurred to me."

Yes, he was enjoying himself again, but that fact no longer

bemused him. He was growing accustomed to the realization that this woman, Corbett Lazlo's crack bounty hunter, stirred his juices as no one had been able to in a very long time. Maybe ever. Since there seemed to be no use fighting it, he reasoned, what else *could* he do but enjoy it?

"I do see your point. I suppose comfort and good manners must occasionally be sacrificed to duty. All right," he said briskly, "so it's the sofa for you, then. I'll just get that blanket...." He stepped toward the bedroom, then paused and turned back to her, one eyebrow lifted deliberately toward his hairline. "I suppose you're going to tell me you're a light sleeper as well."

She narrowed her eyes, watching him the way he imagined a cat might eye a mouse weighing the merits of a suicide dash across open floor. "Very light."

"Ah. So...there's not much chance I could slip past you in the middle of the night, then, is there?"

She smiled, and it was the same smile he'd seen once before, hovering a warm breath above his, just before she whispered the word, *Serendipity.*

"Not a chance," she purred.

"Huh." Pasting on a frown to contain the grin he could feel quivering dangerously through his facial muscles, Nikolas went to fetch his unexpected houseguest a pillow and a blanket.

The next few hours, he thought, promised to be entertaining indeed.

Rhia lay awake in the shadowy darkness, listening to the sounds the rain made in the night. For a time there had been the noises Nikolas made as he prepared for bed—footsteps and scufflings, the gush of water running through pipes, and doors opening and closing—but now there was only the rain, swooshing down the window glass, pattering on the balcony floor, rustling in the vines that covered the apartment building's outside walls.

It should have been a recipe for instant slumber, but instead she was wide awake, tense...restless. Not because the couch wasn't comfortable, but because it was. It was *too* comfortable, that was the problem. She couldn't let herself relax for fear she'd fall asleep. In spite of her arrogant claims, in her exhausted state she was afraid she might sleep soundly enough to allow Donovan to slip away from her. She hadn't been exaggerating when she'd said it had been a long day for her; she'd left the Lazlo Group's headquarters long before dawn that morning—only minutes, in fact, after verification of her target's location had come in around 2:00 a.m. Rhia didn't like delays. Once she had the information she needed, she moved and moved quickly. It was just her way.

She needed rest, and badly; she had a feeling it was going to take all her resources, mental and physical, to keep even one step ahead of Nikolas Donovan.

But she couldn't risk letting him escape while she slept. What she needed, she realized, was some kind of alarm.

She threw back the down comforter Nikolas had generously provided and rose from the couch. Ignoring the robe he'd also given her—nice of him, she thought with a wicked inner smile—she felt in the darkness for the belt she always wore on assignments like this one. Her fingers quickly located the pouch containing the items she needed—nail clippers and a small roll of nylon fishing line, nearly invisible, yet strong enough to land a thousand-pound marlin...so useful in so many ways.

By this time her eyes were well adjusted to the semi-darkness. Working without a flashlight and almost soundlessly, she tied a loop of the fishing line around the front door handle, then threaded it carefully around the leg of a small table nearby. It wouldn't go undetected in full light, but if Donovan decided to run, she doubted he'd be turning on any lamps. She did the same to the balcony doors and then, confident nobody was going to exit or enter the apartment without her knowing about it, Rhia lay down once again on the couch and pulled the comforter over herself with a satisfied sigh.

Nikolas, who had been monitoring this activity from the bedroom, heard the sigh and smiled to himself in the darkness. She hasn't lost her resourcefulness, he thought, as his mind flashed back yet again to his first encounter with her on that Paris hotel balcony. Or her sex appeal, his mind wryly added as his body responded predictably to the memory.

She was a worthy adversary. It was going to be fun out-witting her.

Rhia woke up shuddering with sexual arousal, her body scalded, pulses pounding. *My God, what a dream. Was it... Nikolas? No—surely not. Somebody who reminds me of Nikolas, though, or—no, wait...I think I remember...*

But it was too late, the dream was already slipping away. She remembered a balcony...maybe? Though hazy, it was all she could recall. That, and the same nagging sense of déjà vu that had been bothering her all evening.

Exasperated, she once again threw back the comforter and rose, this time putting on the robe her reluctant host had left lying over the arm of the couch. It felt cool and slick on her skin, and smelled of aftershave and masculinity. Just what her overheated senses needed. Like using gasoline to douse a fire, she thought as she made her way through the shadowed room that was already becoming familiar to her.

The rain had stopped. In the quiet even her bare footsteps on the thin carpet seemed loud, but she made no effort to tiptoe. *I hope I do wake him,* she thought, cranky and jangled from her own interrupted sleep. *Serve him right.* Though just what it would serve him right *for* she didn't try to figure out.

In the kitchen she opened the refrigerator and stared hot-eyed into its depths. Where was that damn wine? Ah—yes. She reached for the bottle of rosé, now barely a third full, and plucked out the stopper with an audible pop. She raised the bottle to her lips, tilted her head back and swigged down what was left of the wine in noisy unladylike gulps. With a violent shudder—she really did not care for wine—she set the empty bottle and stopper in the sink and made her way back to the couch, managing to stub her toe only once.

She was about to reach for the comforter once more when it occurred to her that perhaps she would be wise to use the WC before settling in. To do so, of course, meant she would have to pass Nikolas's door, which she'd noticed he'd left partly ajar. *Figures,* she thought. *He trusts me about as much as I trust him.*

It seemed to her rather like sneaking past the cage of a sleeping tiger—and this time she *did* tiptoe. Having just gotten her libido calmed down, the last thing she needed was a middle-of-the-night run-in with the man who for some reason appeared to be the cause of its recent rampage.

So, when a voice like the deep-chested growl of a tiger came rumbling out of the bedroom just as she was passing the half-open doorway on her return from the bathroom, it was a miracle she didn't jump right out of her skin.

"Trouble sleeping?"

With one hand braced against the wall for support and the other against her chest to keep the adrenaline surge from forcing her heart through her ribs, Rhia managed to make her voice sound almost normal. "No trouble—I'm just…"

"A light sleeper—I know." The voice was a velvety purr, fairly oozing sympathy. "Are you sure you won't change your mind about the bed?" Light flared warm and golden, splashing across the carpeted floor.

Although she tried her best to stop them, her eyes darted like curious children to the door opening. In the rectangle of soft light from the lamp he'd just switched on, she could see Nikolas reclining gracefully on his side with his upper half raised, propped on one elbow. That same half, the only part of him she could see—sculpted muscles of chest, torso, shoulders and arms—wore nothing but smooth tawny skin with an appealing masculine patterning of ink-black hair. His face wore a knowing smile, and one eyebrow raised in deliberate challenge.

A challenge? That was all Rhia needed. It was a bucketful of cold water in the face, that eyebrow—a clarion call to battle. A slug of Jack Daniel's, neat.

Icy calm settled over her as she pushed the door wide open and leaned, with arms casually folded, against the door frame, her focus so narrow now, she barely noticed—or cared—that the lower half of that magnificent body was modestly covered by a blanket.

"No, I haven't changed my mind. The couch is quite comfortable." Her sultry smile changed to a grimace. "If you must know, I was having a rather unpleasant dream." She paused before adding wickedly, "You were in it."

"Really!" She was ridiculously pleased at the genuine surprise in his voice.

"Yes—not all that hard to figure, really, considering you've been pretty much the whole focus of my existence for the past few days. Plus..." She hesitated, frowned, then reluctantly gave in, wondering whether she was going to regret putting these particular cards on the table. She let it out with an exasperated gust of breath. "Plus, I've been trying all evening to think who you remind me of, dammit. Or where I've met you before. Because I'm sure I have, and it's driving me crazy—" She stopped and straightened up, eyes narrowing; his eyes had a suspicious sparkle in them, like someone with a bad poker face and a secret ace up his sleeve. "Okay, wait. You *know,* don't you? We *have* met before, and you know where."

His satisfied chuckle confirmed it. Inwardly grinding her teeth and wearing her most winning smile, she took a cajoling step toward him, her role as his captor and keeper temporarily put aside. "Come on, you have to tell me. I can't believe I wouldn't have remembered you...."

"Hmm...flattering," Nikolas murmured. His eyes had softened with laughter...and something else she couldn't name. His smile grew downright seductive. "I won't *tell* you...but if you'll come here a minute, I'll give you a hint."

"A hint?" She paused, thinking of the limerick again. She really did not trust that tiger-smile.

"Yes, luv, a hint. But you'll have to come closer than that." He shifted, lying back on the pillows, and patted the blanket beside him. "Come, come—what are you afraid of? Surely you don't think a future king would stoop to ravishing an unwilling lady."

"From all I hear, Reginald would have," Rhia said darkly.

"Ah. Yes. But I'm not Reginald. Nor a future king, either, actually, so that's not much help, is it?" His eyebrow rose, his mouth tilted wryly, and his voice deepened with an unmistakable note of mockery. "Miss de Hayes. I never would have taken you for a coward."

She stood where she was, studying him, the challenge ringing in her head. She was far from a coward, and confident enough of that fact not to feel a need to prove it. So why the quickening pulse and heightened senses, the thrum of excitement pounding deep in her belly and shivering across her skin? *This is crazy. Definitely against the rules. Possibly even dangerous.*

Why? Because she'd always loved risk. And hated rules.

Hands thrust deep in the pockets of the borrowed robe, she resumed her unhurried stroll toward the bed and its infuriating and intriguing occupant and stopped an arm's length from both. "Okay, let's have it. The hint."

He shook his head, eyelids half-closed. *Sleepy tiger...* "Sorry, that still won't do, I'm afraid. In fact, you're going to have to come quite a *lot* closer." He patted the blanket again.

"Oh, you can't be serious," Rhia said. "You can't actually think I'm going to get into bed with you."

"Not *into* bed, darling—appealing as the idea may be. Just *on* will do. On *me,* actually. On top of the covers, of course— I did promise not to ravish you."

"No, you didn't."

"Didn't I? Oh, well, all right then, I do now. No ravishing— cross my heart." He drew an *X* over one firm and dusky pec, then said drily, "Anyway, I like to think if I were of a mind to ravish someone, I could manage to do so without resorting to such an idiotic plot."

"Being ravished," Rhia said darkly, "is hardly my greatest fear, at the moment."

"Really? How refreshing. What is, then?"

"Being made a fool of. I don't like being mocked, Donovan."

His eyes and smile softened instantly. "Oh, my dear, that's the last thing I'd want to do to you, believe me. No—you wanted to know where we've met before, and I said I'd give you a hint. I'm about to do so, if you'll allow me, but you're going to have to trust me."

"Trust you?" Rhia said that with a shivery little laugh. But she sat down on the edge of the bed—rather abruptly due to the fact that her legs were suddenly feeling uncommonly weak. Grumpy because of that, she muttered, "Oh, why don't you just tell me? Save all this trouble."

Nikolas chuckled. "I could, I suppose, but this is so much more enjoyable. Now—if you could bring yourself to stretch out here...."

In spite of that weakness in her knees and a giddy, fluttery sensation in her stomach, Rhia had to admit she was enjoying herself, too. She didn't like to imagine what her handlers at the Lazlo Group would make of all this, but the truth was, she always had been allowed a considerable amount of latitude when it came to choosing her methods of operation. So long as those methods resulted in a successful mission, that is. If playing the lighthearted seduction game with Nikolas Donovan was what it took to get him back to Silvershire and into the arms of his royal biological father, then she was willing to make the sacrifice.

The odd thing was, she *did* trust him. Probably more than she trusted herself.

"On top of you, you said?" She turned, arranging herself first beside the long blanket-covered mound that was Nik's body, trying not to think about the part of that body that wasn't covered, the part that was giving off the intoxicating scent and sultry warmth of a clean, healthy man in waves that made her head swim. Catching and holding a breath, she eased her body carefully over and onto the mound. She lifted her head and looked down into those dusky gray eyes, and it was like looking into a very deep well. Fighting an unaccustomed wave of vertigo, she unstuck her tongue from the roof of her mouth and mumbled in a shivery voice, "Like this?"

"Hmm…perfect. Lovely." His voice vibrated against her chest. "Now, then…are the bells ringing?"

Rhia uncrossed her eyes and shook her head. "No…"

His sigh lifted her gently, and she felt an urge to grab hold of something and hold on. Something…like *him*.

"Then I'm afraid you're going to have to kiss me."

Her head rocked back, clearing instantly. She let go a gust of breath. "*Kiss* you! What are you trying—"

Nikolas lifted his head from the pillows and held his arms out wide. "Look—I promised, crossed my heart. No ravishing, see? Arms way out here. I won't even—"

"Oh, just shut up," Rhia said recklessly. She ducked her head and kissed him hard on the mouth. After a moment—a very brief moment—she raised her head and glared at him. "Well? I still don't hear any bells."

He gave a soft, dry snort. "Yes, well, small wonder, with a peck like that. Try it again, luv, and this time put some… hmm, how shall I put it?…some *sex* into it."

She closed her eyes; her heart thumped heavily against the place where her chest met his. "Oh, God—please don't tell me we had a one-night stand. That's impossible. I know I'd have remembered—"

"As someone recently said, do shut up." He lifted his head and his mouth found hers even before she knew she was bringing it down to his once more.

She had no idea how long it was before she raised her head

again; she lost all sense of time. She lost all sense of space, too. She felt the world whirl around her; she was floating, weightless. She needed desperately to hold onto something, or better yet, to have something—strong, masculine arms— holding her. Electricity skated along her nerves; her hands clenched, fisted in the blanket, gathering it in greedy handfuls. Her heart rocked her body with each beat, like hammer blows.

Desperate for breath, she pulled away, finally, and found that her eyes now refused to focus. In a drunken voice she managed to mutter, "What the hell was *that?*"

Nikolas's smile swam into her blurred line of vision, and his breath was soft on her lips as he whispered, "Serendipity."

She opened her mouth and a gasp burst from her throat, but that was all she had time for as his arms came around her and, with one deft and powerful twist of his body, he rolled her under him. Stunned, she looked up at the face suspended above her, the face filling up all her world with its chiseled jaw and patrician nose, its dark brow and brooding eyes, its beautifully sculpted mouth. *That face. That mouth...*

Memories flickered like lightning flashes; a clap of thunder shuddered through her. She whispered, "Oh, my God, was that *you?*"

*She'd never forgotten him, the man who'd saved her career that night. Possibly her life. She remembered every detail of the encounter, from the moment she'd vaulted over that balcony wall, not knowing what she'd find on the other side, knowing only it was bound to be better than staying where she was. The legitimate occupant of the room she'd been searching was known to be a dangerous man—and was evidently unpredictable, too. She hadn't expected him back for another fifteen minutes, at least.*

*When she heard the key card slick in and out of its slot, she hurled herself through the sliding door and onto the balcony, knowing it was only a temporary refuge. Even a blind man or a complete idiot would be able to tell in seconds the room had been searched—and Clive Harrington was no fool. A wife-beater, a child-stealer, a cheat, a liar and a mean-as-a-snake SOB, for sure, but not stupid. The balcony was the first place he'd look.*

*Rhia figured she had three choices: She could go up, down, or sideways. Since the balcony was fifteen floors up and she lacked both wings and climbing gear, that left only one choice, and she took it without hesitation. In roughly two seconds time she was pulling herself over the six-foot wall between her assignment's balcony and the one next door and dropping down on the other side…*

*…Right on top of the unfortunate and unsuspecting person enjoying the view of the lights of Paris and the cool night air.*

*She didn't know what made her do it. She remembered looking down into his face—the face of a man, a young man…and handsome. More than handsome, if she'd had time to think about it. But…she remembered hearing the muffled cry of fury from the room next door, and realizing she had only seconds in which to save herself. And then she was kissing the strange man lying half-stunned beneath her, kissing him as if she'd done it…oh, many times before.*

*She remembered hearing Harrington's voice asking about her, then apologizing for the interruption, and feeling exhilarated…smug…clever. Somehow she'd done it—pulled it off. She was free and clear!*

*But…there was this…man she was lying on…kissing. And his mouth tasted good, tasted faintly of wine…and felt warm and firm and enthusiastic, and—after the first shocked seconds— oh, so skillful. Still tangled with his, her lips formed a smile.*

*Then, slowly, even a bit reluctantly, she separated her mouth from his and gazed down at him, searching for the words to tell him how grateful she was. Searching for a way to say thank you. And good-bye.*

*But…when she lowered her head to touch his lips again in sweet farewell, she felt his body grow hard and quiver with wiry strength...and his arms were around her now, and she felt his head lift and his muscles surge and a moment later she was lying on her back and his weight was pressing down on her and his face was filling the sky above her, blotting out the pale Paris night. She felt his arms tight around her and his heartbeat thumping off-beat against hers. And she thought...*

Foolish Rhia! Stupid—stupid to play with fire this way!

*Her panic lasted only a moment. She was still in control—of course she was. She could stop this any time she chose. The arms holding her prisoner were masterful but not brutal; the eyes burning down into hers were angry, yes, but bright with questions rather than lust.*

What was that? What the hell do you call that? *she heard him demand in a croaking, unexpectedly young voice.*

*And somewhere deep inside her she felt a smile shiver free and bubble up through her chest and emerge with a whispered sigh:* Serendipity.

*He gave a brief huff that might have been wonder or merely acknowledgment, then lowered his mouth to hers for one quick, hard kiss, a kiss that left her with throbbing lips and racing heart and a strange humming in her chest. Then he rolled his weight off of her to lie on his back with one arm across his eyes. She felt his body shake with silent laughter.*

*For one insane moment she thought of staying right there. Wondered what a kiss like that might possibly lead to, and who this young man was who could have a strange woman drop on him from out of the sky and not only keep his cool and play along in her game with life-and-death stakes, but laugh about it afterward. But Harrington was a few yards away in the next room, undoubtedly on the phone to the French police and the British embassy at that very moment. She couldn't count on her good luck holding forever. She didn't know how Corbett Lazlo felt about bailing his agents out of jail—in her case, a second time—but she didn't care to find out, not on her first solo assignment.*

*She sat up, patted her savior's shoulder and breathlessly muttered,* Thanks—I don't know who you are, but I definitely owe you one. *Then she rose, stepped over his body and slipped through the balcony door, moving quickly and nimbly as she always did...moving as if her legs weren't shaky and her stomach jittering with the aftereffects of a kiss she knew even then she was never going to forget....*

"You did say you owed me one," Nikolas said, his voice an amused rumble against her chest. "Although I've never been quite clear on what for, exactly."

"Oh, nothing much," Rhia said grudgingly. "Just possibly my life. Definitely my career."

"Ah—I see. Then I would be correct in surmising that what you were doing in that hotel room was something similar to what I found you doing in mine this evening?"

She tried to squirm, then thought better of it. "Well...yes. I guess you could say that." She focused her eyes on the lock of dark hair that swept across his brow like a black-bird's wing. Studying the silky, glossy blackness of it, she found herself smiling. "But somehow...I don't think that gentleman would have cooked me supper and offered me his bed."

"Hmm...foolish man."

The lock of hair brushed her forehead like a whispered command, and obediently her eyelids fluttered closed. She felt the warmth of his breath flow over her lips, and her heart gave a crazy leap, gave a foolish, giddy leap, like a smitten school-girl's. Her breath caught; unable to help herself, she lifted to him, searching again for that clever, clever mouth. He chuckled; his lips hovered...brushed...nipped...teased. Her stomach dropped sickeningly as she felt herself lifted on a wave of desire, like a roller coaster when it shoots up...up...up to the crest...just before it begins its heart-stopping plunge back down. Down...toward certain disaster.

But, as she teetered there, waiting for the plunge, breathless with exhilaration, trembling with desire, she felt a heartbeat thumping against her palm. And she realized that, without any recollection of having done so, she'd placed her hand against his chest like a barrier.

Roller-coastering emotions bumped and careened over realizations and fears and screeched to a halt just short of panic. *My God, what am I doing? I can't…*

"Nikolas—wait," she gasped. "I can't…do this."

"Mmm…why not?" The soft words tickled her lips and his tongue lightly soothed them. "It's not like we haven't done this before."

"That was…different. There was a reason…circumstances." *And I was young, then. Reckless!* Her voice went breathy with panic. "And I didn't know…who you were."

His laughter was dry with irony. "So…it's okay to kiss a stranger, but not a prince? And you wonder why I'm not exactly thrilled at the thought of being one?"

And he rolled away from her, leaving her just as jangled and shaky as she had been on that memorable night so long ago.

He jerked the tangled blanket aside and got up, and she barely had time to register the fact that he was wearing a pair of black silk boxers that rode low on narrow hips, before he leaned down to brush her forehead with his lips. "Don't get up, luv. I'll take the couch."

He was walking away from her when she fought her way free of the half of the blanket that still cocooned her. "No way. Dammit, I'm not letting—"

He turned back, put his hands on her shoulders and gently but firmly pushed her down onto the bed, clucking to her as he did so like a mother hen to a wayward chick. "Don't get excited. I promise I won't run off while you're sleeping. In fact, I give you my word on it—how's that?"

She eyed him warily, not trusting that smile or the gleam in those pewter-gray eyes, not for a second. "Word of a king?"

His smile vanished. "No," he said coldly as he straightened up, "Word of honor. *My* honor."

He turned and strode from the room. And in that moment, in her opinion—boxers and all—had never looked more like a king.

# *Chapter 4*

*W*ord *of honor.* My *honor.*

Nikolas lay awake, listening to those words whisper in his mind like ghost voices in an empty castle. The words had meant something, once. So had the words of the man who raised him, the man who had been like a father to him. The man who had taught him all he knew about honor. About duty. About love of country.

And hatred of tyrants. Hatred of kings in particular, and of one king, Henry Weston of Silvershire, specifically.

*Silas Donovan.* The man's face flashed before his mind's eye like a slide show on fast forward, in all the ways he'd come to know it in his thirty years. True, it was a hard face in many ways, austere and forbidding, with a mouth that seldom smiled and eyes that often glittered with the light of fanaticism. The man Nik had called simply Uncle had never been warm or affectionate, or even particularly kind. And yet, in his way, he'd been good to Nikolas. Among many other things, Silas had taught him strength, discipline and a will-ingness to sacrifice and dedicate his life to a cause greater than himself. He had taught him so well, in fact, that Nikolas couldn't remember a time in his life when he'd ever been free of the burden of responsibility Silas had placed on his shoul-ders. A time when he'd been allowed to be just a lad: young, carefree, with a whole world of bright possibilities to explore.

*Word of honor. My honor.*

But what value could there be in either his word or his honor when the basis for both was a lie?

It was hard for Nikolas to explain, even to himself, why he wasn't yet ready to return to Silvershire to deal with the cat-astrophic changes in his life. There was a part of him that still clung desperately to the hope that it was all an awful mistake, that at the very least there was some kind of explanation for how his DNA and Henry Weston's could be a close match—distant relatives, perhaps? But in his heart, he knew there was no mistake; as Rhia had pointed out, DNA doesn't lie. The only thing left for him to do now was accept this new reality, and try to think how it affected his future, both immediate and long range.

No small task.

For one thing, there were the questions looping through his mind, flitting in and out among the images of Silas Donovan's face, most of which he couldn't even pin down, much less find answers to.

He needed time. Just a bit more time.

Nikolas turned his head toward the small pile of clothing that had been left carelessly draped over the back of the couch, only a shadowy wrinkle in the darkness, but he caught a whiff of that faint feminine aura that seemed so familiar to him. After a moment he reached out a hand and idly stroked the butter-soft leather jacket with a finger, and smiled grimly to himself in the darkness. *Sorry, luv. I hope you'll under-stand...one day.*

\* \* \*

Rhia had never considered herself a particularly sensual person, and certainly not indolent. Yet, when she came slowly awake in a feather-soft bed to the smell of coffee and the sweet and gentle warmth of a hand caressing her forehead, she wanted only to snuggle down and wallow in the pleasure of it, like a cat in a puddle of sunshine.

*He's here. He kept his word.* She told herself she'd never doubted he would.

Two things happened then. Memories of the events of the night before hit in an all-out sensory barrage, and at almost the same moment, she felt firm, velvety lips brush hers. Her breath hitched and her lips parted, almost without her knowing, and then she was sinking...helplessly drowning in a deep, intoxicating whirlpool of desire.

She couldn't help herself...her body wasn't hers to govern. Of its own volition it arched and curled and lifted...outposts like fingers and toes tingled as blood abandoned them to rush to more exciting, throbbing places. Her hands ventured from their blanket-cocoon...reached...found his...and her fingers spread wide to allow the erotic slide of his fingers between hers—even those ordinary places now suddenly so sensitized his touch there made her moan.

He lifted his head, and hers lifted, too, following his mouth, not wanting to let it go. His chuckle stopped her—and the fact that his hands were holding her captive, pressed into the pillow above her head. She collapsed back into the pillow, panting slightly, trying to focus her eyes, and finally mumbled, "What in the hell was *that?*"

His lips pressed a smile to hers. "What, haven't you ever been kissed awake before?"

"Not by a prince." She smiled lazily at him through the curtain of her lashes...knowing she shouldn't. Knowing full well she was flirting with a smiling tiger.

She became aware, all at once, of the strength in the hands

that imprisoned hers. She squirmed in a testing way and murmured, "Do I smell coffee?"

His eyes rested on her, dark and benign…and so close she could see the twin images of her own tiny self reflected in them. "You do. I've brought you a tray—breakfast, actually."

She watched him narrowly, while her heartbeat rocked her breasts against his chest, against the crisp white shirt he wore. "You didn't have to do that. I need to get up anyway."

"Well, luv, that's not quite true. You see—" he lowered his mouth to hers, and she responded to him as she had before, opened to him even as her mind's sleeping sentinels were finally waking up and sounding the first confused alarms "—you aren't going to be going anywhere for a while, I'm afraid."

She uttered a muffled howl of outrage and began to squirm and writhe in earnest, but the alarms had come too late. Helpless against his greater strength, she felt cold steel around her wrist, and heard a sound she knew all too well—the click of handcuffs locking. She gave her imprisoned arm one furious yank, an entirely futile move, since the other end of the handcuffs was securely fastened to the iron framework of the bed. She lay still, then, seething and glaring up at Nikolas, who was sitting beside her now, placidly smiling—though still holding her uncuffed wrist as a precaution, she surmised, in case she tried to claw his eyes out.

"Please tell me," she said through tightly clenched teeth, "those aren't *my* handcuffs?"

He shrugged, grinned—had the nerve to try to look endearing. And almost pulled it off, having that unmistakable just-showered and -shaved look she normally found irresistible. And dammit, he did smell so good….

"Well, they were *there,* you see—that's quite an interesting belt you have, by the way—most enlightening, really—and since it didn't seem likely you'd be using them in the near future…well, how could I resist?"

"Fine," she said, glowering at him as she twisted her un-cuffed wrist experimentally in his grasp, "you've had your fun, now get this thing off me."

His smile would have been devastatingly attractive if it hadn't been so damn—there was no other word for it—*smug*. He made scolding noises with his tongue. "Now, now, clever girl that you are, I'm quite certain you know that isn't going to happen. Not right away, at any rate. I did try to tell you I needed a bit more time before I'd be ready to go back to Silvershire. I know you have your job to do as well. This seemed the best way to solve the problem—from my perspective, at least."

"You can't seriously be thinking of just *leaving* me here. Like this. You wouldn't." Sheer disbelief kept any traces of fear out of her voice. The implications, the possibilities didn't bear thinking about.

Nikolas looked genuinely shocked. "No, of course I wouldn't. Well—not indefinitely. Not even for very long, actually. Just until the cleaning lady shows up." He shot the shirtsleeve cuff on his free arm and glanced at his watch. "Should be here in about…two hours, I imagine. When she arrives, tell her the key to the handcuffs is on the kitchen table. That should give me enough of a headstart, I think. Well, sorry, luv, but I must be off."

He started to get up—then, almost as an afterthought, leaned down and kissed her instead. Not a quick farewell smack, either, but a long…leisurely…lingering…completely devastating reminder of how lovely his lips felt, how talented his tongue was, how completely powerless she was to prevent her body from responding to their touch. She tingled and tickled and burned in all her most vulnerable places. She wanted to sob with frustration, to scream with fury. But when he released her from that terrible torture and rose at last, she was so shaken that for a moment she couldn't utter a sound.

"*Au revoir*—enjoy your breakfast," he said softly, and left. She sucked in air and found her voice. "*Nikolas—damn you!"* She held her breath and listened so hard her head hummed, but all she heard was his retreating footsteps. "Okay, I'm not allowed to kill you," she screamed after him, "but I promise you I will find a hundred ways to make your life a bloody living *hell!"*

The only reply she heard was the soft closing of the door.

Nikolas dropped a heavy bunch of dusty red grapes into his bucket and straightened up, removing the wide-brimmed hat he was wearing and wiping away sweat with a forearm. "What?" he asked in response to the voice from the next row over that was now swearing softly in French.

"Here comes another bloody tourist," his friend Phillipe replied in English. "Wanting to help with the *vendange,* I expect, like it's an entertainment we put on for them. More trouble than they're worth, most of them, but good for business in the long run, I suppose. The winery benefits a little, anyway."

Nikolas turned his head to follow the progress of the tall figure striding briskly up the dusty lane between vineyards already beginning to shimmer with the heat of the rapidly climbing sun. A woman, he saw now, wearing a backpack and carrying a black oblong case of some kind. As she walked, he could see her head moving from side to side, and he wondered if her eyes, shielded by the dark glasses she wore, were searching among the heads bobbing up and down between the rows—all that was visible of the army of hardworking pickers—searching for one head in particular.

He couldn't help himself; a wry smile tugged at his lips and he chuckled. "That's no tourist, I'm afraid."

There was a rustling sound and Phillipe's dark, interested eyes peered at him through the bronze-tipped leaves of the grapevine separating them. "It is her, then, the woman who chased you out of my apartment in Paris? The one who wants to take you back to Silvershire to become a king? And she has found you so quickly? *Mon dieu,* my friend, you must be losing your touch."

"So it would appear," Nikolas said absently. He was trying to decide whether the odd sensation quivering up through his belly and into his chest was indicative of dismay or delight.

"Would you like to hide under here? She'll never find you among all these vines." Phillipe's teeth gleamed white among the grape leaves. "How is this? I will go and tell her you've gone away to…I don't know where. I'll make up something—something far away. Brazil, maybe?"

"Very funny. You don't know this woman. She wouldn't be fooled for a second. And besides—it would be much too undignified to be discovered crouching under a bush. Here—take my bucket, will you? I suppose I'd better go and face the music—sooner rather than later."

"I'm coming, too—it is, after all, my vineyard. I think I should give a personal welcome to the woman who brought Nik Donovan to his knees, don't you think?" Grinning unforgivably, Phillipe stuck his hand in the air and shouted *"La hutte!"*

A moment later a large cone-shaped basket came bobbing down the row, borne on the back of a wizened fellow with a face like ancient parchment and a grin that displayed several missing teeth. Phillipe bantered jovially with the man in French as he emptied his bucket into the basket, then took the bucket Nik passed over to him and emptied it as well. After waving *la hutte* and its carrier on their way, the two men set off down their respective rows on a course to rendezvous with the visitor coming up the road.

"I am curious," Phillipe said, quickening his pace to match Nik's, "what is this 'music' you face? I know most of your English expressions and quite a few American ones as well, but this one…? Am I correct in assuming this particular music will not be pleasing to the ears?"

"You could assume that, yes," said Nikolas drily. "The last time I saw the lady she threatened me with a hundred fates worse than death."

Phillipe made scolding noises. "You really must work on

your people skills, my friend. Especially if you are to be a king one day. You know—" He broke off with a chuckle as Nikolas threw a fat ripe grape at him and missed.

To Nikolas's bemusement, he felt his heartbeat accelerate as he stepped from the rows of grapevines onto the dusty road. A few dozen yards away, Rhia had come to a halt. Her expression was impossible to read from that distance, particularly with her eyes hidden from view, but he felt safe in assuming it wouldn't be pleasant. The odd thing, though, was the warm little nugget of pleasure he felt forming way down in his belly at the sight of her.

Not that anyone would fault him for that; she was, after all, a sight to warm any man's loins. She wore jeans that sat low on her hips, and a tank top that brought to mind vivid memories of the chemise she'd been wearing the last time he'd seen her…not to mention the circumstances in which he'd left her. Then, her thick, wavy dark hair had been in a sultry tangle tumbling onto her bare shoulders. Now it was caught back by a bandana handkerchief folded into a triangle and tied at the nape of her neck, and the tawny skin of her arms and chest and throat wore a golden slick of sweat.

Without saying a word, she lowered the oblong case to the ground between her feet and took a water bottle from its holder on her belt.

"Mother of God, what do you suppose is in that case? Please tell me she's not come armed."

Nikolas barely heard and didn't acknowledge Phillipe's remark, made in a droll undertone out of one side of his mouth. Rhia had removed her sunglasses, and those cool green eyes had found his, found them and snared them with an intent and unreadable gaze, and his world, his awareness had narrowed until it only had room for her. Phillipe, the vineyards, the army of pickers, the barrel-laden wagons and the tractors pulling them, all faded into background noise, like the busy hum of bees on a summer's day.

She drank long and deeply from the water bottle and returned it to her belt. Watching her, he felt his own throat go dry. Her eyes never left his as he closed the distance between them, though oddly, they seemed to him more puzzled than angry.

He paused a double arm's length away from her and nudged his hat to the back of his head. "That was fast," he said, offering her a smile as a hopeful peace offering. "What did you do, hide a tracking device in my shoes?"

She snorted and said, "I wish I had." But he could tell her heart wasn't in it. She seemed distracted, he thought, as if her mind was on something else entirely. "No, I told you—I just have a knack for finding people."

"Huh. A 'knack,' you say. So…you just *knew* where I'd be? So you *are* psychic."

She shifted her shoulders in an impatient way—again, as though the discussion was interrupting something far more important. "No, I…you'd mentioned your friend, the one whose apartment you were staying in in Paris. You said he had family in Provence. A winery. It seemed like a good bet." She put on her sunglasses, then lifted one shoulder in a dismissive way. "It was where I'd go."

"Ah," said Nikolas. "Empathy."

She'd bent over to pick up the oblong case at her feet. Her shielded eyes came back to him as she straightened. "Empathy?"

"Your 'knack'—that's what it is, you know. Empathy. The ability to put yourself in another person's shoes. To think like he does. Feel what he feels. I can see where that would come in handy in your line of work. Here—let me take that for you."

He reached for the case and she surrendered it to him without an argument, which he thought was a pretty good clue that it wasn't, as Phillipe had suggested, a weapon. He hefted the case. "What's in here? And by the way, whatever possessed you to have the cabby drop you at the bottom of the hill when you had all this to carry? You could have had him take you straight up to the house, you know."

She cut her eyes at him, and her smile was wry. "I thought I'd sneak up on you—in case you took a notion to run again. But I have to tell you, I never expected you'd be out in the vineyards picking grapes." Above the dark lenses of her glasses her forehead crinkled in a frown.

*And I sure didn't expect my heart to go nuts at the sight of you, damn you.*

Rhia studied her assignment moodily from the shelter of her sunglasses. Today he was wearing a pair of blue dungarees and a white shirt made of some kind of loosely woven material, with long sleeves rolled to the elbows. No collar. His neck was deeply tanned and gleaming with sweat, and looked sleek and powerful as that of some dominant male animal— a stag, perhaps, or a stallion. *Or a king?*

*Why did you have to be so damned attractive? Why didn't I stick to finding lost children? They weren't nearly so complicated.*

His lips took on a sardonic tilt. "Not quite the occupation one expects of a prince? No—I suppose not. Though I've picked many a grape in my life—make of that what you will. Come." He took her elbow, and Rhia felt a small electric shock where his fingers touched her bare skin. The dryness of the air, she told herself. Static electricity. And somehow she found herself walking beside him up the dusty road, and they were walking together in casual intimacy, like lovers out for a stroll.

"Let me introduce you to Phillipe. This is his vineyard— or his family's, as I'm sure you already know. Phillipe—come and meet the woman who has promised me the punishments of a hundred hells. Rhia, this is Phillipe, one of my oldest and most tolerant friends. Phillipe—say hello to Rhia de Hayes, bounty hunter."

Nikolas's companion, who'd been waiting for them at a discreet distance, flicked away the cigarette he'd been smoking, removed his hat with a sweeping gesture and placed it over his heart. His hair was a mass of sweat-damp curls, lighter than

Nik's, a rich warm brown that matched his eyes. He had extraordinarily nice eyes. He was, in fact, every bit as attractive as Nikolas Donovan, and his smile was just as charming.

Then why was it, she wondered, that when he murmured, *"Enchanté, ma belle,"* and lifted her hand to his lips, she felt no little shock of awareness, no tingling warmth where his lips touched, no hollow flip-flopping sensation in her stomach, no humming sensation in her chest?

"I am in complete sympathy with you, mademoiselle—it is high time someone gave this man the treatment he deserves," Phillipe said solemnly, still holding her hand. "I can only hope I may be allowed to watch."

Rhia burst out laughing—he was so outrageous she couldn't help it. Phillipe grinned irrepressibly and kissed her hand once more before releasing it.

"Nik, my friend. Take this lovely lady up to the house and make her welcome. We'll be stopping for lunch soon—we're about finished for the day anyway. Tell Elana to make up Maman's room for our guest—she won't be back from Monte Carlo until the *vendange* is finished, I'm sure. That is—unless you would like her to sleep in your room, Nik?"

Rhia didn't have to look at him to know Nikolas was grinning. "Please don't bother," she said smoothly. "I won't be staying long. As it happens, Nikolas and I have an important engagement in Silvershire." She turned her head, then, and gave him a long, deliberate stare. He gazed back at her with cool gray eyes, arms casually crossed on his chest.

Phillipe made a gesture that was extravagantly—almost comically—French. "Oh, but you must stay! At least until the *vendange* is finished. I cannot possibly spare this man at the moment. And for you, mademoiselle, it will be an enjoyment. *Vendange* in Provence is like one big party—like your Mardi Gras. A moveable feast. A few more days, eh? What can it matter?"

She shot Nikolas a dark look. He held out his hands in one

of those half-French, half-British gestures of his. "I swear, I did not put him up to it."

She gave in with a put-upon sigh, and didn't tell him she'd planned to give him several days, anyway. A few more days of freedom....

"Don't think you've won this battle," she said as she and Nikolas resumed their leisurely stroll up the gravelly dirt road toward the oasis of dark green trees that shaded the stone-and-stucco house—not touching, now, and she refused to admit to herself she was sorry. "I just don't want to leave your friend short-handed for his damned *vendange*—what is that, by the way?"

"*Vendange?* That's the grape harvest. Happens every year around this time."

Other than shooting him a quelling glance, she ignored the facetious remark. "I can't believe the vineyard owner is out here picking grapes like a field hand. Is that part of the tradition?"

"It is, actually. Among the small growers, anyway. Most of the pickers you see here are neighbors and other small farm owners from around the area. They all come together to help each other with the harvest, moving from farm to farm, vineyard to vineyard until the job's done."

"A 'moveable feast'?"

Nik smiled. "Partly. You'll see soon enough. You heard him say they'll be breaking for 'lunch' soon? I'm afraid the word *lunch* doesn't come close to describing it. All the farmers sort of compete with each other to see who can put on the biggest and best noonday spread. The wine and local hooch—which is called *marc*, by the way, and unless you've a cast-iron stomach, I don't recommend you try it—will be flowing freely as well."

"In the middle of the day? How does anyone work afterward?"

"They don't. You heard him say they were about done for the day. He meant that."

"Nice short workday," Rhia remarked.

"Like hell it is. When it's hot like this we start at three in the morning."

She threw him a look of horror. "Why?"

"Because the grapes don't like it when you take them out of the nice warm sunshine and toss them into a cooler. It sends them into shock, or some such thing." His easy smile made something inside her chest wallow. As if her heart really had turned over.

Because the implications of that didn't bear thinking about, she said crossly, "You talk about grapes as if they're...I don't know—alive."

His eyebrow went up, and she repressed a shudder. "Really? I suppose I do. You hang around vintners very long and it rubs off on you."

"You spend a lot of time here, then?"

His smile went crooked. "*Spent,* not spend. When I was at university, mostly. Spent most of my holidays here, when my...when Silas was off somewhere."

"Doing...?"

"Whatever it is he does, I suppose. Fomenting rebellion, rousing the rabble." He shrugged and looked off across the vineyards for a moment. "I didn't mind, actually. Phillipe and his family were...like family. His *maman* was pretty much the only mum I ever had." He threw her his lopsided smile, and she felt the most astonishing sensation—an aching pressure at the base of her throat. "I probably have her to thank for civilizing me, at any rate."

Rhia cleared gravel from her throat. "You were happy here."

"I was, yes. At one time I actually considered making a career of it—grape-growing...wine-making. There's a region in my country I've always thought— Have you been to Silvershire?"

"Only to the capital—Silverton."

"Ah—yes, well, it's southwest of there. Carrington's ancestral lands. The climate is quite similar to this—perfect for growing wine grapes."

"Why didn't you? Make a career of it?"

The crooked smile flickered again. "It wasn't quite what Silas had in mind for me. Or fate either, as it turns out."

Nik's stomach went hollow suddenly. Hefting the case he was carrying, he said, "What the devil's in this, by the way? Not, as Phil suggested, some sort of weapon, I hope?"

Her lips didn't smile, and he wondered what her eyes would tell him if it weren't for the damned sunglasses. "Nope," she said, "just a saxophone."

He gave a bark of surprised laughter. "A...*what?*"

"You know...jazz, the blues...it's a horn...you blow it..."

He hadn't thought anything she could do would surprise him, but obviously he'd underestimated her. Again. *Serendipity...* A strange little shiver ran down his spine. How could she have known he'd always had a particular fondness for American jazz? "Don't tell me you know how to play it."

"No, of course not," she replied in a frosty tone, "I just have a really eccentric taste in accessories."

"A bit cranky, are we?" he remarked evenly, hiding all traces of his inner delight.

"That's how people get when they're left handcuffed to a bed," she replied, and he could almost hear her teeth grinding. "Particularly without access to a *bathroom.*"

"Ah. That." He stopped in the middle of the road to look at her. Realizing his eyebrows were doing that thing that annoyed her so, he made a conscious effort to stop them— also to contain his grin—before he walked on. "I really had hoped you'd gotten over that."

"Not a chance, Donovan." He could feel her eyes on him, dark as a threat.

He glanced at her and made scolding noises with his tongue. "Oh, come now, you aren't the type to carry a grudge, surely?"

There was something hypnotic about her eyes... "My mother always claimed one of her grandmothers was

Creole—a voodoo priestess," she said, and hissed the last word like a curse. "It's in my blood."

He wanted to laugh, but the tingle of excitement rushing beneath his skin didn't feel like amusement. He could feel heat and heartbeat intensifying in places they shouldn't have been, not at high noon in the middle of a French vineyard. Not in response to a woman whose avowed mission was to take him into custody and return him to a place he had no desire to go. But…really—*Creole? Voodoo?*

He was mulling over this interesting new tidbit of information about his adversary's background when the convoy of tractors pulling trailers laden with barrels and people began to stream past them. Phillipe shouted and waved from the midst of the crowd on the last one, and it halted in the road beside them. Nikolas looked at Rhia and made an offering gesture. She threw him a challenging look, then took the helping hands reaching out to her from the crowd on the wagon and allowed herself to be hoisted aboard. Nikolas passed the oblong case containing her saxophone up to her as she settled into the midst of the boisterous crowd, then levered himself onto the back of the flatbed. Someone gave a shout and the tractor began to move forward again. Someone began to sing, and most of the passengers on the trailer joined in. And Nikolas, for no reason he could think of, found himself smiling.

## Chapter 5

For the second morning in a very few days, Rhia wallowed her way to consciousness to the smell of coffee, and to find Nikolas Donovan sitting on the bed beside her. This time, instead of gently caressing her face, he was shaking her. Not the least bit gently.

"Rise and shine, luv—time to get up." His voice sounded obscenely cheerful.

She pried open one eye and said, "It's *dark!*" in an outraged tone. And then gasped, cringed and covered her eyes with her hand as light stabbed them cruelly from the lamp on the table beside the bed.

"There," Nikolas said without sympathy. "It's not dark anymore. Come on—get up. I've brought you coffee. We've got about fifteen minutes before the trailers leave."

"Leave? For where, in God's name? At this hour—" Oh, God, was she whining? She struggled to sit up, and Nikolas helpfully drew back the light blanket that covered her. She pulled it back up to her chin and glared in his direction without focusing. "What hour is it, by the way?"

"Two forty-five—well, actually—" he glanced at his watch "—it's two forty-eight, now. I suggest you hurry if you want time to drink that coffee."

She closed her eyes and rubbed at her temples, which did absolutely nothing to diminish the pounding behind them. To make matters worse, when she opened her eyes again Nikolas was still there, and, once she had him in focus, looking sinfully handsome and smiling at her like a beneficent saint. She regarded him for a moment with loathing, then said, "Are you being deliberately cruel, or is this an aspect of your personality I wasn't briefed about?"

His laugh sent involuntary ripples of pleasure through her. It was like rubbing against fur. "My dear, you did say you wanted to pick grapes with the crew this morning."

She gave him a sideways look of stark disbelief. "Impossible."

"Sorry to have to tell you this, but I heard you with my own ears. So did Phillipe and most of the crew."

"I couldn't have…could I? *When?*"

"Hmm…let's see. It was after your third glass of *marc,* I believe—or perhaps it was the fourth—I'm afraid I lost track. Anyway, the crew was very much impressed with you. If you back out now, you're going to suffer an enormous loss of face."

Rhia groaned and collapsed back on the pillows, closing her eyes. "Oh, God. Father Matthew was right."

"Father Matthew?" Nik's voice was vibrant with rather poorly suppressed emotions—laughter, she was sure. And something else. Something that sounded a lot like—oddly—affection.

"Yeah—he was the priest in the Catholic girls' school I went to in Florida. He always told me I'd go to hell. I think this must be it."

He made a smothered sound—definitely laughter. "Oh, come now—it's not so bad once you get outside. Rather nice,

actually." There was a pause, and she felt the touch of something cool and soothing on her aching head—something that
warmed almost instantly and became Nikolas's fingers.
"You're really not a night person, are you?" he said tenderly.
"Who knew?"

She opened her eyes and tried to glare at him, but found
that her eyelids had grown inexplicably heavy. "It's not night,"
she mumbled, "it's morning. Dark, pitch-dark morning." Her
tongue felt heavy, too, and her lips seemed to have swollen.
She had a powerful desire, now, to press them into the nice
warm palm that was cradling the side of her face. "I've always
been a night person, actually. My nights have only become
an ordeal since I met you."

"It doesn't have to be that way, you know." The pad of
his thumb brushed gently across her swollen lips, but
instead of soothing them, set them on fire. The heat and
heaviness began to spread...like melting molasses...into
her arms...her legs...her body. Her breasts felt tight, and
even the kiss of silk and lace was more than her sensitized
nipples could bear.

"You do know," Nikolas murmured, "if it weren't for this
unfortunate hang-up you have about my allegedly royal blood,
you and I would be lovers by now."

Her heart stuttered and her stomach wallowed drunkenly—
roughly the way those parts of her had behaved the first time
she'd jumped out of an airplane during her training for the
Lazlo Group job. Now, as then, pride made her catch a breath
and fight valiantly against the panic. "You're awfully sure of
yourself, aren't you?" *There*...tart, and not *too* breathless.

His reply was wordless. He simply leaned down and
kissed her.

In some buried, weakened part of herself, had she been expecting it? In that same part of herself she'd definitely wanted
it. When she felt his warm lips pillow against hers, she uttered
a single whimpering cry...and opened to him.

And then she was in free fall, the wind rushing so hard against her face she couldn't breathe. Fear gripped her, and then exhilaration. *I've got to stop this! I have to stop...*

But she couldn't stop. And in the end, after she thought she must surely have passed the point of no return, it was Nikolas who pulled the ripcord. "Yes," he murmured, with his lips still touching hers, "I am."

His lips moved, then...along her jawline, riding on the velvety cushion of his sweet, warm breath. Her breasts grew heavier, each breath lifting them intolerably against the chafing fabric of the silk-and-lace camisole she'd slept in, making them yearn for the touch of his fingers instead.

Fighting it, she said in a desperate rush, "It's not just your ancestry—it's my job...Nik. My job—oh, damn."

His mouth found the hollow below her jaw, slid, hot and open, along the side of her neck. She moved her head—didn't want to...couldn't help it—moved it to give him better access to the sensitive places there, the places where her pulses thumpety-thumped like the jazz beat pouring from a Bourbon Street bar. Her fingers ached with the struggle to keep from burying themselves in his hair.

"Your job doesn't need to know what happens between us here," he whispered against her singing flesh.

"*I'll* know." It came on a gasp...or maybe a sob.

Nikolas let go of a breath and fought his way out of the whirlpool of desire like a diver struggling toward the light. He knew he had no business being angry—and he wasn't. He'd had no business doing this in the first place—he knew that, too. At least, not now. Although...someday, someday soon...

He pulled away from her swiftly, the way he'd tear off a bandage or pull out a tooth—because it was less painful that way. Brushing her warm, moist cheek with the backs of his fingers, he said lightly, "You're unusually dedicated to your job, aren't you?" *Or is it your employer you feel such loyalty to?* He wanted to say it, but didn't. He wasn't a jealous man—

or never had been. So why was it he felt a sudden urge to strangle a man he'd never met?

"I am," Rhia said in a voice that was flat and slightly thickened. She sat up and drove both hands, fingers spread wide, into her hair. Holding her head between her hands, she uttered a small and somewhat surprised, "Ow."

"Hangover?" Nikolas inquired, feeling like a wretch.

She nodded carefully. "A wee one, yeah." And he could see her girding herself, and her willpower marching out to do battle with her human frailties. After a moment she drew herself up, pinched the bridge of her nose between a thumb and forefinger, pulled in a long breath and opened her eyes. She reached for the cup of coffee he'd placed on the bedside table, sipped, than lifted her head and leveled a determined look at him. A steady green look from under thick black lashes. "I owe Corbett Lazlo a lot. I'd hate like hell to let him down."

"Ah," Nikolas said. "I see."

She shook her head and set the coffee back on the table. "No, I don't think you do." Throwing back the bedclothes, she pulled her knees up and swiveled them past him so that, for one heart-stopping moment, she was sitting beside him on the bed, with her smooth, sleek thigh touching his, and her body's warmth and musky feminine scent wafting over him, clouding his senses.

While he was still fighting the effects of her nearness, she rose and walked unselfconsciously to the bathroom, and his gut clenched as his gaze followed her. Buttocks...firm and rounded, solid muscle under a delicate veneer of feminine softness, scarcely disguised at all by the skimpy panties she wore. Long, taut legs and a stride of confidence and an athlete's unstudied grace. When the bathroom door closed behind her, he released a breath he didn't know he'd been holding, then laughed silently at himself for his heart-pounding, sweaty schoolboy's lust.

When she emerged from the bathroom moments later, he

had himself in hand…somewhat. It helped that she looked like a well-scrubbed teenager, with her hair in damp strands around her face and her eyes struggling to focus. She didn't look at him as she went straight to the backpack she'd left lying on the floor near the foot of the bed.

"I probably owe Corbett Lazlo my life," she said in a matter-of-fact tone as she hefted the backpack onto the bed and unzipped it. "I definitely owe him for the fact that I'm not in jail right now." And she lifted both hands and clasped them together above her head in a long sinuous stretch that bared a good bit of her lean and supple torso and momentarily robbed Nikolas of his breath.

When he had it back again, he said drily, "Nice try, luv, but you're not going to distract me that way. You can't suppose I'd let that remark go without explanation."

She threw him a look over her shoulder, a look of vague innocence he didn't buy for a minute. "There's not that much to explain, really." She gave him a sleepy-eyed smile, and he remembered the way she'd evaded the question about her association with the Lazlo Group when he'd asked it in Phillipe's kitchen a few days ago in Paris, evaded it with a smile, then, too, and the same subtle little seductions.

He said nothing…watched her take a rolled-up T-shirt and jeans out of her backpack and put them on over the wisps of underwear she'd slept in. Her movements were brisk and efficient, slightly jerky, without any hint of awareness or seduction, now. Socks and a yellow bandana handkerchief came from the depths of the backpack next. She tied the kerchief around her hair the way she'd worn it the day before, then zipped up the backpack, picked up the socks and turned to look for her shoes. He snaked out a hand and caught her wrist.

She went utterly still. Her eyes met his and seemed to shimmer in the lamplight, the way the sea does when the sun strikes it through a hole in the clouds. He felt her wiry strength, and the pulse tap-tapping against his grip, and they both knew very well she could have broken free at any time and done him considerable damage in the process. Instead, for reasons he couldn't imagine, she stood quietly, her hand relaxed in his grasp, and waited.

"It's quite unfair, you know. You know so much about me," he said softly. "And I know so little about you."

He thought he saw something flicker behind her eyes, and for a moment her mouth…her face seemed to blur…become younger. Become vulnerable. Her lips parted, and he held his breath. But instead of words, he heard the reedy beep of a tractor's horn.

"They're here," she said breathlessly. Reaching for the coffee he'd brought her, she gulped down half of it, then bent down and scooped up her shoes from the floor beside the bed. "You'd better have something for me to eat out there somewhere," she threw darkly over her shoulder as she marched barefooted out of the room. "I don't pick grapes on an empty stomach—not even for a prince."

It felt good to have the last word, but it was a hollow victory. As she sang out good-mornings to the work crew and allowed reaching hands to pull her onto the wagon, Rhia's stomach was still jittering with the aftereffects of too much *marc,* and the awareness of how close she'd come to opening up to Nikolas Donovan—emotionally *and* sexually. *My God, Rhee, what were you thinking?*

The picture that flashed instantly into her mind was graphic and unequivocal: Herself…Nik…gloriously entwined. Heartbeats bumping against each other in sultry, syncopated rhythms…sweat-slick bodies gliding together… melding in sweet and perfect harmony…. *Rhee, oh, Rhee— you're not seriously thinking of going to bed with him, are you?*

Someone handed her a fresh sweet roll and she bit into it without tasting it, unable to swallow, unable to think or respond to the friendly babble of voices around her. Unable to hear anything at all but the chorus of happy voices inside her head crying, *Yes! Oh, please, yes!*

The morning went by faster than Rhia had imagined it would. And Nikolas was right—it wasn't so bad once she was out in the fresh cool darkness of the early morning. Floodlights set up at intervals along the road cast long mysterious shadows as the pickers fanned out through the rows of grapevines, men, women and teenagers, all joking and jostling and calling challenges to one another. Competition was fierce among them to see who could fill a bucket the fastest. Fierce, but good-natured.

Rhia was given a bucket and a pair of clippers—secateurs—and shown how to snip each bunch of grapes from the vine and drop it into her bucket. After that she was on her own. She quickly lost track of Nikolas, which was probably a good thing, as she found herself becoming caught up in the friendly competition, too, not wanting to be the last one to fill *her* bucket. She worked as quickly as everyone else did, squatting down to reach the lower vines, snip-snip-snipping until all the bunches had been picked, then rising and moving on to the next vine. In spite of the coolness of the morning air, she was soon sweating, and glad of the bandana she wore which helped keep not only the dust and leaves out of her hair, but the sweat out of her eyes.

She learned to shout *"La hutte!"* as the others did, when her bucket was full, then wait for the person with the cone basket strapped to his back to come down the row so she could empty her bucket into the basket. When the basket was full, it would be carried back to the wagons and dumped into a barrel through a large funnel with a hand grinder, which would break up the grapes, partly crushing them.

It was hard work, but it made the time go quickly, and Rhia was surprised when she discovered that the darkness had thinned to pale lavender, and the hum of the generators that had powered the floodlights was replaced by the chatter and warble of birdsong, and the distant crow of a rooster. She paused to watch, entranced, while the sky became rosy pink, then salmon, then scarlet, and the sun lifted a molten eye above the purple hills and turned them a rich golden brown. The sun's touch felt like a warm hand laid lightly on her shoulders.

She saw that Nikolas, two rows over, had also stopped to watch the sunrise. As if he felt the touch of her eyes, he looked at her and smiled, and she felt a swelling inside, and the inexplicable prickle of tears.

But she refused to let herself ponder the meaning of such unfamiliar feelings, and instead brushed away a runnel of sweat with the back of her hand, pushed her hair impatiently over her shoulder and Nikolas Donovan from her mind and went back to snipping bunches of grapes from vines now sparkling with a diamond dusting of morning dew.

By midmorning, though, she was starving, and her headache had returned with a vengeance under the late-summer sun. She could feel it pounding like a hammer and anvil behind her temples as she reached the end of her row and straightened stiffly, rubbing at the small of her back. Her bucket was nearly full—might as well empty it before starting a new row, she thought.

She was looking around for *la hutte* when she spotted Nikolas over by the wagons, leaning against the tailgate, talking with Phillipe and drinking from a bottle of water. And keeping an eye on her, apparently, because when he saw her looking his way he motioned her over. It was her contrary nature that made her defy the happy little lifting sensation inside her chest and first pause to take off and unhurriedly retie her headscarf…take her own water bottle from her belt and drink…rearrange the grapes in her bucket—completely unnecessarily—before joining him. That made her refuse to look at him, lounging there with unconscious elegance in spite of the sweat that made Rhia feel itchy and dirty but only made his dusky skin gleam like polished wood and his black hair curve in wet spikes over his forehead. Made her refuse to admire the way he managed to look regal in spite of the open-neck shirt and jeans he wore, and the red scarf tied rakishly at his throat like a buccaneer's.

As she approached the two men, she saw Nikolas say something to Phillipe, who clapped him on the shoulder, blew Rhia a kiss, then sauntered off. She hesitated, then walked on, knowing the heat in her face and body wasn't all from the warmth of the sun. She was acutely aware of every inch of her body, the way it moved inside her clothes, the chafe of fabric against her sensitive places, because of the way his eyes watched her…eyes full of knowledge, confidence, and promise. *We would be lovers by now…*

"Taking a coffee break?" she said caustically, furious with the way her nipples hardened and rubbed against the lace that covered them, the way her pulses throbbed in all the wrong places. The way her chest hummed at just the sight, the nearness of the man.

"Nope—quitting time." Nikolas took her bucket from her and motioned with his head. "Job's all done."

She saw then that the other pickers were drifting in from the vineyard, laughing, chattering, teasing one another as they passed their laden buckets up to someone on the wagons to be dumped into the grinders mounted on barrels. Phillipe was there in the midst of it all, bantering and exchanging back-slaps with the men, kisses with the women, as they removed hats and scarves, wiped necks and brows, lit cigarettes or drank from water bottles.

"So, what now?" Rhia closed one eye, squinted up at the sun and added hopefully, "Lunch?"

His smile kindled, and she felt herself responding to it even though she very much did not want to. "If you mean like yesterday's bacchanalia, sorry to disappoint you, luv, but no.

No *marc* for you today, I'm afraid. Everybody'll be heading on home, I should imagine. They've chores of their own to take care of, after all. Things to do…"

"So, tomorrow you all move on to another farm, is that the way it works?"

"Not tomorrow, it's Sunday. Nobody picks on Sunday." He made a scolding noise with his tongue. "Shame on you—nice Catholic girl, you should know that."

Rhia gave him a look as she lifted a hand and pulled the scarf from her head, gave it a shake to let what breeze there was move through her sweat-damp hair. She was too hot and tired to banter with him. And hungry. "Right now, all I know is, I need a sandwich and a shower—not necessarily in that order."

"I think I can arrange that." His lashes lowered, his smile grew lazy and his movements unhurried as he casually reached out and fingered a damply curling lock of her hair off her neck and guided it over her shoulder.

Somewhere, far, far away, bees were humming, birds were singing, people were laughing…and Rhia heard none of it. She heard only the pounding of her heart, felt only the sizzle of the sunlight on her cheeks, and the shivery brush of Nikolas's fingers on her neck. She swayed slightly; she couldn't help it.

"Though…I must say, I like you this way—all wet and wild, hot-eyed and dusty. Rather like a gypsy."

He knew he shouldn't do it. Shouldn't touch her, shouldn't tease her—though it amounted to teasing himself more than anything. But he couldn't seem to help it. Somewhere along the line, his wanting had become need, and since he wasn't in the habit of allowing his physical and sexual needs to get in the way of his commitments and responsibilities, he wondered if he was allowing this particular need to blossom on purpose, as a distraction and a buffer from the chaos of his life.

As good an explanation as any, he thought. A tiny ember of alien emotions flared within him—anger, a touch of fear, touches of bitterness and bleak despair—and was quickly smothered. In a day or two he would face whatever the future had in store for him, but for now...for now, by damn, he would allow himself to enjoy whatever pleasures this beautiful, exotic, intriguing creature might offer him. No guilt, no regrets.

He'd devoted his life so far—his youth, certainly—to a cause, denied himself the comfort and fulfillment of relationships, settling instead for the temporary ease of casual affairs, the willing company of the type of woman that seemed to come his way in endless supply. He had no idea what he might be doing a week or a month from now, but for today, and perhaps tomorrow, there was this woman. Rhia. That the most beautiful and fascinating woman he'd ever met should have come into his life at such a time seemed to him more than chance. More, even, than serendipity. It almost...*almost*... made him believe in fate.

*Fate.* The thought jarred him back to awareness, where he discovered green cat's eyes gazing into his, hazy with confusion, and his hand resting on Rhia's neck, his thumb stroking up and down her sweat-slick throat, and a hot coal of desire in his belly that threatened to set him on fire.

Taking back his hand, he said, "Right, then, let's see what we can do about getting you your heart's desire..." Brisk was what he'd intended, and instead heard his voice emerge thick and furry as woolen mittens. He swiped his hand across the leg of his jeans—as if that could wipe the feel of her skin from his sensory memory—then walked the length of the wagon, checking the load of filled barrels. He paused beside the tractor to give Rhia a come-here gesture with his head and hand. "Here, this rig looks ready to go—come on, up you get."

He watched her eyes get that certain glow and her chin that particular little tilt that he was coming to know very well. It meant her independent nature was about to do battle with her feminine side. He felt a ridiculous surge of purely masculine triumph when she stepped forward and gave him her hand, allowing him to "help" her onto the tractor's high step. And a surge of something much more mysterious, a kind of exotic delight, when she gave him a sideways look as she did so, a look that clearly said, *I'm only doing this to humor your masculine ego, you know.*

She gave her head a toss as she seated herself on the high rear fender. Nik chuckled as he took the driver's seat and started up the tractor. He waved to Phillipe and the other pickers and pulled out of the line and onto the road, smiling to himself, all his senses, his nerves, his whole body sizzling with a particular excitement…alertness…expectancy. He remembered it well, that feeling, though it had been a good long while since he'd experienced it.

*The thrill of the chase.*

# Chapter 6

The shower was primitive by American plumbing standards, obviously a late—though not recent—addition to the old stone farmhouse. It consisted, as so many European showers do, of a handheld device that had a tendency to snake out of control and spray tepid water in unintended directions, usually, Rhia found, when her eyes were tightly shut and her face covered with shampoo. So it wasn't the sensual pleasure of it that made her linger much longer than she should have.

She needed to think. She did some of her best thinking in the shower; something about the gentle drumming on her scalp, the relaxing massage and caress of the water, the shushing sounds that drowned out all distractions. Sometimes she thought it seemed as though the water actually loosened up her mind…washed away clutter…made things clearer. And she desperately needed to think clearly—about many things, but mostly about Nikolas Donovan.

Thoughts of Nikolas were dangerous. Even painful. But

she forced herself to think of him anyway, like pressing on a bruise to assure herself that it really did hurt. The attraction she felt for him that had seemed so entertaining at first—daring…a little wicked, but ultimately harmless—had begun to feel instead like being caught in a flood. The water had risen before she'd realized it, and now she was being swept away by the torrent. Sometimes swimming hard and still fighting it, true. Sometimes, for a moment, giving in and letting the current carry her. Those times, the giving-in times, the letting go of the struggle times, were beginning to feel like such a relief to her, and every second the temptation grew to simply…let go. Stop fighting it. Stop trying to cling to what remained of her sanity and good sense, which were as useless anyway against the rising tide of her feelings as grabbing for twigs in a flood.

She could not fall for Nikolas Donovan. *She could not.* She could see no good outcome for herself if she did.

He wasn't making it easy for her to resist him. Damn him. Of course, he would probably have been irresistible without one particle of effort on his part, but he seemed determined to indulge himself in this lighthearted pursuit of her, as if… as if, she thought, shivering with sudden anger under the shower's cooling spray, it were some sort of *game.*

Though actually, if it were a game she could probably handle that; she'd played them herself, from time to time. Enjoyed them as much as anyone.

*But what if it's not a game?*

*Oh, yeah, admit it, Rhee. That's what's really worrying you, isn't it? That this doesn't feel like a game. Not to you, anyway. Games don't make you feel like you're riding a torrent. Like you're not in control.*

Rhia really hated not being in control, which was probably why she'd never allowed herself to fall in love before. But suppose…just suppose…that was what was happening to her now?

The thought caused a swooping sensation in her midsection, which in turn made her drop the shower wand for the sixth or seventh time. She picked it up and aimed the spray full in her face, head bowed, eyes closed and breathing hard through her mouth, and after a moment was able to make herself face the awful possibility that she might be falling in love with Nikolas Donovan.

*Falling in love with a prince. The heir to the crown of Silvershire.*

Okay. Suppose she was. The way she saw it, there were two possible outcomes.

One, it's just a game to Nikolas, and Rhia completes her mission, delivers him to his father the king and returns to her job with the Lazlo Group with a few bruises on her heart. Not a happy prospect, but she'd survive.

Or two, it's not a game for Nikolas, either. But the prospect of that didn't bear thinking about.

She emerged from the shower physically refreshed and more emotionally exhausted than when she'd stepped into it. She hurriedly toweled her hair and left it to dry in its own way, dressed in the only clean clothes she had in her backpack—khaki walking shorts and a red tank top—and slipped on her dusty running shoes and went to find Nikolas and, she hoped, some food.

She found both waiting for her in the small shaded courtyard off the kitchen. And something else.

"What's this?" she asked, nodding at the bright yellow scooter standing at the ready between Nikolas's outstretched jeans-clad legs.

His eyebrow lifted. "This? Strangely, it's a Honda—evidently, they're quite the thing in Europe these days. Phillipe's, not mine. He's been kind enough to lend it to me, though. Hop on—I want to show you something."

She sauntered toward him, arms folded across her middle, where her stomach had begun to growl uncontrollably. "Is there food in there?" She nodded at the cooler lashed to a small metal ledge on the back of the scooter.

"There is. A repast fit for a—do pardon the expression—king." He held out his hand, waiting with supreme and annoying confidence and a smile tugging irresistibly at his lips.

How *could* she resist? But she did, finger-combing her damp hair back from her face as she replied coolly, "Only if I get to drive."

His smile blossomed and his eyes grew smoky behind sleepy black lashes. Bracing the scooter with his feet, he pushed himself back and up onto the pillion seat and lifted his hands from the handlebars. "She's all yours," he murmured, laughing softly.

"'There was a young lady from Niger…who smiled as she rode with a tiger…'" Rhia muttered under her breath as she settled onto the front part of the seat. A seat which seemed very small, suddenly, altogether too small for two people to sit on at the same time. At least, not without a great deal of body contact.

"What's that?" His voice was a furry growl so close to the nape of her neck that it made shivers cascade in rivers down her back.

"Nothing," she breathed. She tested the reach and the foot pedals, then started up the motor and clicked into gear.

"That's right, you do like to be on top, don't you?" Nikolas murmured in her ear as she guided the scooter skillfully out of the courtyard. "I'll have to keep that in mind."

What had she been thinking? Thoughts that made her scalp sizzle. With him sitting so close behind her, she felt as if she'd been wrapped in a Nikolas-cocoon, steeped in Essence of Donovan. His heartbeat thumped against her back, his body heat melded with hers, his scent filled her head with sultry, sweaty images of tangled bodies…hers and his in wicked disarray….

Her jaws locked and her eyes squinted as she fought to keep her attention focused on the operation of the scooter as it grumbled impatiently through the farmhouse grounds. It whined with excitement as she accelerated down the lane, and came to a purring stop where the dirt lane met the paved road.

"Where to?" she asked in a voice that held strange vibrations not caused by the scooter.

"Left," Nikolas said.

"Right," she said, and pushed off, accelerating into the turn. And felt his arms come around her and hold on tight.

"Watch it," she muttered desperately between clenched teeth. "Do you want us to have an accident?"

His laughter rippled down her spine. "My love, it's precisely in anticipation of that possibility that I'm hanging on to you for dear life."

"That had better not be a criticism of my driving, Donovan." With a grim smile she shifted gears and the scooter leaped forward. The wind snatched the breath from her lungs and forced Nikolas to reply in a shout.

"Not at all. I'm more than impressed, actually."

"I had one of these things when I was in high school," she shouted back. "Well, not a Honda—a Vespa, oddly enough. My father bought it for me for my sixteenth birthday. Oh, hell—" She broke off as her rapidly drying hair began to whip in the wind, lashing her neck and, she was sure, Nikolas's face as well.

*Good—serves him right,* she thought as she slowed the scooter for an approaching crossroads. *Serves him right...for what? Being too damned attractive? You're the one who insisted on driving.*

She let go of one handlebar to try to corral her hair, and felt his hands there already. Felt his hands, both of them, gather her hair and gently twist it...lift it away from her neck.

"Mmm, your hair smells good," he murmured. Something—his lips, his mouth, his breath—brushed her nape.

Her spine contracted involuntarily; shivers shot through her like Fourth of July sparks. And to her embarrassment, the scooter's idling engine chose that moment to sputter and die.

"*Dammit, Nik.*" She'd intended more anger, more force behind it. Why did it have to sound so feeble?

For a long moment, Nikolas didn't reply. Something in her voice... How could he have made this confident, capable woman sound so desperate? So vulnerable? What was driving him, lately, that he kept behaving in ways so out of character for him—or, for the Nikolas Donovan he'd always thought himself to be?

*Blame it on my bad angel, I guess.*

The thought made him smile. It was what Phillipe's maman had called it, on those rare occasions when he'd gotten into mischief during his stays with Phillipe's family. *You have been listening to your Bad Angel, Nikki. You must not listen to him. Listen only to your Good Angel. He will never make you do things you will later regret.*

He let out a short gust of laughter and lifted his arms away from Rhia, shifted so there was space between his body and hers. As if he'd released a switch of some kind, the scooter's engine immediately snarled to life, and as it shot forward, this time he held on to the scooter instead of its driver.

Listening to his good angel, he managed to maintain the distance and keep his hands away from Rhia for the rest of the trip, leaning close only to make his voice heard as he guided her along the familiar route. Strange, though...the more space he put between his body and hers, the more he felt himself drawn to her, compelled by that same odd magnetism he'd felt first in the kitchen of Phillipe's flat in Paris. An attraction he felt certain even now had very little to do with sex—although it did affect him in some of the same ways....

At Nik's direction, Rhia turned the scooter off the paved road and onto a dirt lane that soon dwindled to a rock-studded track. The track wound downhill through thickets of oak trees and pines and around and between outcroppings of granite boulders through which, now and then, she caught glimpses of a meandering river. Finally, obeying another tap on the shoulder and hand gesture from Nikolas, she pulled the scooter into a little clearing of hard-packed earth and turned off the motor.

Still straddling the bike and trying without much success to finger-comb her hair into order, she said, "What is this, the local make-out spot?" It was very quiet, and in the stillness she could hear no sounds of people or vehicles, only the rush and chatter of the river.

Nikolas, who was unbuckling the cooler from the rear of the scooter, didn't look up but merely smiled. "Patience, luv. You'll see in a minute." He lifted the cooler and beckoned with his head. "Coming?"

She drew a shuddering breath, pocketed the key and followed him. Her shoes crunched over a carpet of oak leaves, acorns and pine needles. The air was warm and smelled of pine and earth and…something else. Something that tugged dusty memories from half-forgotten shelves. *River bottoms… bayous…hot sticky summers.*

She nudged the memories to the back of her mind and kept her eyes on Nikolas as he walked ahead of her down the bumpy but well-trodden path. It gave her such pleasure to watch him. He moved with the effortless grace of a leopard—a black leopard, she thought, as the wisp of a breeze lifted and toyed with his glossy black hair. A strange excitement shimmered all through her, and at the same time there was a heaviness in her heart. Which, she reflected, was the way she always felt now, being around him—or even just thinking about him—this terrible mixture of joy and despair, pleasure and pain. And she thought that if this was what falling in love was like, she was glad she'd managed to avoid it for so long.

Up ahead where the path curved around a pile of boulders, Nikolas had paused to wait for her, smiling with a touch of an odd eagerness and endearing self-consciousness. As she caught up with him he tilted his head toward the vista that had come into view just beyond the rocks.

The question hovering on her lips died there, and she said, "Oh, wow," instead.

Ahead of them the river ran wide and shallow, chuckling over rocky patches and lying quiet and leaf-dappled beneath trailing branches of the weeping willows that lined its banks. It would have been a lovely spot even without the towering structure that spanned the river's width a hundred yards or so upstream—a stone bridge, it appeared to be, consisting of two tiers of magnificent arches.

"It's Roman, of course—not as impressive as the *Pont du Gard*," Nikolas said with a modest shrug as he led the way down to the water's edge. "But also not as well-known, and therefore—" he smiled in a way that made her heart quicken "—less apt to be overrun with tourists."

"It looks as if it enjoys its share of visitors, though," Rhia said, glancing around at the hard-packed pathways and areas worn bare of grass by picnickers. Or lovers?

"Kayakers and fishermen, mostly." He nodded toward a small group of the former farther up the river beyond the bridge's arches, their brightly colored kayaks looking, from that distance, like petals of gaudy tropical flowers strewn on the waters. He glanced at Rhia and his smile tilted. "And lovers, of course."

"And which of those were you?" She asked it lightly, her heart tappity-tapping behind her ribs as she followed Nikolas across boulders and through thickets of trees and shrubs, following a pathway only he could see.

"What's that?" He paused to look back at her. "Oh—you mean, when I've come here before? All of the above, I suppose, over the years. Though more of the first two than the third, I'm afraid," he added wryly.

"Oh, come now."

"Sad, but true. I was a studious lad, you see. No time for

the lassies." He held out his hand to help her down the last treacherous steps, and his grin, as he looked up at her, seemed to belie that claim. It might have been only because she knew from his dossier that the words were in fact true that Rhia was able to find the regret in his cool gray eyes.

Thinking of that Nikolas, the quiet, studious, lonely school-boy Nikolas, she put her hand in his. The warmth of it seemed to spread all through her body. She felt his hand tighten around hers as she slipped on a gravelly patch and for a second pulled hard against the strength in his taut muscles. Then, as she regained her footing, instead of releasing her he drew her to him in a motion as fluid and easy as a dance movement between longtime partners.

For Rhia, time seemed to stand still in that moment before he kissed her. All her perceptions seemed heightened…honed. She heard music all around her, in the trickle and chatter of the water and in the songs of birds calling to each other in the trees, in the whisper of leaves falling and the hum of insects, and even in the bass growl of a vehicle of some sort passing on a nearby road. She saw sunlight sparkling on wet rocks and the edges of leaves turning gold and a spider's web hanging between two trees, catching the light and shining like spun silk. She felt the warm breeze on her bare arms and legs, her cheeks and hair like a gentle caress…and it all felt to her like summer saying good-bye. The beauty of that moment seemed unbearably sweet to her, achingly sweet, as though she knew it would never come again, not in just this way, and she knew she would leave a piece of herself behind in this moment forever.

She felt the kiss before he kissed her, as if all the nerves and cells in her body were springing eagerly to meet him. And she knew then that she'd been wanting this, needing this, and that it had been inevitable from the moment he'd lunged for her across a Paris balcony and she'd stood unmoving and let him take her down when she could so easily have eluded him.

When his lips met hers she lifted a wondering hand and

touched his face, and the textures—his textures—on her fingertips…the softness of skin contrasted with the roughness of emerging beard, the delicate play of muscles over the granite hardness of jawbone…the incredible intimacy of that…made it intensely *real*.

And at the same time it seemed an impossible forbidden miracle, and the pain of that contradiction made her lips tremble and tears etch the backs of her eyes.

She felt his hand on her back, firm between her shoulderblades, and another on the nape of her neck, fingers spread wide to burrow through her sweat-damp hair as he brought his mouth to hers, took her lips with a tenderness that made her ache. It was a giving, not a taking kiss, and she held herself still, breath suspended, and let it fill her with all the sweetness and goodness and light and joy she could possibly hold, until she quivered with the surfeit of those things, utterly overwhelmed.

He withdrew from her slowly, still holding her, and she let her head lie in the cradle of his hand as she gazed up at him, seeing him through a haze of light, like fog lit by sunshine. He seemed impossibly beautiful to her then. His hard features had blurred edges and his keen eyes a soft sheen of confusion, and the lock of hair curving down across his forehead made him look like a gentle saint.

His forehead creased suddenly with a frown, and he said in a voice gravelly with awe, "My God, Rhee, I can't believe how desperately I want to make love to you. It's quite extraordinary. Unprecedented, really."

Thus did Nikolas, feeling himself teetering on the edge of a vast unknown, manage once again to pull himself back just in time.

There was a suspenseful moment, though, before she began to laugh, to his profound relief—and laughed until tears glistened in her eyes like tiny jewels. At least, he hoped they were laughter's tears….

"Unprecedented?" she sputtered, wiping her eyes. "That's as bad as *Serendipity!*"

"Yes, I suppose it is." He caught a lifting breath and turned her neatly into the curve of one arm while every muscle and nerve in his body cramped in disappointed protest, then picked up the cooler and hiked it under the other arm. "I don't do my best work on an empty stomach, I'm afraid." He let his glance skim over her hair, the glossy strands so close to his cheek he could smell its elusive but familiar fragrance, and added lightly, "The sentiment's dead-on, though." And quickly, before she could respond, took his arm from her shoulders and caught up her hand instead. "Come—let me show you my private rock."

"If that's a variation on 'Come see my etchings,' I'd say you get honorable mention for originality, at least," Rhia muttered drily.

He chuckled, and after a moment began to sing lustily the line of a song that had been taunting him for the past twenty-four hours or so. *"'Come let's be lovers...'"*

"Simon and Garfunkel," he said when she looked at him curiously. "Come, come—you should know them, they're American. Very popular in the sixties—your mum's era, probably."

She was watching her feet, but he caught the wry tilt to her smile anyway. "During the sixties I think my 'mum' was more into John Coltrane and Cannonball Adderly."

"Ah," he said, "of course. Jazz saxophonists, both of them, right?"

"Right." He felt her head turn and her sharp green gaze touch his face. "Is there *anything* that wide-ranging education of yours didn't cover?"

"I doubt it," he said, striving for lightness but somehow unable to keep an edge of bitterness out of his voice.

What *had* it all been for, he wondered, that education of his? Had he been lied to and groomed all his life for...*this?* To become the one thing he despised above all others? *A king?*

What a joke that would be, he thought, if it were true.

They ate sitting on a flat rock that jutted out over the water, in the dappled, constantly moving shade of the giant weeping willows nearby. The meal Nik had prepared for them was simple—crusty bread drizzled with olive oil and sprinkled with garlic and herbs, topped with a delicious mixture of ripe tomatoes, olives, eggplant, anchovies and capers; a variety of goat cheeses, and wine—rosé, of course.

He cut a slice of the bread and showed her the proper way to anoint it with olive oil and toppings, then offered it to her with a reticence that bordered on shyness and seemed to her almost unbearably sweet. This was a new side of Nikolas Donovan, one the Lazlo Group's extensive dossier had evidently overlooked, and she didn't know what to do with the feelings it roused in her. Tender, nurturing feelings, alien to her nature. Or so she had always believed.

Was that why, instead of taking the piece of bread from him, she opened her mouth and let him feed her the first succulent bite, knowing what a seductive and dangerous thing it was? Or was she simply caught in the golden web of that magical afternoon, and unable—or unwilling—to claw her way out?

So she laughed self-consciously when bits of the vegetable topping escaped and fell onto her shirtfront, and the seasoned oil oozed onto her lips and down her chin. And when Nik flicked away the crumbs, she let herself wallow shamelessly in the pleasure of that casual touch. When his finger deftly caught the riverlet of oil, before she even thought about it, she licked it from his fingers.

His touch was like some sort of magic wand that turned her skin to shimmering fire in an instant. Something thumped in the bottom of her stomach, and her eyes opened wide and looked straight into his. And she wondered if the soft haze of confusion she saw there was only a reflection of what he saw in *her* eyes. She licked her lips and waited, tense and heavy with wanting, for him to kiss her again, and was bitterly disappointed when he leaned away from her instead, and picked up the loaf of bread, whittled off a slice and handed it to her with a smile, then cut another for himself.

And so they ate, sitting at angles across from each other, almost but not quite facing, almost but not quite touching, making little in the way of conversation beyond murmurs of pleasure and muttered requests to pass something or other. A pair of doves fluttered down and waddled shyly about on the fringes of the picnic, hoping for handouts which both Rhia and Nikolas readily provided. The sun came and went, burning hot on their faces sometimes, playing peekaboo with the waving branches of the willows on its slow descent into evening.

When she had eaten all she could hold, Rhia brushed off her hands, picked up her wineglass and gave herself up to the sheer pleasure of watching the man beside her…and wondered how and when it had come to this, that just the sight of him could make her ache with that terrible combination of joy and sadness.

He was sitting relaxed now, one leg outstretched, one arm propped on a drawn-up knee, lips curved in a little half smile as he tossed bits of bread crusts to the doves. As if he'd felt her eyes on him, he spoke for the first time in a while. "This was one of my favorite places when I was growing up, I'm sure you've guessed. Still is, I suppose."

"I never would've guessed that," Rhia said drily, not letting him hear a trace of softness in her voice.

He gave a short, gentle laugh that reminded her of the chuckling sound of the river. "I always felt good here, you see—didn't seem to matter what I was doing or who I was with—fishing with Phillipe, canoeing with a bunch of his friends, or…"

"Necking with a girl?"

"Once or twice." He flicked her a glance, then shrugged. "First time I've been here with a woman, though."

"Oh, my," Rhia murmured, "should I be honored?"

"Oh, definitely," he said, and his smile grew in a slow and sensual way. "After all, I've brought you to my special place."

She studied him for a long, simmering moment before asking, with solemn curiosity, "Why did you, Nikolas?"

His forehead crinkled in that puzzled little frown that told her he was about to tease her again, which she was beginning to realize was his way of easing back when things threatened to become too intense.

"I'm not quite sure, actually. I suppose there's something primitive involved—caveman-ish, you know? Some sort of male imperative where I show you, the female of my choice..." he trailed a finger lightly down her bare thigh as his eyes drifted over her face "...that I am capable of providing you with a safe, secure and lovely place in which to consummate—*what?*" She was laughing and shaking her head.

What else could she do?

His eyes slipped downward to study the movement of his finger on her thigh, as if fascinated by the goose bumps its stroking had raised there. When they lifted again to hers there was a softness in them, like the sky before it rains. "We *are* going to be lovers," he said softly. "I know it, and so do you."

She turned her head quickly to hide the tears that had sprung unexpectedly to her eyes. Her throat ached.

"The idea doesn't appear to make you happy. Why is that, Rhee?"

She swallowed...shook her head, tried to laugh. Then, instead of answering him, heard herself say in a husky Cajun accent, "I had a place like this when I was growing up. A place where I always felt good, no matter what I was doing or who I was with."

He didn't speak, and his hand lay quiet on her thigh, waiting...as if he knew there was more to what she was telling him than reminiscence.

*Chapter 7*

"My cousins—well, they were my mama's cousins, actually—had this place down in the bayous." He wondered if she even realized she'd lapsed into the cadences of her childhood. "We used to go down there and visit, now and again…sit and fish, play music, eat…just generally have fun, you know? We Cajuns are good at havin' fun." She flashed him a smile, and the wave of tenderness that rose inside him when he saw the pain in it stunned him to utter silence.

"It was the nighttime I loved best," she went on after a moment. "When the darkness came down, you couldn't see the squalor, the poverty, all you could see was the moonlight dancin' on the water, and lightnin' bugs twinklin' out in the trees, and the soft yellow light from the porch where the grown-ups were sittin', playin' music. One of the cousins— or maybe his daddy—played the mouth organ—harmonica, you know? Played it so it would just about make you cry without you even knowing you were sad. Mama, she could play just about anything, but she liked alto sax best. And there was always a fiddle and a banjo, and maybe some spoons…I don't know what all else, but together they made a beautiful sound. It just sort of filled in the spaces between the frog and cricket sounds and the slap of the water against the pilings, and the 'gators bellowin' off in the swamps. And the air was so soft and wet it seemed like it got inside your skin…made you feel gentle all over, like nothing could ever rile or upset you and you'd just stay this happy for always and forever."

"But you didn't stay that way, did you?" Nikolas said softly when she paused. "Because your father came and took you away."

Her head jerked around and she stared at him with wide startled eyes. "How did you—"

"You told me—in Phillipe's kitchen, in Paris—remember?" For no other reason except that he desperately needed to touch her, he reached out and with one finger guided a stray lock of her hair away from her cheek and nudged it behind her ear. Her skin felt like warm satin against his fingertip, and he ached to feel its softness on his palms…his lips…with every part of him.

His fingers, trailing wistfully down the side of her neck, snagged on the thin silver chain he'd noticed the day she'd arrived in Phillipe's Paris flat. He hooked it and drew the tiny silver charm from its nest between her breasts. He watched it swing from his extended finger for a moment, then lifted his eyes to hers. "A saxophone," he said softly. "I get it now."

He relinquished the charm as her fingers closed protectively around it. "My mother gave it to me," she said in a thickened voice. "For my twelfth birthday. She told me it was to remind me that no matter what happened, I'd always have music. That was right before my father came for me. That's why—" She stopped, shook her head and looked away.

"I didn't ask you to tell me about that in Paris," Nikolas said, watching his fingers skim lightly over her shoulder. "I barely knew you, then. I thought I hadn't the right. But now that we know we're going to be lovers..." He took his gaze from the place where his finger touched her skin to meet her somber green eyes...and smiled.

Her eyes darkened as he watched. "I'll tell you," she said gravely, not returning his smile, "so maybe you'll understand why that notion doesn't make me happy. But—" her lashes quivered and fell and she caught a quick breath "—it would be a whole lot easier to talk about this if you wouldn't touch me."

He felt a surprising stab of pain, but lightly said, "I'll give it a try." He lifted his hand from her shoulder and stretched out sideways, propped himself on one elbow and gave her a go-ahead nod.

She looked at him warily along her shoulder as she drew up her knees and wrapped her arms around them, and it seemed to him she was building a fortress around herself—a fortress meant for one purpose: to keep him out.

"Mama was working in a jazz joint on Bourbon Street when she met my father—playing music, mostly, but between sets she'd serve drinks...tend bar. My...father—" her mouth and even the tone of her voice changed shape when she said that word "—was in the real estate business—in a big way. Like—think Donald Trump, okay? Only Southern-style—based in Miami. He was in New Orleans for a couple of months getting some new project going, and one night he happened to walk into the place where my mama worked." She paused to give him a sideways look, lifted a shoulder and tried to smile. "I guess he liked her looks and her music—she for sure liked his looks and his money.... Anyway, sparks flew. By the time he was ready to leave New Orleans I was well on the way. He did marry her—I'll give him credit for that. And he took her home with him to Miami. That's where I was born."

She was silent for a while, but he didn't prompt her, just listened to the river sounds and watched the setting sun paint her hair with reddish light. The wistfulness in her face as she gazed into her past made his own throat tighten with a sadness he didn't quite understand. Nostalgia, maybe? Thinking of—and lonesome for—a past he'd never had?

She let go a soft, sighing breath. "She was miserable in Miami—wasn't happy with *him*. No big mystery why—she was warm-hearted and a free spirit, and he was a cold-hearted control freak. Anyway, when I was about two, she took me and ran off—went back home to her folks in New Orleans. Naturally, he followed her, not because he loved her—or me—so much, I'm sure. He's not capable of that. It was because he just couldn't stand that she'd left him. And worse, because she'd taken something that belonged to him, *he* thought. Me."

She lifted her head and shook her hair back and glared at him, and there was an angry fire in her eyes. "He was rich and powerful. In a custody fight you'd think my mama wouldn't have stood a chance, right? But you'd be wrong. She was no dummy, she filed for divorce in Louisiana, and a Louisiana judge—a Cajun judge—gave her full custody of me. My father had to go back to Miami empty-handed, and for ten years, Mama and I were as happy as could be."

She fell silent again, and this time Nikolas didn't wait for her to pick up the thread. He shifted restlessly and sat up. "Ten years…and then he came and got you? What did he do, take your mother back to court? Why did he wait so long to do it?"

In the golden light he could see a bitter little half smile, her only answer—then—to his second question. "Nope, just showed up one day in his Mercedes and took me."

"*Took* you? As in…kidnapped? My God. What did your mother do? Didn't she—"

"Mama wasn't home at the time. I think—" Her voice went high and then broke, startling them both. She waited a moment, fingering the little gold saxophone. "I think she knew he was coming. I think she made sure she wasn't there when he showed up."

Nikolas just stared at her, The question—*Why?*—in his mind so deafening he couldn't even say it.

She stared defiantly back at him and answered it anyway. "Hey, I was twelve. And growing up fast, if you know what I mean." She hunched one shoulder in a shrug that reminded him of a wounded bird. "Maybe she felt like she wouldn't be able to handle me. Maybe she decided she wanted her freedom—who knows? I don't know if she contacted him or he contacted her, but I'm positive they made some kind of deal. Anyway—" her lips spasmed briefly, then firmed "—he came and got me, and I went to live with him in Miami. I wasn't given a choice. End of story."

He cleared his throat and said harshly, "Oh, I seriously doubt that. More like the end of a single chapter, and I can't wait to hear the rest. But I'm already beginning to get the gist, I think. You said you were telling me this now to explain why you aren't happy about the otherwise delightful prospect of making love with me, so I must assume it's because of this complete jackass of a father, right? He's turned you against men, or some such bilge?"

"Not all men," she corrected. "Just…very rich and powerful men."

"Ah," said Nikolas.

"And who is richer and more powerful…"

"…than a king. Yes, I see."

Silence and purple twilight wrapped them in its gentle cocoon.

Hunched and wretched, Rhia watched Nikolas lean away from her to open the cooler. Reaching for the wine, she thought, wishing there was something a good bit stronger in that cooler—Jack Daniel's maybe. But instead he took out a shallow crockery bowl covered in plastic, and then a short fat glass jar containing something thickly liquid and amber in color. In silence, and with almost ceremonial reverence, he uncovered the bowl and opened the jar, then selected a cut section of ripe fig from the bowl and dipped it in the contents of the jar. He turned it to corral the drips, then held it out to her.

"Come 'ere," he said softly when she looked at him askance. "I want you to taste this."

"What is it?"

"Dessert. Open up."

"Oh, Nik. I don't think I can eat another bite…" Not because she was full, but because her throat was so tight, and aching like sin. But she opened her mouth anyway, because when he smiled at her that gentle way, she'd have done anything he asked. She let him place the sticky morsel on her tongue. An incredible sweetness burst inside her mouth, figs and honey flavored with lavender and…orange blossoms. "Oh, my God," she murmured. "It's delicious…heaven." *No—* this *is sin. Decadent…sensual…*

He was already leaning toward her. He had only to lean a little farther to kiss her, and at first she could hardly distinguish the sweetness of his mouth from the honey already clinging to her lips. Then there was a blending of the two sweetnesses that seemed to turn liquid and run into every part of her, filling her to bursting with a sweetness so intense she couldn't bear it. She felt a building pressure inside her chest, a rising whimper…and just when she thought she wouldn't be able to hold it in another second, he pulled back from her, wiped his essence and the stickiness of honey from her lips with his thumb and murmured, "I'm just a man, Rhee. Not rich, not powerful. I'm a rebel, I suppose. But definitely not a king."

"But," she whispered, "you will be."

"Unless I choose not to be." His eyes were grave and very close to hers.

She stared back at him. Her lips felt chilled and bereft without his, with all the sweetness gone and her stomach doing cold flip-flops under her ribs. At the same time her heart was quivering eagerly, doing happy-puppy dances and crowing, *Yes, oh yes! Choose not to go back! We'll run away to-*

*gether—or stay right here in this sunny valley among the vineyards. I will even learn to like wine!*

While her head, heavy with the weight of duty and responsibility, sternly chided, *Are you insane? It's your job to take him back. You must take him back. His country needs him.*

Then he kissed her again, and both of those voices went silent, the only sound inside her head now the hushed and daring love words she knew she could never say.

With one hand between her shoulderblades and the other cradling her head, he slowly laid her back. His mouth followed her down, and then his body, as his hands lifted her to meet him, bringing her hard against him, and somewhere amidst the shock waves of pleasure rippling through her came the realization that it was the first time she'd felt the full strength and warmth of his body like this, touching, pressing all along the length of hers, without blankets or layers of clothing between.

*The first time?* Then why did her skin seem to know his touch already? She felt his hand slip under her top, slide rough and warm over her skin, pushing the soft, giving fabric ahead of it until it found and nested one tight and aching breast. Her breast felt so good in his hand…and so familiar…so right. She let her head drop back, baring her throat to him, offering him that and any other vulnerable part of her he cared to conquer. Complete and unconditional surrender.

Her breast lifted eagerly into his palm, and when she felt his mouth encapsule the tender tip and his tongue begin its exquisite torture, waves of desire all but overwhelmed her. She felt like a fragile shell around a liquid center…her inside sweet and melting, like honey in the sun.

She heard herself whisper—whimper—his name. Her fingers were tangled in his hair.

He took his mouth from her breast, pressed his lips briefly, warmly against hers and whispered back, "I know…I know, luv. But not here."

She was dazed with arousal, shivering with wanting... wanting to do anything to keep from stopping this...sick with knowing it had to stop. "Do you really think," she asked, her voice bumpy from the shivers, "anybody's going to come along?"

"Probably not." Laughing softly, he kissed the tip of her nose, then her chin, then each eyelid. "But I know you like to be on top, and I'd hate to think what this rock would do to my tender bum."

Then she was laughing, too, pushing furiously at him, clinging helplessly to him, tears seeping between her lashes. Wondering how she could still laugh when she was about to charge headlong into sure disaster.

The house was quiet and dark when they returned. Nikolas had expected it would be; Phillipe would be out carousing with his friends on a Saturday night and unlikely to return before morning, celebrating the end of *vendange*. Maman wasn't due back from Monte Carlo until tomorrow.

He dropped Rhia off in the courtyard near the kitchen door, then returned the scooter to the garage. When he came back to the house he found her standing in the hallway, looking un-characteristically uncertain. She watched him as he came to her, and her eyes followed his as he cupped her cheek in his hand and tenderly asked, "So...is it still yes?"

She smiled then, her lashes dropping across her eyes with what might have been relief, and huskily replied as she swayed into him, "Against every ounce of good sense and judgment...it's still yes. I guess I'm my mother's daughter after all."

A fierce little jet of protective anger spurted through him and hardened his voice. "You may well be, but I'm bloody well sure I'm not like your father."

Her lips parted with an almost inaudible gasp, and he caught whatever response she might have made with his own mouth. He kissed her without restraint, knowing there was no reason now to hold anything back, and found that he was hungrier for her than he'd thought, hungrier than he'd thought he could be. His need for her was a fist in his belly, a burning weight in his loins, and something else the exact location and nature of which were far less easy to define. He knew he'd never felt its like before with any woman. It emptied his head of all coherent thought and filled him instead with feelings too vast and complex to articulate, so that when he lifted his mouth from hers at last he could only gasp and hold her close to him, like a dazed shipwreck survivor finding a raft to cling to.

So it was left to her to mumble, her words a moist warmth on his throat, "My place or yours?"

Cobbling his scrambled wits together, he gave a shaken laugh. "Well, since technically yours belongs to Phillipe's maman, I think I'd prefer mine, if that's all right with you."

She tipped her head back, searching for his mouth, and managed to get as far as, "Fine with—" before he gave her what they both wanted.

He never did know quite how they got from there to his bedroom, or how long the journey took. It might have been seconds or uncounted hours. He remembered shutting the door at last, closing them into the quiet embracing darkness of his bedroom, and after that his only reality was the woman in his arms, the taste of her mouth, the shape of her breasts pillowed against his chest, the firm round weight of her buttocks in his hands…her hands pushing under his shirt, their warm thrusts impatient on his skin…yet no more impatient than he was for her touch.

He'd never felt such a hunger, such impatience before. Lovemaking, liaisons, sex…had always been simple for him. A lighthearted—sometimes intense—experience, no more complicated than the enjoyment of a good meal or a fine wine, indulged in whenever he'd felt the need of relief from the pressures and demands of school, work, *the cause*. One or two had been…memorable; none had ever consumed him. None had ever obliterated thought, overridden judgment. None had made him consider, even for a moment, shirking his duty to his country or abandoning the task he'd set for himself of releasing Silvershire from the burden of medieval monarchy and guiding her kicking and screaming into the twenty-first century.

But he wasn't thinking of any of that now. What was he thinking? He wasn't thinking. He only *wanted…felt…needed.*

With greedy hands he pulled her against him, and was shocked to discover that at some point he—or she—had divested her of her clothes—most of them, all but the thin scrap of nylon that still stood as a barrier to her most vulnerable and guarded places. Her nakedness in his arms was both a delight and a torment, his need to bury himself in her like a vast and terrible thirst.

And yet, though his skin felt feverish and his clothing an intolerable abrasion, though pulses hammered in every part of his body, he felt himself holding back. *Why?*

It stunned him to realize that it was *she* who was the brakes on his runaway passion—her need, her desire, her vulnerability. He understood that he wanted the same things for her that he wanted—needed—for himself, and he wanted to be the one to give them to her. Wanted to watch her face light with joy and her eyes grow hazy with sated passion, her lips curve with a smile of feminine mystery.

This, too, was something new—not that he cared for his partner's pleasure; he'd always made that a priority, and available evidence suggested he'd done it rather well. But this was different—he wasn't sure how, exactly, only that it was.

So he slowed himself down, even though there was urgency in his every heartbeat, and touched her with tenderness, even though his own skin felt on fire. He whispered to her passion words he didn't recognize and wouldn't remember, even though his own need was a screaming pressure behind his eyes. He held her gently from him while her clever hands stripped him naked and then traced patterns across his skin that left him all but blind and quivering like an infant.

'It was then that he laid them both down. He ran his hands over her powder-soft skin, dipped them under the lacy edges of the last nylon barrier and pushed it away, and her gasp when his exploring fingers found her warm, protected places made him swell with a fierce masculine triumph, and at the same time, something like…awe.

He regretted, then, that he hadn't turned on the lights so he could see her, too. Regretted, but only a little. His senses were already on overload with the taste, the smell, the feel of her; adding sight to the feast would have been gluttony.

Besides, he already knew she was beautiful—though at the moment, strangely, that didn't seem important to him at all.

Sound, too, was muted, limited to breath sounds and sighs, and those passion-whispers that aren't really words. Both of them were lost in the wonder of discovery like small children on Christmas morning.

The rhythmic push of her body against his hand…the sweet, soft powder-scent of her breast, the bud-like tip blossoming in the warmth of his mouth…her quick lifting breaths, the momentary stopping of them when his fingers found her hidden depths…it all seemed new to him somehow. Her body in his arms, sleek and lithe as an otter's, her hands weaving pleasure-spells over his skin, her lips murmuring love words she probably didn't realize she was saying…it all seemed like a miracle to him, and at the same time as natural as the sounds of the river running along its bed.

It felt natural, too, when passion had obliterated thought, when murmurs had become whimpers of desperate demand, that he should bring her to *him,* drape her over him so that her long, supple body covered his from chest to toes. Natural that her legs should move apart and her knees come up to straddle him, and her hair slip forward and fall around his face and hers like a curtain...natural as the rain falling.

He felt her body shaking as she lifted her head to look down at him in the darkness. "You really did mean it, didn't you?" She leaned down to him again, but it was her forehead that touched his lips and it was then he realized with a surge of dazed delight that she was laughing. Laughing in the broken, breathless way of someone overwhelmed. "About me being on top..."

"Always..." His tongue could barely form words. They were whispers, mere puffs of air. "You have the power...but I think...if you don't plan to let me inside you now...you should just kill me at once...put me out of my misery."

He heard her breath catch...felt her body shift...her hand gently encircle him...the first exquisite giving of her tenderest places. He gasped when he felt resistance. "Rhia—luv—are you—" But she silenced him with a quick, breathless kiss, and slowly, slowly her warm body accepted...adjusted...enfolded...welcomed him.

She drew a shuddering breath and whispered, "Are you still in misery?"

His hands held her hips as he set himself more deeply inside her, and his silent laughter jolted him...and her. "Misery? No...but did you kill me after all? Because I think...this must be Paradise."

Her shaken laughter joined his and then was extinguished in their merging mouths...in hungry, questing, greedy, heedless kisses. His arms encircled her, brought her down to him, held her as close to him as he dared—and then, almost before he knew what she was doing, she was leaning back, bringing him with her so that they were both sitting upright, still holding each other, still together, still entwined. She wrapped her legs around him and he felt himself nested deep inside her, as deep as he could possibly go. And he felt her mouth blossom into a smile.

"Now…neither one of us is on top," she murmured, teasing his moistened lips with the words. "That's the best way, isn't it?"

"The best way possible," he agreed, and bringing one hand up to cradle her head, brought her mouth deeply to his again.

She began to move then, a smooth undulation of spine and muscles, a sensuous rocking that stroked every part of him at once, and he was dizzy with the pleasure of it…lost in desire. He felt his mind leave him, aware only of building pressure, an urgency like nothing he'd ever known before. His hands moved over her back and his body thrust against her rocking, hard…and harder…and her breaths became frantic whimpers. She tore her mouth from his at last and he buried his face in the hollow of her throat and pressed his mouth against the leaping pulse there while her back arched and tightened like a bowstring.

He said something to her…he didn't know what. She gave a little sobbing cry and he felt the tension inside her break and her body ripple with the shock waves, waves that caught him up and carried him with her, helpless as a rag doll in a flood.

When his mind came back to him he was in a quiet, peaceful place, dazed and battered but exhilarated, too.

He lay back slowly, bringing her with him. Her body was still wracked with shivers, so he reached for the edge of the comforter that was folded across the foot of his bed and flipped it over them both, wrapping her in its warmth and his arms. Then he lay silently holding her. Unknown emotions were swelling inside him, making it impossible for him to speak. He wondered about her silence, wondered if it was because she felt the same emotions, and what she would call them if he asked. Knowing he wouldn't ever ask.

Finally, when her body had stopped quaking and the comforter's warmth became too much, he folded a corner of it back and kissed her damp forehead, and she stirred and slipped to one side, leaving her head pillowed on his shoulder, her arm across his torso and one leg companionably tucked between his.

"Sorry, luv," he murmured as he stroked a hand idly up and down her back, "I hate to say it, but…I'm afraid the word that comes to mind, once again, is…unprecedented."

Her body rippled with laughter. "Works for me," she said in a sleepy purr that made him think, for the first time in a while, of a cat.

He woke to find himself alone, the comforter smoothed and tucked against his side where Rhia's body had been. He realized, though, that it wasn't her absence but a sound that had awakened him, a sound that came from somewhere far off, like a cry in the night. That's what he thought it was, at first—someone crying. Then he realized it was music, and he thought it was the most beautiful and at the same time the saddest sound he'd ever heard.

He knew he wasn't dreaming it; certain demands and discomforts of his body left him no doubt that he was fully awake. Throwing back the comforter, he got up and walked naked to the bathroom he shared with Phillipe, noting as he did that Phillipe's bedroom door was still open a few inches, indicating he hadn't, as Nikolas had expected, returned from his evening's celebrations. Nikolas quickly took care of the demands and discomforts, washed himself and put on a bathrobe, then went in search of the music, and Rhia. He was certain he'd find both in the same place, and he did.

She was in the courtyard, sitting on a low semicircular stone wall that skirted the base of a fountain set into the courtyard wall. The fountain wasn't running at that time of night, and the water lay still and dark at her feet, reflecting the moonlight in turgid undulations. She was wearing a light robe that must have been Maman's that hung open to reveal the scrap of lace she called panties and a sleeveless top like the undershirts some men wear. It hugged her breasts and slender torso like skin only slightly paler than her own. Her back was propped against the courtyard wall and her bare legs were drawn up, cross-legged under her. Moonlight lay around her like spilled milk and glinted subtly on the instrument in her hands.

He stood in the kitchen doorway and listened to the saxophone's mournful wail, not wanting to interrupt her, letting himself fill up with a sweet melancholy, the kind only a sad song could make him feel.

He must have made some movement, or maybe she only sensed him there. In any case, she let the music die to a whisper, then lowered the saxophone and sat waiting for him, her head back and resting against the wall.

Unable to read her expression and not knowing why she was out here in the courtyard playing the blues alone in the moonlight, he went to her slowly, hands in the pockets of his bathrobe to keep from reaching for her.

"Regrets, luv?" he asked softly, a sharp little pain lodging near his heart.

She shook her head. Reaching out a hand, she caught the belt tie of his robe and pulled him closer. Then, instead of lifting her face for his kiss, she simply leaned her head against him. Unfathomably moved, he stroked her hair for a moment, then sat behind her on the fountain's base and settled her against him. With his arms wrapped around her and his lips against her hair, he murmured, "Then why the sad song?"

"It's called the blues," she said with a hint of a smile in her voice. "You don't need to be sad to play the blues."

He kissed the top of her head, closed his eyes and inhaled the sweet fragrance of her hair. "But you are, aren't you." It was a statement, not a question.

She let out a breath, and it was a minute or two before she answered, in a voice that was husky and soft. "Yeah, I guess I am. A little."

"Why, luv?"

"I don't know. I think—" He felt her body strain as she hauled in another breath, as if she had vast spaces inside that air couldn't reach. "I came here to bring you back. It's my job to bring you back. You are the crown prince of Silvershire. It's your duty to go back. But…" her voice became a breaking whisper "…dammit, I can't help it. I don't want you to go."

He tightened his arms around her and rested his cheek on her head. "I don't want to go either."

"But you're going to…aren't you." She didn't make it a question.

He let out a breath, and it was a long time before he answered, "Yes, I guess I am. I think…I must."

She turned her face into the hollow of his neck. "Yeah. That's why you're going to make one helluva great king, you know that, don't you?"

He was shocked to feel a warm wetness on her face that could only have been tears.

## Chapter 8

The Lazlo Group's sleek black helicopter churned across the waters of the channel on the morning sun's glistening path. Rhia, watching the wakes of ships and the Channel Islands—Alderney, Guernsey, Jersey—drift by below, thought it was like being the lone traveler on a broad superhighway paved in gold.

She tore her gaze from the sparkling vista and glanced again at the man sitting silently beside her, narrowed eyes focused intently on the hazy outline just coming into view on the horizon. A cold little frisson of misery rippled through her. This morning there was no sign of the Nikolas Donovan she'd come to know, the cynical charmer from the Paris apartment, the carefree, flirtatious grape picker—somewhat more earthy than expected. The skillful and incredibly tender lover. This, she thought, must be the man Corbett Lazlo had warned her about, the hard man, the rebel who for years had organized and led a powerful and dedicated opposition to the monarchy in Silvershire. A man both respected and feared.

The man who'd made love to her, made her feel things she'd never felt before, the man who'd made her laugh…and cry, was a stranger to her now.

She was glad the clatter of the chopper's rotors and the headphones they both wore made conversation difficult, if not impossible. What would they have talked about? Impersonal things, probably, fit for the ears of the chopper pilot—an unnecessary recap of plans for the coming reunion with Nikolas's father, King Weston, perhaps. It was to be a private meeting, held in strictest secrecy, not at the royal palace in Silverton, or even at the official royal retreat in Carringtonshire, but at a little-known hunting lodge in the Lodan Mountains in the province of Chamberlain, the king's ancestral home. Those present at the historic meeting would include King Weston, Nikolas, Rhia and a few trusted members of the king's security staff. Those were the terms both the king and Nikolas had agreed upon. The details had been left to Rhia and other representatives of the Lazlo Group to work out.

And after the reunion…what then? Rhia's job would be done, another difficult assignment successfully completed. And Nikolas…what would become of him?

Bleakly, she watched a muscle work in the side of his jaw, his steely gray eyes fixed on the approaching coastline. Would he accept the charge that had been taken from him at birth and assume the crown he'd always despised? Become king…and thus forever beyond her reach? Would she ever again feel his hands on her body, taste his mouth, smell his skin?

Pain knifed through her and she drew a sharp, gasping breath, just as the chopper swept over the lacy edge where the lapping Channel waves met the rocky shores of Silvershire.

The helicopter's route brought them into Silvershire's airspace just north of the town of Dunford, in Danebyshire. As they crossed the gleaming ribbon of the Dane River, Nikolas nudged Rhia with his elbow and pointed; she nodded in reply. It was an acknowledgment, nothing more. He knew it wasn't necessary for him to tell her Dunford was where he'd lived and worked for the past five years, teaching history at Dunford College of Liberal and Fine Arts. She would have learned that fact, and just about everything else there was to know about his life, from the Lazlo Group's dossier. Though right now, looking down at the slate roofs and church spires of the town and the campus, he felt as disconnected from that life in spirit as in body.

That was his past. No matter what happened at the coming meeting, he had to accept that he could never go back to the way things had been.

Though he stared out his side of the chopper, watching its shadow flit across the forested landscape below, he was intensely aware of the woman sitting beside him. She was dressed once again in the black pants and leather jacket she'd worn for breaking and entering Phillipe's flat in Paris, though the chemise had been replaced by a black pullover embroidered just above her left breast with the green-and-gold plaited pentagram that was the Lazlo Group's logo.

Rather ironic, he thought, that she should be the one bright spot for him in all of this, when she was the one who'd yanked him out of his former life and pitched him kicking and screaming into this new one he'd never dreamed of nor wanted. In any case it would have been idiotic to blame her for it, and he didn't. She'd only been doing her job. And as for what had happened between them, he acknowledged that was more his doing than hers, and furthermore, in his selfishness he'd caused her some degree of pain.

Still, he couldn't bring himself to regret what had happened…making love with her. Or to contemplate the possibility that it might never happen again.

To block that thought, he turned his mind instead to the coming meeting. Another irony, that was. He'd tried so many times, as head of the Union for Democracy, to arrange a meeting with His Majesty, to discuss his plan for phasing out the centuries-old and outdated monarchy and ushering in a form of democratic government based—in his opinion quite reasonably—on that of their neighbor, Great Britain's responsible monarchy. In the past, he'd never gotten past Weston's advisors—not hard to understand their diligence, perhaps, since most of their jobs no doubt depended on keeping the status quo. And now…here he was, on his way to a private, one-on-one meeting with the king at his secret mountain hideaway. But not to discuss politics.

What, he wondered, as his heart lurched and a pulse began tap-tap-tapping in his belly, does a man say to a long-lost father who is not only his sworn adversary, but his king?

The chopper churned on across the Dunford Wood, the province of Perthegon, and crossed the Kairn River into Chamberlain. *My father's lands. I suppose that makes them my lands, too?*

His mouth curved in a sardonic little smile as the chopper banked sharply south over the Lodan Mountains.

The helicopter settled onto the grassy clearing, a little meadow surrounded by pine trees not far from the lodge. As the rotors slowed to a lazy swishing, Nikolas opened the door and stepped down onto the yellowing grass. He paused to wait for Rhia to do the same, and then they both hurried at a half crouch through the turbulence to meet their welcoming committee.

Three people had emerged from the woods on the edge of the clearing. Two were men, obviously security guards, resplendent in the king's livery and looking gloriously out of place in that rustic setting. The third person, Rhia was startled to see, was a woman, casually dressed in slacks and a windbreaker. Her auburn hair was pulled back in a ponytail, and it was a moment before Rhia recognized the king's personal physician, Dr. Zara Smith—or was it Shaw, now? she wondered. Lady Zara had recently become the wife of Dr. Walker Shaw, the Lazlo Group's chief psychologist and an old friend of Rhia's.

While the two guards stood stiffly at attention, Lady Zara, whom Rhia had met only briefly at her wedding reception, greeted her with a smile and a brisk handshake. "Hello, Rhia, it's good to see you again."

"Likewise, Lady Zara," Rhia said, returning the smile. "Good to see you looking so great. Married life must be good for you."

"Walker is good for me," Lady Zara replied, with the soft eyes and satisfied smile of a woman deeply in love, and Rhia couldn't help feeling a small, treacherous stab of envy.

"I'm surprised to see you here," she said. "I thought you were still on your honeymoon."

Lady Zara's forehead creased momentarily with a tiny frown. "Lord Southgate suggested I be here for the meeting," she said in an undertone. "He is…concerned. But it was His Majesty who insisted on it."

She turned curious, champagne-colored eyes on Nikolas and offered him her hand. "Mr. Donovan, I must tell you that I have strongly advised against this meeting."

"I imagine you have," Nikolas said drily as he shook her hand. "You, and I'm sure many others as well, considering I'm suspected of murder for hire—among other things."

"That's for others to determine," Lady Zara said without smiling. "My concerns are for His Majesty's health. The king is still recovering from his recent illness, as you know. He is still not entirely himself, which is to be expected given the series of shocks he's had to deal with. His son—ah, Reginald's death, then surgery for a brain tumor, and the hospital bombing and his subsequent coma on top of it. The news that Reginald wasn't the king and queen's biological son, and the fact that he was murdered…and now…" she shook her head "…learning his biological son and the true heir to his crown is none other than the man who's been trying to take it from him—" She broke off, realizing, perhaps, that she'd been a bit too frank.

Nikolas said with a touch of impatience, "Of course. I'll try not to say or do anything that might upset His Majesty."

Rhia winced at the note of sarcasm, but the doctor only said mildly, "Your presence alone will upset him quite enough, I expect. If you will come this way, please. He's been waiting for you—somewhat on edge, as you can imagine."

She turned and led the way to a broad pathway that wound through the pine forest. One of the guards fell in behind them while the other took up a sentry's position at the edge of the meadow—to keep an eye on the helicopter and its pilot, Rhia guessed. She turned once to look back at the chopper, sitting motionless now, like a great black insect, the pilot leaning relaxed against the Lazlo Group logo on its door.

The path beneath her feet was spongy with pine needles, the air pungent with the scent of the pines and the dusty earth. She breathed deeply as she walked, filling her lungs with that warm dry air, hoping it might help to quell the butterflies rampaging through her middle. Wondering whether Nikolas had butterflies, too.

If he does, no one would ever know it, she thought, stealing glances at him as they made their way along the pine-carpeted path. His eyes were cool as rain, his face might have been chiseled from the earth itself. There was only the tiny muscle working in the side of his jaw to tell her of the turmoil inside.

*Oh, yeah. He definitely has butterflies.*

Was this what Nikolas would call empathy, she wondered? Or was it only her newborn feelings for him that made her feel his turmoil too, and ache to take his hand?

The mountain setting was idyllic and beautiful, no doubt a perfect place for healing both body and soul, if Nikolas had taken notice of it. But he had gone far away for the moment, retreating inside the chilly isolation of his analytical mind. It was where he often took refuge from the chaos of his emotions or circumstances beyond his control. The meeting ahead, the current upheaval in Silvershire, the unanswered questions, even his new and unsettling feelings for the woman walking silently beside him, all these things were manageable, he believed, if he could simply reduce them to problems to be solved.

*Focus,* he ordered himself sternly, as his mind whirred dizzily through a blizzard of thoughts, unable to see any of them clearly. *One thing at a time. First things first.*

*Get through this meeting first. After that...who knows where I'll be? In prison, maybe.*

*You will naturally conduct yourself with dignity,* he told himself.

Yes, he would be courteous. But not cordial. Weston was the sovereign ruler of his country and as such, deserving of respect, no matter how Nikolas might feel about the monarchy itself.

*But no amount of DNA will ever make the man my father.*

And, he reminded himself, Weston no doubt had the same reservations about him. After all, the man had raised that twit Reginald as his son and heir for thirty years, and undoubtedly felt a father's love for the blighter in spite of his rather considerable shortcomings. That sort of feeling didn't disappear because of a few mismatching strands of double helixes.

Nikolas told himself he wouldn't expect a thing from this one-on-one meeting with His Majesty, except maybe a chance to begin to clear his name of those insane suspicions of murder and mayhem. No, all that would happen today was that he and Weston would take each other's measure, ask and answer whatever questions might occur to them, and that would be that.

He just wished he could do something about the bloody butterfly convention taking place in his stomach.

He stole a glance at the woman beside him, sleek and lithe in her uniform black, silent and intent as a hunting cat, green eyes focused on their guide up ahead as if she were some fascinating species of mouse. He wondered what she was thinking—feeling—right now, and whether she had butterflies, too.

He wished he could reach over and take her hand.

* * *

The Weston family's so-called hunting lodge was in fact a sizeable manor house built in the Georgian style out of natural stone. It was only two stories in height, with leaded windows, a slate-tile roof and towering chimneys, a large one at either end and several smaller ones scattered between. Rhia, who'd been picturing something more on the order of a log cabin, or maybe a Swiss-style chalet, thought that if this was what royals called a modest hunting lodge, she couldn't wait to see the palace.

The house seemed oddly out-of-place here, tucked among the towering pines. Such an imposing house, Rhia thought, deserved a proper setting, with sweeping lawns and curving driveways and magnificent formal gardens. Here, it reminded her of Sleeping Beauty's castle under the spell of the evil fairy, left at the mercy of creeping vines and rampant vegetation…neglected, abandoned, forgotten.

However, any signs of neglect—real or imagined—ended at the mansion's front door. Their approach had evidently been observed, because as they mounted the wide stone steps, the massive double doors were opened and held for them by two more of the security guards in full dress uniforms. Lady Zara, being accustomed to the trappings of wealth and position, swept through the doorway without a glance or a pause; Rhia and Nikolas followed, with their escort bringing up the rear.

The doors swung shut behind them with a quiet thump, and they found themselves in a great hall with a high vaulted ceiling, paneled in gleaming wood and lit by the soft glow of lamps tucked in alcoves along the walls and recessed high up near the ceiling. The atmosphere was peaceful, filled with the scent of wood polish and pine and an indefinable aura of elegance.

They were given no time to admire the portraits, tapestries and carved-wood panels along the walls, however. Their escort led them on at a brisk pace, her footsteps tapping on the parquet floor and instantly swallowed up in the vastness of the hall. Around them the house seemed deserted, and eerily still.

Lady Zara paused in front of a door near the far end of the hall. With her hand on the doorknob, she looked over her shoulder at Nikolas. He nodded almost imperceptibly, and she lifted one hand to knock while opening the door with the other. "Your Majesty," she said quietly, "Mr. Donovan is here."

She stood aside, then, and gestured for Nikolas and Rhia to enter ahead of her.

Neither the room nor its sole occupant were what Rhia had expected.

The king had elected to meet his son in what was obviously a private retreat, with none of the trappings or ceremony of royalty. The room was informal, even cluttered. The walls were lined with cabinets—cupboards below, and above them shelves filled with books that had obviously been read, not selected for the elegance of their bindings. The chairs arranged in casual groupings looked comfortable, even a little shabby, and there were reading lamps conveniently situated beside each one. There was a large cluttered desk, a comfortable couch, several small tables and ottomans, and in one corner, incongruously, a stationary exercise bicycle in gleaming chrome. There was a fireplace—unlit—and flanking it, twin French doors that stood open in invitation to the pine-scented breeze.

In front of the doors and the fireplace, with his hands resting on the back of a large leather chair, a tall but frail-looking man stood waiting.

She'd been prepared, but even so the king's appearance shocked her. In tapes she'd seen of his last public appearances before Reginald's death and his own surgery and subsequent collapse, Henry Weston had been a robust and vigorous man, much younger-looking than his age, which she seemed to recall was somewhere in his late sixties, with strong, handsome features, silver hair and fierce dark eyes, and the same regal bearing she'd seen in Nikolas. Now, his face was much thinner, those still-magnificent eyes were sunk deep in shadowed sockets. Although he was plainly making an effort to stand erect, he appeared to have aged a decade in less than six months.

Lady Zara closed the door, then hurried to her patient's side. "Your Majesty, please. You must—"

But the king waved her aside with a regal gesture and came around the chair, leaving one hand on its back for support. Rhia found herself stepping quietly aside and leaving Nikolas to go forward and face his father alone.

For a long moment there was absolute silence in the room, while the two men took each other's measure. Then His Majesty, King Weston of Silvershire, spoke in a soft and rasping voice:

"By God, it's true. You have your mother's eyes."

Looking back on it later, Nikolas was able to recall very little of what was said in those first moments. He felt…not so much numb as insulated. As if his mind and emotions had been carefully packed in cotton wool. He remembered being shocked, on some level that didn't involve his emotions, at the king's appearance; even knowing of Weston's illness, he hadn't been prepared to see the powerful monarch he'd considered his adversary looking frail and old.

He remembered hearing the words, …*your mother's eyes*… and seeing Weston's mouth spasm with emotion and the sudden glaze of moisture in the fierce dark eyes. He remembered hearing Rhia's soft intake of breath, as if she'd felt a stab of unexpected pain. But he himself felt no reaction whatsoever. Weston might have been referring to someone Nikolas didn't even know.

There must have been awkward moments—there was no rush of prodigal son to his father's welcoming arms, for one, and…did one offer to shake hands with a king? But if there were, he was immune to self-consciousness. He did recall introducing Rhia, and requesting that she be allowed to stay, and being formally introduced in turn to the Lady Zara. He remembered Weston seating himself, at his physician's urging, and he and Rhia being invited to do the same. He even allowed himself to acknowledge the pride and strength of will that had compelled the man, in spite of his obvious physical weakness, to insist on standing to greet this long-lost son who was also, possibly, his enemy. But he didn't allow any of it to touch his emotions.

Not then.

"I know how difficult this all must be for you—as it is for me," King Weston said when they were seated and Lady Zara had left to arrange for tea. He lifted a hand, and only the slightest tremor betrayed the emotional and physical strain Rhia knew he must be under. "I am aware of your…political position, you know—and of your…activities during the past decade." He lowered his head and aimed a scowl of mock sternness at Nikolas. "They tell me you want to do away with my crown, Mr. Donovan." And then, to Rhia's amusement and delight, the king arched an eyebrow. *One only.* "How ironic it must be to find now that you are destined to wear that crown yourself, one day." His lips twitched, and there was a gleam of humor in his eyes.

"Ironic…yes, I suppose it is," Nikolas replied coolly, and Rhia marveled again at his calm, his iron self-control. "Whether or not that is my destiny is another matter."

King Weston merely chuckled. He regarded Nikolas intently for a moment. "I didn't want to believe it myself, you know, when they told me. I know, I know—" he waved a hand impatiently "—DNA doesn't lie. However, I had to see for myself. I felt—I believed, you see, that I would know my own son even if I had never set eyes on him before. And I was right…I was right." His face seemed to spasm, then stiffen with its effort to contain what must have been overwhelming emotions. He coughed, then added gruffly, "You *are* the image of your mother, you see."

Nikolas didn't reply. He sat in utter silence, and only Rhia could see the tiny muscle working in the side of his jaw.

King Weston placed his hands on the arms of his chair and pushed himself to his feet. Both Nikolas and Rhia rose immediately, as royal protocol demanded, but the king waved Rhia back to her seat. "No, no, my dear, don't get up. Nikolas, my boy, walk with me for a moment, if you will—while my doctor isn't here to forbid it." He added the last with a sly smile and arched eyebrow for Rhia, as he held out his hand to his son.

After a moment's hesitation and a quick, questioning glance at Rhia, Nikolas offered his father his arm. As the two men moved slowly to the open French doors, Rhia could see that the king was making an effort to walk erect, leaning only slightly on that support.

Watching them, she felt some unknown emotion ripple through her and emerge in a silent, quivering laugh. *My God,* she thought, *how alike they are: proud, iron-willed, both of them...born to be kings.*

As he and Weston stepped through the French doors onto a small terrace of shade-dappled slate, Nikolas could feel his protective cloak wearing thin. It was one thing to keep a man at arm's length in the abstract, or while listening to his voice and watching his face from half a room away. It was quite another when the man's hand was resting on one's arm and one knew that the warm blood pumping beneath the thin, age-spotted skin was the same blood that ran through one's own veins.

The whole insane thing was in danger of becoming real to him. He wasn't at all certain he was ready for that.

Beyond the terrace, a path thick with bark mulch and pine needles wound through a garden of perennials and shrubs in an autumn state of blowsy disarray, rose hips and berries of various shades clinging to sparsely-leafed branches, a few sturdy asters and chrysanthemums still blooming among the browning stalks of last summer's lilies. They strolled slowly along the meandering path, the king evidently in no hurry to disclose his purpose in requesting this moment of privacy, Nikolas mentally bracing for whatever might come.

Weston paused finally, plucked an autumn rose from an overgrown bush and tucked it almost absentmindedly in the breast pocket of his jacket. "First, I must tell you," he said, in a voice that seemed to have regained much of its power and authority, "that most of my advisors were strongly opposed to my meeting you alone like this." He gave Nikolas a glance along his shoulder, one eyebrow arched. "Seemed to think I might be in some danger."

Nikolas, distracted by the eyebrow—*So that's what she was talking about. Strange, I don't seem to find it quite as annoying as she did*—frowned and muttered, "I can imagine." He drew a quick breath and pulled himself back to the moment. "I hope you don't believe me capable of murder, as so many others seem ready to do," he said, narrowing his eyes.

"Carrington—Lord Southgate—seems to think you are a man of principle and honor. He trusts you, and I trust him. Which is why…" Weston paused and turned to face Nikolas, meeting his eyes with his intent black stare. "Why I must ask a favor of you, Mr. Donovan—one I suspect you will not be happy to grant me."

Startled and a bit wary, Nikolas began a murmured protest. Weston lifted a hand to silence him.

"I want you to know…Nikolas…that I've learned a great deal about you since this whole incredible affair was revealed to me. By all accounts, Carrington's evaluation of your character is on the mark." His frown turned fierce, his voice gruff. "In fact, my boy, I think you are everything a man might wish for in a son, and I will be proud to call you that one day, when we've both had some time to get used to the idea. I suspect your mother would have been proud as well." He paused to clear his throat loudly, while Nikolas squinted intently into the woods and swallowed hard several times.

"However," Weston went on after a moment, with a quiver of anger in his voice, "in spite of his shortcomings, I raised and loved Reginald as my son for thirty years. Nothing he did could have changed that—as I hope you will find out for yourself one day, a father's love is unconditional. But...blood will tell, evidently. And it did concern me, as the time approached for him to assume my crown, that he hadn't matured and, er...hmm... settled down to the degree I had hoped he would. Nevertheless, I believed..." He shook that off, and when he turned once again to face Nikolas, his face had hardened.

"Someone murdered him, Nikolas. Someone did this—to him, to you, to me. Someone has plotted against me for more than thirty years. Thirty years ago, someone took you from me and put that poor boy in your place, a child ill-equipped for the life he'd been thrust into, thus dooming him to failure, to a lifetime of expectations he wasn't equipped to meet, and, ultimately, to a terrible and much too early death. Someone robbed him of his life, me of my true son, and you of your father. Your mother, the queen, God rest her—" He broke off, shaking his head.

He took the rose from his pocket and regarded it for a moment with such unfathomable sadness that Nikolas felt his own throat tighten. Then Weston crushed the petals in his fingers and placed his closed fist on Nikolas's arm. When he spoke again his voice was strong and vibrant, like that of an orator. "This is the favor I ask. I ask it of you as my son, as my heir, as the future king. Find the person or persons responsible for these heinous acts. Find out who has done these things to you, to me, to Reginald...to Lady Zara—yes, she was nearly killed, as well, you know. I want the wretch found and brought to justice. I want this…this cloud that has hung over Silvershire since Reginald's death lifted. Will you do this for me, Nikolas…my son?"

# Chapter 9

*My son.*

Nikolas was surprised by a contrary surge of resentment—contrary, because he knew hearing the words should be a cause for joy, not anger. And he did feel anger, though not with Weston, not even for such a blatant assault on his emotions—perhaps even deliberate manipulation. He was angry with himself for the way his heart kicked when those two words replayed in his mind. For the way they'd arrowed right through his protective shields and found the hidden desires of his soul.

"I'll be happy to do as you ask, sire," he said evenly. "Or at least try. Not, however, as your heir, and definitely not as 'future king.' Understand this—I don't want anything from you, least of all your crown."

Weston inclined his head slightly. His eyes were shielded, but his lips had twitched into what wasn't *quite* a smile. "I must accept that, I suppose—for now. Why, then?"

"Because I was planning to do so anyway, for one thing. And then—" he smiled sardonically, making a valiant effort to keep his eyebrows level as he made a little mocking bow "—there is the small fact that you are my king, and as such, your wish is my command."

Weston's features spasmed briefly, as if he'd felt a twinge of annoyance, or maybe pain. He made a dismissive gesture with his hand and said gruffly, "When I give you a command, Nikolas, you will know it. However…" He drew a breath and straightened his spine. "Whatever your reasons for accepting this charge, I thank you for it. And now, there is something I would like—" He turned as if to retrace their steps, then halted when he saw Nikolas had remained in place, feet firmly planted in the thick layer of garden mulch. "Yes? Is there something more you wish to discuss?"

"Two things," Nikolas said bluntly, folding his arms on his chest. "First, I'd like to have Rhia—uh, Agent de Hayes—the woman who came with me today—working with me on this. And second…" He hitched in a breath. "I'd like to see the evidence—the 'proof'—whatever it is that makes you so certain all this is true—that I am, in fact, this missing heir."

Weston's eyebrow shot up. "Proof—other than your appearance, you mean?" His smile tilted, and his strong bony hand closed on Nikolas's elbow. "That 'proof' is what I am about to show you. Come.

"Of course," he added grandly as they strolled back through the overgrown garden, "you may have whoever and whatever you need to assist you in solving this mystery of ours—the resources of my kingdom are at your disposal."

They walked on, footsteps crunching on garden debris and pine straw, releasing earthy scents into the warm autumn air. "This agent of Corbett Lazlo's…de Hayes. She seems like a capable young woman. A competent agent, I assume?"

Nikolas kept his expression and tone neutral. "More than competent."

"Yes, yes…I suppose she must be, if Lazlo chose her to find and bring you back." Nikolas didn't reply. Their footsteps crunched slowly on, keeping step. Weston threw him a sideways glance, and his tone became…could it be *sly?* "She is also, I observe, an extraordinarily attractive young woman."

Nikolas opened his mouth, then closed it again. He was almost certain, above the crackle and scuffle of footfalls, that he heard King Weston chuckle.

"Don't you wish you were a little bee out there in that garden right now?"

Despite its softness, Lady Zara's voice startled Rhia. She was standing beside the open French door, so intent on watching the two men outside that she hadn't realized anyone was behind her. She gave a little spurt of laughter and placed a hand over her quickened heartbeat. "Oh—I didn't hear you come in. Sorry."

"That's okay—I can see you have…someone else on your mind." Zara's smile and sympathetic eyes left no doubt as to her meaning.

Rhia closed her eyes and sagged against the draperies. "God…is it that obvious?"

Lady Zara laughed. "I'm a newlywed, remember? I know how it feels—and what it looks like, too. I get to see it every day in my husband's eyes."

"Great," Rhia muttered on an exhalation. "That's all I need." Her eyes returned to the two figures in the garden as if pulled by forces beyond her control. "I can't let him know," she added bleakly.

"He doesn't feel the same way?" Lady Zara's voice was half-curious, half-sympathetic.

Rhia gave her head an impatient shake. "It's not that—well, actually, to tell you the truth, I don't really know whether he does or not. But…it wouldn't matter if he did. In fact, I think that would make it worse."

Lady Zara's forehead creased in a physician's concerned frown. "I can't imagine why."

The ache in Rhia's throat kept her silent for a moment. Down at the far end of the garden, Nikolas and the king were facing each other, deep in what was obviously a tense, even passionate conversation. "Look at them," she said at last, and left it there as that were explanation enough.

Following her gaze, Lady Zara nodded. "They *are* very much alike, aren't they? Anyone seeing them together like this would know them for father and son, without a doubt."

The ache spread into Rhia's chest. "He's born to be king— will be, one day," she whispered, then laughed and said flatly, "And I for sure am not ever going to be anyone's queen."

Lady Zara's mouth opened—in surprise, perhaps—then closed and curved into a knowing smile. "Oh, Rhia. Never say never. If there's anything I've learned from all that's happened in the past few months, it's that *anything* is possible. Anything. Trust me on this."

Rhia didn't bother to argue, or to explain to Lady Zara, daughter of a duke, whose husband had just been made a baron, that it was *she,* Rhia de Hayes, daughter of a blues musician who'd grown up barefooted in a Louisiana trailer park, who wanted no part of royalty. Instead she remained silent, her gaze focused once more on the two men in the garden. They had turned and started back toward the house, now walking side by side like old friends out for a Sunday stroll.

Lady Zara, watching them, too, spoke softly. "What *does* a man say to a son who was stolen from him, after thirty long years?"

Rhia touched away a single silent tear. "Or a son to a father he's been taught to despise?"

The other woman placed a gentle hand on her arm. "They'll be back here in a minute, but…a word of advice—from one who's been there? The man himself will probably be too dense to notice—it's everyone else you have to worry about."

She tapped the pocket of Rhia's jacket and smiled. "With those eyes…I suggest you wear your sunglasses, darling—at all times."

Rhia and Dr. Smith appeared to be comfortably settled in a pair of matching tapestry armchairs when Nikolas and the king reentered Weston's study. The women were drinking tea—and they might present the very picture of genteel ladies, Nikolas thought in some amusement, were it not for Rhia's sleek black leather, and the fact that he recalled her saying once that she didn't care much for tea. When his eyes had adjusted to the indoor light, though, he could see they were both smiling, and that their eyes were bright with laughter, and he felt a momentary twinge of envy for that lightness of spirit.

Both women instantly put down their teacups and popped to their feet when the king entered the room, but as before, Weston gestured impatiently for them to be seated. He touched Nikolas's arm. "Mr. Donovan, if you would please…open that door over there and ask the gentleman standing outside to bring in the chest—he'll know what I mean. Then come have some tea—Zara, my dear, if you would pour, please…"

While Nikolas went to comply with his king's request, Weston lowered himself heavily into the big leather armchair, then immediately leaned forward to accept a steaming cup from the doctor's steady hand. "Ah, yes…thank you, my dear. And do stay," he added, when she stood up and turned as if to leave the room. "You are the one who found it, after all. I'm sure Nikolas will have questions."

Weston waited while Nikolas returned and took his seat in the chair he indicated—a twin to his own brown leather, set beside and at a slight angle to it. Then he took a sip of tea and grimaced at the heat, placed the cup and its saucer on the table beside his chair and turned his keen black eyes on Rhia. "Miss de Hayes, I must ask you to forgive me."

Nikolas saw her give a small start, like a wool-gathering

student called upon unexpectedly by the teacher. She hastily lowered her teacup and produced a hoarse, "Your Majesty?"

Weston smiled, although his eyes remained intent. "I haven't thanked you for finding my son and bringing him back to me—although thanks alone don't seem adequate for what you've given me. If there is anything I can offer you in return…"

Rhia's cheeks turned dusky pink beneath her tan. She muttered, "Oh—no—sire…I was just doing my job." Then she reached to put her cup and saucer on the table and added in a dry tone more like her own, "And I didn't 'bring' him." Her eyes flicked toward Nikolas but didn't quite make it all the way. "Nikolas—Mr. Donovan agreed to come. Entirely on his own."

"Yes, yes, I'm sure he did." Weston sounded amused, and with the chuckle he'd heard in the garden still fresh in his mind, Nikolas felt an inclination to squirm. "Nevertheless," Weston went on "I am grateful to you for whatever part you may have played in influencing his decision—which," he added, with a glance at Nikolas, "if my son is anywhere near as headstrong as I think he is, I imagine was considerable." He inclined his head in a gesture of honor. "Thank you, my dear, from the bottom of this father's heart."

During an awkward pause filled with throat clearings and rustlings and birdsong from the garden outside, Nikolas became conscious of an odd stiffness in his jaws, and at the same time a restlessness…an edgy sense of isolation…an unaccustomed need to make contact, to touch or lock eyes with another human being.

With one specific human being. Rhia.

But she was too far away to touch and seemed to be avoiding his gaze, and it came to him that the cramping in his jaws was tension, and that its source was the frustration he felt at being denied what he wanted. Needed.

*I need her.*

The thought was so new to him, so shocking, he was barely aware of the knock on the door…of the door opening to admit one of the uniformed guards—rather incongruously wearing latex gloves—carrying a medium-sized wooden chest. Still half dazed, he watched the guard march across the room and place the chest on the oriental rug between Weston's feet and Nikolas's. The guard then saluted, did a crisp about-face, and left the room.

As he blinked the chest into clearer focus, Nikolas felt a strange prickling in his scalp. Then a chill flooded him from head to toe, and the room and everyone in it receded, leaving him alone in a whirling vortex. Memories came at him like flying debris, and voices from his past filled his head, blocking thought:

*Nikolas, it's past your bedtime. Put your toys away this minute.*

*Do I have to, Uncle?*

*Nikolas, are you still reading, boy? Put that book away and lights out. Tomorrow's a school day.*

*Yes, Uncle.*

*Nikolas, how do you think you'll do at Eton if you persist in playing games instead of studying?*

*I'm putting it away now, Uncle.*

He became conscious of a choking sensation in his throat, and his lips moved as he silently said the only clear thought in his mind: *Impossible.*

It was very quiet in the room as King Weston took a key from his jacket pocket and inserted it into what appeared to be a new and very efficient lock. Everyone's eyes were focused intently on the chest—everyone's eyes but Rhia's.

At that moment hers were on Nikolas, which was why she was probably the only one in the room who saw his face drain of all color, his body jerk almost imperceptibly before going still as stone. She was the only one aware that the knuckles of the hands gripping the arms of his chair were bone-white... and that the eyes staring into the chest had gone glassy with shock.

In her concern, she almost...*almost* spoke to him, said his name aloud. Instead, with her pulses pounding in her ears, she swallowed hard and shifted her gaze to the chest, forcing herself to think about it, focus on it, catalog every detail in her mind as she'd been trained to do.

In spite of some dirt and wear, it was actually quite attractive, she thought. And obviously very old. Rhia, who had a fondness for old things for their history and character, beautiful or not, felt a strong desire to explore it with all her senses...run her fingers over the smooth wood—cedar, perhaps?—and brass fittings...smell the old-wood-and-dampness smell that always reminded her of the French Quarter in New Orleans. An innocuous, innocent-looking little chest, to contain the cause of so much turmoil...so much grief.

"Where did you find it?"

Nikolas's calm voice startled her. Her eyes jerked back to his face, and she could hardly believe it was the same one they had been focused on a moment ago. His eyes, resting on Lady Zara, were merely curious, now, his face completely composed. Only a hint of white around his mouth and the muscle working near the hinge of his jaw gave evidence—and to her alone—that he'd just received yet another emotional body blow.

Lady Zara glanced at King Weston. "In a moment, Mr. Donovan. I think you should see whatever is in the chest first—don't you agree, Your Majesty?"

King Weston didn't reply. His eyes were shielded, his jaw intent as he leaned over, turned the key and opened the padlock, then removed it from the chest and placed it in his jacket pocket. He lifted the lid, which gave an obligingly gothic creak.

Then the only sounds were the incongruously joyful warble of a bird outside in the garden, and some faint rustlings as the king carefully lifted something wrapped in tissue from the chest.

"Before I show you these things, Nikolas, I must explain," the king said. "Naturally, the essential items of evidence are in Lord Southgate's custody, locked safely away in a forensics lab somewhere. I will tell you that they consist of a lock of hair, and a baby's, er…nurser—uh, bottle—from which they were able to obtain both fingerprints and DNA."

"But that doesn't—" Nikolas all but exploded.

The king lifted a hand to silence his protest. "The fingerprints on the bottle," he said patiently, "though an infant's, are a verified match to yours—" his lips twitched "—which I regret to say are on file with our police department, as well as national security. Your DNA is not. However, since the DNA recovered from the bottle, as well as from the hair follicles, is a close match to mine, it was considered necessary to obtain a sample immediately. Which Mr. Lazlo's agents—" he gave Rhia an acknowledging nod "—were able to do quite easily, from materials found in your office at Dunford College."

Nikolas stiffened and threw Rhia a look that stung. "You… broke into—"

"I did no such thing," she shot back, more calmly than she felt. "The dean was more than glad to—"

"Be that as it may," King Weston said, in a crackling voice that instantly reclaimed everyone's attention, "Your DNA was obtained, Nikolas, and it, too, was found to match the samples from this chest. But there is more." He took a breath, and his voice wavered and lost some of its volume. "There were…two items which I withheld from the forensics scientists. Lord Southgate—the Duke of Carrington—and I—and one forensics expert sworn to absolute secrecy—are the only ones who know of their existence." Almost reverently, he lifted the tissue-wrapped object he'd held concealed in his hands and folded back the paper to reveal a small silver box, quite tarnished but exquisitely carved. "And now…the three of you."

He opened the lid to reveal, nestled in a bed of royal purple velvet, a baby's silver cup, the kind once given to every newborn infant by doting aunts and uncles, engraved with the child's name or initials and date of birth. King Weston removed the cup from its velvet nest and held it up for all to see, turning it so the monogram HRW—Henry Reginald Weston—was plainly visible. Then he rotated the cup.

"This," he said softly, tapping the engraved crest on the other side with one index finger, "is the royal crest of my predecessor, King Dunford. This cup was given to my parents by His Royal Majesty on the event of my birth. I, in turn, gave it to my son, on the day of *his* birth. This—" with hands that shook slightly he held up the second item—a black-and-white photograph in a gilt oval frame "—is a photograph taken on that day." He handed it to Nikolas, quickly, as if it burned his fingers, and went on in a breaking voice, "That is your mother, Queen Alexis. This was taken just two days before she died—I know, because I took it myself—she would have no one else except the doctors see her. She thought—" He smiled slightly. "She didn't like the way she looked, you see. However, I thought she looked quite beautiful, as always, and I convinced her to let me take this one photograph. The babe in her arms, Nikolas, is you. And the cup you see in the picture, here—your mother was holding it for you—is this one." He held up the silver cup with an air of triumph. "This very same one."

The ringing voice seemed to hang in the air…in the ears… like the tolling of a bell. Nikolas shook his head to dispel the echoes and stared narrow-eyed at the photograph in his hands. Through the clouded glass he could see a gaunt, exhausted-looking woman with heavily lashed light gray eyes, her dark hair hastily arranged in a style he recognized as having been popular in the 1970s. She was propped on a massive pile of pillows, smiling bravely and holding what seemed to him an uncommonly ugly baby with a smashed-in face and puffy, slitted eyes. The child's most remarkable feature was a shock of jet-black hair.

In a harsh voice very unlike his own, he asked, "What makes you so sure I'm the child in this picture? He looks—it could be anyone."

Weston smiled gently. "I am sure, my boy. Absolutely

certain, even without the DNA. Do you see in the photograph, the way the infant's hand is open and touching—holding, one could almost say—the cup? When I saw the photograph I asked Lord Southgate to have the cup tested for fingerprints. Remarkable as it seems, they were able to match the prints left on this cup by that tiny hand…to yours, Nikolas. *To yours.*"

Dazed and fighting for control, Nikolas cleared his throat and handed the photograph over to Lady Zara. Ignoring her faint gasp as she looked at it, he croaked, "How could—how did this happen? Didn't you—didn't anybody notice it wasn't the same kid?"

It was brutal, but he was beyond caring. Sometime during the past ten minutes or so, the relentless assault on his emotions had evidently achieved what all the scientific evidence in the world could not. Nikolas was no longer speaking to a king; he was merely a son like so many other sons, having heated words with his father.

Weston leaned back in his chair with a sigh. "Ah, yes. I assure you, I have asked myself that a thousand times since…all this came to light." He shot Nikolas a fierce glare. "I am certain it would not have been possible if your mother had been alive. She would have known her own child. But…" His face spasmed with that same terrible grief, and he closed his eyes and shook his head. "But, shortly after I took that picture, she…there were complications. She was rushed into surgery, but she lapsed into a coma. Two days later, she was dead, and I—I'm afraid that in the days that followed I wasn't aware of much of anything. It was days—God help me, maybe even weeks—before I saw you—before I saw my son again. If I noticed changes, I wouldn't have thought anything of it— children change from one day to the next at that age."

"What about…I don't know—nurses, nannies?"

Weston's face hardened. "I imagine at least one of them had to be part of it, but they're all long gone, I'm afraid. Anyone who might have known about the switch is dead…" He paused and aimed his black stare at Nikolas. "Good God. You don't think—"

"I think," Nikolas said softly, "it's time Lady Zara answered my question. I'll ask it again. Where did you find the chest? And how?"

Mystifyingly, she blushed. Clearing her throat, she replied, "I'd rather not say *how* I found it. It's complicated, and... somewhat personal. Suffice to say, Walker—Dr. Shaw—and I found it in a vault under the collapsed ruins of an old pavilion on the grounds of an abandoned estate. The estate..." she glanced at the king and drew a steadying breath "...belongs—belonged—to Benton Vladimir, the Duke of Perthegon."

"Vladimir!" Nikolas exclaimed. "But...he's been—"

"Missing, yes—exiled, vanished," Weston said grimly. He waited a beat before adding in a deliberate tone, "For thirty years."

"Perthegon..." Nikolas shook his head, which was swimming with implications, with possibilities, with scenarios he didn't want to think about or look at too closely. Not now. *Not now.*

"Uh, excuse me," Rhia said, holding up her hand like a shy child in a classroom, "can somebody take pity on the ignorant American in the crowd and explain what all this means?" She knew quite a bit about recent developments in Silvershire, of course, and the name Vladimir sounded familiar, but she still felt like the only one in the crowd who didn't know the people being gossiped about.

Lady Zara gave a little spurt of laughter. Weston arched an eyebrow at Nikolas. "I believe we have time for a short history lesson. Professor Donovan, will you do the honors?"

She felt his reluctance like a stiffening in her own muscles as he turned toward her, and a shiver went down her spine at the hard, set look of his mouth, the cold glitter of anger in his eyes.

*Empathy. Remember, it's not you he's angry with.*

"The Duke of Perthegon—Lord Benton Vladimir," Nikolas

began in a voice that grated with poorly disguised impatience, "was supposed to have succeeded Pritchett Dunford as king of Silvershire." He acknowledged his father the king with a formal little nod. "When Lord Henry Weston, Earl of Chamberlain, was chosen instead, this country was very nearly plunged into civil war." He paused to take a gulp of tea. When he continued he seemed to have relaxed a little, as if finding some small refuge from his rampaging emotions in the familiar role of teacher.

"The trouble began when King Dunford and his wife, Queen Eloise, were unable to produce an heir to succeed him on the throne. You know, of course—"

"A *male* heir, I assume you mean?"

"*Any* heir...actually," King Weston said, looking mildly amused at the interruption, as if Rhia had been a favorite child guilty of some minor misbehavior. "King Dunford and Queen Eloise had no children. If they had had, perhaps the issue of female succession would not have had to wait until this past decade to be resolved."

It was a moment before the meaning of that statement caught up with her. "You mean, a woman can—"

"Oh, yes, a princess can succeed to the throne," Lady Zara put in, glancing at the king with a smile of apology and sympathy. "It hasn't happened yet, but it will. Someday." She looked at Rhia...and *winked.*

"To return to our history lesson," Nikolas said, tapping a finger on the arm of his chair and looking stern. "In the Charter of Lodan, which was adopted in the thirteenth century following the Battle of Lodan—in the two centuries prior to that, you see, Silvershire's nobles had been trying their level best to annihilate one another—the rules of succession were set forth. One rather unique article states that the heir shall succeed to the throne on his thirtieth birthday, rather than waiting for the current ruler to kick off—thus, it was hoped, preventing the possibility of an interminable reign by a tyrannical or doddering monarch. And also, I imagine," he added drily, "reducing the temptation on the part of an impatient heir to hurry his predecessor's departure along.

"In any event, the system has worked quite well for a good many centuries—I will give it that." Nikolas aimed a fierce glare at his father. "But times do change. The world has changed. It's high time Silvershire entered the twenty-first—"

"That may be," King Weston interrupted gently. "However, my reign is at an end, and that, my boy…is an issue for my successor to decide. Now, if you will, please continue…"

Nikolas cleared his throat. "Of course. Forgive me. Anyway, as I said, King Dunford had produced no heir. The Charter provides, in that event, for the king to chose a successor from among his nobles. In this case there were two candidates—cousins, very near in age—Lord Vladimir and Lord Weston. Vladimir, by virtue of being two months the elder of the two, and from a slightly more exalted lineage—" Nikolas's mouth tilted sardonically "—was the obvious choice to inherit the crown."

King Weston nodded and picked up the narrative. "I had always assumed that would be the case, even though King Dunford made it a point to include me in his royal tutorials with Benton—Lord Vladimir. He wanted us both to have as much knowledge as possible about the running of the kingdom, you see, assuming that I would serve the kingdom in some position or other." He paused to rub his eyes, as if, perhaps, he had a headache, and Lady Zara gave him a look of concerned appraisal.

Ignoring her, the king went on, with a wave of his hand, "Unfortunately, Vladimir felt threatened by King Dunford's insistence in involving me at every level. Perhaps he believed the king was considering me for the crown instead of him… who knows?" Again the king paused. To Rhia, he looked like a man carrying a heavy burden of sadness.

"The sad thing is," King Weston said at last in a musing tone, "the circumstance that finally pushed Benton into acting as he did had nothing whatsoever to do with the succession. My father was dying, you see. He didn't wish that fact to cast a shadow over the coming coronation ceremony and the attendant festivities, so he had asked that his illness be kept secret. Only my mother and I and the king and queen knew the truth. It was, naturally, a difficult time for me, and I often sought my king's counsel.

"But Benton—Lord Vladimir—misunderstood these private meetings, and incorrectly assumed King Dunford had changed his mind about whom he would choose to succeed him. Fearing he was about to lose his chance to become king, Lord Vladimir—" King Weston made a grimace of distaste and an abrupt dismissive gesture with his hand. "I dislike speaking of it, even now. Suffice to say, Lord Vladimir made an attempt to discredit me by framing me for acts of high treason. Reprehensible acts. Thankfully, his plan was discovered before it could be carried out. I was chosen by His Majesty, King Dunford, to succeed him as King of Silvershire, and the Duke of Perthegon, just as he was about to be imprisoned and prosecuted for his crimes, vanished into thin air. He has neither been seen nor heard from in the thirty years since. It has always been assumed he fled the country. Now…I am not so sure."

Rhia, who had been listening intently to the king's story, stiffened to attention. "Are you suggesting he—the exiled Lord Vladimir—is behind these recent acts of violence and sabotage? And that it was he who switched the babies—replaced Nikolas—uh, the prince with an impostor?"

Again the king rubbed a hand over tired eyes. "I can think of no one else who would do such a thing. And," he added with a wry smile, "he did vow to make me pay for robbing him of his 'birthright.'"

The smile vanished and he brought his closed fist down hard on the arm of his chair. "God help me, though—I am at a loss to see how he could have done it! If he did not leave this island, if in fact he's been living right here among us all this time, how in blazes has he managed to do it? How has he managed to come and go at will, even invade the heart of the palace itself, without being seen? *Where is he? How has he hidden himself? Who is he now?*"

King Weston clutched the chair's arms and pushed himself to his feet. Lady Zara went instantly to his side, but he shook off her help. Holding himself tall and erect, he lifted a hand that shook only slightly, and when he spoke his voice held the vibrant timbre Rhia remembered from his television appearances. "This, Nikolas—and you, my dear—this is the task with which I now charge the two of you. *Find that blackguard Vladimir.* Wherever he is, whoever he is pretending to be, the wretch…must…be…found!"

# Chapter 10

"Nikolas…" Rhia halted in the middle of the path and touched his arm. "Hold up a minute."

The two of them were alone, for the moment, making their way unescorted through the sun-dappled forest to the meadow where the helicopter waited. Lady Zara had stayed behind to see her exhausted patient to his chambers, and the security guard who had accompanied them on their arrival had returned to his regular post. The hunting lodge had been swallowed by the woods behind them and up ahead the meadow was still only glimpses of gold between dark trunks of trees.

Nikolas paused and turned his head toward her. His eyes were crinkled in a questioning frown, but their focus was on something only he could see.

"We have to talk." She spoke in a low voice, though there was no one to hear her. Her heart had begun to beat hard and fast, and she didn't know why, only that something was dreadfully wrong. "Now. Here—before we get back to the chopper." She heard him exhale, and his gaze lifted and slid past her head. She could feel the tension vibrating through the muscles in his arm, radiating up through her fingers like a low-voltage current of electricity. She gripped his wrist harder, and the urgency she felt was in her voice, now. "What the hell happened back there? Something about that box—that chest—hit you like a ton of bricks. I saw it, so don't try and deny it. And unless I misunderstood him completely, His Majesty just asked me to work with you to find this guy, this…Vladimir. Look—if I'm going to do that, I'm going to have to know what's going on. *Everything,* Donovan. I don't go into a job blindfolded."

She was completely unprepared when he pulled her to him and wrapped her in a bone-crushing embrace. Unprepared…but her flesh responded to his like thirsty earth to a sudden shower of rain. She felt her blood rise beneath her skin, felt the heat of it and the pressure, and she thought she might burst from it. She gave a sharp gasp that turned into a whimper when his mouth covered hers.

His mouth was hard, the kiss deep, demanding; there was a kind of desperation in it, and an unfathomable hunger. Pressed tightly against his body, she could feel the rapid thud of his heart and the tension quivering in his muscles. Overwhelmed herself, she could only cling to him while her pulses rocketed into warp speed and the earth beneath her feet ceased to exist. She felt her legs buckle and might have fallen if she hadn't been wrapped so tightly in his arms.

He ended the kiss as abruptly as he'd begun it, tearing his mouth from hers with a gasp that was like a small explosion, an escape of passionate and powerful emotions held prisoner too long. Heedless of clips and fastenings, he clutched a handful of her hair in one big hand and buried his face in the curve of her neck. He groaned softly. "Ah…Rhee. You have no idea how much I've needed to do that."

"Yes…I do." Her lips felt numb; she could hardly get the

words out. "Because I've needed it, too. Dammit." She could feel herself trembling. Furious with herself for her inability to stop it, she pounded the hard, ungiving muscle of his arm with her fist. "But don't think this is going to distract me, Donovan. I still want to know what it was about that box that upset you. Tell me, dammit. Or—"

He cut her off with another kiss, this one almost playful. "God, I love it when you're assertive," he said huskily against her mouth, sounding like the Nikolas she knew. "It's such a turn-on." He kissed her again, long and slow and deep. Her insides went liquid and warm and she could feel a moan rising dangerously in her throat.

Then he drew back and looked down at her, and his eyes were shadowed and grave. "I wish I could, but I can't. Not now. Not yet. I don't know myself…there's something I need—" He broke off, dropped a kiss on the tip of her nose and said firmly, "I need you to trust me, luv, okay? And…I need your chopper. D'you think Corbett Lazlo would mind if we kept it just a bit longer?"

"It's yours to command," Rhia said, but her voice was bumpy as he turned her and pulled her against his side. He held her close with one arm while they continued along the path.

"Good—let's go wake up our pilot, shall we?" His tone was light again, but his eyes were hard, and she could see the tiny muscle working in his jaw.

"The old Perthegon Estate? Sure, yeah, I know where it is. No problem." The helicopter pilot, whose name was Elliot, spoke with an American accent—from New York or there-abouts, Nikolas guessed. The pilot tucked the wrapper from a package of cream-filled cupcakes into the pocket of his uniform shirt and levered himself nimbly up from his lounging position in the doorway of the chopper. "Hop in and buckle up. I can have you there in a jiff."

Nikolas waited for Rhia to climb aboard, then followed.

She took the jump seat opposite the door, leaving the seat beside the pilot for him. The chopper's rotors began to spin while he was still strapping himself in.

"That old place is pretty much a ruin, now, but from what I hear it used to be somethin' else," Elliot shouted above the noise of the chopper's turbine engine. "Ever been there?"

Nikolas shook his head. "Seen pictures—that's about it."

"Real showplace, I guess it was like something out of Disneyland."

"Yeah," Nikolas said.

*Disneyland...yeah, that's what this whole thing is like— some kind of fairy tale. Not the happy, chirpy, singing-mice kind, though. The scary kind with wicked stepparents and evil villains and all sorts of blood and gore.*

Elliot spoke into his radio and the helicopter lifted into the air. Nikolas's stomach and the golden meadow dropped away, and in minutes the forest had vanished into cloud haze.

As they left the mountains behind, the clouds thickened, becoming patchy fog as they neared the capital city. Situated as it was, on the Kairn River plain just thirty kilometers or so inland from Kairn Bay and the Port of Perth, Silverton was frequently blanketed by the marine layer as it crept inland following the low river valley like a crooked, beckoning finger. Elliot spoke often into his radio mike now, in constant touch with the tower at Silvershire International.

Once across the river and out of the city's busy airspace, Elliot keyed off the mike and jerked a thumb back over his shoulder. "Gonna need to gas this thing up—we're runnin' on fumes. After I drop you guys off at the castle, I'm gonna head on back here to the airport and refuel."

Nikolas nodded. Rhia leaned forward and tapped him on the shoulder.

"Tell him to bring us back some burgers and fries—I'm starving."

He gave a little laugh half of surprise, half chagrin. He

was hungry, too, and hadn't realized it. He'd been too tense, his stomach tied in too many knots to feel anything so mundane as hunger.

As if awakened by the power of suggestion, or out of pure contrariness, his stomach gave a loud growl.

Elliot did another thumb-jerk. "Got a buncha stuff back there in my duffel—keep it handy for times like this when I don't get to make a pit stop. Help yourselves—in fact, take it with you if you want. I can grab a bite at the airport."

"What kind of stuff?" Rhia was already reaching for the duffel.

Elliot grinned. "Junk, mostly. Chips, chocolate bars…stuff like that."

"Yum," said Rhia happily.

The helicopter banked sharply and plunged down through a hole in the clouds.

Elliot deposited them in a field of waving grass plumes and fading meadow flowers on the back side of the house—or castle, more like—and immediately took off again. Holding her hair with one hand against the chopper's turbulence, Rhia turned in a slow circle and said, "Wow."

Nikolas didn't reply. He took off his sunglasses and tucked them in his jacket pocket, then stood gazing at the castle—Perth Castle, ancestral home of Lord Benton Vladimir, the Duke of Perthegon. He didn't know what he'd expected—some kind of blinding revelation, maybe? A vision? At the very least, a clue that would help provide answers to the questions swirling inside his head. Instead there was the same restless stirring all through his body, that had been with him since he'd boarded the Lazlo Group's helicopter in Paris. And at the same time a cold hollow feeling of dread.

The day, it seemed, had turned to match his mood. Tendrils of gray-white fog were coiling up from the river, wrapping themselves around the castle's stone turrets and cupolas and blotting out what was left of the sun. A damp chilly breeze touched the back of his neck like ghost-fingers.

"I don't know about Disneyland," Rhia said, gazing up at the castle, head back, thumbs hooked in her belt. "I'm thinking more along the lines of Dracula."

"The fog does lend it a certain atmosphere," Nikolas said absently. He nodded toward some scaffolding that could be seen climbing the wall far off to their right. "Looks like someone's been doing a bit of work on the place, at least."

"Doesn't appear to be a soul around at the moment, though." There was a pause, and then: "Are you going to tell me now just what it is we're doing here? Because whatever it is, I vote we explore whatever's in that goody bag of Elliot's before we do anything else."

He let go of a breath he didn't know he'd been holding, and to his surprise, a laugh came with it. Peeling his gaze away from the castle, he looked at Rhia instead, and felt the knots in his stomach begin to loosen. Her tilted green eyes were studying him intently, and he had the feeling that if she'd had a tail it would have been twitching. Laughing softly, he reached for her with one arm and pulled her against his side.

"That's not what I'd like to explore," he murmured into her hair. His hand crept around her waist and flattened over her stomach…then inched its way upward under her jacket to cradle and measure the weight of one firm round breast.

She socked him smartly on one of his pecs—though her nipple had already hardened treasonously beneath his palm.

"Ow. That's hardly the response I was hoping for, luv." But he'd felt a shudder ripple through her body—just before she twisted away and out of his reach.

"Stop trying to distract me, damn you. I told you, that's not going to get you off the hook with me. I want to know what we're doing here. What is it you're looking for? If you'd tell me, maybe I could help you find it."

"That would be somewhat difficult," Nikolas said in a musing tone, "considering I haven't got a clue myself."

He turned his back on the castle and gazed out across the meadow, which lay like a messy bed coverlet on the gentle slope. Farther down, closer to the river, it was dotted with copses of trees that almost hid the marshes and the island where the pavilion had once stood, the ruined pavilion where Zara said she and Walker Shaw had found the chest.

The pavilion had been demolished and the vault beneath it filled in, Zara had told him. There was nothing left there now. And in any case, he wasn't keen on the idea of wading through a swamp just to look at an empty ruin, and was pretty sure Rhia wouldn't be, either.

"There's nothing out here," he said, turning back to the castle. "I need to get inside. D'you suppose it's locked?"

Rhia looked over at him and her lips curved in a kitty-cat smile. "Shall we go and see?"

She set off up the hill toward the castle, moving ahead of him with her long athlete's stride. He didn't try to catch up with her; the view from where he was was far too enjoyable.

Their circuit of the castle confirmed Nikolas's fears: All the windows were either locked from the inside or firmly painted shut, and the doors were sporting what appeared to be new and very effective padlocks.

"Well, that's that, I suppose," he said, having given the lock on the massive front doors a fruitless yank. He stepped back and craned his neck to study the upper-story windows. "I guess we can try the scaffold, see if any of the upstairs windows—what are you doing?"

Rhia had taken a small black leather case from her belt and was unzipping it. As he watched with dawning apprehension, she selected several small metal objects from the assortment laid out inside, then tucked the case in her pocket and stepped forward. "Excuse me," she murmured, picking up the lock in one hand and weighing it appraisingly, "this might take me a minute. It's been awhile…"

He said in flat disbelief, "Rhee…those aren't *lock picks?*"

"Yep." She was intent on the task now, the tip of her tongue clamped between her teeth, eyes narrowed in concentration.

It was hard to tell whether the strange shimmery feeling inside him was wonder or dismay. Stifling laughter, he managed to choke out, "Rhee…luv…are you insane?"

"Shh! Be quiet. Almost…*there.*" She gave the lock a tug and it opened in her hands. She straightened and threw him a triumphant look—a bit of a smug one, too.

He gave an incredulous snort. "Where did you—did Lazlo teach you that?"

She was suddenly very busy returning her tools to their case and not looking at him, but he saw when her smile slipped awry. "No, not hardly—though he did provide me with this nice set of tools." She gave him a sideways look from under her lashes. "Guess I forgot to tell you—I used to be a cat burglar in my former life."

"Come on…seriously." He'd given up trying to stop the laughter, though a cold little breath of unease was wafting across the back of his neck. Or was it only the fog?

"He thinks I'm kidding," Rhia muttered to the brass lion's head on the door.

She pushed the door open all the way, then leaned her back against it and watched him as she waited for him to pass through it ahead of her, chin lifted in unspoken challenge.

He hesitated…almost reached for her…almost touched her. Almost asked the questions he knew she expected, with that look of defiance that couldn't quite hide the vulnerability underneath. But then something—the chill stale wash of air from the closed-up castle, the musty smell of abandonment, perhaps—reminded him of where he was and why he'd come there, and the questions floated away like cobwebs to the back rooms of his mind.

Rhia pushed away from the door and closed it carefully behind her, enclosing them in gloomy darkness that was only slightly diluted by the pale light slipping through the cracks in dusty draperies and the panes of stained glass high in the stone wall above the entrance doors. Feeling vaguely abandoned, she tucked her hands in her jacket pockets and ambled unhurriedly after Nikolas, who was working his way down the vast hall, jerking doors open and looking briefly into rooms.

"What are we looking for?" she asked when she caught up with him, peering over his shoulder at a gray darkness filled with the ghostly shapes of shrouded furniture.

"You remind me of a small child on a long road trip," he said tartly, narrowed eyes still studying what appeared to be a lady's sitting room. He pulled the door shut, shot her a look and mimicked a child's falsetto: "Are we there yet?"

"Oh, very amusing." She folded her arms on her chest and gave him a quelling look. "However, I ask because we *are* trespassing, and our ride is going to be coming back to pick us up soon, and whatever it is we're here to do, I suggest we get it done quickly. Oh, yeah—and did I mention I'm starving? And that I tend to get bitchy when I'm hungry?"

His soft laughter reached for her in the gloom, then his arms and his warm mouth. "Sorry, luv…" The words of remorse brushed her cheek like a caress, and she melted inside. Her arms found their way around his waist all by themselves. His arms crisscrossed her back and he wrapped her close against him so that she felt the slight jerking of his body when he laughed. "I'm a pig…an absolute prick. I forgot. Of course we should eat something. Where did I leave the bloody duffel?"

"It's back there…by the door." Her reply was muffled against his shoulder, and she released a long, uneven breath that snuggled her even more comfortably against him. Hunger forgotten for the moment, she felt a strange reluctance to let go, a premonition, perhaps, of a future she dreaded and didn't want to acknowledge. A future without him. A shudder rippled through her, and tears burned the backs of her eyes.

*Low blood sugar,* she told herself. With clenched teeth and willpower, she pulled herself away from him and half ran back across the hall to retrieve the duffel bag from where Nikolas had thoughtlessly dropped it on a huge mirrored hall tree just inside the entrance.

When she returned with the bag, Nikolas had seated himself on a step about halfway up one side of a matched pair of curving staircases that rose like gracefully spread wings to a second-floor landing. As she mounted the stairs to join him, she could feel his eyes drawing her in, almost like a guiding hand. Her eyes had adjusted to the dimness, and in that shadowy light his face looked grave and bleak.

She halted a few steps below him, her eyes on a level with his and a cold, undefined fear coiling in her stomach. "Nik, what—"

"Shh…" He took the duffel bag from her and patted the stairstep beside him. "Food first. Questions later. Let's see what sort of goodies our Elliot has squirreled away."

"You want to eat *here?*" She was eying the dusty steps.

Nikolas had the bag open and was sorting through its contents. "Good a spot as any. The whole place is dust and cobwebs… Ah—look what we have here. Something called… Cheese Doodles. D'you suppose they actually have cheese in them? That would be protein, I suppose."

"Gimme." Rhia snatched the bag from his hands and plunked herself down on the step below his, squeamishness and premonitions both, for the moment, forgotten. "Oh, my God," she breathed as she tore open the bag and inhaled the familiar smell, "do you have any idea how long it's been since I've eaten a Cheese Doodle?"

"None whatsoever," he murmured as she popped a handful of the dusty orange crunchies into her mouth. She closed her eyes as she chewed, shutting out his expression of horrified fascination.

She opened her eyes and dusted her fingers on her pants, leaving orange-ish streaks. "Mmm-mmm—that was tasty— I used to love these things. What else is there?"

"What? Oh—yes, of course…" Tearing his gaze from her mouth, he dug once more into the bag. "Well, okay, here's something else for you, peanut butter crackers."

"Mmf—hand 'em over. I love peanut butter."

"Of course you do. You're an American. Ah—here's something for me—crisps! That's chips to you, I suppose. Hmm… onion-flavored—not my favorite, but beggars can't be choosers, can they? Oh, and look—the fellow has a sweet tooth, it seems. Here's a tin of biscuits."

"Biscuits? Oh—right. You mean cookies. Goody—hand 'em over." She licked her lips, wiped more orange Cheese Doodle dust on her pants leg and reached for the red plaid tin of Scottish shortbread cookies. Wonder of wonders—they were dipped in chocolate.

He laughed and held the cookies out of her reach. "You are a little glutton, aren't you? Sorry—no dessert until you've had your dinner…" He leaned down and kissed her, just in time to catch her mouth opening in protest.

She felt the kiss all the way down to her toes. Had she ever craved a man's touch so much? If she had, she couldn't recall it. Her head fell back and the world tilted….

Nikolas lifted his head, licked his lips and said thoughtfully, "Hmm…I believe I'm actually acquiring a taste for Cheese Doodles. Let me just see…"

He lowered his mouth to hers again, his hand gentle on her arched throat, lips and tongue firm and clever as they tasted the cheese dust clinging to her lips in teasing nibbles. It tickled, but she felt no desire to laugh. She wanted him with a boundless yearning that made those unfamiliar tears prick at her eyelids again, and helpless anger rise quivering into her chest. And what was this *crying* thing all of a sudden? She wasn't a crier—never had been. She'd been eighteen years old the last time she'd cried.

A chuckle jerked beneath the hand she'd placed, without realizing it, against his chest. Words whispered softly across her lips. "Mmm…lovely. Wonder if it works with peanut butter as well…"

She pushed hard against his chest, contrary to her heart's desire. Laughing, she scolded in a voice that tried hard to be stern, "Sorry—no dessert until you've eaten your supper," and turned her face away so he couldn't see how desperately she wanted him to kiss her again…and again…and never stop.

"Ah—yes, I suppose you're right." He drew back, wearing a look of mock seriousness, though a grin of appreciation tugged at his lips and his gray eyes were alight with laughter.

Gazing at him, watching him pop open the bag of potato chips, Rhia felt bedazzled. She thought, *If he wasn't born to be a head of state, he could be one anyway. With that charm, that charisma, in America he could be a movie star.* Hungrily, she watched him put a chip in his mouth and chew, then lick the salt and crumbs from his lips, and she understood the impulse that had made him kiss her.

"You know," he said between munches, giving her an appraising, sideways look, "I must say I'm surprised. I never would have taken you for a junk-food junkie."

She swallowed a mouthful of Cheese Doodles and licked her fingers, then picked up the package of peanut butter crackers. She gave her head a little throwaway toss and said lightly, casually, "I'm not, anymore. Used to be, though. A bad habit I picked up in juvie."

"Juvie?"

"Juvenile detention—you know, jail for kids?" This moment had been inevitable from the beginning, she realized now, but that didn't mean she was prepared for it. She felt her heart racing, her nerves twitching, urging her to jump up and

run away from it. Foolish thought; there was no running away
from destiny.

"You're kidding."

She shook her head and concentrated on opening the
package so she wouldn't have to see his face while she told
him. "Nope. That's where I spent a good part of my teenage
years, actually."

"What on earth for?"

"Truancy, running away, shoplifting—that sort of thing. I
wasn't a good person, Nik. I ran away for the first time
about…oh…three days after I got to my dad's house in Palm
Beach. Got as far as the bus depot in Miami, that first time,
before his security guys picked me up. After that he bribed
me to stay—first it was a bicycle, then a wave runner…a
scooter…you name it, I had it. I still ran away, though—every
chance I got. So, eventually, I wound up in juvie." She
shrugged and popped a cracker into her mouth, though her
mouth was too dry already.

"And…the shoplifting?" His voice was gentle. She risked
a glance at him and wished she hadn't; the sympathy and
kindness in his eyes were almost her undoing.

She swallowed the bite of cracker, then took a breath that
hurt her chest. "Ah. That. Well…when the running away
didn't seem to be working, I thought I'd become a big enough
pain in his ass that he'd be glad to get rid of me." She laughed
harshly and threw him a bitter smile. "Didn't work, of course.
That would have been admitting failure. My dad didn't believe
in failure. So…" she wrapped up the remaining cracker in its
cellophane packaging paper and began systematically crushing it to smithereens "…on the day I turned eighteen I left for
good. Left everything—took some clothes and enough money
for a bus ticket to Louisiana and to eat on until I could start
earning a living, and that was all. I told my father I was an
adult, and if he tried to stop me or come after me I'd get a restraining order." She dropped the pulverized cracker into the

duffel bag and leaned back on her elbows, tilting her head back to glare up at him. "And, I know what you're thinking."

His eyebrow shot up. "*Do* you now?"

Guilt made a hard lump in her chest; rejection of the guilt made her breathlessly angry. "Yeah. You're thinking I was too hard on him—my dad. After all, he didn't abuse me, he gave me presents, put up with all my crap, and I was a spoiled, thankless brat. Well...you'd be right. But there are two things—two...things, okay? One, I was just a kid. And two... he robbed me of my mama. *My mother.* I can't forgive him for that. I won't forgive him for that."

She was shaking, suddenly too angry to sit still. She would have jumped up, paced up the stairs, run down them...anything to release the pent-up emotions...the rage and the sorrow. But Nikolas's hands were resting on her shoulders, massaging, kneading, compelling...keeping her firmly anchored. And so she gave in to their gentle prompting and leaned her head against his thigh instead, and sighed and closed her eyes. And it felt so good...*so safe* there...the tears that had been threatening all day came seeping through and puddled beneath her lashes.

"And did you find her?" Nikolas asked softly, his fingers lightly stroking. "Your mum?"

"How did you know—"

"Hush—" a chuckle stirred through her hair, like a sweet warm breeze "—d'you think you're the only one with empathy? Obviously you went to find her. It's what I'd do."

"I did." Her whole body ached now with the memory... memories of the last time she'd cried. She gave a liquid, hic-cupping laugh. "I guess you could say it was...my first missing persons case. And my first failure. Because I was too late. Mama was gone. She died just a few months before I got there. She'd left me..." she drew a shuddering breath "...her saxophone. It's all I have of her now."

Nikolas stared at the stained-glass window at the opposite

end of the great hall until his eyes burned dry in their sockets. He asked himself when the conviction had come to him that what he felt for the woman sitting quietly nestled against him, her head resting on his thigh, her soft hair wafting like a baby's breath over his hands...that what he felt for this woman, perhaps the sexiest and most desirable woman he'd ever known...wasn't at all about sex. Well, at least, not *all* about sex.

Had it ever been?

He thought about that magical long-ago encounter on the balcony of a Paris hotel, and the events that had brought that fantasy creature back into his life, this time as a very real, very human, flesh-and-blood woman. Was she a part of it, this destiny with which he seemed to be on a collision course?

His mouth tightened and a little quiver of resolve skated down his spine. She *would* be a part of his future. He would make sure of that.

With that resolve came emotion, emotion so powerful he didn't know what to do with it, except wrap the cause of it tightly in his arms and bury his face in the soft curve of her neck, close his eyes and breathe the sweet scent of her into his lungs, let her warmth seep into his pores and the shape of her body and the texture of her skin imprint themselves eternally on his mind and his senses, make her his in every way he possibly could. *In every way...*

The wave of desire that hit him then was unlike anything he'd ever known. It grew out of those overwhelming emotions like a tsunami out of an earthquake...a natural force, impossible to ignore or defend against or deny.

"Memories," he said, and she turned her face up to him, eyes tear-glazed and questioning. He touched her face...cradled her cheek in his hand and answered in a thickened voice, barely able to get the words out, "Memories of your mother—the ones you told me about. You have them, too." *At least you have those...*

But he didn't say that aloud.

# Chapter 11

Rhia stared at him, stared at him so hard her eyes burned, as if his image were being laser-printed on her retinas. *Memories...* Her whole body ached with the thought: *That's all I will have of you, too, one day...soon.*

And then, through the blur of unshed tears, she saw the pain in his shadowed eyes. She hadn't believed it possible to hurt more than she already did, but in that moment her own sense of grief felt as if it had doubled. *Oh, selfish Rhee! Thinking only of your own loss. Talking about your own past. What about his? This day, this trip, this time—it's for him, not you!*

She placed her hand over the bigger one that lay warm on her cheek and whispered brokenly, "I do have memories. But you don't. You don't have anything of your—"

"Hush..." His voice sounded harsh, even angry. "Can't miss what you've never had."

They both knew it was a lie.

She started to say something—to tell him so, maybe—but

his mouth came down and she let it take hers, so desperately, achingly glad to have him touching her that nothing else mattered. *I'll have this, at least,* she thought, and as she opened her mouth to him she gathered the memory up and tucked it away in her heart like a greedy child hiding candy.

Was it just her natural gift of empathy that made her respond to his kiss like dry tinder to a match, Nikolas wondered, or could she possibly be as hungry for him as he for her?

What did it matter? He only felt the burn of it, the heat of her body colliding with his as she turned in his arms and reached for him…the sting and sizzle of her fingers on his skin as she half lay across his lap, her mouth surging up to his, meeting the rhythmic thrusts of his tongue with little whimpering pulses of her own. Desire—his need of her—ripped through his body with cruel force, doubling him over like a bad cramp. A groan slipped unguarded from his throat.

Rhia tore her mouth from his and gasped, "Nik, what—"

But he caught her to him, hid her face against his throat and whispered hoarsely, "Nothing…nothing, my love. I just want you so badly…." It wasn't what he wanted to say.

She could feel his body shaking with silent, rueful laughter. "I want you, too," she whispered back, shaking, too, though not with laughter.

"This is insane…" But his hand dove under her jacket, plucked her shirt free from the waistband of her pants, and then his fingers were thrusting beneath it and spreading urgently over her flesh…and the abrasion felt so sweet and good it made her want to weep. "I feel like a bloody teenager."

"Nik, we're on the damn *stairs*. We'd prob'ly kill ourselves." She was laughing now, clinging to him, spotting his shirtfront with her tears.

"And I, for one, would die blissfully happy."

"And…Elliot's going to be back any minute."

A heavy groan rumbled from his chest. "Woman, you are entirely too practical-minded for my—" He stopped.

As tuned to his moods as she was, she felt the change in him instantly. She tensed and drew back to look at him. "What? Nikolas?"

He was looking over her head, his expression a study in conflicting emotions. His eyes flicked down at her and he smiled, if somewhat crookedly. "I don't think Elliot's going to be coming for a while." He nodded toward the front of the hall.

She lay back in his arms and turned her head reluctantly to follow his gaze. "What…"

"Look at the stained-glass window. The light's gone."

"It can't be that late." She was struggling to sit up.

"It isn't, dear heart. We appear to be fogbound."

"You're kidding." She was squirming in his embrace, trying to reach the cell phone on her belt.

"Trust me," he said, "if there's one thing I know about, it's fog." There was a cryptic note of irony in his voice.

She paused…stared at him, thinking she should feel dismay, trying hard not to grin, understanding fully the ambiguous look on *his* face. "So…" she said in a low voice, thoughtfully weighing the slender device in her hand, "you're saying we're stuck here? As in…stranded?"

He gave her a sideways look and nodded. "Uh-huh. For the night, at least."

"Bummer," she said somberly. And deliberately tucked the phone back into its case.

He caught her to him, taking her breath away, his laughter gusting into her hair. Then, for a few minutes they simply held each other, rocking slightly, laughing in wonder at the unexpected gift they'd been given. A gift of time, Rhia thought… like happening upon a lovely little tropical island in a sea of chaos.

When the laughter died, finally, they drew back and looked at each other. Just…looked. Nikolas let his fingers trail down the side of her face, tracing the curve of her cheek…the velvety line of her jaw…the incredibly, impossibly perfect shape of her mouth. And he shook his head, dazed to silence by the enormity of what he felt inside.

"What?" She was gazing at him, her eyes as guarded as he knew his must be.

"Nothing," he murmured. "It's just that you're so damned beautiful."

She gave a tiny squeak of laughter, and laid her fingertips against his lips, reverently, the way people do when they petition a saint. "I think you're beautiful, too."

He closed his eyes and exhaled gustily. "*God,* I want to kiss you so badly. But if I do, I'm absolutely certain I won't stop, and intriguing as the idea of making love to you on the stairs of Vladimir's castle might be…I think we'd better find a place to spend the night while we can still see our hands before our faces."

There was a long pause during which neither of them moved. Nikolas kissed her nose and said tenderly, "Rhee— my dearest—I need you to be strong and get up, because I don't think I can bring myself to let go of you otherwise."

"Me! What makes you think I'm stronger than you are?" Her eyes narrowed. "What about that legendary willpower of yours?"

He snorted. "Evidently I have none whatsoever where you're concerned. All right, then—we'll do this together. Ready? One…two…"

Separating from him left her feeling cold, as if she'd gotten thoroughly chilled and would never be completely warm again. And shaky…hideously vulnerable—an appalling weakness she tried to hide from Nikolas by pretending not to notice the helping hand he offered, busying herself gathering up snack papers and brushing off cracker crumbs instead. Fooling no one. Wondering, as she handed him the unopened tin of shortbread cookies and the half-eaten bag of Cheese Doodles, what had happened to her appetite. Now, she was hungry for nothing at all except him.

It grew lighter as they climbed the stairs, pale gray light from curtainless windows spilling from open doorways all along the landing. In the large common rooms nearest the stairs, Rhia caught glimpses of stepladders and draping drop-cloths, and smelled the faint but unmistakable odor of fresh paint. Farther down the landing, though, shadowy hallways led to wings that housed the private rooms, where the work of renovation hadn't commenced yet. They poked their heads into all of them, while Nikolas provided commentary and hurried them from one to the next like a tour guide in desperate need of a bathroom break.

"Bedroom…bedroom…hmm, with adjoining sitting room, I see—*and* a dressing room as well… Lovely. This would be the nursery, I suppose. And a schoolroom—what fun. Hmm… bathrooms seem to be in rather short supply, don't they? Ah— what do we have here?"

He had opened the last door, which seemed to be wider than the rest. As Rhia caught up with him, he pushed it back and strode into the room like the returning lord of the manor. "The master suite, I believe. What do you think, my love? Will this do?" He turned to smile at her, a strange tense smile that showed his teeth but didn't reach his eyes.

"Do? This room is bigger than my whole apartment," Rhia muttered as she wandered past him, threading her way among the shrouded furniture shapes to the tall multipaned windows that graced two adjoining walls. A corner room, obviously. The view would be breathtaking, she thought, without the fog.

She heard a thump behind her, and turned to see that Nikolas had dropped the duffel bag onto a sheet-draped chair. Before she could stop him, he had energetically whisked the dust sheets off the bed—typical man!—sending a small dust blizzard into the air. They both erupted in laughing, coughing fits, and Rhia was about to choke out a teasing remark of some kind—*Good job, Donovan!*—when he suddenly went still. Simply froze, with the back of one hand touching his mouth and his eyes staring over it at something she couldn't see. Something near the foot of the bed.

"What is it?" She pushed her way back to him through the shapeless mounds of furniture, heart already quickening, nerves and senses snapping to full attention.

The shocked and frozen look on his face was the same one she'd seen there when the king's guard had carried in the chest that held the proof of his identity.

She touched his hand—not surprised to find it cold as ice—and said softly, "Nik, what's wrong?"

Instead of answering, he moved slowly toward the foot of the bed, which was the old-fashioned kind, small in width by modern standards, but so high it would require steps to get in and out of easily, with four tall posts and a canopy frame soaring toward the shadowed ceiling. It was made of some kind of dark wood, maybe mahogany? And in a style Rhia—no expert—thought might be Queen Anne. At the foot of the bed was a large chest, made of different wood than the bed—cedar, surely—and studded and bound with brass, probably meant to store blankets and comforters during the warm summer months. It was much bigger than the chest King Weston had shown them, the chest that held the proof of Nikolas's identity. But even Rhia could see that it had been crafted by the same hands.

Slowly, as if it were some sort of alien and possibly dangerous artifact, Nikolas reached out his hand to touch the chest's vaulted lid. "I thought maybe…I had hoped…" he murmured as he watched his fingers brush settling dust from the intricately inlaid wood. A smile tugged painfully and unsuccessfully at his lips, and he finally just shook his head. "I thought there was a chance, at least…that it could have been someone else who put it there, in the old pavilion. Someone who simply happened by and thought it would make a convenient hiding place…" He looked at her then, and the pain in his eyes struck her like a blow. "You know?"

She shook her head, bewildered and obscurely frightened. "No, I don't," she said flatly, folding her arms to keep them from reaching for him, tapping her foot like an angry wife. "I don't know because you haven't told me, Nikolas. What *is* it, dammit? What was it about that chest—and now this one—that has you looking like...like...I don't know—like you've seen a *ghost?*"

He exhaled, drew a hand over his face and slowly lowered himself onto the chest. "A ghost? Maybe I have, at that." Again, he tried to smile. "Except...I don't think inanimate objects can have ghosts, can they?"

"Dammit, Donovan—"

"Rhee...my love." He reached for her hands and drew her to him, guiding her between his knees as his eyes roamed her face with a tenderness that made her ache. "Don't you know, it's not because I want to keep this from you that I haven't told you. It's just...difficult for me to talk about it at all, you see. I think...because saying it out loud...saying the words...makes it real." His eyes held hers as his legs pressed inward, locking her hips between them. His hands slipped under her jacket and skimmed upward along the sides of her waist. "Then, once I've said it, I can't keep dodging around it any longer. Do you understand?"

When she nodded, he released a breath that sounded like a pressure valve letting go, closed his eyes and drew her close. And he seemed to relax then...like someone walking into his home after a long hard day. She stared past him into the deepening twilight until her eyes burned, fighting a powerful desire to weave her fingers through his hair and cradle his head against her breasts. Instead, she gripped his shoulders hard and said very softly, "Do *you* understand that if you don't tell me this instant, I *will* strangle you?"

He drew back from her, laughing, sounding like himself again, as if holding her for just those short minutes had recharged him. "Ah—my little pit bull terrier. Yes. All right then." He caught a quick, exaggerated breath and said with a lightness that didn't fool her a bit, "The reason seeing the chest sent me into a bit of a tailspin is because I'd seen it before."

"*What?*"

"Or one like it, I should say. *Almost* like it."

"But, Nikolas, that's not—"

"Hush." He silenced her with a finger pressed gently to her lips. "Let me explain. When I saw this one, I knew. They were obviously made as a set, identical except for the size. This is the largest, I would think, the one Weston has would be the smallest, unless, of course, there are more than three. Mine—the one I saw—is a size between the two. They must have been meant to nest inside one another, do you see? Like Chinese boxes."

Rhia nodded automatically...then shook her head, because she didn't see at all. "But why should that upset you? So, they're a set—even I could see they're the same. So what? Where did you see this other one? Are you sure it's even the same?"

His lips curved in an odd, bitter smile. "Oh, yes. I'm absolutely sure. It was mine, you see. Or rather, my uncle's. When I was a child, growing up, I kept my 'stuff' in it—my bits and pieces. My favorite toys, books, the odd treasure I'd found. So I could hardly mistake it, could I?"

He watched her face as he said it, amazed at how easy it was to utter the words after all, and how swiftly the unthinkable became reasonable and logical when shared with someone else. And how relieved he felt, as if a great burden had been lifted from his shoulders.

He saw her eyes narrow slightly and take on a kind of glow, like a hunting tiger's. "So...your uncle must have been working for Lord Vladimir—he had to be." Her voice was hushed, vibrant with excitement. "He was probably someone very close to him, too—a valet, maybe. His right-hand man. Someone he trusted with *your* care and upbringing, anyway. You know what that means? It means..."

Nikolas nodded. "If anyone knows where the bounder is..."

"It's Silas Donovan. We have to talk to him, Nik."

For a long moment they simply looked at each other, her

hands tense on his shoulders, his on her sides, his fingers curving around her slender torso, his head tipped slightly back. And as he gazed at her shimmering eyes and raptly parted lips the thought finally came clear to him like a gentle explosion, the pop and sizzle of a Chinese fireworks candle, to sear itself forever into his consciousness: *I love this woman.*

The pain that had twisted like a knife in his belly for weeks was gone. Now, instead of dread when he thought about the future, he felt full of optimism, even excitement. If his becoming king was what it was going to take to bring democracy to Silvershire, he'd do it, by God—as long as Rhia de Hayes consented to be his queen. With her by his side, he could face any challenge, defeat any foe. Never mind the fog outside the windows, the growing darkness in the room; in Nikolas's soul the sun had come from behind the clouds and was shining warm and bright.

"Nik?"

"Yes, luv?"

"Do you know where he is—Silas—" Her voice seemed to snag on a breath. "Why are you looking at me like that?"

"I'm bedazzled. It's merely one of the hazards of being this close to you—another is that I keep getting this dangerous desire to make love to you on the spot." He saw a lovely pink flush creep across her cheeks and thought of soft, sweet things…like kittens and rose petals.

"I do know where we might find him," he said softly as he moved his hands stealthily upward under her jacket. "But there's nothing we can do tonight…not until Elliot gets back with the chopper. And in the meantime…didn't we leave something rather important unfinished?"

"You mean…supper?" Her lips curved with her kitty-cat smile.

He laughed and said huskily, "No…dessert."

Inside the jacket her body was warm and humid, and her breasts seemed to swell when his hands covered them, to make a perfect fit. He watched her eyes as he spread his fingers slowly, absorbing her softness, learning the shape of her, rejoicing at the eager leap of her nipples into the cups of his palms, and the way her eyelids grew heavy with desire.

Rhia felt herself sway into him, though her hands were stubbornly braced on his shoulders, and she'd told herself she couldn't possibly think of sex right now, that her mind should be occupied with the search for Vladimir, and her feelings caught up in the tangled skein of Nikolas's emotions. But her body wasn't buying it. Instead, it did impossible things: her heart turned over, the bottom dropped out of her stomach, her knees turned to water.

"How do you do that?" she asked in a thickened voice.

"This?" Catching an erect nipple between each thumb and forefinger, he teased them gently…then harder, his lips slowly curving into a smile as he watched her eyes.

She gasped; sensation, sharp, bright and fierce, arrowed straight down through her body and converged on the pulse-spot between her thighs. "No—I mean…how do you just… forget it? Put it all aside? How can you think of sex with all that's— Oh…my g—*Nik*—"

"It's my Y chromosome," he said softly. "We men can compartmentalize. For example…right now…" His fingers were doing incredible things to her breasts, things she felt with every exclusively female nerve ending in her body. "Right now…the only thought in this awful male brain of mine is how much I want to put my mouth here…feel your softness on my tongue…taste you…"

She couldn't think…couldn't see. And she gripped his shoulders now, not to fend him off, but to keep herself from toppling over.

"My sweet Rhia…tell me—are you thinking of sex right now?"

Her laugh was almost desperate. She barely managed to produce a whisper. "You know the answer to that."

"Then…will you take this off for me? Please, my love…" Holding her eyes with his, he brought his hands upward under the two halves of her jacket and moved them apart…peeled them slowly back…pushed them over her shoulders. The soft leather whispered as it slid to the floor. "And this?" He teased her pullover up just far enough to bare a wide strip of her torso to his warm, exploring hands, leaving it for her to take from there. He closed his eyes and drew a rapt breath. "Ah…luv… you feel so good to me."

A shudder of desire jolted her as she pulled her sweater over her head. He murmured something soothing and moved his hands around and spread them wide across her back to support her as he brought his mouth to her unguarded breast. Freed of clothing, her arms settled like wings around him, and a fine velvety warmth enveloped one nipple…then the other, leaving the abandoned one cold and bereft, and hardening painfully against the moistened lace of her bra. A moan slipped from her lips almost unnoticed.

His wandering fingers found the clasp of her bra. "And this, my love…will you take this off, too?" His face swam before her in deepening shadows…his voice was a low, hypnotic murmur, almost felt rather than heard. It seemed to weave a web of enchantment over her, leaving her powerless to speak or to move.

But not to think.

My love…my sweet: *does he even realize he's saying those words?*

His fingers slipped under the straps of her bra and eased them down her arms, turning even that into a caress so tender and erotic it made her stomach quiver. And when, on their return journey, those same fingers traced a new path along the under-curve of her breasts, and his mouth, exploring…tasting… discovered a bared nipple chilled and longing for its return embrace, she felt pressure swell in distant nerve-rich places…and her neck muscles melt and her eyelids drift down like velvet curtains.

*And if he does realize it...does he mean them, or are they just...words?*

She swayed dizzily...her fingers burrowed deep in his hair while his parted lips feathered downward over her stomach and his clever fingers released the buckle on her belt.

"I want to see you...taste you...touch you...all of you. Will you let me, sweet Rhia? Do you want that, too?"

"Yes...oh—please..."

His fingers...magic fingers...eased the zipper down... slipped between flesh and fabric and shucked away the last of her barriers, and in the same swift motion, claimed what he'd uncovered for his own. She stepped out of her clothes, clinging to his shoulders for support, and felt his knee push between her trembling legs.

He tilted his head back to look at her and whispered hoarsely, "Kiss me, now, my dearest Rhia...come to me, love."

*And if he does mean them? Oh...what if he does mean it...?*

She remembered, then, what she'd said to Zara. *Was it just this morning? I told her it would be worse if he did...and it is...oh, it is!*

She gave a shaken, whimpering cry; had she ever made such a sound before? Blindly, she lowered her mouth to his, and it was a little like hurling herself into a bottomless sea. Immersed...lost...she scarcely felt it when a second knee pressed between her thighs, barely knew when her trembling legs gave way and his strong hands guided her down and settled her naked onto his lap.

While she waited in quivering anticipation, legs apart, her feminine places open like a blossoming flower, exposed and vulnerable to his clever, questing fingers, his hands moved unhurriedly, almost lazily over her body, scattering hot-cold shivers across her skin wherever they touched. The rough fabric of his shirt abraded her tender nipples, and her hands gathered it convulsively across his shoulders, tugged at it in frustration, wanting only his naked skin touching her. Anything else was torture.

And his mouth…his mouth consumed her. His tongue slid rhythmically over the sensitive surfaces of her mouth, venturing deeper, filling her, blotting out thought. There was only *feeling,* searing sensation…and Nikolas, his mouth, his hands, his body.

And a desperate need. A terrible emptiness waiting to be filled. She *wanted,* with an urgency unlike anything she'd ever known before. And yet *asking* for what she wanted… needed…seemed beyond her. She seemed capable only of tiny breathless whimpers.

Then…even that was stilled. Her breath stopped as his fingers found her swollen petals at last, and with incredible gentleness slipped between them…then inside her. Just a little, at first…then deeper…filling the emptiness…filling her with a fierce dark heat that drove the breath from her body in a shuddering gasp. She tore her mouth from his as her spine convulsed and her body arched back, and she uttered his name in a sharp, piercing cry.

Instantly, his arm came across her back, strong as steel, protective as a bird's wing, shielding her, supporting her. His hand came to cradle the back of her head, bringing her face into the comforting hollow of his neck and shoulder, and he held her there, held her in warmth and safety while his fingers moved rhythmically inside her and the throbbing pressure built to its inevitable breaking point.

"Nik—" Her voice was silvery with panic, her breath like a knife in her throat.

Instantly, his whispered words were there, cooling the damp hair above her ear. "Too much, sweetheart? Shall I stop?"

"No! But I can't…I—" *…can't say I love you!* "I need you to…hold me. Please…"

"I am, my love. This is me, holding you. I've got you…it's okay…it's *okay…*"

And for that moment, as she finally let go of reason and tumbled headlong into the vortex, she let herself believe it could be…

*I've got you...* But Nikolas wondered for a time, as he felt the strongest, most capable woman he'd ever known tremble like a frightened fawn in his arms, just who was holding whom. The cataclysms he felt rippling like small earthquakes through her body were only echoes of the shock waves tearing through his soul.

*I love you, Rhia de Hayes.* The thought came, not with fire-works now, but as a steady drumbeat deep in his heart, a pulse that would be a part of his life force from this day forward for as long as he lived.

While he was holding her, tightly...tenderly...and her hot and swollen flesh still throbbed in his hand, darkness came at last and settled over them both like a chilling mist. He felt Rhia shiver as the passion-heat subsided, but when he shifted her slightly and gently withdrew his hand from her body, she gave a tiny cry of protest and shuddered convulsively, as if trying to burrow closer to his warmth.

He knew how she felt. He hated to let go of her, as well, even though he knew that, in order to find relief from the growing discomfort in his nether regions, he was going to have somehow to find a way to extricate himself from his clothes.

"Forgive me, my love," he whispered to the sweet-scented dampness of her hair. "Poor planning on my part, I know, but...in my defense, I simply couldn't wait another minute to have you... We need to find a better place for this. Warmer...at least."

From the hollow of his neck her voice came, a muffled and unsteady version of his own British accent. "Ahem...I seem to recall seeing a perfectly lovely bed around here some-where. Seems a pity not to use it..."

He started to laugh, then winced. "Ow. Dearest...before I do myself permanent injury, d'you think..."

"Don't worry," she said as she lifted her head, sounding both husky and giddy at the same time, seemingly caught up in a strange half-dazed euphoria, "if you do, I shall kiss it and make it well."

Laughter gusted from him as the same lightness of being washed over him, too. He kissed her and then, holding her tightly still, managed to get both of them to their feet.

He was relieved to discover the chest he'd been sitting on wasn't locked. As he'd hoped it might, it yielded up a treasure trove of feather bedding, relatively dust-free and reeking of cedar. Uncounted seconds later, he and Rhia were up on that high old-fashioned bed, both wrapped in one great cloud-soft comforter, naked and breathless, laughing and shivering like naughty children.

The laughing and the shivering died quickly and together as the passion-wave engulfed them again. And like a tsunami's second wave, it was just as devastating as the first—more so, since there were no barriers left in its way, nothing at all to slow it down. Hands and mouths were free to roam where they pleased, and they did, taking and giving pleasure in equally greedy measures. Sensation layered upon sensation until the heat, the pressure, the passion became something like agony.

"Darling...I—" Nikolas couldn't say more. He was on fire, in pain, stretched to the stinging point.

From somewhere in the nest of feather bedding came a fat, smug little chuckle—the Rhia he'd first come to know and adore, pleased, he imagined, to be back on top and in control, with him completely at *her* mercy. Then all thought fled, as her lithe, warm body slithered upward over his in one excruciating all-over caress.

*Yes!*

He caught her legs and drew them upward along his sides and lifted his head and shoulders to meet her, joy and the anticipation of sweet relief making starbursts of heat in his belly and chest. Her fingers tangled in his hair as her mouth found his and took possession of it, breathtaking as hot, honeyed brandy. He slid his hands along the back of her thighs to grasp her firm round buttocks, one breath away from sinking his aching flesh into her sweet softness....

But it wasn't to be, not yet. Her hands clutched at his shoulders, and she murmured something against his mouth he couldn't hear. Her legs tightened around him and her body tensed…and he thought: *Of course.* Remembering the way she'd positioned them before—neither one on top— *The best way…*

Only, this time he felt her body tighten and twist…and a moment later, in a move that reminded him of the way he'd turned the tables on her the first time he'd ever held her in his arms, that long-ago night on a Paris hotel balcony, he found himself above her, looking down at her face in the darkness.

She didn't say a word, but there was tenderness in the way her hands reached up to touch his face, and he could feel her body trembling with some vast unknown emotion. Moved himself without fully understanding why, he braced himself on his elbows and cradled her face between his hands, and when he brushed her cheeks with his thumbs, found them damp with tears. He kissed her, then, lightly at first, then deeply, as her arms and legs…her whole body embraced him, and wordlessly invited him in.

As before, penetration wasn't easy, though he knew she was moistened and ready for him. And, as before, he could feel her body brace for the invasion, determined, in her passion, both to ignore and to hide from him any pain he might cause her. But he was just as determined as she was; no matter how urgently he wanted to be inside her he was determined *not* to cause her pain. And, she had given him the control.

So, when she opened to him, he introduced himself into her body only a little, until he felt the slightest resistance…then held himself back, though his arms, his whole body quivered with the strain. When she pushed against him, he lowered his head and whispered, "Relax, my love…let me take it slow…okay?"

"But I—" Gasping.

"Shh…" He kissed her, then, deeply, rhythmically…penetrated her with his tongue, made her mouth hot and slick with his essence…drove his tongue into her until she whimpered… until her mind abandoned her, and her body, left unguarded, warmed and softened and bloomed around his aching flesh. He slipped into her smooth, sweet depths with a sigh that became a duet, her breath and his, woven together in perfect harmony.

And his release, when it came, was like a crescendo of the same song, one she joined to make a climax that, though soulstirring, was only a part of their own beautiful music.

Rhia woke to find light streaming through the multipaned windows, and Nikolas's chuckle stirring warm across her lips.

"Rise and shine, my sweet…"

As the notes of a blues song, achingly sad and lovely, slipped rapidly from her dream memory, she lifted her arms around his neck and sighing, tilted her mouth to his kiss.

"Mmm…love, don't tempt me. Fog's lifting—you can see the river. I expect our friend Elliot will be arriving shortly, and—" he dropped a delicate kiss onto the tip of her nose "—not that *I* mind, but I thought you might prefer not to have your colleague catch you in such an…ah…exposed, albeit delectable—"

"All right, already…I'm up, I'm up…okay?" She opened her eyes, sat up and threw back the comforter, trying hard to scowl, but the image that filled her sleep-fogged vision made her smile blissfully instead. Nikolas…elegant as ever, even when wearing nothing but a day's growth of dark beard stubble. His body was so lean and lithe and beautiful…her heart stumbled, and her body's tender places tingled to wakefulness. Well-being filled her, and she lifted her arms over her head in a glorious stretch, like a cat in a pool of sunshine.

"Stop that, you shameless minx!" Nikolas thrust one arm around her waist and the other under her knees and hauled her, laughing, into his arms. He kissed her once, hard, then lowered her feet to the floor. "Get dressed—*now.*"

Muttering dark Creole curses under her breath, Rhia

obeyed. And as she did, she felt the sunshine fade and a chilly little cloud come to darken her heart instead. *If only…*

*If only it could be like this for us always. If only it didn't have to end.*

But it did. She knew that. The night just past had been an enchantment…a fantasy interlude…a day at Disneyland. Time now to wake up and return to the real world beyond the gates. And as before, she grieved secretly for the end of the dream…the loss of something wonderful she knew would not come again.

Once up and awake, she dressed with her usual efficiency—inspired, no doubt, by the need to find a bathroom as quickly as possible. While she did that, Nikolas, who had finished dressing even before she, folded the bedding and returned it to the chest, then turned out the contents of Elliot's duffel bag. They were wolfing down chocolate-dipped Danish butter cookies and bottled water when they heard the distant clack of a chopper's rotors.

Hastily stuffing what was left of the snack goodies back in the bag, they gathered it up along with their jackets and ran. Rhia, a few steps ahead of Nikolas, was halfway down the curving staircase before she realized he wasn't following. She stopped, gripping the banister railing, and looked back.

Up on the landing, Nikolas was standing absolutely still, frozen in place, like someone caught in a tractor beam.

"Nik?" She started back up the stairs, her heart already beginning to pound, though she didn't yet know the reason.

Light from the window at the far end of the landing had flooded across the wall directly in front of him, bringing into full glory the gilt-framed portraits hanging there. As she came closer, she could see that Nikolas was staring, apparently transfixed, at one portrait in particular. It was a large dark portrait—of one of the previous lords of the castle, she assumed—probably from the Victorian Era, judging from the gentleman's severe clothing, longish hair and full beard and mustache. His only visible features were a knife-bridged patrician nose, and eyes of a fierce and steely blue that glared frostily down at them from under thick, bushy eyebrows.

"Who's that?" Rhia asked sharply. "One of the former Lord Vladimirs, surely."

Without taking his eyes from the portrait, Nikolas shook his head slowly. Words came, barely audible, whispering from lips that might have been carved from stone.

*"It's Silas."*

*Chapter 12*

"I don't understand. If Lord Vladimir *is* Silas Donovan, how could he just…slip on a whole new identity and for thirty years live right here in Silvershire, in plain sight, and not leave any kind of trail?"

"People do it," Nikolas said grimly. "All the time."

"Not to us," Rhia said, gritting her teeth as she clutched at the dashboard of Nikolas's middle-aged Opal. "The Lazlo Group's resources aren't that easy to outwit."

He threw her a glance, then brought his narrowed gaze back to the road ahead—a great relief to her, since their speed had been hovering somewhere between suicidal and insane ever since they'd left Nik's apartment in Dunford. At the moment, they were careening along an almost deserted highway that followed the rugged coastline from the town of Dunford to the northeasternmost tip of the island kingdom. It would probably be a spectacular drive, she thought, under calmer circumstances. Walls of white that were a smaller version of the famed White Cliffs of Dover towered above the road on one side and on the other, dizzying drop-offs plunged to rocky shores and crashing surf. At the moment, however, she was too busy careening back and forth between nausea and fear of imminent death to appreciate the view.

She could see the muscle working rapidly in the hinge of Nikolas's jaw. Sympathy for him tugged at her like a child begging for attention. Ignoring it, she said impatiently, "Dammit, Nik, people know what Vladimir looks like!"

"Do you?" he asked, without looking at her.

"Do I...what? Know what Lord Vladimir looks like? Of course I do—what he used to look like, anyway. I've seen pictures."

"Okay, describe him for me."

She stared straight ahead, concentrating on the pictures in her head and trying not to think about the precipice hurtling by a few feet from the car's tires. "All right, let's see. Tall—over six feet, if I remember right. Strong build. Bald head...blue eyes...aristocratic features—thin lips, high-bridged nose, hollow cheeks, prominent jaw—" She let the words trail off into nothing as the portrait of Vladimir's hirsute ancestor floated into her mind. She turned her head slowly to look at Nikolas. He was nodding, lips curved in a grim little smile.

"It didn't occur to me until I saw that picture. I don't know whether Vladimir was naturally bald or shaved his head, but all he'd have had to do to disguise himself was acquire hair—his own or a wig—and grow a full beard. The rest would be a matter of stance—changing his walk, stooping instead of standing tall. Things like that." He paused, and the smile tilted wryly. "My uncle always stooped. And he walked with a pronounced limp—from an old boating injury, he told me."

Rhia was silent. Her mind was racing madly, trying to take it all in. There'd been no time, until now, to talk about it, work out all the implications, make sense of it. Immediately after Nikolas's stunning announcement, they'd had to dash to meet the chopper. Conversation had, of course, been next to impossible during the short flight to Dunford, and at Nikolas's apartment they'd taken time only to shower and refuel themselves on canned soup and crackers from his meager larder before heading up the coast to a destination he had yet to reveal.

"I take it you know where he is—your, uh…Silas?" Rhia had asked him as they were leaving, trying to curb her annoyance at being left in the dark, hating the distance he'd put between them, the distracted way he spoke to her, the way he carefully avoided her eyes as he replied.

"I believe I know where he might have gone, yes."

They would take his car, he said, rather than the helicopter, which Elliot had told them was at their service for as long as they needed it. He offered no more explanation, and Rhia, looking at his stony jaw and cold-steel eyes, had decided not to argue the issue.

Now, she rather wished she had.

She also wished she'd insisted on acquiring a weapon.

Rhia seldom carried a gun, although she was skilled in the use of firearms and fully licensed to carry concealed. Naturally, bringing a weapon of any sort along on this particular assignment—accompanying Silvershire's crown prince to a clandestine meeting with his father the king—had been out of the question.

She'd asked Nikolas before they'd left his apartment if he was bringing a gun along—it seemed a reasonable question to her, considering they were heading off to confront a possible kidnapper and murderer. He'd told her flatly that he didn't own one. Sorry.

She wished now she'd taken the time to insist on getting herself one. But they'd been in such a hurry….

"There's something else I don't understand," she said, again striving for distraction after a particularly hairy turn had caused her stomach to lodge itself temporarily in her throat. "Lazlo has a pretty extensive dossier on Silas Donovan, including family history. The information goes back a good long way—generations, in fact. A couple of hundred years' worth. How is it that an imposter can come along and insert himself into the Donovan family tree, and nobody be the wiser? What about kinfolk? Neighbors?"

His smile broadened, though there was no more humor in it than before. "Patience, my love," he said softly, the first words of endearment he'd spoken to her since they'd left Vladimir's castle. "All will become clear in due time, I promise. Very soon now, in fact…"

Except for one sharp exhalation, by clenching her teeth and counting silently to ten Rhia managed to keep her seething impatience locked inside.

The car sped on, hurtling around corners on a road that wound steadily downward, ever closer to the foaming surf… then climbed steeply up again, arrowed through a cut in the shallow cliffside to emerge at last onto a barren plain. The plain, studded with scrubby vegetation, stretched ahead to a cloudless blue sky and ended in a rocky point that jutted like an arrowhead into a churning sea. At the tip of the arrowhead, a lone structure rose like a stubby white candle from a gray stone holder.

"It's a lighthouse," Rhia said, with a little hiccup of surprised laughter, and then went silent as Nikolas pulled the car to the side of the road and stopped, leaving the motor running.

He'd had to stop. For a minute. His heart was racing and his hands were cold and sweaty on the steering wheel. Though, at least his voice seemed gratifyingly normal as he said conversationally, "It's called the Daneby Light. A few centuries ago, wreckers made a pretty good living here, using lanterns to lure unwary sailors onto those rocks. The crown put an end to that activity sometime in the mid nineteenth century when they built this lighthouse and appointed someone as full-time keeper. Someone named Donovan, I believe."

Beside him, Rhia was staring at the lighthouse, slowly shaking her head. "My God, Nikolas...*this* is where you grew up? You must have been—" her voice slipped away from her and she snatched it back with a hard, hurting breath "—so *lonely.*"

She turned her head to look at him, and he saw her throat ripple and the intense shine of her eyes beneath sooty lashes, and he felt something hard and cold inside him soften and warm. For the first time since they'd left Perth Castle, he smiled a real smile. "Darling," he said softly, stroking her cheek with the back of his finger, "your empathy is showing."

He shifted gears abruptly and pulled back onto the road. He felt renewed...strengthened, suddenly, all the tension and dread in him gone. "Actually, it wasn't all that bad. You don't really need chums, you know, when you're just a little tyke. And then, I had all this as my backyard. Silas used to take me out on the moors, or along the beach, or exploring the tide pools, and he'd teach me the names of everything we found. And at night, when it was clear, there were the stars—he taught me their names, too. On a moonless night...you wouldn't believe the stars—there aren't any lights out here to compete with them, you see. Can't say I was fond of the storms, though. Or the fog."

"This is what you meant when you said if there's anything you know about, it's—"

"—fog," Nikolas joined in, wryly. "Yeah...I did have my fill of that. But then...I went off to school." He paused, looking back, then let out a breath. "*That* was the only time I was really lonely, I think. The first year was rough, but at least I had the solace of company. There was a lot of sniffling that went on in the first-term's dormitory after lights out, I can tell you. But...it got better. And later on I met Phillipe and started spending summers and holidays with him, and after that I didn't come back here much at all, actually."

"But...wait." She tilted her head, frowning. "Silas doesn't still live out here, does he? According to his file, he lives and works in Dunford. At the college."

"He does. He moved to Dunford when they closed down the lighthouse—or automated it, which amounts to the same thing. That happened when I was at Oxford. After I started teaching at the college, I got him a job there as a custodian." He gave a sharp bark of laughter as it struck him. "My God—can you imagine it? The Duke of Perthegon—working as a *janitor?*" He paused, then said in a voice with no humor in it whatsoever, "He's been AWOL from his job, and he's not at his apartment in Dunford, either. Believe me, the first thing I did when I heard about…all this, was go looking for him. Figured he owed me some sort of an explanation. Didn't think of it then, but it has occurred to me that he might…just possibly…have come here to hide out. He'd done it once before."

They were both silent for a moment, watching the lighthouse loom steadily larger in the car's windshield. Then Rhia said slowly, "Okay, I get how Vladimir could have disguised himself as the old lighthouse keeper and escaped notice all these years—I mean, living way out here, no neighbors—especially if he hadn't any family. There's just one thing I don't understand." He felt her head swivel toward him…felt the burn of her eyes. Felt a chill wash over him before she even asked the question.

"What happened to the *real* Silas Donovan?"

He turned his head and met her eyes—briefly—but couldn't say the words. He knew he didn't have to.

She closed her eyes, let out a hissing breath. "*God,* I wish I had a gun."

The feeling of lightness and optimism left him as quickly as it had come. "Silas would never hurt me," he said stiffly, and felt her eyes turn on him again.

"Nik, the man is very probably a sociopath—you do know that, don't you? He has no feelings, for you or any other human being. People only matter to him if he can use them. Otherwise, they're disposable. He used you—"

He hit the steering wheel with the palm of his hand, surprising himself as much as her. It was a child's anger, stubborn and irrational. He knew that, but it made no difference. "*Dammit,* Rhee! The man was a father to me!"

"He *stole* you from your father. And raised you, groomed you, planned to use you to fulfill his own sick agenda for revenge. You think you know him? How can you know what he'll do?"

He stared bleakly through the windshield. He didn't want to quarrel with Rhia; quarreling with her made him feel cold and sick inside. But he couldn't let himself agree with her. He couldn't. "He was both mother and father to me," he said in a voice that hurt his throat. "The only parent I ever had. I can't forget that."

She didn't reply.

The car topped the last rise and began the long gradual descent toward the tip of the arrowhead. And although outside the sun continued to beat down from a cloudless sky, inside the car Nikolas felt the way he had as a child when the fog rolled in from the channel and shrouded the lighthouse and its two lone occupants in a blanket of white—chilled, isolated...*alone.*

It seemed fitting, somehow.

"Doesn't look like anyone's here. I don't see a car," Rhia said in a low voice that was a measure of how tense she was rather than fear of being heard by anyone outside the vehicle.

Nikolas had parked the Opal nose-in to a row of white-painted rocks separating a bare gravel parking area from an overgrown garden. He was staring through the windshield at what had once been a charming lightkeeper's cottage, built of white-painted stone with a slate-tile roof to withstand the buffeting of storm and sea. Now, wind and rain had scoured away most of the paint, so that the cottage seemed almost to be trying to return to the rock that surrounded it. Windows set deep in the thick stone walls were clouded with cobwebs and salt spray, and wooden shutters bearing slivers of blue paint hung crookedly from rusting hinges.

"There's a garage around the back," he said absently. "If he's been living here for a while and doesn't want that fact known, I expect he'd keep his car in out of sight."

She nodded, but didn't reply. Her throat felt clogged with emotions she couldn't express...words she couldn't say. Oh, how she wanted to reach out to him...touch his cheek...take his hand. *What are you feeling now, Nikolas, my love? This must be so hard...and you are so far away from me.*

He turned his head to give her a lopsided smile. "I must say, the place has gone to ruin a bit since I saw it last. A pity, really. A lot of history here..."

She cleared her throat and returned the smile. "I think it definitely ought to be preserved. When you're king, you should turn it into a museum, or a national monument." Nikolas snorted and reached for the door handle. "Sure," she said as she followed suit, "you know, turn it into a tourist attraction, like they do the childhood homes of presidents back in the States. You could—" The rest froze solid in her throat.

The door of the cottage had opened partway—no more than a foot or so. Through the crack came a pair of arms holding a rifle, and a voice that was cold and hard as steel.

"Ye have 'til I count ten to get back into your car and drive away. On the count of eleven, I start shooting. One..."

"Nik—" *I knew it—I should have insisted on bringing a gun.*

"Shh—it's all right." He pushed the door open and called cheerfully, "Don't shoot, Uncle—it's me, Nik."

The rifle barrel wavered, but didn't withdraw. "Show yourselves—the both o' ye," the voice commanded. "And keep your hands where I can see them."

Rhia eased herself out of the car slowly, hands on the top edge of the door but keeping most of the rest of herself barricaded behind it. Nikolas, meanwhile, stood up boldly, unconcernedly slammed his door and held his hands out to his sides.

"Come on, Silas, what are you doing? This is a fine welcome. For God's sake, put that thing away."

While Rhia held her breath, the gun slowly lowered, then abruptly disappeared. The door opened wider, and a man emerged, scowling into the sunshine. He was tall, but stooped and gaunt—a big-framed man losing flesh to age, though he looked strong and wiry still. He was wearing olive-green wool trousers tucked into knee-high boots, a black knit long-sleeved sweater and an open brown leather vest. He also wore a black wool fisherman's cap over long graying brown hair that had been pulled back into a clubbed ponytail. His beard, moustache and bushy eyebrows were almost entirely gray, and what visible skin he had was weathered as old leather.

"Nikolas, me boy—is that you? Ah—" he made a gesture of impatience with his hand "—forgive an old man. I don't see as well as I used to." As if daring her to challenge the statement, eyes as sharp and blue as steel knives flicked at Rhia before returning to Nikolas, and she winced involuntarily, to her inner fury, as if stung by a lash.

"Thought you'd be Weston's men, come to arrest me for trespassing in me own house," Silas Donovan went on, thin lips drawn into a sneer. Then he laughed—a single harsh sound, like the crack of a whip. "But I hear that's who ye be, ain't it? Weston's man? Henry Weston's whelp, so they're saying. Who'd've thought it, eh, boy? If I'd known who ye were when I found ye on me doorstep thirty years ago, I'd've drowned ye like a runt pup, I would." Baring strong teeth in a wolfish grin, he clasped Nikolas's hand and pulled him into a hard embrace. The two men thumped each other soundly on the back for a moment or two, then Silas turned and aimed his fierce glare at Rhia. "And who is this ye have with ye?" And he bowed his head and doffed his cap in an oddly charming gesture. "Aye, I must be getting old indeed, me lass, to have mistaken ye for Weston's, or any sort of *man.*"

Rhia was rarely tongue-tied, but the bombardment of conflicting thoughts and impressions she was experiencing had her reeling. It was all she could manage just to mutter her own name as she placed her hand in Silas Donovan's leathery grip.

*Who is this man? Can this crusty old seadog possibly be the exiled Duke of Perthegon, cousin to King Weston and erst-while heir to Silvershire's throne? This is the man who raised Nikolas, nurtured him as an infant, was both teacher and companion to him when he was a little boy. Can this be the same sociopath who plotted against the crown for more than thirty years, kidnapped an infant prince, arranged one murder and committed another...and who knows how many more?*

*Could we...could Nikolas...be wrong? What is a picture, after all—a portrait painted more than a century ago? A couple of chests made by the same craftsman? Can it have been as this man says? Was he only a lonely lighthouse keeper who chose to raise the foundling infant left on his doorstep?*

"...a friend of mine," Nikolas was saying.

She felt the brush of whiskers and warm breath on the back of her hand, and a shiver ran down her spine. She lifted her eyes, seeking Nikolas's, and found them resting on her, their gray gaze calm and reassuring.

"Well, come in, come in," Silas said, straightening with a beckoning gesture. "I've just put the kettle on—about to have me tea and a bite, I was. You're welcome to join me, if ye don't mind tinned meat and a bit of bread."

"Nothing to eat, thanks," Nikolas said. "I wouldn't mind tea, though. Rhia?"

She mumbled something in acquiescence, feeling a little like Alice in Wonderland as she followed him into the cottage. And she took care to note, as she did, that the rifle was propped against the wall beside the door.

The front door of the cottage opened directly into a large room that was all but bare of furniture, although a large stone fireplace at one end still held the remnants of a recent fire. It was dim inside; the only light was that seeping in through the small, dirt- and salt-encrusted windows. The place smelled of stale ashes and abandonment.

"I stay mostly in here in the kitchen," Silas said as he led the way with a sprightly step across the room and through a doorway opposite the fireplace, his boots making echoing footsteps on the dusty wood-plank floor. "Make me fire in there at night, when ye canna see the smoke." He swept off his cap and favored them with his wolfish smile as he gestured toward a wooden table and chairs. "Rather not advertise me presence here, if ye take me meaning."

"Why *are* you here, Uncle?" Nikolas sounded merely curious. He pulled out a chair and sat down, leaving Rhia to do the same while Silas turned his attention to the teakettle steaming on a portable gas camping stove that had been placed on the warped linoleum-covered countertop. "I've been looking all over the map for you, since I found out I'm not who I thought I was."

Silas nodded without looking away from his task. "Aye, ye'd be wanting answers, I'll warrant." He spooned tea leaves into a pot and poured boiling water over them. "Ask your questions, lad, and be done with it. We have important things to talk about, ye and me."

"Is that how it happened?" Nikolas asked, and though his voice was quiet, something in it made Rhia feel chilled. "You just…found me abandoned on your doorstep?"

The old man gave his whip-crack laugh. "You think the likes o' me crept into the royal palace one fine eve and stole the royal babe from its mother's arms? Am I a ghost, then? A will-o'-the-wisp?"

"No, not a ghost," Nikolas said softly.

Silas seemed not to hear that as he carried the teapot and three crockery cups to the table and set them down with a thump. His eyes were aglow with a feverish light. "And what does it matter to ye now, eh? That's in the past and done with. *This* is the time that matters. It's *our* time now, boy—everything we've worked for, planned for—it's here now—" he made a fist with one hard bony hand and shook it in front of Nikolas's nose "—right here in our hands. Not quite the way I'd planned it…but either way, that conniving thief Weston's done. Silvershire's ours, Nikolas—*ours. At last…*"

The countryman's lilt had disappeared from his voice, Rhia noticed. He spoke now in the clipped accent of Silvershire's upper class—British, only more so. She reached unnoticed for the heavy crockery cup, weighing it in her hands, assessing its possibilities as a weapon.

Nikolas leaned casually back in his chair. "*Ours,* Uncle? Exactly how is Silvershire 'ours'? I thought we were working to build a new democracy here."

Silas straightened and drew back, his eyes suddenly wary and his smile more fox, now, than wolf. "Why, that's what I meant, lad…what did you think? Democracy, aye, that's what we've been about, ye and me, t'be sure 'tis."

"Is it?" Nikolas's voice had gone deadly quiet. His eyes, Rhia noticed, were iron-hard, and were fixed unwaveringly on the other man's face. "I know what *I've* been working for, but somehow I don't think we've had quite the same goal in mind…*Lord Vladimir.*"

For the space of a half dozen heartbeats, everything stopped—all sound, all movement…even breath. The air itself seemed to freeze solid.

The older man broke the stillness first, cracking it like a stone thrown onto an ice-covered pond. But before his harsh croak of denial could form into words, it was overridden by Nikolas's cold and implacable voice.

"Don't. I've just come from Perth Castle. I've seen the proof with my own eyes." He leaned forward and placed his hands on the tabletop, and to Rhia, watching with suspended breath, he seemed almost to grow taller…broader. *Every inch a king…* "The only thing I want to know, Lord Vladimir, is how you did it. And *why.* Was it all about revenge?"

"*Revenge?*" Every muscle in Rhia's body tensed as Vladimir swooped down like a hunting hawk, eyes fiery with rage, fingers curved into talons. Hers clenched around the crockery teacup, relaxing only slightly when he grabbed hold of the table's edge. She could see droplets of spittle on his lips, shining like tiny diamonds. "You call it revenge? *I* call it justice! *I* was King Dunford's choice! *I* was supposed to inherit his crown. That weasel…Henry Weston…he plotted behind my back…poisoned the king's mind against me. He took what was mine! Took my crown, my life…left me with *nothing!*"

On the last word he pushed back from the table, and Rhia started to breathe again, though she kept her eyes riveted on the man's face the same way she would a coiled-up rattlesnake. *He's insane,* she thought, watching his glittering eyes. *Completely mad.*

*Why, then, does he seem so familiar to me?*

Vladimir drew himself up and glared down at them from his full height with the haughty bearing of an emperor. "So, I took what was his—I took his son. Is that not *justice?*"

"Brilliant," Nikolas murmured, studying him with thoughtfully narrowed eyes. "How on earth did you manage it? Must have had help from inside the palace, I imagine."

"Help? Pah—never needed it." His face took on a crafty look, and his eyes shifted to a distant place only he could see. "I have my ways…come and go from the palace any time I please, yes, I do…and no one the wiser. Took the babe from under their noses…" He laughed—a thin, gleeful snicker. "Raised the boy to despise his father, too…taught him to hate everything the man stands for…educated him…" His gaze snapped back to Nikolas, sharp and bright again. "Oh, and you were a fine boy, a clever boy, Nikolas. Blood will always tell. That was my one mistake you know—that brat I put in your place. Low-class genes…should have known better…"

"Who was he—Prince Reginald?" Nikolas asked softly.

A sneer curved Vladimir's lips. "Bought him. Didn't cost

me much—mother was a prostitute and a drug addict. She was glad to get the bit I offered her."

"What happened to her? Did you have her killed, too?"

"Didn't have to," said Vladimir with a disdainful sniff, looking as if he'd gotten something foul on his hands. "Naturally, the bitch took the money I paid her and bought drugs—too much, as it turned out. Just as well—saved me the trouble of getting rid of her."

He seemed so pleased with himself, seemed not to realize how damning his boasting was. Rhia wondered whether he didn't care if they heard his confession—and the implications of that were chilling—or whether he was simply relieved after so many years of silence finally to be able to let the world know how clever he'd been.

"Wait," Nikolas said, shifting forward in his chair like an interested student at the feet of the master, "I don't understand. If you can get into the palace whenever you want, why didn't you just kill Weston and be done with it?"

Vladimir grimaced. "You disappoint me, boy. Think—what would that have gained me? If the king dies, the crown passes to a child—Reginald, and the power to a regent. I'd have my revenge, yes, but not the rest that I'm entitled to. The *power,* lad." He clenched a fist as if plucking that elusive commodity from the air. *"The power that should have been mine."*

"So…what was your plan? And why kill Reginald, after all those years? I thought he was your ticket to the power."

Vladimir snorted. There was a pause while he picked up the teapot and lifted the lid to inspect the brew. "Why, indeed. As I said, the boy was a lowlife, and stupid in the bargain. I'd kept the proof of your identity, of course—hidden safely away until I had need of it. I meant to use it to blackmail Reginald into doing my bidding—he'd inherit the crown, but I'd be the real ruler of Silvershire—the power behind the throne. But alas, the twit got a bit too big for his britches—tried to have me killed, if you can believe it! Stupidly, too—

fortunately for me, I suppose." He leveled a glare at Nikolas from under bristling eyebrows. "Well, after that, what could I do? The nitwit left me no choice. Ah…but this is so much the better. We can have it *all* now, Nikolas, my boy, don't you see?" He was smiling again, that wild, insane light glittering in his eyes.

He seemed to have forgotten Rhia, who sat rigid in her chair, fighting a disgust so intense she could feel her nails biting into the palms of her hands.

She looked at Nikolas, caught his eye…and the instant flash of communion between them was like electricity in a dark night, a beautiful light flooding her soul. The message in his eyes was plain as spoken words, calming as a touch.

She cleared her throat…pushed her chair back. "I'm afraid that's not going to happen, your lordship, or…whatever. You see, I'm a licensed bounty hunter with the Lazlo Group. I've been commissioned by His Majesty King Henry Weston and his regent, Lord Russell, Duke of Carrington, to take you into custody and return you to Silverton to answer charges of kidnapping, extortion, murder, attempted murder, treason…let's see, what else? Oh, a bunch of things. Anyway, now—" she rose, hitched in a breath "—I'm going to have to ask you to put your hands behind your head—"

Vladimir's whip-crack laugh cut off the rest. "*You?* Think you can arrest *me?* Tell me, *wench,* how you mean to do that, precisely." His sneer was almost audible. "You don't even have a weapon!"

Rage sizzled behind her eyes…twisted cold in her belly. But it was the flash of recognition that took her breath away… turned her body to stone. *My God…that's who he reminds me of. Except for the madness, he's my father.*

Nikolas was smiling without a shred of humor. "Trust me, Vlad," he drawled, "the lady doesn't need one. Make a move on her, and you'll find that out soon enough. I'd do as she says, if I were you. And, by the way…" His voice took on an edge of steel.

"In the unlikely event she *should* need an extra set of hands, she's got me. It's been awhile, but I've found that my commando training does come back to me when I need it. I don't think you'd get far against the two—" That was as far as he got.

Rhia had quietly slipped her handcuffs from the back of her belt where they'd been hidden by her leather jacket. She was bringing them into view when Vladimir, shrieking curses, hurled the teapot full of scalding hot tea at her face and bolted from the room.

*Chapter 13*

Rhia's scream cut through Nikolas like a bolt of lightning, deafening him to everything else. As he dove for her he didn't hear his own bellow of rage or the crash of his chair hitting the floor or the tinkle of shattering crockery. Silas/Vladimir vanished from his mind like a puff of smoke.

Then his hands were touching her...fearfully...feathering over her cheeks, her hair, the sleeve of her leather jacket, slick now with already-cooling tea. Shaken to the core, he whispered, "God...Rhee—are you..."

"Dammit...*dammit!*" Her eyes blazed at him with rage and pain as she tried to shake him off. "*Go!* He's getting away— I'm *fine,* dammit—leave me—just go—don't let him—"

"Let him go." His voice was jerky, uneven. "It's an is- land—how far can he get? And you're *not* fine, you were drenched with boiling water. How bad..." He had to stop; he felt light-headed, all of a sudden. He drew an unsteady hand across his brow, wiping away ice-cold sweat. "My God...I'm sorry…I knew he'd never hurt me, it just never occurred to me he'd go for you instead…" *Because you are a part of me now.*

"I really am fine," she said in a tight voice that was itself proof positive of the lie. She was bent forward at the waist, breathing shallowly, one hand braced on the table, the other holding her black knit pullover away from her body. "Did he…does he have the gun?"

Nikolas nodded absently; he had himself in hand again, his attention focused now on getting Rhia's leather jacket off her without causing more damage. "He went out the front, so I'm guessing he's taken it with him. Can you let me have your hand for a minute, love? That's got it…now the other one… there's a good girl." He eased the jacket away from her and tossed it onto a chair, then took her by the arms and turned her gently to face him. "Which is another reason why I don't want you haring madly after him, my darling. He's got the gun, we haven't. There's only one way out of here, and we'll be on his trail soon enough. First, I want to see—"

They both jerked as a shot rang out—then quickly, before either of them could react, two more.

"What—"

He felt her muscles tense under his hands and tightened his grip. "No, you don't—you stay right here. *Don't…move.*" He set her firmly aside and in two strides was at the window, flattened against the wall beside it. He leaned over for a quick peek, then sucked in a breath. "Bloody *hell.*"

"What?"

"He's shot out our tires. I heard three shots, so it's nice of him to leave us one, I suppose." He said it with a jauntiness he was far from feeling. He knew better than anyone just how isolated they were.

And he didn't know, yet, how badly Rhia was injured.

"Guess that means he's got a car," she said, slurring her words a little.

They both froze once more as an engine roared to life

somewhere nearby. Tires squealed and spat gravel. Nikolas watched through the grimy window as a nondescript gray hatchback of unknown vintage raced away on the windswept highway, trailing a plume of smoky exhaust.

"Which is another thing he has and we haven't," he said lightly as he returned to Rhia, hoping his face wouldn't give away the helplessness and frustration he felt...the crushing sense of self-blame. The anger—at Vladimir, of course, but mostly at himself.

He was shaking inside as he took her face between his hands...frowned tenderly while he studied it feature by feature for damage. His knees went weak and he let out a breath of profound thanksgiving when he found it apparently untouched. Her skin was definitely paler, though, than her usual vivid coloring, and when he kissed her forehead, it felt clammy and cool to his lips.

"Sweetheart," he said huskily, "I am so sorry. This is my fault—I underestimated him. You were right. I was still thinking of him as my father—the man who raised me...."

Her head jerked quickly from side to side—she was beginning to shake all over, now. Through chattering teeth, she mumbled, "No, no—I was distracted, too. I let him get to me. Wasn't on my guard. He...just reminded me so much of someone..."

Startled enough by that to tear his eyes away from his examination of her neck and throat, he said, "Really? Who?"

"Dammit, Nik." She hauled in a breath and her eyes flared hot, bringing some of the color back into her cheeks. "Except for being totally insane, I swear the sonofabitch is just like *my* father. Cold, arrogant, supercilious...so bloody insufferably *certain* every thought in his head is gospel, his every opinion a *fact*. Stop it, damn you, I'm not joking!"

He was shaking with silent laughter. "Rhee, my love, I'm not laughing about your father—believe me, I'm not. Just... hearing a Louisiana Cajun swear like a Brit...got to me.

Sorry." He touched his lips to hers and said tenderly, "I want to hold you so badly, but I'm afraid I'll hurt you. Will you let me have a look at the damage?"

She closed her eyes and gave a shivery laugh as she swayed slightly toward him. "I'm almost afraid to look. It hurts like such bloody *hell.*"

"I hate to say it, but…that's probably a good thing. Third-degree burns don't hurt—the nerves are destroyed." And she would never know, from the blithe way he said the words, that he was half-dizzy with nausea at the thought of the destruction of even the smallest part of her. "So, tell me, dear heart, at the risk of cliché…where does it hurt?"

"I got my arm up in time to keep the teapot from hitting me in the head…deflected most of the water away from my face, at least." Her teeth were chattering again, and her nipples stood out in sharp relief under the wet—now cold—pullover. Naturally, his ignorant body, oblivious to anything but that familiar signal, insisted on reacting to it in the usual way as he slipped his hands under the bottom edge of her shirt. "I think…the jacket may have protected me, too," Rhia said. "Some went down inside…down my front. That's where it hurts the most."

Her breath hissed sharply between her teeth as he pulled the clinging fabric away from her skin. He had to hold his own breath to keep it from doing the same when he drew the shirt slowly and carefully up and over her head and saw the splash of angry red welts across her chest and the tops of her breasts, down the valley between and on to her stomach. He looked away, swearing viciously.

"This, too," she said in a choked voice, tugging at the front of her bra where it met scalded skin.

With unsteady fingers he unsnapped the front clasp and eased the two halves apart, then slipped the straps over her shoulders, all the while keeping his gaze focused on the little silver replica of a saxophone hanging from its thin chain nestled between her breasts, lifting slightly with each muted breath. Rage stung his eyes and the saxophone seemed to shimmer as if in agreement.

"Anywhere else?" His voice sounded cold; he had to make it so in order to maintain even a small measure of control.

She shook her head. "Just a little bit in my scalp…not too bad. Nik…" He lifted his eyes to her face, and they felt like deadweights. She was gazing at him, eyes soft…the color of whiskey. Her fingers touched his face.

A tremor shook him. He said harshly, "I can't remember— what the devil is first aid for burns?"

Her lips trembled into a smile. "Cold water…antibiotics…something to make it stop hurting…" She leaned in and touched his mouth with her smile. Her lips were cold…he felt them warm and soften against his, and juices pooled at the back of his throat as if he'd tasted something unbearably sweet. "There," she whispered against his lips, "that's the best painkiller there is…"

An easing breath poured silently from him as he took her head between his two hands. Holding it like a priceless treasure, he closed his eyes and let his mouth find its way to hers again…sank into it, and felt it begin to heal his wounded soul.

But even without touching her body he could feel her shivering. She was cold, hurt, possibly in shock, and his muscles ached to hold her close, to warm, protect and nourish her, make her all right again. The fact that he couldn't do any of those things brought the rage simmering inside him to a boil again. He'd been a believer in nonviolence all his life; it astonished him that he could feel such a powerful urge to kill.

He left the sweet solace of her mouth reluctantly, pressed his lips to her forehead instead. "My love, you're shivering. There's a blanket in my car, I think. Not much of a heater, though. You're better off staying here while I go and see what I can find. Here—sit down. Maybe see if you can raise Elliot on your cell phone." He pressed his lips to her forehead. "Back in a flash."

He let go of her and strode jerkily from the room, only then discovering how badly shaken he was.

Outside, he retrieved the blanket from the car's boot—dusty and smelling damp—and confirmed his suspicion that the tires were indeed casualties of war. He shook out the blanket as best he could, then wadded it up and headed back to the kitchen. "Here, luv—not terribly clean, but at least it's warm. I'm going to see if there's anything in the garage to patch a tire—" He halted. Rhia wasn't sitting where he'd left her, but was standing beside the window, frowning at the cell phone in her hand. "What is it? No signal?"

She shook her head and made a little grimace of annoyance. "Not even a smidgen."

Nikolas pulled in a careful breath and tried to make his tone light. "Then I'm afraid we're—pardon the expression—royally screwed. This place has been shut down for years—no power, no telephone…I suppose I might try building a fire, perhaps send up a few smoke signals…."

"You can…" Rhia paused, biting her lower lip in concentration as she tugged at something on the back of her belt "…I guess, if you have a really strong desire to practice your Boy Scout merit-badge skills. Or, we can use this." She held up a little black box about the size of a deck of playing cards.

"Don't—" he did a double take and stared at the thing sideways "—tell me that's a—"

"Yep—emergency radio beacon. All we have to do is open it like this—" she was demonstrating as she spoke "—and hit this little button right here…and we're in business." Her valiant efforts to hold back a gleeful smile produced a dimple he'd never seen before, and her eyes had the glow of aged brandy.

He could only gaze at her and slowly shake his head. "A man could easily develop one hell of an inferiority complex hanging around you—you know that, don't you?"

"Donovan, I doubt you're in danger of ever having an inferior anything." The sultry look she gave him from under her eyelashes quickened his pulse and reminded him graphically of the fact that she was naked from the waist up—something *she'd* apparently forgotten. "Anyway," she said with a shrug, "I can't take the credit. It's standard issue for all Lazlo's agents. First time I've ever used mine—I've always considered it kind of a nuisance, to tell you the truth. Just one more thing to carry."

She looked around at the thick stone walls. "I suppose we ought to take it outside. I don't know exactly what the range is, but I'm sure the less interference the better."

She was on her way to the door, looking like an artist's rendition of Athena off to the hunt, when Nikolas cleared his throat and said, "Uh...sweetheart...aren't you forgetting something?"

She paused to throw him a questioning look over one bare shoulder, saw the direction of his gaze and glanced down at herself. "Oh," she said. "That. So what? There's nobody around for miles."

"*I'm* around," he pointed out as he picked up her jacket and draped it carefully over her shoulders. He stroked a strand of damp hair away from her ear and with his lips almost touching its delicate shell, murmured, "Have a little pity, love. You have no idea how rotten it makes me feel, having lusty thoughts about you when you're injured and in pain." It wasn't the time, he knew, to tell her how far beyond lust—light-years beyond—his thoughts about her had gone.

She leaned against him, her head bumping onto his shoulder, her body's curves seeking his. "But I told you—a little lust is like an all-over shot of morphine."

"Rhee, I adore you," he said, laughing weakly, his lips in her hair and her scent, lightly flavored with tea, filling his senses. "But...forgive me, sweetheart, I don't know where to put my hands."

She groped for and found the windowsill, set the transmitter box on it and reached for his hands. She placed them on her hips and covered them with hers, her fingers warmly stroking the backs of his as she turned her face to his neck and whispered, "Anywhere below the waist seems to be fine…"

He groaned. Her warm, firm flesh taunted him, safely protected from his lascivious touch beneath layers of fabric and a belt like something medieval knights put on their women when they went off to war. "My love, you're killing me, you know. You can't possibly—oh…g—" His breath hissed between his teeth as her hands reached behind her, slipped between her backside and his front side to stroke the growing bulge behind his zipper.

"Tell me you don't just want me for my medicinal qualities," he said in a grating voice. Holding himself rigidly still, aware that she was trembling, now. Not the tight shivers that meant she was cold, or breathless ripples of passion, but shudders of overwhelming emotion that racked her body from head to toe.

"I don't…just want you…for your medicinal qualities. I want you…for *all* your qualities."

"So, you do want me, then…"

"Yes…oh, yes…more than want. I think…I need you. I need—" She broke off with a dry sob. Nikolas caught her tightly to him with one arm across her waist, and with the other pressed her head into the curve of his neck and shoulder.

"It's okay," he crooned as he rocked her, "it's okay…"

"Dammit, Nik. Dammit, dammit, dammit…"

"I know…I know."

"I want to kill him. Seriously. I…want…to…kill…him. If I'd had a gun…"

"It's probably a good thing you didn't." He kissed her temple. "Have you ever killed anyone, my love?"

She shook her head. Sniffed. "No. Have you?"

"No." He rocked her silently for a moment. "But I have an idea it's not an easy thing for a good person to do."

She sniffed again, a longer one this time, more an indrawn breath. "No, I suppose not."

She stirred in his arms, and when he let her go she pulled away from him, raking the fastenings from her hair, combing it with her fingers—carefully, because of her scalded scalp. "I'm okay now—really," she said, sounding breathless. "I'm sorry, Nik. I hope I didn't—I mean…" She made an embarrassed little gesture. Avoiding his eyes.

"I may be crippled for life," he said somberly. Her eyes flashed at him, bright with dismay. He smiled and brushed her cheek with the back of his finger. "I'm kidding, my dearest. Contrary to what most adolescent males would have you believe, I don't know of any documented evidence of permanent damage caused by unfulfilled lust." He nodded toward the window. "Let's get our little Mayday box outside where someone might actually hear it, shall we?"

"I think somebody has," Rhia said in an odd voice, going motionless with her head cocked at a listening angle.

Then Nikolas heard it, too—the steady thump of a helicopter's rotors. "Well, well. I suppose that's Elliot?" He lifted one eyebrow. "Lazlo does take good care of his people, doesn't he? I must say, though, I'm rather glad the cavalry didn't arrive a few minutes earlier, aren't you?"

"Sorry I didn't get here sooner," Elliot shouted as Rhia took the hand he offered. "I was outside taking a—uh…sorry—taking care of…uh, personal business—didn't catch the signal." He glanced at but didn't comment on the way she held her jacket together loosely with one hand when she let him help her into the chopper. As she settled into the jump seat, he yelled over one shoulder, "Don't tell Lazlo, okay? He'll have my head. I had strict orders not to take my eyes off your six."

She reassured him with a smile, the best one she could manage with her teeth clamped together. The pain raking down the front of her body no longer made her nauseated, at least. Now, it just stung like bloody hell.

Nikolas's tall form filled the doorway of the chopper. She

watched him toss in Elliot's duffel bag and the other odds and ends he'd brought from the car, then grip the sides of the opening and lever himself gracefully through. His eyes found hers immediately, asking if she was okay, telling her everything would be all right. And as he slipped past her and into the shotgun seat beside Elliot, he let his hand lie for one brief moment on the top of her head.

She felt the warmth of it slide all the way down through her pain-wracked body. An ache filled her throat and she closed her eyes…wishing. *Wish his touch didn't feel so damn good. Wish I didn't love him so much…*

"You must have been pretty close by," Nikolas said to Elliot as he belted himself in. "How'd you know where to find us? Didn't we leave you at the airport in Dunford?"

"I've been on your tail pretty much since you left Dunford. Like I said, I had orders from the man himself—s'posed to stick to you guys like glue." The chopper swooped upward, lifting a swirl of fine sand into the air with it. "I was hunkered down a couple miles from here—didn't want to get too close, 'fraid I might spook the target." Elliot jerked his head toward Rhia. "Looks like I missed some action."

Nikolas nodded his head. Rhia could see the side of his jaw twitch with his wry smile. "Little bit."

"She okay?"

"She will be."

"The target?"

"Got away."

"Ah. Figured that when I saw that oil-burner hightailin' it down the road," Elliot said with a small headshake. "Maybe I should've gone after 'im, but like I said, I had my orders."

Rhia didn't hear Nikolas's reply. Exhausted by pain and emotional turmoil, she closed her eyes and let her head fall back against the headrest. Inexplicably, as a new wave of anger rippled through her, the image imprinted on the backs of her eyelids wasn't the murderous Lord Vladimir's. It was her father's.

* * *

Later that evening, in Nikolas's seaside apartment in the college town of Dunford, Rhia lay in his bed propped up on a pile of pillows, wearing only a pair of his black silk boxers. As she listened to the sounds coming from the adjoining bathroom—the hum of an electric shaver...the rush of water in the shower...the thump of a dropped bar of soap—she was in serious danger of engaging in what for her was a rare sin: self-pity.

And why not? She was entitled, dammit. She couldn't have a shower...couldn't wash her hair. Her chest and stomach hurt; so did her scalp, in places, so she couldn't even give her hair a decent brushing. And the burns looked awful. Sickening, she thought as she lifted her head to look at the angry blisters one more time. Yes—truly ugly. Blood would have been better.

Scowling, she reached for the tube of antibiotic cream lying on the table beside the bed and unscrewed the cap.

The bathroom door opened. Nikolas emerged, freshly shaved, water-spangled, black hair falling in damp commas across his forehead, a towel loosely knotted around lean hips...and every cranky negative thought flew right out of her head. Something warm and sweet enveloped her, like delicious perfume carried on a soft summer wind. She felt her face being taken over by a smile she knew was besotted, even goofy, and there seemed to be nothing she could do to make it leave. In a daze, she watched him come toward her, and felt herself filling up with a tingly, effervescent joy.

"Hello, you," he said as he sat on the edge of the bed beside her, smiling with such undisguised tenderness it made her throat quiver. Warmth radiated from his still-damp body, along with the scents of aftershave and soap. He took the tube of cream from her and sniffed it. Lifted one eyebrow. "This the stuff the doctor gave you?"

She nodded; speech was beyond her just then.

He squeezed a bit of the cream onto his finger and touched

it gently to a welt just above her collarbone. "Shh..." he said when she winced. And then, to distract her, she suspected: "Did you get all reported in?"

She nodded, then countered in a tightly controlled voice, "Did you get through to the palace?"

"I did." He was watching his fingers, intent on his task. Gazing down at him, she forgot about pain...thought how utterly beautiful his lashes were...thick and black and long. *A woman would kill for those lashes...* "Spoke with Russell— Lord Carrington—himself, actually. He's increased security...put the palace on high alert."

"Do you really think Vladimir's going after the king?" He was so near...she had to clutch the sheet in handfuls to keep from touching him. She wanted so badly to touch him...to smooth away the frown of concern that had gathered between his eyebrows.

But if she touched him, she wouldn't stop there, and that wouldn't be fair to him. She squirmed inwardly, thinking of the way she'd behaved earlier, in the lighthouse cottage. She wouldn't do that do him again.

He flashed her a look and a wry smile. "You were a wee bit preoccupied, so you probably didn't hear what Vlad was screaming when he tore out of the cottage. It was all pretty insane, but I did hear some dire threats against the king's person." The smile faded. "It wouldn't surprise me, since all his plans have fallen apart anyway, if he's decided to go out with a bang and take the man he blames for his misfortune along with him."

"I don't see how he could get to him. He'd have to get past the palace security, which I'd think would have a difficulty factor along the lines of...oh, I don't know, breaking into Fort Knox or stealing the British crown jewels."

"He's done it before," Nikolas said grimly.

Rhia watched the tiny muscle working in the side of his jaw, and after a moment said softly, "You're worried about him, aren't you? King Weston, I mean. You really do care about him."

He lifted a shoulder, watching his fingers tap cream onto a blistered patch of her chest with the delicacy of a watchmaker. "Of course I care. He's the king. His murder would be a national tragedy."

"A personal one, too, I think. You haven't even had a chance to get to know him yet—your *father*." She caught a breath, trying so hard not to flinch. "He's a good man, Nik. And you're very much like him, you know. You should be there with him. If we leave now, we could—"

"Tomorrow's soon enough."

"But—"

He leaned over and kissed her, just thoroughly enough to make her tingle all the way down to her toes. Then he pulled back just far enough to murmur, "Do shut up and relax, won't you? Right now, all I want to do is make you feel better. Let's see...didn't you tell me this is what works best?" His lips, firm and warm, the texture of satin, slid across hers...nibbled at their sensitive insides. He caught the lower one between his teeth when she pouted and sucked it gently, laughing low in his throat.

Her hands fisted in the sheets. Freeing her mouth from that exquisite torment, she whispered, "You're supposed to kiss the owie. But I don't think I could stand..."

He lowered his head, and his hair, cool and damp from the shower, tickled her throat. "Hmm...how about if I kiss it close to the owie? Like...here? Would that hurt?" And she felt the warm, liquid laving of his tongue on her neck...then a hot, drawing pressure.

"Oh—" She drew a shuddering gasp. Then, faintly whispered, "No..." How had her hands escaped from the knotted sheets and found their way to his hair, touching it half fearfully, as if it were soap bubbles, or thistledown?

"Hmm...how about here, then?" And again...the gentle stroking, first, then the heat. She felt it in her breasts, the soles of her feet, and between her thighs. "And here..." It was all she could do not to moan. "And…this lovely little nipple seems quite untouched…"

Same thing—tongue caress…gentle sucking—but this time the sensation that arrowed through her to the swelling, heating place between her legs was sharp and raw, and the gasp slipped from her throat before she knew. The muscles in her back and legs contracted. Her chest rose and fell with her quickening breaths, lifting her distended breast to him, pushing her nipple deeper into his mouth. Pain was forgotten completely; she clutched at his shoulders, wanting him…on her… inside her…everywhere. Never mind the blisters. Nothing else mattered.

He lifted his head…his hair in silky feathers on his forehead, eyes full of a shimmering softness…and smiled at her with such—the word that came into her mind, like the lyrics to a well-loved song, was *sweetness.* And she giggled— couldn't help it—because it seemed such an unlikely word to apply to the next king of Silvershire.

"Ah, feeling better already, are we?" His voice was a husky growl that only fed the fire inside her.

"You're a very good doctor," she whispered, threading her fingers through the longish hair on the back of his neck.

"Hmm…and I've always wanted to play doctor." The angelic smile tried hard to turn itself into a leer.

"You have a very nice bedside manner, but I think… you've left some of my injuries…oh—" Her voice hitched to a new octave as he lowered his mouth to the hollow below her rib cage. She sucked in air and her stomach muscles tensed.

"Relax, my love…" His breath flowed like warm oil over her taut skin. His hands moved slowly down her sides, stroking…gentling…following the curve of her waist and hips… then retreated to the waistband of the boxers. His fingers hooked into the elastic and drew them down, baring her belly to his questing mouth.

She held his head in her hands, glorying in the silken flow of his hair over her fingers. Her eyes closed…her eyelids felt heavy and warm, as if the sun was shining brightly on her face. She felt her whole body swell and ripen…and her heart did, too, until she felt it would surely burst inside her, and all the love she felt for him come pouring out. *I can't…I can't. Can't let him know…* She bit down on her lip, fighting to keep the words inside. And focused intently…fiercely…on the physical sensations that were nearly tearing her apart.

She scarcely felt it when he slipped the boxers off. Her legs, obeying his gentle command, parted as easily, as naturally as a flower opening at the behest of the sun. It felt like the sun's touch, too, the way his hands seemed to heat all of her skin at once…a sizzling heat that spread over her body…her stomach, her legs and her buttocks. She arched and stretched in the lovely warmth, sensuously, like a cat.

And then his mouth found her center…moved to claim it for his own. His tongue licked over her…into her…and the heat coalesced into a searing white-hot ball that exploded through her like a supernova. Time ceased; she lost all sense of place… didn't hear herself cry out as her body rocketed through a pulsing void, completely out of control…

…until she felt herself gathered in, held fast in powerful arms, felt her back cuddled against a strong chest and her whole body rocked by a steadily thumping heart. Satin lips touched words of reassurance to her temple and the sweat-damp place behind her ear. She felt safe and warm and loved. Why, then, were her cheeks wet with tears?

She lay quietly in the grip of a dream, content to let the happiness she knew was ephemeral as a rainbow bathe her in its lovely light…until it dawned on her that the hard male body pressed against her back was no longer swathed in a towel. She moved her bottom experimentally. Yep, definitely Nikolas and nothing whatsoever else.

He stirred restlessly, one rock-hard leg hooking around hers to hold her still. The muscles in the arm supporting her head bunched under her cheek as he lifted his hand to caress her hair. "It's all right, my love…go to sleep."

"But—you—"

"Shh… You've been injured, you need to rest."

"But…don't you want—Nik, I can feel—"

"Don't worry about me. I'll be perfectly fine…if you'll just stop doing that…"

"You mean…this?"

"Dar—" breath hissed between his teeth "—stop that this instant, minx—I mean it."

"Or…what?"

"Or…" His tongue licked into her ear and she went limp, every inch of her skin spangled with goose bumps. He drew his hot, open mouth down along the side of her neck and chuckled when she gasped…squirmed closer, fitting her buttocks into the nest of his body. He raised himself on one elbow and leaned down to ask in a growling whisper, "Are you sure, my love?"

She nodded, already beyond speech. His lips pressed against her temple as his hand reached around to cup the mound of damp curls between her thighs. Finding her moist and ready, he slipped his hand under her leg and lifted it. She shifted, adjusted, making it easy for him…and he slid into her body slowly, like the sweetest of homecomings…filled her body with heat and her heart and mind with an aching joy.

His hands were strong and sure, holding her steady against his rocking thrusts, his fingers gentle as they stole between her swollen petals and found the sensitive place hidden there. Sensation bolted through her once more; she whimpered… gasped…cried out…and hurtled headlong into climax.

It was every bit as intense as the first orgasm had been, but instead of a terrifying void, she felt surrounded in love and warmth; instead of aloneness, a deep communion. She did feel lost…as if her *self,* her heart and soul, had become inextricably joined with his, and she would never be the same Rhia again. Somewhere in her fractured self was the thought that this should be a frightening thing…but it wasn't.

Tears of overwhelming love and joy sprang to her eyes when she felt his release follow hers, and afterward she floated into sleep, still blissfully wrapped in Nikolas's arms.

# Chapter 14

He watched her come awake, and was steeped in the same sense of wonder with which he'd once observed, as a very small boy, the emergence of a butterfly from its leafy chrysalis. First, the delicate flutter of eyelids…a hint of green sparkling through dark lashes…a tiny frown gathered between bird's-wing brows…the quivering of rose-petal lips on the verge of a yawn…and once again, as then, he couldn't resist reaching out to touch the miracle with an unsteady finger.

She twitched her nose…brushed at her cheek where he'd touched it. Then her eyes opened and looked directly into his, and he thought no sunrise had ever been so beautiful.

"Whazza matter?" she mumbled, her eyes crossing slightly in their effort to focus on his face. "What're you doing?"

"Just looking at you, my love," he said tenderly, stroking her hair back from her forehead. "Watching you sleep."

She rolled her eyes and gave a husky laugh. "Oh, *that* must have been lovely."

"It was, actually. I was going to do the whole Prince Charming thing and awaken you with my kiss, but you seemed about to return to life without it, so I've enjoyed watching the process. Quite fascinating."

"Oh, God…" She put a hand over her eyes, then scrubbed it across her face and glared at him—or tried her best to. "At least you didn't handcuff me to the bed this time." But he could see the smile and the answer to his deepest wishes shimmering in her eyes.

"Never again," he whispered, and leaned down to kiss her. Then he drew back and added thoughtfully, "Not without your permission, at least."

"Seriously…how come you're all dressed already?" Too early in the morning for humor, evidently. She frowned, yawned hugely as she pushed herself up higher on the pillows, then winced and sucked in her chest when the sheet dragged across her burns. "I must look like bloody hell. Feels like I haven't showered in *days*. Can't imagine what you must be thinking…"

Smiling at her grumpiness, he hooked a finger in the sheet and lifted it away from her breasts. "Actually, I was thinking how very much I should like to see your face on my pillows every morning when I wake up."

*Yes, and I should love to see your face grow rosy and your body plump with my child. I want to watch our sons and daughters suckling at your lovely breasts. I want to watch the joys and sorrows we share etch lines in your face, my love, and your skin grow ever softer, more fragile and even more beautiful in old age.*

Those things he thought but didn't say. And because he was too steeped in love and his own fantasy, he failed to notice that Rhia's eyes had gone wide and dark with dismay.

"Marry me, sweetheart." The words slipped from him without thought. He didn't feel them pass his lips; it was as if they had simply gone straight from his heart into the air.

And her response came back the same way—a recoil that pierced him like an arrow. *"What?"*

*Too soon, you imbecile!* But that realization came too late; the words were out there, hanging suspended between them, and could not be unsaid.

"Yes. Marry me." Nothing to do now but forge ahead. Leaning casually on one elbow to hide the crazy pounding of his heart, he looked into her horrified eyes and smiled. "You must know I adore you—I've hardly made a secret of that. I intend to spend the rest of my life with you, anyhow, and quite frankly, I can't think of any reason why we couldn't…shouldn't make it legal."

"Oh, I can think of at least one really good one." Her voice was dark and soft.

"You don't love me…" He was sure enough of her feelings to say the words, but they quivered in his throat regardless. "Is that it, sweetheart?" He lightly stroked the soft white undercurve of her breast with the back of one finger.

"No!" She batted his hand away…hitched in a breath. "You know that's not…it." Another breath, and she gathered the sheet to cover her nakedness again. "You're about to become king. Or have you forgotten? You can't marry me."

"Why not?" He sat up suddenly, and swiveled to face her. "Oh, wait—don't tell me it's because you're a 'commoner'? Good God, woman, this is the twenty-first century—didn't that crap get done away with somewhere along in the twentieth? Besides, if you come down to it, I'm a commoner myself, in everything but blood. No, love—sorry, that excuse won't wash. The people of Silvershire are going to fall for you as madly as I have. They're going to think you're an absolutely smashing queen."

She stared back at him in stony-eyed silence for a moment. Then swallowed, and said in a voice to match her eyes, "Yes, I'm sure the good people of Silvershire would be positively thrilled to have a convicted felon as their queen."

He shook his head and gazed at her indulgently, laughing. "What on earth are you talking about?"

"I told you, but you didn't believe me. If you had—"

"Told me what? When? You mean, about your juvenile record? Don't they seal those?"

"No. Not that. Back at the castle. When I was picking the lock. I told you I used to be a burglar, but you just laughed."

"Now, wait a minute—"

"See? You're doing it again. Maybe if you'd taken me seriously the first time, you wouldn't be entertaining crazy ideas about something that just ain't—gonna—happen." She was scrambling off the bed, still clutching the sheet. He could feel her body trembling as she slid past him.

"Okay, hold it right there." He shook his head again, no longer feeling the least bit like laughing. "Good God—I think you *are* serious. Do you mean to tell me you actually were a burglar? Convicted? As in…jail?"

She nodded, chin lifted, arms folded across the wadded-up sheet she was holding to her chest.

"Does Lazlo know? Okay—foolish question—of course he'd know—he knows everything."

Her mouth tilted wryly. "Where do you think he found me? I don't know how, but he got me released—paroled into his custody, actually. He convinced me there were better uses for my talents than stealing rich people's jewelry…made me clean up my act, get healthy, get in shape. Sent me to college, trained me, gave me a job—one I happen to love, by the way. One I…don't want to lose."

She watched his face change as it hit him. The pain.

Though none of it showed in his voice as he said softly, almost gently, "That's it, isn't it? Not that I can't marry you. It's that you don't want to marry me."

"Not you! Don't you understand? I don't want to marry a *king*." She paced angrily, dragging the sheet like an oversized toga, furious with him for being hurt, with herself for hurting him, and with him again for making it necessary, for bringing up the subject she'd been dreading, trying so hard not to think about. "Look—to you, being king is a simple matter of obligation. Of duty. Not to mention the opportunity to fulfill your lifelong dream for your people. But for me…my God, Nik—" she whirled, trembling, to face him "—the idea of being queen, being married to a king—it would be like being trapped. Put in a cage. I know what royals' lives are like—I've seen it firsthand, in my job. They're *on,* all the time. They have no privacy, no personal freedom. I couldn't live like that. I'm sorry, I just couldn't." She gave a desperate, hiccupping laugh. "And, I know the romantic thing is supposed to be, all for love, right? Well, I've seen how that works out firsthand, too. Up close and personal. My mother gave up everything to marry my father, and look what happened. She was miserable. In the end, she messed up both her life and mine. It doesn't work, Nikolas!"

He'd watched her diatribe in patient silence, with set expression and glittering eyes. Now, he lifted one shoulder and said stonily, "Then I won't be king."

She gave another helpless, hurting laugh and stared past him for a few moments, fighting for control. When she was sure she had it, she drew a breath and said in a low, husky voice, "Yes, you will. You know you will. You have a duty to your country, your father…maybe even to destiny." She laughed again, lightly, this time. "You'll go down in history, Nikolas…the father of Silvershire's democracy. Future generations of schoolchildren will be required to memorize your birthday."

"Rubbish," Nikolas snapped, then got restlessly to his feet. "Okay, you're right. I suppose I'll have to be king, but not forever. Just long enough to bring about free elections. Then my duty's done. I'll be free—"

"Elections? Free? Are you kidding me? In any election you'd win in a landslide. With your charisma, King Weston's long-lost son, the kidnapped prince? If you didn't run, they'd write you in. Probably proclaim you king by acclamation!"

"Okay, fine—" he folded his arms on his impressive

chest and drew himself up to his equally impressive height "—if I'm the king, I can bloody well choose who I want to be my queen."

"Listen to you!" She threw up her hands in exasperation, then had to grab hastily for the sheet. "My God, you sound like a king already!"

"What's that supposed to mean?"

"It's all about power, Nikolas. When men have power, they think they can have everything their way. Just like my father."

"Oh, okay—that's what this is all about, isn't it?" It was his turn to throw up his arms. "Your father. You're still mad at the jerk for taking you away from your mother. Well, let me ask you something, sweetheart. Where do you think you'd be, if he hadn't done that? If you'd stayed in that trailer park with your mum—what would you be doing right now? Working as a cocktail waitress, playing blues in some New Orleans pub? Do you think you'd have gone to college? Would you be working for the Lazlo Group? How many abducted kids do you think you'd have saved? Would you have met me?"

She could only stare at him, holding herself rigid while furious unreasoning tears gathered in her throat.

"Think about it." He reached out to brush her cheek with the backs of his fingers. "Ask yourself if you like your life the way it's turned out. Then, ask yourself if you'd have anything you have now if your father hadn't come for you and taken you back to Florida. Ask yourself if you'd have anything different, if you could go back and change it. Think about how mad you are at your father for giving you this life." He let his hand drop away from her, and his voice hardened. "Think about it, Rhia. Then get over it."

She gave a gasp of rage, whirled and made for the bathroom—an exit that would probably have been much more satisfying if she hadn't first had to untangle her legs from the sheet.

In the sanctuary of the bathroom, she gripped the edge of the sink and leaned on her hands, staring blindly down at them and breathing hard, teeth clenched. Refusing to let the tears come. Thinking, *I'm right, dammit—I know I'm right!*

While hovering anxiously over her, another Rhia—a heart-broken Rhia—was wailing, *What are you doing, you silly fool? The last thing you wanted to do this morning—the last thing you'd ever want to do—is fight with Nikolas!*

The angry Rhia, self-righteous Rhia, turned her back on the sink and the mirror and squeezed her eyes tightly shut. *Dammit, Nikolas. Damn you. Why did you have to go and ruin things? Why did you have to ask me to marry you?*

*I can't...just can't. I don't want to be a queen. It would never work, no matter how much I love you.*

With that thought the heartbroken Rhia and the angry Rhia coalesced into one, with a shaft of pain so intense it doubled her over. *Oh, Nikolas, I do love you. I do...* She rocked herself, arms folded over her breasts like broken wings, heedless of her unhealed burns, refusing to allow herself the solace of tears. *Maybe it's just as well. Yes—it's good this happened now, while I'm still strong enough to say no.*

She sniffed, and slowly, experimentally, unfolded herself. Discovering that she felt stronger, quieter inside, she washed her face and dressed in the clothes she'd worn the day before and washed out last night in Nikolas's sink. Except for the bra—no way could she wear that. She'd have to do without. The pullover was still damp, but the coolness felt good on her burns.

When she opened the door, Nikolas was just disconnecting the telephone. He glanced at her and said, in a voice as neutral as his expression, "I've summoned a cab. Rang Elliot on his handy, as well—he's warming up the chopper. All right with you if we grab coffee and a bite at the airport?"

"Sure, that's fine. Coffee's all I want, anyway." She wasn't hungry; Nikolas had fed her well the night before...in more ways than one. But the memories that tried to sneak into her mind through that door were too fresh, too raw, and she slammed it firmly shut on the beginning ripples of pain.

She picked up her utility belt, which, along with her leather jacket, she'd left draped across a chair. She buckled it on over her pullover, then reached for her jacket. Taking a nine-millimeter Walther from the holster built into the jacket's lining, she proceeded to check the weapon over thoroughly and with the efficiency of long practice. She'd asked Elliot to get her a weapon, and he'd given her his own backup piece. It was a little lighter than she was used to, but it would do the job.

She slapped the magazine back into place and looked up to find Nikolas watching her, eyes darkly intent. A sardonic little smile tugged at the corners of her mouth as she imagined the struggle being waged behind his carefully controlled features. She knew what he was thinking…what he wanted to ask her…

*You're going to visit a palace, Rhee—the royal palace, home of kings, the most beautiful and elegant building in all of Silvershire, one of the most beautiful in the world—and you're wearing* that?

But he didn't ask it. Probably he'd already realized what it meant even to think it, and stopped himself in time.

Instead, he nodded at the gun and said mildly, "Do you think they'll let you take that into the palace?"

On that safe ground, she allowed her smile to bloom into full irony. "Nik. I have a permit and my Lazlo Group credentials. With those I could probably take a weapon into *Buckingham* Palace."

He said nothing, only nodded. She felt his gaze following her every move as she returned the gun to its holster, picked up the jacket and slipped it on…shrugged it into a more comfortable fit on her shoulders and tugged down the sleeves. Thus armored, she looked up at last and met those hooded, pain-filled eyes.

"This is who I am," she said softly.

From the street below came the beep of the taxicab's horn, saving him the necessity of a reply.

* * *

Rhia's reaction to her first glimpse of the royal palace was everything Nikolas could have hoped for. One word that pretty much said it all:

"Wow."

He smiled wryly and didn't reply, but the words *gilded cage* slipped unbidden into his mind as the car swept up the long drive toward the sentry boxes at the main front gates.

Beyond the heavy wrought-iron gates and the concrete security barriers, he could see the graceful stone spires of the palace outlined against a clear blue autumn sky, the yellow painted walls gleaming like gold in the morning sun. He'd been to the palace—the public part of it—more than once, the first time as a very small child, brought there by his "uncle" Silas Donovan to see where the man who'd murdered his parents lived. He'd tried, then and on each subsequent visit, to feel the anger and disdain he knew his uncle expected, but deep inside, even as a child he'd thought it must surely be the most beautiful place in the world. Now, for the first time in his life he allowed his throat to swell with a lump of pride.

The unmarked limousine that had brought them from the airport had tinted windows, an amenity Nikolas was profoundly thankful for when he saw the reporters and paparazzi staked out along both sides of the drive.

"Do you suppose it's always like this? The media, I mean?" Rhia had torn her gaze from the palace to look at them, too.

"I have an idea there are always a few lurking about. With all that's happened in and around the palace lately, though, it's probably to be expected there'd be a crowd."

"Especially since the rumors broke about the existence of a long-lost prince," Rhia said drily. "Good thing they can't see who's in here. We'd probably have a riot on our hands."

"Oh, come now," Nikolas said, laughing uneasily, "I think you're exaggerating my popular appeal. Not so very long ago, they were sure I was guilty of murdering the crown prince."

"And, now they know you're not. Care to put your 'popular appeal' to the test?" Even in the shadowed car, he could see her kitty-cat smile. "Go ahead—stop the car, get out and introduce yourself."

He snorted and said, "No thanks." But deep inside he felt a small shudder, and the same voice that had spoken of gilded cages now whispered, *Are you sure you're ready for this?*

He'd thought he was ready…had even looked forward to the challenges of running a country. That had been when he'd let himself dream that he'd be doing so with Rhia at his side. Now… He'd do it, of course, because it was his duty. His country needed him. But it loomed as a lonely and daunting task.

As soon as the limo had cleared the security checkpoint, Rhia ran her window down—partly so she could gawk unhindered as the car wound its way through the magnificent grounds, but also because she was finding Nikolas's silence oppressive. She knew the silence probably had nothing to do with the fact they'd quarreled; Nikolas wasn't the type of man to sulk. She had an idea it was finally beginning to hit him— the enormity of what had happened to him, and the changes that were coming. And the overwhelming responsibility. But still…the silence, the tight, thin line of his mouth, the muscle working in his jaw…were all reminders to her of the way she'd hurt him, like a toothache that wouldn't go away.

The limousine prowled past the palace's magnificent formal entrance, with its three-tiered sweep of gleaming marble steps leading up to the wide double doors that had been hand-carved from ebony and inlaid with silver and ivory, and the grand balcony above from which generations of Silvershire's monarchs had greeted their loyal subjects. Rhia would have liked to have taken a tour of the great halls and public rooms she'd heard so much about, but that would have to wait for another day. A day when there was no longer a madman on the loose. A madman with a chilling ability, it seemed, to enter and leave the most secure parts of the palace at will. She wasn't here as a tourist, she reminded herself, or even as a friend of the prodigal prince. She was here as an agent of the Lazlo Group, the most exclusive and highly regarded private security organization in the world. And her job was to catch a killer—before he killed again.

After what seemed to Nikolas enough twists and turns to have brought them back to where they'd started, the limo slipped beneath a beautiful stone portico and rolled to a stop in front of the entrance to the royal family's private wing. Standing at parade rest on either side of the doors were a matched set of uniformed guards armed with two-way radios and automatic rifles. As the limo driver got out to open the door, a fit-looking silver-haired man in a dark gray business suit with the royal crest emblazoned on the jacket pocket came briskly down the shallow steps to meet them. He took Rhia's hand to help her from the car, then stood stiffly at attention as Nikolas followed.

"Maximillian, chief of palace security, at your service, sir," the man said, addressing the air to the right of Nikolas's ear.

Nikolas held out his hand. "Hi—I'm Nik Donovan, and this is Agent Rhia de Hayes."

There was a sound that may have been smothered laughter from the limo driver, then a moment of startled silence before Maximillian, looking faintly bemused, took Nikolas's hand, bowed over it with a muttered, "Your Highness." When he looked up, his eyes met Nikolas's and his lips twitched into a smile. "Welcome home, sir. His Majesty is waiting for you in the Bourbon Rose Garden. I can take you there now, if you wish. Or," he added, with a pointed look at Rhia's militant black leather, "to your quarters, if you would prefer to, er… freshen up first."

"We'll see the king straight away, if you don't mind," Nikolas said with what he hoped was an absolutely blank face, still trying to get over the shock of hearing himself addressed as "Your Highness." Taking Rhia's arm, he met her mutinous look with an elevated eyebrow, and she snapped her mouth shut on whatever indignant retort she'd been about to make.

"Bourbon roses? Did I hear that right?" she said in a stage whisper out of the side of her mouth as they followed Maximillian through elegantly appointed rooms with high ceilings and walls covered with gleaming carved wood paneling or murals painted in soft pastels.

Nikolas smiled. "I doubt that means what you're thinking, love."

Maximillian had heard the exchange, and answered over his shoulder in the chatty but rather formal manner of a docent. "Bourbon roses are named for their place of origin, not the alcoholic beverage, Agent de Hayes. They were developed on the Ile Bourbon, an island in the Indian Ocean now known as Réunion. They're quite old—from early in the nineteenth century, I believe." He paused to unhook a velvet-covered chain barrier and waved them through, then followed, replacing it behind him. "The palace's rose garden originated in the 1860s, when Bourbons had become quite the thing in Paris."

"This is the first I've heard of it," Nikolas said. "I gather it's not part of the public tour?"

"No, Your Highness. In the first place, it is located in the oldest part of the palace, which, although having undergone some renovation in recent years, is still not considered safe. A regular maze, dark and confusing passages…not quite the place you'd want tourists wandering about. Then, there's the fact that His Majesty likes to spend time there." He paused again, this time to throw Nikolas a look of apology. "Since the queen passed, God rest her soul, he's the only one who does. It's been let go a bit, I'm afraid."

The security chief had been leading them at a brisk pace through increasingly dim and dusty corridors festooned with cobwebs and rank with the smell of damp and decay. Now, he preceded them down a short flight of stone steps to a small vestibule, where a thick and ancient wooden door stood open to the courtyard beyond. Here, too, a pair of uniformed guards equipped with two-way radios and automatic weapons stood at ease in the rectangle of brilliant autumn sunshine, and snapped to attention when they heard footsteps on the vestibule's stone floor. They saluted the captain, flashed curious surreptitious glances at Rhia as they bowed to Nikolas, then stepped aside to let them pass.

The first thing Rhia noticed was the smell. Not roses, which she'd expected—something darker, earthier, more mysterious…but to her every bit as sweet. So sweet, and so achingly, wrenchingly familiar it brought a soft gasp to her lips and an unexpected stinging to her eyes. For the second time in the past week she found herself inundated with memories of her childhood, of the bayous…of slow-moving water and thick black mud…of rotting leaves and moss and all manner of growing things. It must be the river—the Kairn, she thought, Silvershire's largest and most important river, which she knew flowed right through the heart of the capital city. Quite nearby, too, perhaps just beyond the thick courtyard walls. But even standing in that sunlit rose garden, she felt that if she only closed her eyes she would feel the soft humidity on her skin… hear the frogs and cicadas singing their shrill duets…see fireflies winking against the blackness of her eyelids.

The pressure of Nikolas's fingers on her arm as he guided her around the arched and swaying branch of a gigantic climbing rosebush dragged her out of the past, back to the present. And it hit her then—the thing he'd tried in his own way to tell her earlier that morning. The bayous *were* her past. *This*—old roses in a palace courtyard…the familiar weight of a nine-millimeter handgun against her side…Nikolas, close to her…touching her, holding her hand—this was her *now*. Like the river beyond the walls, her life flowed on…always and only onward; it could never go back. And childhood had been left behind long ago.

The ache in her throat felt like a whispered good-bye.

King Weston was waiting for them at the far end of the courtyard, in a shaded alcove created by two stone arches and a tangle of nearly leafless rose canes. Beneath the thicket of canes, two carved stone benches had been placed facing each other. The benches were thickly upholstered with leaves and the fallen petals of a scattering of autumn blooms, evidence the king had not been making use of them before they arrived. As he came to greet them, leaning only slightly on an ivory-handled ebony cane, the bouquet of densely petaled blossoms in his hand—and several more spilling from the pockets of his jacket—gave a hint as to how he'd been occupying his time.

As before, Rhia found herself hanging back to observe the reunion between royal father and son, keeping a distance—a physical one, at least. Impossible, though, not to feel the pressure of colliding, conflicting emotions as she watched the two men greet each other with a typically awkward masculine embrace. Impossible not to feel her heart flutter when both men turned to her wearing the same unbelievably appealing smile. Impossible not to feel shivers all through her body—shivers of love—when she thought how beautiful Nikolas was, and how good. Yes—he was a *good* man. He would be a good king, too. Like his father, good to the core.

Unlike *her* father.

*...I'm bloody well not like your father.*

"Rhia, my dear!" King Weston held out his arms, cane in one hand, roses in the other, and to her utter astonishment— and Nikolas's obvious amusement—embraced her and kissed her soundly on one cheek. "So very sorry to hear about your injuries," the king said, drawing back to study her with a concerned frown. "I trust you'll heal quickly, my dear. That blackguard Perthegon must be caught! And soon—before he does any more harm."

"Yes, uh, sire—er, Your Majesty..." *Damn.* She was all but

stammering. She took a breath and felt the calming press of the Walther against her ribs. "We're doing our best."

"Yes," the king said, with a wry and glittering look at Nikolas, "I expect you are—and everyone else as well. I feel as if I'm a prisoner in my own home—a prisoner on…what do they call it? Huh—lockdown, I believe. Yes. Anyway, I came out here to get away from it all. For a breath of freedom. And fresh air." He waved the rose bouquet in a sweeping gesture. "How do you like my rose garden?"

Rhia coughed. "Uh…it's…beautiful."

King Weston laughed. "You lie rather badly, my dear. It's a neglected mess." His eyes creased in a squint of sadness as he gazed around him. "This was the queen's favorite spot, you see. After she died, I'm afraid I let it go to ruin. Lately, I've begun to think about putting it right again. This one here—" he held up a blossom of rich rose-pink, sniffed it, then pointed it at the tangle of canes overhead "—was her favorite. Zepherine Drouhin, it's called. It has no thorns, you see. That's why she liked it—she loved roses, but was always pricking herself on the thorns." He touched the blossom to his lips, and to Rhia's complete bemusement, presented the rest of the bouquet to her. "These are for you, my dear. Welcome to the palace."

"And now," he said, taking Rhia's arm and turning to walk a few slow steps back toward the vestibule, "I expect you'd like to see the rest of the place."

"Uh, yes," she said, clearing her throat in a valiant effort to pull herself out of the Disney movie she seemed to have wandered into. "As a matter of fact, I'd like to go over security arrangements—"

The king waggled his cane. "No need for that. Between my own palace guard and the extra security forces Corbett Lazlo has provided, everything has been well taken care of, I assure you. We are all safe here."

*Safe as a babe in his mother's arms?* Rhia glanced at Nikolas and suppressed a shiver. His gray eyes were glittering as he looked back at her, and she wondered if he'd had the same thought.

"Forgive me," he said, in a tone that was probably a bit more abrupt than should have been used to address a king, "but Vladimir—Lord...Vladimir—has gotten into the palace before."

King Weston nodded. "Through the old tunnels, yes. But that's all been taken care of now. The tunnels have been closed off or filled in. At any rate," he said firmly, drawing himself up and gesturing again with his cane, as if it were an eraser, "*you,* my dear girl, are here as my guest, not my bodyguard. Nikolas—have Max get someone to give her the grand tour, won't you? And show you to your rooms. Then later on I should like it very much if you would both join me for dinner in my chambers."

Rhia could actually feel herself blushing. "Oh—but...Your Majesty...I'm not—I'm honored, but...I didn't exactly..." Oh God, and stammering, again, too. She didn't dare look at Nikolas; if he was grinning, she'd have no choice but to kill him. *I can't believe this,* she thought. *I can't believe I'm going to say it...* "Your Majesty, I'm sorry, but I don't have anything to wear!"

King Weston halted and turned to her with smiling eyes. "Quite frankly, I think you look smashing just as you are." He lifted her hand to his lips and kissed it. "However, I do know all women like to dress up, put on fancy things now and then. Don't worry, Miss de Hayes, I shall see to it that you have something to wear."

He turned to Nikolas and clasped his hand. His voice seemed to deepen and grow husky. "My boy, I'm glad you're here at last. I shall look forward to our visit this evening—perhaps we can begin to get to know one another. I'll send someone to escort you to my chambers—shall we say...five o'clock?"

Nikolas murmured, "Yes, of course. That will be fine."

The king waved them on, then pivoted and returned to his roses.

"Will someone please just kill me now?" Rhia ground out

between clenched teeth, as she and Nikolas made their way back across the courtyard. "Could I possibly *be* more embarrassed? And don't you *dare* laugh, or I swear I will kill you."

"I'm not laughing," Nikolas insisted, while doing exactly that. Then he shrugged, and the grin faded. "I'm not even going to claim credit for 'I told you so,' because I didn't."

"No, but you thought it. God, I hate it when you're right..." They were almost to the vestibule. She caught his arm to stop him and whispered, "Nik—am I insane, or did the king—your father—just flirt with me?"

"Oh, you're not insane," he said drily. "Although I may be—with jealousy."

She shot him a sideways look, pretending disgust. "Now I know where you get it from. You can't help it—it's in your genes."

# Chapter 15

"My God," Rhia whispered, "I can't believe I'm actually wearing a Givenchy. Me—the former Miss Trailer Park of New Orleans."

Nikolas didn't comment; he knew how sappy he'd sound if he told her the truth, which was that in his opinion no queen or empress had ever looked more regal. Besides which, if he told her *that,* he was fairly certain it would only make her mad.

Although, to be truthful, lately he couldn't be certain of anything where Rhia was concerned. Since they'd arrived at the palace, she'd seemed…different. Edgy, nervous…lacking her usual poise and self-confidence.

"Are you sure I look okay in this thing? It's not too…*you* know…"

He didn't know what to make of her. It was the first time he'd ever known her to be insecure about her appearance. It was also the first time he'd seen her wearing a dress and high heels, and he did know what he'd *like* to make of that. Take them right off her again, as soon as he could possibly manage it.

He let his gaze slide over her—quickly, which was as much as his libido could stand. "No, love," he said gently, "it's not too…anything. It's just exactly right."

"I don't know…it *is* from the nineteen sixties, after all." She heaved in a breath, twisting and turning in front of the window in a way that made his mouth go dry as she tried to catch a glimpse of her reflection in the dark glass. She paused to throw him a look of bemusement. "I still can't believe he let me wear his wife's—Queen Alexis's—your mother's clothes. I'm amazed he'd even still have them."

"Yes, well I suppose it would be rather difficult to dispose of something like a queen's wardrobe," Nikolas said drily, and to remove himself as far as possible from temptation, paced to the opposite end of the informal reception room in the king's private chambers, where they'd been left to await his majesty's pleasure. "It's not as though one can simply drop everything off at the Oxfam shop. I should imagine some will eventually go to a museum."

She gave a breathy little laugh. "In the meantime, I'm wearing Givenchy. I feel like…who is it?" She snapped her fingers. "Audrey Hepburn—*Breakfast at Tiffany's*. You know—the little black dress?"

He folded his arms on his chest and pretended to give her a critical once-over. Truth was, she did look a little like Audrey Hepburn—from the neck up: Dark hair piled high on her head, exotic eyes and luscious mouth…long, elegant neck. But from there down…from what he could recall, for all her grace and beauty, Audrey on her best day had never had curves like that.

Avoiding the issue, he frowned at his watch, then glanced at the doors that led to the king's inner sanctum. "Wonder what's keeping our royal host?"

Her eyes jerked to his and her lips parted. The look that came over her face was one he'd never seen before—frightened, even confused. His heart began to pound as he asked hoarsely, "What? Rhia, what's wrong?"

She shook her head—a quick, erasing motion—and pivoted away from him. "Nik—it's nothing. I…"

He was at her side in an instant, gripping her arms and turning her to face him. "It's obviously not nothing. Tell me."

She gazed at him…opened her mouth. But the words wouldn't come. *It's hard…I don't think I can…I'm sorry.* She'd never tried to put it into words before—*the feeling.* The sizzling under her skin, like static electricity…the flashes of *something* just on the edges of her consciousness that never came into focus…the hum in her head that wasn't quite sound.

She swallowed…took a breath. "I know this is going to sound…weird. I thought it was just nerves—you know, I'm wearing this dress, having dinner with the king, for God's sake. Anyway, I've been feeling it ever since we came in here. And then, when you mentioned him, I *knew* what it was. It's…"

"Your sixth sense," he said quietly. Not mocking, not questioning. The relief that flooded her almost made her knees buckle. And she knew she'd never loved him more than at that moment.

She nodded and clutched at his arms. "Something's wrong, Nik. Don't ask me how I know, I just do." She twisted to throw an anguished look at the closed door to the king's private rooms. "We can't just go barging in there—he's the *king.* What—"

"Who says we can't?" Nikolas crossed the room in long strides and gripped the ornate brass door handle. He pushed it, then looked at Rhia, who was right behind him. "It's unlocked. Do you think that's normal?"

"I don't know," she murmured through rigid jaws. The sizzling was more of a crackling now; she could feel it running along her scalp, lifting her hair. Her chest was tight with the certainty that she needed to get through that door. "But I think we should find out."

He nodded grimly. "I'll go first—"

"Like hell you will. I'm the one with the training here."

"Look, you don't even have your gun. If anything—"

"Who says I don't?" She lifted up her skirt to show him the Walther strapped snugly against her thigh. "Now—are we going to stand here and debate, or open this door?"

He shook his head wonderingly. "Have I mentioned you're giving me an inferiority complex? Okay…you first, but go low. I'll cover your back. And…maybe you should leave the gun where it is until we know…"

"Right. Ready…let's go."

Adrenaline surged into her veins as Nikolas pushed down on the handle and silently opened the door; she scarcely felt her feet touching the floor as she slipped through. She was a breath of wind, nothing more. A wide paneled hallway stretched ahead of her…empty. She moved swiftly along it, glancing into open doorways as she went, aware that Nikolas was right behind her, and that what she was looking for was somewhere ahead of her…somewhere close.

And so was danger. She could feel it lurking, like something watching from beyond the firelight….

The Walther lay heavy against her flexing thigh muscle as she crept closer to the end of the hallway. There was only one door left, the one door that wasn't standing open. She approached it like a cat stalking her prey…took her position to the right of the door. Nikolas moved silently to the left side, facing her.

On her nod, he lifted a hand, knocked sharply on the door panel and called out, "Your Majesty, it's Nikolas. Are you all right in there?"

They waited, frozen, listening to the pounding of their own hearts.

Rhia held up three fingers, and he nodded, then pointed to her skirt and lifted one eyebrow. She shook her head; something told her it wasn't yet time to reveal her hidden ace. She held up one finger, then two, then three.

Again Nikolas gripped the handle and pushed open the door, but this time he managed to slip through before her, effectively shielding her from whatever might be waiting for them on the other side. The irresistible force that was her adrenaline-charged body collided with the immovable object that was his, and as the resulting explosion burst from her lungs in a gasp of helpless fury, she heard a cold, quiet voice.

*Vladimir's.*

"Come in," he said pleasantly. "I've been wondering when you two would decide to join us."

Nikolas barely heard the words. For those first seconds he seemed to be swathed in a gauzy film that muffled sound, paralyzed muscle and cloaked vision so that he saw the impossible scene before him through a reddish fog: Henry Weston, his father, sitting in an upholstered Queen Anne chair that had been positioned to face the door. Behind him, Lord Vladimir, clean-shaven now, and dressed in black fatigues and beret, holding a handgun with the barrel pressed to the king's temple.

Nik came abruptly back to the moment when he felt Rhia try to slip past him. Catching her arm, he pulled her against his side and stretched his lips in a smile. "Silas…"

"How did you get in here?" Rhia's voice could have etched glass.

King Weston's smile was wry. "It appears not quite all of those tunnels have been found and disposed of, after all. The blackguard came right through the wall in my library, if you can believe—"

Nikolas felt Rhia jerk as Vladimir's whip-crack laugh slashed across the last word. "Believe it, *pretender.* You can't keep me out. I know this palace better than you do—better than anyone does. And why shouldn't I? It's *mine.*"

Holding himself in a grip of steel, Nikolas said, "What do you want, Silas?"

"My name is *Vladimir,*" the intruder thundered, grasping Weston's arm and jerking him to his feet. "*Lord* Vladimir—

Duke of Perthegon! I want what is *mine*—what was stolen from me. Nothing more, nothing less. And I shall have it—or die. But if I die, before I do, this—this *thief* will die, too!"

"Lord Vladimir," Rhia said quietly, "you must know it's over. Your secret is out—you can't possibly get what you want now. But if you give yourself up, you will have a chance to tell your story, get it out there for the people to hear, so everyone will know what was done to you."

Nikolas edged closer, still holding on to Rhia and trying his best to keep himself between her and the madman with the gun. He could feel her muscles vibrating and bunching under his fingers. It would be just like her, he thought, to do something unthinkable—like go for her weapon, or put herself in front of Vladimir's gun to save him or the king.

Vladimir's glittering eyes flicked at Rhia like the tongue of a snake. "Give myself up? So they can put me in a cage? What, *wench,* do you think I'm stupid enough to barter my freedom for my story? No—I'll die first, and die a happy man, so long as *this*—" he gave Weston's arm a vicious yank "—dies first. And before he dies…he will know the worst pain a father can feel." A terrible smile stretched his lips. The barrel of the gun slowly shifted.

Nikolas went cold. He felt Rhia's muscles gather under his fingers.

But before anyone could move or speak, there came a thunderous booming from the far end of the hall. From the reception area. Someone was pounding on the outer door.

Vladimir froze, teeth bared in a grimace of madness. He looked quickly one way, then the other, like a cornered animal, and then began backing in a tight circle toward the door to the sitting room Nik and Rhia had just come through, dragging Weston with him, the gun once more pressed tightly against the king's temple.

Henry Weston's face was pasty gray, but his eyes were calm as they met Nikolas's.

Nik didn't think. He just let go of Rhia's arm and stepped forward, hands out to his sides. Heard himself say harshly, "Let him go. Take me with you."

"No!" Color flooded back into the king's face as it contorted with anguish. "I'm the one he wants. I'm old, my reign is over. You're my son, Nikolas. You mean more to me than my crown. More than my life…"

The pounding was louder, now. A preemptory voice was shouting, "Maximillian—security. Your Majesty, is everything all right in there?"

Vladimir's eyes flicked from side to side, then narrowed. "This way—all of you," he hissed. Gesturing with the gun, he herded them through the door and into the hallway. "In there—hurry!" He pointed toward the first open door on the left.

Nikolas pulled Rhia with him into what was obviously the king's private study. Like his mountain lodge, the room contained floor-to-ceiling bookcases filled with obviously well-read books. Vladimir shoved Weston in after them and followed, slamming the door behind him just as a loud bang and running footsteps were heard in the reception room down at the far end of the hallway.

"Don't move—any of you," he snarled, "or I kill him now." He backed across the room, still holding the gun on Weston, then let go of him long enough to grasp the carved molding that framed one of the bookcases and give it a mighty yank. Ancient gears creaked as the section of shelves slowly began to move.

To Rhia, it seemed that an eternity passed before the gap in the wall of shelves widened enough for a body to squeeze through. Everything, even her heartbeat, seemed to be moving in slow motion. Beyond the library door she could hear voices and running footsteps, but their rescuers, too, it seemed, were coming at the speed of growing grass. Meanwhile, she needed only a moment to go for her weapon, but it had to be the right moment. She didn't dare risk it as long as Vladimir had his gun to the king's head. She had to wait for her chance. Maybe, once they were in the tunnel, in the darkness...

But her chance didn't come—not then. Vladimir shoved her through the opening first, then Nikolas, then the king, with the gun jammed ruthlessly against the base of his skull. Once they were all crammed into the small dusty space behind the wall, Vladimir activated some sort of mechanism that reversed the door. Then, while there was still light coming through the opening, he took a battery-operated torch from a niche in the stone wall, turned it on and thrust it at Nikolas.

"Here—take this. She's going first—your lady friend. Keep the light pointed at her back. Don't move it, or I shoot her first." He didn't sound mad, now, only terrifyingly purposeful. Efficient. Like a stone-cold killer. "That way. Go on—move."

With a final groan, the panel clicked shut. In a darkness alive with jumping shadows and the sounds of breathing, Rhia moved forward, the Walther like a hot brick against her thigh.

The passageway seemed endless, following a bewildering succession of twists and turns, short ups and downs, until she had lost all sense of direction. Finally, at the end of a short stretch of passageway, she came to a flight of stone steps that seemed to disappear into the darkness beyond the glow of the flashlight. The steps led...not down, but *up*.

"So that's it." Nikolas's musing voice came from close behind her. "They found all the underground tunnels, but nobody thought to look up."

"Shut up," Vladimir hissed. "Climb."

"Just out of curiosity," Nikolas said in a conversational tone, as Rhia started up the steps, trailing one hand along the wall of ancient stone, "where does this go? To the roof, I assume? What do you do after that—fly?"

"You'll learn soon enough," Vladimir said with a sneer that didn't have to be seen. "Keep moving."

At least it's not a tunnel, Rhia thought with a shudder as she climbed steadily upward into the leaping shadows. The air was close, but reasonably cool, and smelled of ancient dust and rat droppings rather than mildew and damp. But she was worried about the king. How much more stress could he take?

*I have to find a way to stop this. I have to get to my gun. Maybe...when we get to the roof...*

Nikolas watched the flashlight beam dance across Rhia's slender back, swaying skirt and well-muscled legs. As he followed her up the stairs, he thought he could almost see the gun strapped to her thigh. It was within reach of his hand. Maybe...if they were to pause for a moment...if he could get to it...

*I have to find a way to stop this. I don't know how much more my father can take. Maybe...when we get to the roof...*

"This seems to be as far as I can go." Rhia's voice came drifting down from the shadows above him. "What now?"

"It's a trapdoor," Vladimir snapped. "There's a latch. Find it. Open it."

Nikolas moved the light higher and heard a grunt. "Ah—I see it. Okay..." There was a loud creak, then a thump, and a rectangle of starlit sky appeared overhead.

"I trust you will remember that I'm holding a gun, and that I will kill Nikolas first if you do anything I don't like," Vladimir said coldly. "With that in mind, please...ladies first. Nikolas, keep the light on her so I can see her clearly, or I will shoot this old man in the leg."

They emerged, one after the other, into the fresh air, like survivors creeping out of a bomb shelter. The night was chilly and clear—and where was the bloody fog when you needed it? Nikolas wondered, as a brisk autumn breeze penetrated the silk fabric of his evening jacket.

They were on a flat surface, stone, from the feel of it, not slate. He could see the lights of the old town, Silverton-upon-Kairn, twinkling festively just across the river, looking almost close enough to touch. He could smell the river, too, and hear the murmur of it as he turned in a slow circle, trying to get his bearings. How could the river be so close—almost beneath his feet, from the sound of it? And the spires of the Renaissance part of the palace so far away?

"Douse the light," Vladimir ordered. "Move on—down there. Go on…"

It came to him, then. This was the old part of the palace, the part built on the ruins of a medieval abbey. He remembered the docent on one of the tours he'd taken telling about the original structure, which had included a stone footbridge connecting the abbey to the market town of Kairn across the river. The bridge had long since crumbled and fallen into the river, leaving only the ruins of an ancient guard tower in one corner of the thick stone walls of the abbey courtyard. They had emerged from the passageway, he realized, not onto the roof, but the top of the six-foot-thick wall itself. Behind them was the king's special refuge, the Bourbon Rose Garden. Straight ahead, the remnants of the old bridge jutted out over the glittering water.

"Looks like a dead end to me," Nikolas said, holding his hands out to his sides. "Come on, give it up. There's no place to go. It's over."

"It's not over!" Vladimir was panting, his voice shrill with fury. "We can still do it—I can kill him for you—right here. It's what you always wanted—Weston dead. The people—they'll know it was me—they'll follow you, Nikolas. I have a boat—"

"It's over," Nikolas said softly. "Let him go."

*"No!"* It was like the roar of an enraged lion. "I'm taking him with me—he's my way out. If you try and stop me, I'll kill you *and* the woman. Maybe…" He paused, breathing audibly. "Maybe I *will* kill you—you betrayed me, boy. I raised you! I taught you! And you went back to this—"

"That's enough, Benton." Weston's quiet voice cut through the shrill babble like a knife. "Kill me, if you wish—I've lived my life. Nikolas, my son…I'm grateful to have had a chance to meet you. My only regret is that we didn't have more time. You will be a good king. Come, Lord Vladimir—leave them, and let's be gone."

"No!" Nikolas shouted, his voice shaking. "Father—"

While Weston had been talking, Vladimir's head had swiveled toward Nikolas; he could see the glitter of hatred in his foster parent's eyes. Now, those eyes flicked at Weston, and his lips pulled back in a smile. When the eyes returned to Nikolas, the barrel of the gun came with them.

"My son…" Vladimir said in a sneering voice, and laughed his whip-crack laugh. "Yes—this *is* a more fitting revenge, I think. Weston, say good-bye to your precious *son*. I took him from you once—now I do so again—forever!"

Nikolas never saw it coming. He heard a cry of pure anguish, a bellow of rage…threw up his hands in an instinctive and futile attempt to hold back the inevitable. Instead, something flashed into his line of sight from out of nowhere, hit him hard. He felt himself falling.

Even as his mind was screaming *Rhia… No!* he heard two shots, one after the other. And then he was lying on his back on the cold stones with Rhia half on top of him, and her gun was slowly drooping, falling from her limp hand.

Dazed, he lifted his head, straining to see beyond her inert body. And his heart stopped. A few yards away, Vladimir was crouched, swaying, blood dripping from one hand. The other still held the gun, which he brought slowly around until it was pointed directly at Rhia. Nikolas could see his teeth gleaming in a grimace of pure malice. And all he could do was fold himself over her body and brace himself once again, waiting to feel the impact of bullets tearing into his flesh.

Once again, that particular horror was spared him. Instead, he was forced to watch in dreadful slow motion as King Weston, summoning all his reserves of strength, lashed out and struck the gun from Vladimir's hand, then crumpled slowly to the ground. He had to watch helplessly as Vladimir, blind with rage and pain, swooped down on the helpless man, his fingers curved into eagle's talons, going for the king's throat.

"Nik…"

He almost didn't hear the whisper.

"Nik…take it. My gun…here…I can't…"

Moving as if in a dream, he picked up Rhia's gun from where it had fallen…found it sticky with her blood…aimed and squeezed the trigger.

Vladimir jerked as the first bullet hit him. Spun around and staggered backward with the second. With the third, he toppled slowly over the edge of the ruined bridge and disappeared into the dark water far below.

The silence that followed was like a blanket of ice. Nikolas could feel it encasing his body, his mind, his soul. He wondered if this was what death was like. The death of all hope and love and joy.

He didn't feel the gun slip from his hand. He was folding Rhia in his arms, holding her close and rocking her, trying desperately to force his own life-forces into her still, still body. Praying.

*Stay with me, Rhee…stay here, my love. I need you. I love you. You don't have to be queen…I don't want to be king, not without you…*

Again, he almost didn't hear her whisper.

"Nik…" Her fingers were touching his face, wiping something from his cheeks. "I'm not going to die."

"You'd bloody well better not," he said fiercely, brokenly. "You're going to marry me. I'll give up the crown. We'll go and raise grapes in Provence, if that's what you want. Just… don't leave me."

"You…don't have to give up the crown." She drew a rasping breath that sent cold ripples of fear through his body. "I'll marry you…one condition…"

"What, my dearest? Anything."

"I get…to keep my job. The…pro bono stuff…at least."

Nikolas was laughing helplessly, unable to speak, when he realized, suddenly, that he wasn't alone. That someone was there beside him, helping him support Rhia's body, lending them both his warmth and courage and strength.

"I believe that can be arranged," King Weston said.

Maximillian and an army of palace guards found them there a few minutes later, the three of them so tightly entwined they made a single silhouette against the sparkling lights of the city.

# *Epilogue*

## I.
*Royal Palace, Silvershire, one month later*

"Do stop checking your tiara, my love."

His Majesty, Nikolas the First, newly crowned King of Silvershire, spoke to his wife of three weeks and queen of scarcely three hours out of one side of his mouth as they made their way slowly along the royal purple carpet that stretched the entire length of the great reception hall, smiling, nodding and waving at the glittering crowd of specially invited guests. "I've been assured that it is firmly attached. It's not going to come loose and tumble over one eye. And if it does," he added tenderly, patting the gloved fingers curved around the crook of his elbow, "heads will most certainly roll."

"Don't joke," Rhia snapped. "I can't believe I let you talk me into wearing it."

"I'm rather surprised about that, myself, actually. I imagine the chief of protocol was greatly relieved, and I know the citizens of Silvershire—your loyal subjects—loved it."

"I didn't do it for them," she muttered darkly behind a rigid smile. "I did it for you and nobody else. This is our first public appearance together. I didn't want you to be ashamed of me."

The king's chest fluttered with emotions he was still trying to get used to as he let his gaze rest briefly on his bride…his queen. Sometimes the miracle of her was almost more than he could bear, especially when he thought how near he'd come to losing her. It had only been a month since Vladimir's bullet had ripped into her chest, collapsing her lung and narrowly missing an artery. And scarcely three weeks since he'd married her in a small—very small, very private—ceremony in the newly renovated royal suite in the palace's medical facility. Only Lady Zara, Lord Shaw and King Weston had been present as witnesses. Lord Russell Carrington, in his capacity as regent and acting head of state, had performed the ceremony. Immediately afterward, Nikolas had taken his wife off to the south of France for rest, recuperation and TLC. *Lots* of TLC. Which seemed to have done the trick, he was pleased to note. The vibrant color had returned to her cheeks, and the kitty-cat glow to her eyes.

"I'm touched, my darling, but there is no way on earth you could possibly shame me. I'm insanely proud of you, you know. Not to mention madly in love."

"Yes, well…just wait until the paparazzi catch me climbing up someone's balcony—oh, look, there's Zara and Walker. I haven't seen them since we got back from Provence. We really must invite them over for dinner soon, Nik."

"Don't try to distract me, minx. If you think I'm going to let that outrageous remark go by…" He aimed a kingly smile over her head, while his eyes burned down at her from under his lashes with a husband's stern authority. "There will be no more balcony-climbing for you. Not for the next several months, at least. The doctor said—"

She gave a soft gasp. "Hush! Don't you dare tell anyone. Not yet. You know I want to keep it secret, at least for the first few months. I hate it when people start counting the months."

"They'll do that anyway, you know. And if you intend to keep our secret, you're going to have to do something about that glow...."

They reached the end of the reception line at last. The orchestra struck up a waltz, the carpet was rolled up and carried away. Nikolas turned to Rhia and bowed over her hand.

"My queen...my dearest love...may I have this dance?"

Her heart fluttered and tears pricked—she was still a little weak from her injuries, she supposed. But to be truthful, in spite of her griping and grumbling—which they both knew was all for show—as she allowed herself to be swept away in her husband's arms, she felt as though she were waltzing on clouds.

*How did this happen? How did I get so lucky? Look at them—all the crowned heads and dignitaries of the entire world—watching me—me!—dance with the most beautiful, wonderful man in the world, and all of them—the women, at least—envying me in their hearts...*

And then, in that glittering sea of faces...one jumped out at her. Familiar. *Impossible.*

A shaft of cold stabbed through her. She gasped...stumbled. Nikolas's arms tightened around her, and his concerned whisper touched her ear. "What is it? Are you in pain?"

"I—no. No, I'm fine. I just...thought I saw...someone. Never mind." *Impossible.*

The waltz ended and another began. Nikolas tucked her hand in the bend of his arm and led her to the sidelines, as behind them other couples began to drift out onto the dance floor. They moved together through the throng, accepting congratulations and well wishes, greeting friends and dignitaries...until Rhia suddenly halted, her fingers tightening on Nikolas's arm.

"Nik, who is that man—the silver-haired one talking to

King Weston? I can't tell who it is, from the back, but I feel as if I should know him." Her voice was breathless. The still-healing surgical scar on her chest tingled and burned like fire.

"Let's go and see," her husband said, in an expressionless voice that was a dead giveaway in itself.

But she let him lead her through the crowd anyway, her feet moving of their own volition, it seemed. Her heartbeat pounded mercilessly against her aching chest.

And then...the man turned. The shaft of ice stabbed through her again, then melted instantly in the heat of fury. "Bloody hell. What's he doing here?" she hissed, turning her face to Nikolas's shoulder. "Who invited him?"

"I did," he said, smiling crookedly and lifting an eyebrow as he looked down at her. "I know you're angry, dearest, but I also know you will forgive me, in time." His eyes softened, and the smile faded. He lifted her hand to his lips. "My wedding gift to you, my love. You gave me back my father. Now, I return the favor."

He turned, keeping a firm hand on her elbow, to greet King Weston and his companion.

The tall, tanned, silver-haired man shifted his flute of champagne hastily to his other hand in order to shake the one Nikolas offered him, but his vivid green eyes came right back to Rhia. He looked slightly dazed, and, to her utter amazement, uncertain as he shook his head and said wryly, "Well, Rhee, looks like you've grown up a bit since I saw you last."

She drew an uneven breath. She could feel her husband's hand, strong and steady on her elbow, feel his warmth and love all around her...enfolding her. She could hear his words, telling her what she'd needed for so long to hear. She took another breath, and felt the tension inside her ease.

"Hello, Dad," she said, and walked into her father's arms.

## II.
*University Medical Center, Silverton*

Zara, Duchess of Perthegon, and her husband, Lord Walker Shaw, stepped past the security guards at the door and advanced into the room on tiptoe, eyes shining, faces wreathed in smiles. Dr. Shaw shook Nikolas's hand while Zara, being a creature of tradition, dropped him a quick curtsey before she bent to kiss Rhia's cheek.

"Dear, you look absolutely beautiful. And so does this little angel." Her voice had dropped to a whisper in deference to the newborn princess sleeping soundly in her father's arms.

"She is beautiful, isn't she?" Rhia hadn't been able to take her eyes off of her daughter from the first moment she'd laid eyes on her. "I think she looks like her daddy, don't you?"

"Oh, no," said the King of Silvershire, gazing down at his daughter with a besotted grin. "She's absolutely the image of her mother—thank God."

"I don't think I've ever seen so many flowers," Zara said, gazing around at the room, which had begun to look more like a hothouse than a hospital room. "Who are they all from?"

"Oh, everyone—those over there are from Prince Charles and the Duchess…that obscenely huge one is from my father, naturally." Rhia rolled her eyes. "He seems to think money spent equals love."

"For some people, it does," Dr. Shaw remarked.

"Well…anyway. Those little pink rosebuds are from Chase and Sydney—they were here earlier. Sydney's baby is beautiful, too, isn't she?"

Zara nodded. "We saw them as were coming in. Yes, she's just adorable. Whatever else you can say about Reginald, he was a very handsome man."

Her husband gave a warning cough. Rhia rushed on, "Oh—and these right here are from Russell and Amelia—oops, I mean, Their Royal Majesties, the King and Queen of Gastonia." She grimaced apologetically; she was still getting used to the protocol of titles. "They're coming for the christening, by the way."

"Did you check the bouquet for rubber snakes?" Zara asked tartly, and her husband chuckled.

"She's still ticked because Lord Carrington got her with a water balloon the last time he was here. Personally, I think it's great that even a king can have an inner child."

"Well," Zara said, touching a finger to the sleeping baby's downy head, "we'll leave you three alone—we just stopped by to say hello and greet the new arrival. We're on our way to the opening of the Alzheimer's and Dementia Center at Perth Castle. King Weston is supposed to cut the ribbon. I hope—"

Nikolas nodded. "He's been here already. Stopped by on his way to the ceremony as well."

"Oh, good. Okay, then, I guess we'll see you at the christening." Zara dipped another curtsey as she turned to go, then paused in the doorway. "Speaking of which, have you two decided on a name yet?"

Rhia and Nikolas looked at each other. Nikolas nodded.

"Yes, we have," Rhia said, drawing a breath that quivered with happiness. "It's…Sarah."

Zara looked startled for a moment, then brightened. "Oh— *Sarah*. That's lovely. Is it *for* anyone in particular?"

Rhia looked into her husband's eyes and smiled. "For serendipity," she whispered.

# Author's Note

In addition to abolishing by royal decree the restrictions of gender on the laws of primogeniture governing inheritance of property and titles, in the first year of his reign, King Nikolas the First established Silvershire's first democratically elected parliament. He also appointed a special committee to draft a new constitution for the country, to include articles providing for the future of the monarchy. Popular opinion being in favor of retaining Silvershire's monarchy as a cherished part of its history and traditions, provisions are being considered whereby future rulers may be chosen or deposed according to the will of the people.

\* \* \* \* \*

# Available Next Month

### Closer Encounters
Merline Lovelace

### The Heart Of A Mercenary
Loreth Anne White

### Fully Engaged
Catherine Mann

### The Lost Prince
Cindy Dees

### Detour
Sylvie Kurtz

### Never Look Back
Sheri WhiteFeather

**MIRA**

**_New York Times_ bestselling author**

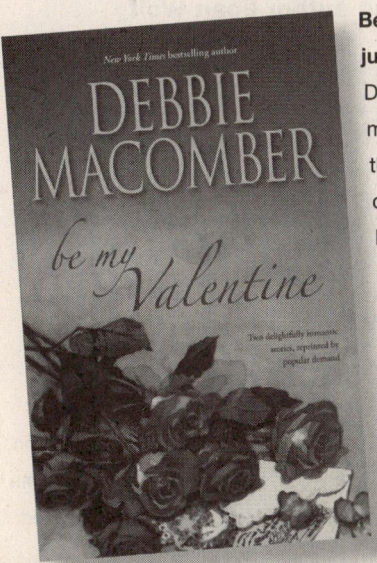

Be my Valentine... and not just on February 14!

Dianne Williams needs a man. But only for one night—the night of the community centre Valentine dinner, to be precise. So after her children's relentless efforts to get her a date, Dianne finds herself approaching a handsome stranger named Steve and making him an outrageous offer. One that might lead to more than just one night...

"Debbie Macomber writes characters who are as warm and funny as your best friends. She's earned her place as one of today's most beloved authors" – _New York Times_ bestselling author Susan Wiggs